# LIBERTY

## Also by Kimberly Iverson
## (writing as Kim Headlee)

*Dawnflight*

# LIBERTY
## KIMBERLY IVERSON

HQN™

HQN™

ISBN-13: 978-0-373-77134-9
ISBN-10:    0-373-77134-7

LIBERTY

www.HQNBooks.com

**Printed in U.S.A.**

To Dad, who showed me the modern world,
and to the Great Dover Street Woman,
who showed me the ancient one.

# I

FINGERS CRAMPING AND shoulders aching from having wielded the pitchfork all day, Rhyddes ferch Rudd tossed another load of hay onto the wagon. Sweat trickled down her back, making the lash marks sting. Marks inflicted by her father, Rudd, the day before because eighteen summers of anguish finally had goaded her into speaking her mind.

Mere physical pain couldn't compare with the ache wringing her heart.

Her father despised her.

She slid a glance toward the author of her mood. He stood a few paces away, leaning upon his pitchfork's handle in the loaded wagon's shade to escape the July heat as he conversed with her oldest brother, Eoghan. She couldn't discern their words, but their easy camaraderie spoke volumes her envy didn't want to hear.

Her father's gaze met hers, and he lowered his eyebrows.

"Back to work, Rhyddes!" On Rudd's lips, her name sounded like an insult.

In a sense, it was.

Her name in the Celtic tongue meant "freedom," but the horse hitched to the hay wagon enjoyed more freedom than she did. Her tribe, the Votadins, had been conquered by the thieving Romans, who demanded provisions for their troops, fodder for their mounts, women for their beds and coin to fill the purses of every Roman who wasn't a soldier.

And if those conditions weren't bad enough, for all the kindness her father had demonstrated during her first two decades, Rhyddes may as well have been born a slave.

She scooped up more hay. Resentment-fired anger sent wisps flying everywhere, much of it sailing over the wagon rather than landing upon it.

"Hey, mind what you're doing!"

Owen, her closest brother in age and in spirit, emerged from the wagon's far side, hay prickling his hair and tunic like a porcupine. Rhyddes couldn't suppress her laugh. "'Tis an improvement. Just wait till the village lasses see you."

"Village lasses, hah!" Sporting a wicked grin, Owen snatched up a golden fistful, flung it at her and dived for her legs.

They landed in the fragrant hay and began vying mightily for the upper hand, cackling like a pair of witless hens. When Owen thought he'd prevailed, Rhyddes twisted and rolled from underneath him. Her fresh welts stung, but she resolved not to let that deter her. He lost his balance and fell backward. She pounced, planting a knee on his chest and pinning his wrists to the ground over his head.

Victory's sweetness lasted but a moment. Fingers dug into her shoulders, and she felt herself hauled to her feet and spun around. Owen's face contorted to chagrin as he scrambled up.

"Didn't get enough of the lash yestermorn, eh, girl?" Rudd, his broad hands clamped around her upper arms, gave her a teeth-rattling shake.

When she didn't respond, he turned his attention upon Owen. "And as for you—"

"Da, please, no!" Rhyddes stopped herself. Well she knew the futility of pleading with Rudd. Still, for Owen's sake, she had to try. Her father's scowl dared her to continue. She swallowed the lump that had formed in her throat. "'Twas not Owen's fault. I—" Sweat freshened the sting on her back, and she winced. "The fault is naught but mine."

Rudd eyed her for an interminable moment. "Aye, that I can well believe." He grasped each sibling by an arm and strode across the hayfield toward the family's lodge. "Owen can watch you take his lashes as well as yours. We'll see if that won't mend his ways." The thin linen of her ankle-length tunic failed to shield her from his fingers, which had to be leaving bruises. Rhyddes gritted her teeth. Rudd seemed disappointed. "I doubt anything in this world or the next will make you mend yours."

"You don't want me to change. You'd lose your excuse to beat me." Sheer impertinence, she knew, but she no longer cared.

"I need no excuses, girl."

The back of his hand collided with her cheek. Pain splintered into a thousand needles across her face. She reeled and dropped to her hands and knees, her hair obscuring her vision in a copper cascade. Hay pricked her palms. Owen would have helped her rise, but their father restrained him. He blistered the ground with his glare, obviously not daring to turn it upon Rudd for fear of earning the same punishment.

Not that Rhyddes could blame him.

Rudd yanked her up, cocked a fist…and froze. "Raiders!"

Rhyddes turned. And wished she hadn't. Picts were charging from the north to converge upon their farm, their battle cries growing louder under the merciless afternoon sun. One of the storage buildings had already been set ablaze, its roof thatch marring the sky with thick black smoke.

Rudd shed his shock and sprinted for the living compound, calling his children by name to help him defend their home: Eoghan, Ian, Bloeddwyn, Arden, Dinas, Gwydion, Owen.

Every child except Rhyddes.

Determined not to let that stop her, she ran to the wagon, unhitched the horse, found her pitchfork, scrambled onto the animal's back and kicked him into a jolting canter. The stench of smoke strengthened with each stride. Her mount pinned back his ears and wrestled her for control of the bit, but she bent the frightened horse to her will. She understood how he felt.

As they loped past the cow byre, a Pict leaped at them, knocking Rhyddes from the horse's back. The ground jarred the pitchfork from her grasp. The horse galloped toward the pastures. Frantically, Rhyddes fumbled for her dagger. Although her brothers had taught her how to wield it in a fight, until now she'd used it only to ease dying animals from this world.

But the accursed dagger wouldn't come out of the hilt. Sword aloft, the Pict closed in.

Time distorted, assaulting Rhyddes with her attacker's every detail: the lime-spiked hair, the weird blue symbols smothering face and arms, the wickedly sharp sword, the ebony leather boots and leggings, the breastplate tooled to fit female curves.

*Female?*

The warrior-woman's sword began its deadly descent.

From the corner of her eye Rhyddes saw her pitchfork. Grunting, she rolled toward it, praying desperately to avoid her attacker's blow.

Her left arm stung where the sword grazed it, but she managed to reach her pitchfork and scrambled to her feet, thankful for the shaft's familiar solidity. Unexpected eagerness flooded her veins.

As the Pict freed her weapon from where it had embedded in the ground, Rhyddes aimed the pitchfork and lunged. The tines hooked the warrior-woman's sword, and Rhyddes twisted with all her strength. The Pict yelped as the sword ripped from her hand to go flying over the sty's fence. Squealing urgently, the sow lumbered for cover, trying to wedge her bulk under the trough.

With a savage scream, the warrior-woman whipped out a dagger and charged. Rhyddes reversed the pitchfork and jammed its butt into the Pict's gut, under the breastplate's bottom edge, robbing her of breath. Quickly she reversed it again and caught her under the chin with the pitchfork's tines. As the woman staggered backward, flailing her arms and flashing the red punctures that marred her white neck, Rhyddes struck hard and knocked her down.

The warrior-woman looked heavier by at least two stones, but Rhyddes pinned her chest with her knee, hoping it would suffice. She dropped the pitchfork and grasped her dagger, thankful that it slid free this time. Grabbing a fistful of limed hair, she jerked the woman's head to one side to expose her neck.

The Pict bucked and twisted mightily, trying to break Rhyddes's grip. 'Twas not much different than wrestling a fever-mad calf.

Rhyddes's deft slice ended the threat.

Blood spurted from the woman's neck in sickening pulses.

Rhyddes stood, panting, her stomach churning with the magnitude of what she'd done. 'Twas no suffering animal she'd killed—and it just as easily could have been her lying there, pumping her lifeblood into the mud.

Bile seared her throat, making her gag. Pain lanced her stomach. Bent double, she retched out the remains of her morning meal, spattering the corpse.

After spitting out the last bitter mouthful and wiping her lips with the back of her hand, she drew a deep breath and straightened. As she slowly turned in a full circle, her senses taking in the sights and sounds and stench of the devastation surrounding her, she wished she had not prevailed.

The news only grew worse as she sprinted toward the lodge.

Of her seven brothers, the Picts had left Ian and Gwydion dead, her father and Owen wounded, the lodge and three outbuildings torched. She ran a fingertip over the crusted blood of her wound. It was scarcely more than a scratch, and she couldn't suppress a surge of guilt.

Mayhap, she thought through the blinding tears as she

ran to help what was left of her family, it would have been better had she died in the Pict's stead.

The surviving raiders were galloping toward the tree line with half the cattle. The remaining stock lay stiffening in the fields, already attracting carrion birds.

Three days later, the disaster attracted scavengers of a wholly different sort.

MARCUS CALPURNIUS AQUILA sprawled on his belly across the linen-draped marble massage table, head pillowed on his crossed arms, shins and feet jutting over the table's edge. As the male slave worked eucalyptus-scented unguent into the aching muscles of Marcus's shoulders, Marcus could feel the tensions of combat seep away.

Too bad the man couldn't work out the knots in Marcus's relationship with his father, Sextus Calpurnius Agricola, governor of Britannia province.

Citing "official business" yet again, Agricola had declined to witness Marcus's gladiatorial bout in Londinium's amphitheater this afternoon. Marcus's opponent had fought well, causing Marcus in his scanty armor to work up a sweat that surely had all the women swooning with delight.

Never mind that Marcus, who fought under his cognomen, Aquila, the "Eagle," remained a perennial favorite with the crowd. Agricola never missed an opportunity to point out that Marcus's public exhibitions—and the resulting private liaisons with adoring female spectators—flirted with the precipice of social acceptability and could damage Marcus's political aspirations.

While exceptions were made for aristocrats, everyone

else who plied their violent trade in the arena was considered *infamia:* "infamous ones," a step above condemned
criminals and grouped in the same class with undertakers,
prostitutes and actors. Infamiae could never become
citizens, and mere association with them had destroyed
many an otherwise stellar reputation.

As the slave's strigil scraped gently across Marcus's back,
removing dead skin and excess salve, Marcus snorted. He
had no political ambitions. In fact, he proudly considered
himself free of all ambitions whatsoever, save convincing his
father to accept him for who he was, not for how he could
enhance Agricola's career.

An uphill battle, to be sure.

A knock sounded on the chamber's door. At Marcus's
bidding, the slave opened it and exchanged a few murmured
words with another man. The blast of cool air and the sound
of two sets of footsteps told Marcus the slave had admitted
the visitor.

Marcus sat up, thrust out a hand to request a towel from
the slave, and draped it across his loins. Tribune Darius
Caepio, Agricola's chief of staff, who had officiated today's
bouts, entered the sudatorium. He looked even more dour
than usual, as if he wished he could fan himself but his
military decorum forbade it.

"Let me guess." Marcus raised an open hand. "I am late for
my father's dinner party." He asked the slave to towel his back.

"In your father's view, sir, that is the least of your trans-
gressions today." Darius stepped a pace closer to Marcus.
"Someone of importance saw you fighting in the arena."

"Fagh." Standing, Marcus made a dismissive gesture,

wrapped the towel more securely about him and strode past Darius into the comfortably cooler outer chamber where a freshly laundered loincloth, tunic and toga awaited. "I care not if Jupiter himself watches me." He dropped the towel, girded on the loincloth, and tugged the tunic over his head and arms, yanking it into place with savage pulls.

Only one being's opinion did Marcus crave, and he had yet to grace any of Marcus's bouts with his presence.

Darius almost smiled. "Jupiter is not dining with you at the praetorium this evening."

Caught in the midst of draping the blue-trimmed white woolen cloth about his six-foot frame, Marcus froze. "Not Senator Falco?"

"The same." This time Darius indulged himself in a rare smile. "And his daughter, the lovely Lady Messiena."

Darius, already three years past customary retirement, probably viewed every young woman in such kind terms. Marcus's recollection of Messiena, when their families had been neighbors in Rome before Emperor Marcus Aurelius had appointed Agricola as governor of Britannia, was anything but "lovely."

The senator's presence had been expected for several weeks. The emperor had dispatched him from Rome to investigate citizens' complaints of the Pictish coastal raids.

That Senator Falco had brought his daughter, however, was an unexpected development that boded ill for Governor Agricola's unmarried son.

**2**

RHYDDES STOOD SCOURING the last of the barley porridge from the cast-iron cauldron, still feeling numb, after three days, from the shock of losing Ian and Gwydion, when she heard the mounted troop clatter up to the hastily rebuilt lodge.

She didn't need to see them, didn't need to understand their accursed tongue. The bile burning her throat warned her who had arrived.

After working up a mouthful, she spat into the cauldron, grabbed fresh sand from the barrel and attacked the spot as if she could scour these visiting vermin and their ilk from the face of the earth.

She would have wagered three wagonloads of hay that the Picts must have torched some of the buildings in town, and the Romans had come to collect coin for repairs.

As if they could squeeze blood from a corpse.

Rhyddes scrubbed the cauldron with renewed vigor.

She had hung up the pot and was turning her attention toward the griddle when Owen burst, panting, into the kitchens. She grieved to notice lines furrowing his brow as deeply as those carved on their oldest brother.

Burying Gwydion and Ian had made Rhyddes feel ancient, too. Ancient and vulnerable.

To lighten his mood, she offered a thin smile. "If you've come for more food, you're too late."

"Nay." He beckoned. "Da has sent for you."

Indeed. Had the sow learned to fly, too?

Without bothering to shed her food-stained apron, she dusted the sand from her palms and strode toward the door.

Owen caught her arm, his face a study in anxiety. "He wants you dressed in your best."

A nameless fear clutched at Rhyddes's stomach.

Nay, not nameless. Her father must be planning to marry her off to one of these invaders. She felt her skin crawl.

But Rudd's word was law on this farm, and his daughter had no choice but to obey. She didn't need Owen's admonishment to hurry; she had no wish to feel the lash again.

"Dressing her best" meant exchanging her patched but serviceable overdress for one that hadn't experienced as much wear. After reaching her cramped quarters in the lodge, she removed the overdress from her clothes chest and gave it a peremptory shake. Not a fine garment by any reach of the imagination, it was in good repair, with only a small stain marring the front—stewed apples Owen once had lobbed at her—invisible save under the harshest sunlight.

She pulled off the dress that reeked of the kitchens and donned the better one. No sense in giving the bridegroom the impression he ought to keep her in the sty. Briefly, she considered whether to rebraid her unruly hair but decided it would be better to respond quickly to Rudd's summons.

Upon emerging from the lodge, she received her first surprise to find most of the sixteen Romans had already mounted. Only the soldiers' leader, apparent by his fancier armor, stood conversing with Rudd while another soldier scratched black marks on a brittle scrap of sheepskin.

The door banged shut behind Rhyddes, causing her to start. Rudd looked at her with an unreadable smile.

And well he might smile, she thought bitterly, since he would soon be rid of her by her marriage to one of these brutes.

"Hurry, girl!" Rudd called. "These men have other farms to visit."

The leader fixed upon her a penetrating stare. The other men, while obviously trying not to look, were sliding glances her way, too.

Cheeks aflame, she ran toward them.

"Is there not to be a ceremony, at least?" she dared to ask her father while eyeing the strangers warily. "Which is to be my husband?"

Rudd's peal of laughter chilled her.

"Pay her no mind, good sirs," Rudd told them. "Her wits may be feeble, but she works well, I promise you that."

"She had better."

The commander approached her and seized her chin. Alarmed, she stepped back, but his other arm whipped around her waist and held her fast. As if judging horseflesh, he moved her head from side to side and forced her mouth open to bare her teeth.

"Small, but she appears healthy enough," he said to Rudd. "Is she a virgin?"

The soldier's leer sent a warning prickle down her spine.

"What do you take us for," said Rudd, "rutting rams?" The commander glared at Rudd, who put up both hands and displayed an ingratiating grin. "Good, my lord, she has lain with no man."

Rhyddes failed to understand why the soldier looked disappointed. He released her face, strode to the soldier with the sheepskin and uttered something in their language. The underling made a few more marks on the skin, handed it to Rudd and mounted.

"Da, this sounds less like a betrothal than a—"

"Slave sale," Rudd finished for her. "You see, my lords, she is cleverer than she looks."

Horror coursed through Rhyddes in sickening waves as the chief soldier ordered one of his men to dismount and bind her wrists with rawhide strips.

"No, Da, please!" She tried to jerk free, but the cords bit into her flesh. "Don't sell me! I won't cause you any more trouble, I promise!"

Rudd's laugh froze her soul. "True enough, girl. You won't."

The soldiers' leader picked her up as one might heft a sack of grain, deposited her onto the back of one of the remounts, lashed her wrists to the saddle horn, collected her horse's reins in one gloved fist and handed them to one of the other mounted soldiers before vaulting astride his horse.

As the troop moved forward, she twisted back for her last look at her home. Furious tears blurred her vision, but she could never forget Rudd's smug look. Her brothers appeared from the fields to watch her pass out of their lives, every one looking as anguished as the last. Especially Owen.

She wanted to scream, cry, murder, anything to release the betrayal-forged fury in her heart. But the only litany to settle in her brain, mile upon jolting mile, was: *Da, how could you?*

After they had stopped to make camp, she learned why the commander had seemed disappointed to hear she was a virgin. According to the Romans' laws, since she was a virgin when the tax collectors acquired her, she had to be a virgin when they delivered her to the slaver who would bring her to market.

The chief ordered his men to tie her arms and ankles to a tree, facing its trunk, and his intentions became horrifyingly clear. As he hitched her skirts to expose her body below the waist, she felt his fingers lightly caress her inner thigh—almost lovingly—spiraling slowly upward until they reached the threshold of her warm, moist core. For a moment she thought that might satisfy him. How wrong she was.

Encouraged by his men's grunts and hoots, he probed deeper until it felt as if he was impaling her on his entire hand. She gritted her teeth and willed her mind back to the farm and the shelter of her brothers' love....

The soldier withdrew his hand and the real torture began. He spread her buttocks and slammed into her to become the first of several to slake his lust upon her without sacrificing her virginity. Screaming curses and pleading herself hoarse, she writhed in a futile attempt to escape each new assault, but that only goaded the men deeper into their depravity.

After they'd released her for the night, while the ache in her heart robbed her of sleep as surely as did the aching of her body, she stared at the cold, comfortless realm of the gods and changed her question.

*Da, why couldn't you have flogged me to death?*

MARCUS PAUSED UNDER the arch leading into the dining chamber, his fingers playing across the fluted column's cool ridges as he surveyed the room and its occupants.

Everyone appeared to be comfortably arrayed on the dining couches, set radially around the circular marble table and attended by more servants than flies on fresh horse dung. Strains of lyre music wove through the air from behind a gauze curtain. The mingled aromas of lamb and salmon wafted toward him on the freshening breeze, making his stomach rumble. From the contents of the slaves' trays he realized dinner had advanced to the beef course.

Small wonder his parents weren't seething at his tardiness.

He attributed the miracle to the presence of their distinguished guests, Senator Publius Messienus Falco and his raven-haired daughter, Lady Messiena.

The graceless girl with the pimply face and toothy, silly grin had indeed grown into a lovely young woman. Not what Marcus would call a stunning beauty, but the pimples had vanished, and the womanly curves visible from beneath her stola's drape pleased the eye. He caught himself wondering whether they would be equally pleasing to the touch.

The sound of clapping startled Marcus from his reverie. "Well," said Senator Falco, continuing his ovation. "The Eagle has returned from the kill."

Marcus squared his shoulders, as if preparing for a gladiatorial bout, and strode into the chamber.

Agricola regarded Marcus sharply. "You killed your opponent?"

"No, Father." A thousand barbed retorts demanded release, but in the interest of family unity, he held his peace.

"No," echoed the senator, "but a finer stoop I have never seen, by man or fowl."

Marcus wasn't sure whether to take the remark as a compliment or an insult. Diplomacy forced him to settle on the former, and he expressed his thanks.

Messiena favored Marcus with a coy smile that hinted at her opinion of his fight. He inclined his head in her direction.

Agricola cleared his throat as Marcus took a hot, damp towel from a slave for cleaning his hands. "Senator Falco, Lady Messiena, I can see you remember my son, Marcus Calpurnius Aquila."

Marcus returned the towel to the slave's tray. Hand to chest, he bowed slightly and advanced to take his place on the sole remaining couch, between his mother and the senator.

Messiena's gaze, through demurely lowered lashes as she reclined on the other side of Falco, never left Marcus.

"We were discussing the threat posed by these northern Pictish devils," stated the senator as servants loaded delicacies onto Marcus's gold-embossed silver platter, and Marcus attacked the pile with as much gusto as decorum allowed. "Have you an opinion of what should be done, Aquila?"

He did not. Governing this backwater province was his father's task, thanks be to all the gods. Marcus savored a mouthful of poached salmon while he decided upon the most tactful response. "I am sure," he said at length, "that my revered father has matters well in hand."

"Indeed, he would, given ample resources," Falco said between swallows of wine, "which the emperor cannot spare, at present, because of the disastrous Armenian campaigns."

The senator gave Agricola a measuring look, but if he was hoping to find even a hint of consternation, Marcus knew he'd be disappointed. Agricola was too new to this governorship, too grateful for the appointment, and thus too loyal to Emperor Marcus Aurelius, to be subverted that easily.

"I've heard our fortunes are finally improving along that frontier," Agricola said, "thanks to the brilliant military leadership of our venerable coemperor, Lucius Verus."

Marcus shifted to more easily regard his father. "Resources for Britannia? Do you mean soldiers?"

"In part, yes," Agricola replied. "The Picts have been attacking coastal farms from the sea—or, more precisely, across these infernally wide estuaries the locals call 'firths.'" As Agricola warmed to his topic, the gravy-smothered beef cubes on his platter cooled. "I would like to build a series of fortified lighthouses along the northeast coastline, between the walls of Hadrian and Antoninus, both to aid mariners and to serve as troop garrisons, so our men can respond to attacks faster."

"But won't the lighthouses help the raiders, too, Governor Agricola?" Messiena asked. Her father glared at her, and she averted her gaze, her cheeks flushing prettily.

"Lady Messiena raises a valid point," Marcus insisted, earning a raised eyebrow from Falco and an approving nod from Marcus's mother, Loreia.

Agricola shrugged. "These barbarians attack at all hours

of the day and night already. If they know the lighthouses are manned by more than a lone soul with a torch, it should deter them from mounting seaborne raids." Agricola popped a dried, pitted apricot into his mouth, chewed and swallowed. "The main issue, as the esteemed senator has observed, is funds."

"But if these Picts remain determined to raid their Celtic neighbors, they could change their tactics," Marcus said.

"Why not simply send in a legion or two and kill them all, Sextus?" Loreia asked.

Agricola favored her with an indulgent smile. "Because, dear wife, it is not that simple." His expression sobered. "The Picts are an unbelievably savage race. The general for whom I am named needed *four* legions to succeed a hundred years ago, and even with far superior numbers, weapons and equipment, General Agricola couldn't subdue them entirely. I possess stacks of reports telling a common tale: the Picts hit hard and fast, take what they can, burn or kill the rest, leave their dead to rot and vanish into the hills. Even the best legionnaires cannot fight ghosts."

Messiena and Loreia exchanged worried glances, prompting Agricola to apologize for offending their delicate sensibilities.

Loreia beamed. "Apology accepted, Sextus. And as penance, we shall now discuss why our honored guest has consented to bring his charming daughter so far from home."

Marcus suppressed a groan; he could all but hear what was coming. So he spared everyone the trouble of dancing around the issue. Looking squarely at his father, he asked, "Where is the betrothal contract?"

The elders laughed. Messiena blushed.

"Hold on, Aquila," admonished the senator. "No contract has been drawn up."

"Yet," Agricola added meaningfully. "You see, Falco, my son's hasty words prove my point, if his arena actions weren't convincing enough. He stands in sore need of a good woman to settle him down."

"The question remains whether my daughter should be the one to perform this task." Falco shifted onto his side to face Marcus. "What are your ambitions, Aquila?"

It was an admirably subtle way of asking what Marcus could contribute to this proposed union, and what advantages Senator Falco could derive from it. That Marcus had never considered the issue was a gross understatement.

Marcus drank deeply from his goblet, but the wine turned rancid in his mouth, and he swallowed hard. The only possible answer he could give was the one that would curtail his freedom:

"Whatever my esteemed father thinks is best." The words nearly made him choke.

Loreia smiled her appreciation.

Agricola all but openly gloated. "Excellent, Marcus. You may begin by ceasing this gladiatorial foolishness at once."

"But, Father—" Agricola's warning glance cut him off, but he stiffened his resolve. "Just hear me out, please. I have a match scheduled in eleven days, and it would be very awkward to withdraw at this late date. Besides, the people—your people enjoy watching me compete. This increases your popularity."

"Hah. I very much doubt that you think about my popularity as you prance, half-naked, about the arena."

Marcus gave a conciliatory nod. "Point taken, sir. Still, when they cheer for me, they cheer for our family."

Agricola looked toward Falco, and the senator nodded. "The crowd does love your son, Agricola. Do you agree, Daughter?"

Messiena returned, with a slight shake of her head, from whatever world she'd been occupying. "Yes, Papa." Her smile, no longer toothy or silly, looked wistful. Hopeful, even.

His foreboding mounted; time to try levity. "Besides, the games give me excellent exercise." Marcus grinned. "You would not want a future leader of Rome to become soft, would you, Father?"

"If exercise is what you seek, Marcus, I can always appoint you as a military tribune and attach you to one of Britannia's legions." That pronouncement earned Agricola a low, warning hum from Loreia. They exchanged a look. "On the other hand, the legions are plagued by spoiled, wealthy sons who don't possess the first clue about soldiering. I would be doing our emperors a favor by keeping one more out of the ranks."

"Ah, but your eagle does harbor ambitions," crooned the senator. Marcus mistrusted the calculating glint in the man's flinty eyes. "Perhaps even to become the Eagle of Rome one day?"

"Most certainly not," stated Agricola flatly before Marcus could reply. "Emperor Marcus Aurelius and his brother are good men. Surely their reign shall make Rome prosper."

"If it doesn't bankrupt her first," muttered Falco.

It was Agricola's turn to give Falco a measuring stare. "And it is my duty as a provincial governor, and yours, Senator Falco, along with the rest of the empire's highly ranked servants, to ensure that calamity does not come to pass. Would you not agree?"

Falco spread his hands and inclined his head in a noncommittal pose. Marcus glanced at his father but could not discern how Agricola had interpreted Falco's gestures.

Marcus had developed the rudiments of a theory, but he submerged his suspicions. Such speculation could get him killed.

"Perhaps I have not made myself clear," Agricola continued. "I cannot tax the residents of Britannia into oblivion to support my plan for defending them. I was hoping, Senator Falco—" his tone sharpened "—to enlist your assistance in the Senate with regard to obtaining appropriations. Since you do not appear to be interested in backing Britannia's cause, then perhaps you and I have no further business to discuss."

Lady Messiena looked downright crestfallen. Marcus masked his relief with a swig of wine.

Falco grinned ingratiatingly. "Now, Agricola, I did not intend for my silence to be construed as a refusal."

"Then you accept my earlier offer?"

"Earlier offer?" Marcus suspected the answer.

"Why, to display solidarity before the Senate by joining you and my daughter in marriage, of course," Falco replied. "Providing that you agree to a permanent withdrawal from the arena first, Aquila. Your father is correct. Such frivolous behavior is not seemly for a fledgling politician."

Refusal wasn't an option. Every Roman father possessed the legal right to do whatever he deemed necessary to punish a disobedient child—even execution.

And yet acceptance would seal Marcus's personal and public fate in one cunning stroke.

He glanced at his parents, but their beaming countenances denied reprieve. Not that he had expected any.

Marcus sucked in a breath, feeling like a drowning man fighting for air. "As you wish, Father, Senator Falco. I shall speak with Lanista Jamil on the morrow."

"But what of your upcoming match?" Messiena asked.

"I am sorry to have to disappoint you, Lady Messiena," Marcus said glumly, already framing the words of the withdrawal he would have to give the gladiators' owner. In spite of their friendship—or because of it—he was not looking forward to Jamil's reaction.

A plea glittered in Messiena's liquid brown eyes as she turned toward Agricola. "I cannot speak for the citizens of Britannia, but I would very much like to watch him compete again, Governor Agricola, with your permission."

Agricola set his jaw, no doubt unhappy at being publicly backed into a corner. Marcus kept his eyes trained upon his dinner plate. Its cold contents had lost all appeal.

"Very well. One final match." Marcus gave him a sharp, questioning glance. Agricola responded with a slight shrug. "It will give me a chance to see you compete, too. Afterward, you retire your sword, is that clear?"

"Yes, sir." Marcus felt too stunned, as much by Messiena's daring as by his father's response, to do more than murmur his thanks to both of them.

Falco extended his hand to clap Marcus on the back. "Then I am pleased to accept you as Messiena's betrothed, Aquila."

If Messiena or Loreia could have looked any happier, Marcus couldn't fathom how.

Agricola inclined his head toward the senator. "Please

convey my assurances to Emperor Marcus Aurelius and the Senate that the residents of Britannia—citizen and non-citizen alike—shall be well served by my plan." He turned a fatherly smile upon the senator's daughter. "I bid you welcome to our family, Messiena."

Marcus marveled at his father's control; in Agricola's place, he would have been demanding to know what had caused Falco's apparent change of heart.

Throughout the animated banter that followed—wedding details, led mostly by the ladies—he couldn't shake the notion that he'd just signed his own crucifixion order.

3

JAMIL OF TANIS, Egyptian by birth and a Roman citizen by right of having survived two decades of compulsory military service, including a stint as a centurion of the Praetorian Guard, flicked his horsetail whisk much as its original bearer had done, to chase off flies as he strode past Londinium's wharves toward the slave market. Lord Ra shone auspiciously bright on this, the nineteenth day of July by the Romans' reckoning and the first day of the Egyptian New Year.

Word on the street buzzed that a ship had arrived with captives from northern Britannia. As owner of Villa Britanniae, Londinium's gladiatorial school, and the gladiators' principal trainer, Jamil kept a constant watch for promising candidates. And on such a propitious day as this, he hoped the goddess Maat would deign to be generous.

Years ago, while fighting to quell the massive Pictish uprising that had convinced Hadrian's successor, Emperor

Antoninus Pius, to build a second wall across northern Britannia, Jamil had observed fierce women warriors swelling the barbarians' ranks. Perhaps some had been captured at long last. Female gladiators had become quite the rage across the empire—and not always for their fighting skills.

But even if Jamil could add a gladiatrix to his collection and she became the provincial champion, he had no wish to take her to Rome. There certain death awaited him.

"Sir! Were you born that way?" A young boy, already being shushed and pulled away by his mother, pointed at Jamil's pox-ravaged face.

He shook his head to answer the child but also to banish his evil memories—and the guilt. He resolved to concentrate on the present.

Londinium's slave market, situated on the northern bank of the river Tamesis, within easy litter distance of the city's wealthiest district, was always a riotous affair of slavers displaying their goods to everyone from the serious buyer to the mildly curious. The troops looked faintly bored as they stood in full armor under the July sun, clutching their spears and attempting to stay alert. Sweat, perfumes and meat cooking at the prolific vendors' stalls mingled into chaotic scents. Equally chaotic were the sounds as people of all classes and ages milled about, stepping forward at intervals to examine a particular specimen or ask questions of the slaves' handlers, competing to be heard over the auctioneer's battlefield timbre.

The slaves being sold were easy to identify: they were naked, save for the brass plate inscribed to identify the slave's age, regional origin and an abbreviation indicating occupation, such as *DOM* for household help or *AG* for a farm laborer. Some of the younger women bore an additional descriptor: *V* to certify their virginity. Monetary penalties for misrepresenting a slave's description were high and rigorously enforced.

After making a cursory circuit of the square, Jamil noted two or three men who might make promising gladiator candidates, but no women. Perhaps the divine Lady Maat had not destined him to have an auspicious year after all.

As the auctions proceeded and owners began leaving with their new possessions, a large crowd remained in one corner of the square. On his way to investigate, Jamil noticed the governor's son heading in the same direction.

"Hail, Aquila," he called, waving his whisk.

Marcus Calpurnius Aquila stopped, turned, and favored Jamil with a regretful smile. "You're still speaking with me in spite of my—shall we say, involuntary retirement?"

"You're not retired until tomorrow night." Jamil mirrored Aquila's smile and stowed the whisk in his belt. "After that, I will still be permitted to greet a friend, will I not?"

The young man clapped him warmly on the shoulder. "Thank you for understanding, Jamil."

What was to understand? Jamil had known that Aquila would have to abandon the arena sooner or later. That it had to happen sooner, because of a woman, came as no surprise.

Rather than sharing those thoughts, Jamil asked, "Buying a sparring partner?"

"It depends on what sort of sparring you mean." Aquila's smile became a mosaic of rebellious triumph and lust as he nodded toward a trio of attractive virgins standing roped together under the shade of a mutton vendor's awning, guarded by a soldier. Aquila had already bought them each a plain, ankle-length tunic for transporting them to the praetorium modestly. "I call it shopping for wedding presents."

The veteran of the three-year Judaic revolt during Hadrian's reign chuckled. "Wedding presents to serve your future wife, or for yourself?"

"Guess." Aquila's expression sobered. "But with your permission, I would like to continue sparring with your men."

Jamil agreed. "Their moves become too predictable if all they do is practice upon one another."

By this time, Aquila and Jamil had reached the crowd's fringe. The taller Aquila could peer over most people's heads, and Jamil studied him for a reaction. His patience was rewarded with a glimpse of that unique expression of a man who sees what he wants and resolves to obtain it at any cost.

The center of this crowd's attention had to be female and perhaps deserving of Jamil's consideration. He stepped behind Aquila as the lad invoked his rank to open a path through the throng.

No, not female, Jamil silently amended: a goddess. A decidedly short goddess, however. The top of her head barely passed Aquila's bicep. But, unlike the other women, she posed defiantly, as if challenging anyone to find fault with her body.

As WITH SURVIVING her treatment among the soldiers, Rhyddes found anger to be an excellent ally for masking her fear and embarrassment. To be forced to strip and parade naked in front of this leering crowd—a plague on all Romans! How she yearned to spit in their faces.

Fixing her gaze on a point at the top of the far wall while she dwelled upon happier days helped her weather the humiliation.

A pair of hands cupped her breasts, sending tingles scurrying through her body. She shifted her gaze to stare into the most alluring hazel eyes she'd ever seen, set into a tanned, ruggedly handsome face topped with closely cropped, curly black hair. The face of a god.

A Roman god, if the scarlet-bordered bed linens draped about his tall, muscular frame was any indication.

But, Roman or no, he was making her feel like a pampered goddess with his warm caresses. She closed her eyes and parted her lips in a soft sigh. When his touch became more firm, she regarded him again, puzzled by the change.

His face seemed lost in concentration. In the next breath Rhyddes realized he was kneading her flesh as dispassionately as a woman evaluating the ripeness of peaches.

She worked up a mouthful of spittle, fantasizing about how it would look adorning that arrogant face. Deciding it would buy her more trouble than she could afford, she swallowed and steeled herself to the Roman's touch. His haughty grin raised the hackles of her anger, suppressing other emotions he'd awakened.

Even so, 'twasn't easy.

The female slave's confidence proved well-founded, Jamil mused. Aside from her height, which could be used to entertaining advantage against a larger opponent, she possessed well-muscled limbs, very little spare flesh, except where it would most please a man, and a gorgeous face framed by bright, coppery hair. Keen intelligence glinted in her sea-green eyes.

Jamil glanced at his competitor.

Only serious bidders were permitted to touch the merchandise, and Aquila had wasted no time in exercising this right. Jamil watched the slave as Aquila fondled her in the usual places. Although she looked furious enough to bite off Aquila's head and spit out his teeth, she did not flinch. Her iron self-discipline earned her another point as a candidate gladiatrix.

Rather than mutely announcing his intent to bid, as Aquila had done—although it would have been prudent to test the slave's strength—Jamil contented himself with performing a visual inspection. When she met his gaze, he thought he saw a flash of fear displace the simmering anger, something he had not observed when her attention had been fixed upon Aquila.

Jamil shrugged off her reaction as a typical response to his face, which smallpox had disfigured years earlier.

He made a mental note of her description: an eighteen-year-old virgin Celt from northern Britannia, tagged as a farm laborer, which was unusual for a female. Not Pictish, then, as Jamil had hoped, but he found her occupation promising.

The right armor and weaponry could create an illusion for an audience eager to believe what they craved.

When he moved behind her, what he saw stopped him short.

A dozen fading welts marred the creamy perfection of

her skin across her shoulders and upper back. Aquila, who had stepped back for the bidding, probably had not seen the injuries.

Jamil drew her handler aside. "Did you inflict those?"

"No, sir. She had them when I bought her." The slaver's passable Latin bore the distinctive drawl of the residents of northern Britannia.

"And you bought her from—?"

The man, clearly not happy at being pressed to disclose this information but required by law nonetheless, nodded, frowning, toward the governor's residence, the praetorium's whitewashed perimeter walls visible beyond the slave market. "She was sold to pay a tax debt. The tax collectors certified that they did not inflict any harm upon her."

"Indeed," Jamil muttered with disgust. "That depends upon how one defines *harm*." He'd heard of many cases, especially regarding tax sales, where a female slave was used in degrading ways while preserving her virginity and thus her value.

But when the slaver began digging through a pouch hanging from his belt, presumably to produce the requisite proof, Jamil touched his arm. "No need for that, friend. I believe you."

It was just as well, for the auctioneer called for this female slave to step onto the block. To her credit, she obeyed with minimal prodding.

As required, she pivoted slowly to give all bidders a full view. Women gasped and made sympathetic sounds when they saw her welts. A few of the men called out lewd remarks, which went steadfastly ignored by the slave. That proud, defiant demeanor never left her face, even after the handler cuffed her to make her appear more submissive.

The average citizen would want no truck with a potentially rebellious slave. This woman's attitude and stripes trumpeted rebellion.

Her spirit didn't disturb Jamil; silently, he applauded it.

A prosperous-looking young man opened the bidding at a thousand brass sesterces, earning him a disapproving glare from the pretty woman standing beside him. Aquila raised the bid to the more typical amount of twelve hundred, the equivalent of a month's wages for a common laborer.

Jamil jumped the bid to two thousand, shutting out all but the most serious bidders. A novice gladiator could earn his owner a hundred times that amount for winning his first bout.

While the opening bidder seemed disappointed, his lady looked distinctly relieved.

A new bidder joined the fray for this intriguing female slave, raising the bid to five thousand. Although Jamil couldn't see the man clearly through the crowd, his spine tingled a warning. He shook it off as foolishness and doubled the bid.

Aquila seemed content to let Jamil and the other bidder fight to forty thousand.

"A bit expensive as a toy for your gladiators, don't you think, Jamil? Or do you plan to keep her for your bed?" Aquila said as he signaled fifty.

"It's obvious how you would like to use her, Aquila. How do you think your betrothed will react to the competition?" The auctioneer asked for sixty, and Jamil nodded.

Aquila's joviality evaporated. "You have no right to drag my betrothed into this conversation." He jumped the bid to seventy-five.

With a dismissive wave, the third bidder stalked away.

Jamil smiled serenely and nodded the next increment. "Now, Aquila, are you certain you wish to pay more than that…to your own father?"

Aquila shot Jamil a perplexed look. "What do you mean?"

"She was sold to pay a tax debt," Jamil answered, "so if you were to buy her, you would, in effect, be paying the governor for the privilege."

"Your bid, sir?" asked the auctioneer of Aquila, probably extending the courtesy only because the aristocrat had proven himself such a good customer already.

The governor's son shook his head. Jamil purchased his first candidate gladiatrix for a staggering one hundred thousand sesterces, probably twenty times the tax her father had owed.

As Jamil settled the deposit with the auctioneer and led his acquisition from the slave market, he prayed to Lady Maat that this woman wouldn't prove to be a foolish investment.

RHYDDES COULD FOLLOW enough of the proceedings to realize the two primary bidders shared cordial ties, although she'd have sacrificed her right hand to learn what the man who'd purchased her had said to anger his rival.

Privately, she had cheered to see that arrogant—if intoxi-catingly handsome—Roman lose the bid to the older, darker skinned man with the pox-pitted face. The prospect of becoming the arrogant one's bed-slave, only to be cast out when she no longer interested him, had frightened her, though she had taken care to bury her fear.

The older man had disturbed her when she'd caught a

glimpse of his poxy face. And yet, oddly enough, his countenance had heartened her. In a society whose people placed
great value upon beauty and physical perfection, he had
somehow managed to carve himself a comfortable niche.

If he could do it, then by all the gods, Rhyddes—in spite
of her wretched circumstances—could, too.

The losing bidder approached them, carrying a length of
fabric draped over one arm. His smile made Rhyddes's heart
stutter, and she chided herself for her weakness. The man
embodied everything she despised about Rome, and she
fervently hoped never to see him again.

That infuriatingly charming smile, as he proffered the
garment to her after exchanging a few words with her new
owner, suggested otherwise.

Rhyddes had never felt more thankful to don clothing.

By the time she had poked her head and arms through
the proper holes, the affluent Roman was gone. She didn't
expect that to disappoint her as much as it did. Neither did
she expect to be pricked by a pang of jealousy as she spotted
him across the square, herding his newly purchased female
slaves toward the heavily guarded set of buildings dominating the riverbank nearby.

The tug of ropes binding her wrists broke her reverie, and
she glanced down. To her surprise, her owner had tied the
bonds comfortably. A quick jerk, however, affirmed the
knots' strength.

Sternness invaded her owner's gaze, reminding her of her
dreaded father. "No escape," he said in the Celtic tongue.
"You try, you die."

Rhyddes's eyebrows shot up. His message had been

crudely formed but unmistakably clear. "Aye, my lord," she murmured, gaze downcast.

She felt her owner slip his fingers under her chin and pull, gently yet firmly, upward.

"Not lord. *Lanista.*"

"Is that your name, sir?"

Frowning, he shook his head, lips pursed. "Means 'master of sword.'"

Though she couldn't fathom why a "master of sword" would have bought her, she nodded, which seemed to please him.

They started forward, and she almost forgot her plight amid the myriad fascinating sights, sounds and smells of this madly pulsing collection of tile-roofed buildings peopled by what seemed to be every race known to heaven.

Cooking odors—some she recognized, like beef, mutton and pork; many, she didn't—reminded her she hadn't eaten a hot meal in days.

Wagons vied for passage among the riders and the swarms of people traveling on foot. Children frolicked with dogs in front of impossibly clean-looking houses. Bairns squalled in their mothers' arms. Cats chased rodent prey into alleys.

Soldiers loomed everywhere. Some were stationary, like those guarding the slave market; some patrolled afoot and on horseback. Each time the sun glinted off a spearhead, helmet or breastplate, she fought the overwhelming urge to run.

Her owner halted. Rhyddes stumbled into him. She uttered an apology but realized he wasn't heeding her.

All color had drained from his face. She followed the line of his gaze toward a man who wore the robes favored by wealthy Romans but carried himself warily, as befitting a warrior visiting unfamiliar territory. The man's gaze seemed distant, as if he were seeking someone.

Her owner laid a hand on her waist, drew her close and kissed her. The gesture was devoid of passion.

Panic welled. It felt as if she was kissing her father!

She tensed but bridled the urge to push away. This man owned her body, she reminded herself.

Rhyddes had endured enough ill treatment in the past ten days to fill three lifetimes. If her new owner wished to use her to avoid detection, well, that was better than being used for baser reasons. She willed herself to relax in his embrace.

He broke contact, glanced nervously about the square, and began ushering her away from the town's center more swiftly than before. Of the wealthy man—if indeed that was the person her owner had been trying to avoid—there was no sign.

Softly, and a mite awkwardly, he expressed his thanks.

Not knowing how to respond, she remained silent, though curiosity pricked her to learn what had troubled him so.

As they trod the road leading toward the city's fortress and a massive, turf-and-stone structure with a group of buildings squatting nearby, she felt unmistakable twinges of caring toward this man.

**4**

RHYDDES'S OWNER LED her through a massive gate. The complex was guarded within as well as without, though these men wore iron-studded leather jerkins rather than the silvery, metal-banded gear favored by the soldiers, thanks be to all the gods.

The women all seemed to be servants, carrying water urns, platters of food, baskets of laundry and bandages, sweeping, scrubbing or scurrying about on some errand. In addition to the guards, menservants and craftsmen, many men were occupied with fighting drills, wielding a dizzying array of weapons in the central courtyard, which, strangely, was separated from the colonnade by a sturdy iron fence, thrice man-height.

The fence reminded her of a cage, and she shivered.

Rhyddes, presuming she was fated to join the servants' ranks, was astonished when her owner turned into a cavernous room adjoining the courtyard and ordered her to follow him inside.

Hooks and racks supported weapons of every description: daggers, war-knives, swords and spears, each blade honed to gleaming perfection. Stranger weapons resided here, too: spiked clubs, staffs, weighted nets and three-tined tools similar to the pitchforks used on her father's farm. Armor, shields and helmets of various styles hung from pegs driven into the walls.

The man strode to a section of wall displaying one of each type of weapon, stopped and faced her.

"Your name, woman?"

"Rhyddes ferch Rudd, master." She sighed. "Freedom, daughter of Red."

He said her name a time or two, as if practicing. "You fight, Rhyddes?" He pronounced it "ree-this," rather than the proper way, "hree-dthes," but she appreciated his effort.

She jutted her chin. "I killed a raider."

He looked impressed and...pleased? "Kill—how?" His gesture indicated the wall.

Rhyddes stepped forward and pointed to the trident and the war-knife.

Stroking his chin, he nodded slowly. "I, Jamil of Tanis, teach you to fight good. Make people cheer." He turned to lift a short sword off the wall and posed with it in an attack stance. "This, *gladius:* sword. You—" he extended the sword toward her chest "—*gladiatrix:* sword-woman. You learn to make good fight show, kill clean, no pain." His countenance darkened as he slapped the blade's flat against his palm. "If you do not learn, do not obey, you die."

She took the proffered weapon and hefted it, finding it heavier than the war-knife her brothers had taught her to wield, but much more elegant and dangerous than a pitchfork.

Mayhap with this sword she could win back her freedom....

"Obey or die. Say it, woman." His tone forbade disobedience.

Rhyddes looked up from the sword, mystified. "Master?"

"Do this." He thumped his right fist over his heart and held the pose. Clutching the sword, she complied, the sword's point extending past her shoulder. "Now say, 'I will obey or die.'"

*Obey or die.*

Even under her tyrant father, discipline hadn't been that strict. She swallowed convulsively. The fist gripping the sword's hilt began to tremble, and she hated herself for the weakness. She tightened her grip, and the trembling stopped.

"Say it!" thundered Jamil of Tanis.

Her head reeling with a thousand implications, she blurted, "I will obey!" She drew a shuddering breath and let it out slowly. "Or...die."

"Good." He laid a hand over her fist and pried the sword from her grasp. She felt only too happy to surrender it to him. "Well come to *Familias Jamilus*." She wanted to ask him what those last words meant, but he had turned to replace the sword on its pegs. Regarding her again, he gave an impatient wave. "Come, Gladiatrix. Learn your new home."

Outside the armory, he beckoned to one of the guards, who had been standing in the walkway's shade with his companions and watching the warriors mock-fighting within the cage. From his graying hair and weathered face, Rhyddes judged the man and her father to be of an age, though where Rudd had started growing a paunch, this man's work kept him trim and fit.

But his leer reminded her of her first captors, and she recoiled in alarm.

Jamil of Tanis yelled a string of words, and the guard's leer instantly yielded to contrition. Apparently not content with that, Jamil shouted something else. Everyone came running. While the caged warriors dropped their weapons and wedged as closely as the bars would permit, the guards, craftsmen and servants crammed into the open-air walkway around Jamil and Rhyddes. Jamil resumed his rant, waving his arm toward her with adamant gestures.

One word emerging time and again out of the jumble Rhyddes recognized, for it was the only word of the Romans' language the soldiers had bothered to teach her: *virgo*.

Virgin.

Only they had used it in scorn, for it was the one thing that had prevented them from fully defiling her.

She studied the faces: some openly hostile and resentful, others neutral or mayhap a wee bit friendly. And yet the tax collectors' actions had taught her another vital lesson:

Trust nobody.

Her owner uttered something that caused every man and woman to bark a single word and salute him. He nodded, apparently satisfied, and regarded Rhyddes earnestly. "No fear. You safe, Gladiatrix. Them, you…no touch." As she tried to puzzle out what he meant, his smile turned sardonic. "They do not obey, they die."

He intended to enforce her virginity upon pain of death?

Was he saving her for himself? Not if his actions in the slave market were any sign.

Probably, she mused bitterly as he dismissed the crowd except for one female servant and the guard whose leer had ignited Jamil's rage, her owner intended to auction her virginity to the highest bidder. That handsome Roman from the slave market, perhaps....

Unbidden rose the memory of his hands cradling her breasts, and she felt a rush of moist warmth between her legs.

Soundly she denounced her womanish weakness. These Romans had turned her into a slave; she'd be damned by all the gods before she let anyone turn her into a whore.

Her guard grasped her arm, though not hard, and propelled her through the thinning crowd toward a shadowy corridor, lit by torches mounted between each pair of rounded doorways. The guard guided her into the first of these doorways, which opened into a large, deserted chamber filled with niches and benches. A clever pattern of dolphins, fish and waves, wrought in tiny tiles, decorated the floor. The guard spoke something to the woman who had followed them and departed the chamber.

The woman led her into an alcove, with its own bench, pegs and niches, where they wouldn't be visible from the doorway. Hands on hips, she gave Rhyddes a long appraisal. Abruptly she spun and began pulling several items from the niches: an undyed tunic, two narrow lengths of linen, a stack of towels and tiny vials filled with the gods alone knew what.

Mayhap the woman could read Rhyddes's thoughts, for she

set aside her burdens to pull the stopper from a vial and hold it to Rhyddes's nose. Rhyddes took a tentative sniff and was rewarded with the scent of roses…and the memory of the dense canes arching across the pastures' hedgerows back home, bursting forth in a dizzying profusion of tiny white blooms….

Don't cry, she sternly reminded herself, blinking.

The entire time, the woman's actions were chorused by soft words Rhyddes wished she could understand, for they sounded motherly and reassuring.

Rhyddes had never known the comfort of a mother's love; her mother had died birthing her, and Rudd had never remarried.

The instinct to trust nobody began to seem too harsh.

Offering a sympathetic smile, the servant gestured for Rhyddes to undress. With "obey or die" echoing in her brain, she complied. The dress puddled on the stone floor, followed by her breast band and the cloth girding her loins. The servant wrapped her in towels, collected the vials in one hand, and guided her through a doorway that opened onto a rectangular stone pool.

Mist drifted across its surface, reminding Rhyddes of the ponds at home in the quiet stillness of dawn, her favorite time of day.

*Don't cry.*

The servant emptied the vials of rose oil into the pool and motioned for Rhyddes to shed her towels and step in. 'Twas without doubt the strangest bathing place she'd ever seen, but after a fortnight without having the chance to clean herself properly, she'd have bathed in Lugh's divine spittle.

She stepped onto the lip and dipped her foot into the water.

And jerked it out, gasping.

Rhyddes whirled toward the woman, who had knelt on the pool's rim. "What manner of sorcery is this?" She held no hope of the servant understanding her, but she couldn't bridle the outburst. The water was hot, with nary a flame in sight.

"No sorcery, Gladiatrix." Rhyddes glanced up to see her owner standing framed under the doorway. She felt the blush but chided herself; he'd already seen her fully naked once this day, as had half the residents of this accursed Roman town. Jamil flicked a hand toward the pool. "Bathe."

He didn't have to add the "or die" clause. Her brain had already ruthlessly reminded her.

Squaring her shoulders, she turned and swallowed her fears to step into the water, while Jamil and his servant spoke in low tones. She had to admit the water's warmth—not nearly as hot as she'd first imagined—felt blessedly good. Inhaling deeply of the rose scent, she unbraided her hair and sank up to her chin. Her coppery tresses fanned out around her.

"Servant woman name Materia," said Jamil of Tanis.

He departed the chamber, and the servant—Materia, Rhyddes supposed—grasped a smaller towel to begin scrubbing Rhyddes's head and hide.

Too bad Materia possessed nothing with which to scrub away the painful memories. Her soft singing helped a little, though. Rhyddes closed her eyes and slipped back to a happier time, when she and Owen, as young children, had cavorted across their father's fields in carefree delight.

*Don't cry!*

She pressed a wet hand to her face, breathing deeply.

Rhyddes wasn't sure how much time had passed before

she felt Materia's fingertips pry her hand away. She twisted to regard the servant, whose expression had shaded from sympathy to compassion. Rhyddes partook of the unspoken gift for a long moment before Materia smiled an apology and tugged on Rhyddes's hand in a clear command for her to leave the bath.

Having no idea how far this "obey or die" directive extended, Rhyddes didn't resist. As she emerged from the pool, Materia cloaked her in towels, helped her step down, and led her back into the chamber where she'd undressed. She bound Rhyddes's breasts and loins with clean strips of linen, blotted her tresses, and gave her the tunic.

Cut for a man, the garment extended only halfway down her thighs. After tapping her chin thoughtfully, Materia bustled to a niche and withdrew a pair of knee-length linen breeches. While Rhyddes donned those, the woman visited a different niche and returned with a leather belt for Rhyddes to cinch the tunic around her waist.

This new attire, unlike anything she'd ever worn and yet no different than the garb sported by the warriors sparring within the cage, suffused her with a sense of their power.

Her first sight of the guard waiting outside the bathing chamber, however, reminded her that she continued to live only at the sufferance of her owner, and her position as his newest slave was anything but powerful.

Rhyddes nodded her thanks at the servant woman, who smiled and hurried off. She hoped to see Materia again soon.

The guard escorted Rhyddes around the far side of the training enclosure, which now stood empty, to another large, vaulted chamber where the warriors were eating, seated in long rows. He directed her to a bench, said something to cause the men to shift down, and Rhyddes sat while her escort assumed a post standing against the nearby wall with the other guards. A servant set a wooden bowl of barley and bean porridge on the table in front of her, along with a wooden spoon and a pitch-sealed leather flagon of ale.

She dipped the spoon into the bowl and sampled the porridge. It was warm if bland, the ale was half water, and Rhyddes didn't have much of a stomach for either, but since it seemed to be the only fare to be had—and mayhap the only meal of the day, at that—she forced herself to partake.

At some unknown signal, the men put down their bowls and flagons, stood and raised their fists toward Jamil, who was sitting on a raised platform although he hadn't appeared to be eating. Not knowing what else to do, Rhyddes followed their example, if half a beat late. He lifted both arms and chanted something. The men, and Rhyddes, lowered their arms and began filing toward the doors to be paired with guards.

The guard who'd escorted Rhyddes to and from the bathing area fell into step beside her. She wished she could ask him what was happening.

It became clear soon enough.

While the warriors entered the bathing chambers, Rhyddes's guard took her past a series of stone pools to the latrine, which he let her use, unaccompanied, and on through a final, guarded door that opened onto another set of buildings.

She heard a set of footfalls behind them but dared not turn, lest that be interpreted as disobedience.

The buildings, she quickly learned as they entered the

first one, contained hideously narrow cells. Most, in the form of rumpled blankets or cast-off clothing, appeared occupied, if presently empty. All had vertical bars, like the training area in the other courtyard, running the width of the cell.

No secrets abided in this place.

The guard halted in front of an unoccupied cell, its barred door standing open as if enticing the unwary to enter. Rhyddes felt plenty wary, but she had no choice other than to heed its mute invitation. She stepped between the gray slate walls, careful not to bark her shins on the cot. If she stretched out her arms, her fingertips came within a forearm's length of brushing both walls at once.

Aside from the cot, its straw mattress and a scratchy wool blanket, the cell was devoid of furnishings. And of natural light.

"Like new home, Gladiatrix?"

She whirled and looked at the guard as if he'd grown a second nose. "You know my language?"

Grinning, he positioned thumb and forefinger to indicate how much.

'Twas good enough.

As he began to swing the door shut, she laid a hand on his arm and gazed earnestly at him. "I am sorry if I caused trouble for you earlier."

"No trouble." His short laugh sounded rueful. "Deserved it."

"Are you my guard now?"

"This—" he swept an arm to indicate the cells from hers to the end of the corridor, a dozen in all "—my duty."

"Alone?" It didn't seem to fit, with as many guards as she'd seen this day.

He shook his head and swung the door, backing her into the cell. "I must go."

The door shut with a terrifying clang.

"Sir!" She clutched the cold bars, failing to block the raw panic from her tone.

The guard paused with the key in the lock and regarded her curiously.

A hundred questions clamored for release. Every one started with, "Why?"

He frowned as if trying to discern what she'd asked. She wasn't sure herself. "Why the lock, Gladiatrix?"

'Twould do, for a start. She nodded.

He scrunched one shoulder. "Lanista Jamil's orders." He twisted the key. The lock engaged with a preternaturally loud click. "For all warriors—gladiators. And you, Gladiatrix." He withdrew the key, hooked the ring on his belt and turned away.

"May I know your name, sir?" It felt ungodly strange, asking that of a captor, but she hoped to reclaim a hint of humanity in this inhumane place into which the gods had thrust her.

"Vederi," he said without breaking stride.

He had already disappeared from sight before she realized he hadn't bothered to ask hers in return.

So much for humanity.

She sank onto the cot, head in hands and heedless of the straw poking her thighs through the mattress's canvas cover, and sobbed out all the rage, fear, despair and grief that had harried her for the past fortnight, feelings pride had forbidden her to show the soldiers or the slaver, denying them any chance to wield those emotions against her. Pain as visceral as any blade's thrust sliced into her gut. She dropped to her knees and pressed her cheek to the wall, painting it with her tears and pounding the cool slate with the heel of her hand.

"Da, how could you?"

Each futile thump knelled like another nail driven into the coffin housing the remains of her freedom.

"Da!"

THE GLADIATRIX'S PLIGHT bared wounds long buried in Jamil's past, as the desert winds scour away the sands burying a centuries-forgotten relic, exposing it to harsh scrutiny.

"Da!" she howled in her native tongue. *Father.*

Jamil winced.

The only child who would have known him by that title had not lived long enough to learn the word.

He had followed Vederi and the gladiatrix to make sure she was comfortably settled in her quarters, but two gladiators who'd decided to pick a fight in the baths had commanded his attention. By the time the guards had restored order, and Jamil had sent the offending gladiators to isolation cells, Vederi had already resumed his normal duties.

Now, with the woman's anguish echoing throughout the wing, he stood a few paces from her cell, lost in the uncharted territory of wishing he could help her but knowing he could not.

Jamil possessed a fair idea how his gladiatrix felt, if for different reasons.

Paralyzing grief had smitten him upon the death of his beloved wife and their only child, an infant daughter. His fingers crept up to rub the pits and wrinkles on his cheek. The pox had taken the lives of his wife and daughter, and left him a disfigured face as a permanent reminder of his dear ones' deaths.

Why Anubis hadn't claimed him, too, he couldn't begin to fathom.

Neither friends nor family could supply a mote of comfort during his mourning. Their well-intentioned words had sounded less like wisdom than inept platitudes.

He lowered his hand and knotted it into a fist.

Inept platitudes were all that leaped to mind at present. The gladiatrix—doubtless suffering from curtailment of what little freedom she'd previously enjoyed, and probably fear of the unknown, as well—did not need to hear ineptitude expressed in her own language, or any other.

Her sobs quieted, and Jamil withdrew. The guards soon would be escorting the men to their quarters for the night. Some of his gladiators seemed to resent the presence of a woman competitor; no sense in fostering discontent by appearing to show favoritism to an untried candidate.

As for her grief, Jamil knew the perfect remedy, which had worked for him while he'd served in the army. His gladiatrix would find little time for indulging in grief within the confines of the rigorous training regimen looming before her.

For if he did not train her hard enough, he would forfeit today's investment at the first blow struck against her upon the arena's sands.

5

AFTER A FITFUL night, guards rushed Rhyddes through a regimen of running, bathing, dressing and eating. Along with some other gladiator-slaves, who appeared as confused as she felt, and a dozen guards, Jamil of Tanis led them out of the training grounds and a quarter mile down the broad avenue to the arena.

The round earthen structure—topped by a crown of stone seats and surrounded by towering, fragrant, mushroom-shaped trees the likes of which Rhyddes had never seen—had not been visible from the slave ship. Yestermorn, when her owner had taken her past it on their way to the buildings where his gladiators lived and trained, the structure had stood empty and she had not grasped its significance.

This day, her first glimpse of the place where she would meet her gods nearly made her revisit her meal. Bile scalded her throat as she heard the crowd's cheers rise and fall from within.

Had her owner changed his mind about training her? Did he mean to sacrifice her, instead?

They approached a tunnel guarded by city soldiers, causing her gut to convulse again. When the troops turned away a clot of visitors but allowed the fledgling gladiators and their guards to pass, her dread ratcheted into panic.

Her owner laid a hand upon her arm. Flinching, she gasped.

"No fear, sword-woman," Jamil of Tanis said in his fractured Celtic. "Watch. Learn."

He snapped out a command, in that other language, to the guards who'd escorted them from the school. The guard to whom she'd spoken yestereve, Vederi, did not number among them.

Looking at Rhyddes and the rest of the gladiator-slaves, Jamil of Tanis pointed at a room, constructed to the left of the tunnel's arena-side arch, which was devoid of furnishings and featureless save a bank of barred windows facing the combat floor. While half the guards assumed posts outside, the rest ushered Rhyddes and the other slaves inside the slate-walled chamber that reminded her, except for the windows, of a larger version of her cell.

The clang of the barred door banging shut, followed by the lock clicking into place, worsened her gut's writhing.

Rhyddes wished somebody—her owner, a guard, anybody—would explain what was happening. But Jamil of Tanis had left them, and none of the guards responded to her tentative inquiries, except with looks of bored annoyance as they made shooing motions with their hands and spoke more foreign words.

Stymied, she returned to the windows like a moth to

flame as the first combatant entered the arena. Strangely, he was dressed less like a warrior than a hunter, in supple leathers dyed a dark shade of green, with only a hunter's long-bladed knife strapped to his bare left thigh and two rope coils tied with leather thongs to his belt.

As she wondered about the man's opponent, it emerged from a far tunnel, snapping at its handlers and crawling in a weird gait that bent its body this way and that as if it were a banner in a breeze. The grotesque gray lizard stood half as tall as a pony and stretched twice as long, if one included its tail, which appeared powerful enough to knock down a bull.

With uplifted snout and undulating tongue it scented its prey and, hissing menacingly, closed upon the hunter-gladiator with astonishing speed, mayhap goaded by the people's shouts.

The gladiator avoided the charge with a powerful spring that landed him beside the beast. Bellowing, it faced about to find its escaped prey. Another leap put the gladiator atop the lizard, infuriating it further.

What followed was a series of charges, sudden stops, twists and bucks as the lizard tried to dislodge the man flattened to its back, his arms wrapped about its neck. Just as it seemed the beast would win, the gladiator freed a rope, twined it around the lizard's neck, tied a knot and pulled back hard to tighten the noose. The gladiator's muscles quivered, and from her vantage Rhyddes could all but count each sweat droplet glistening upon his brow.

The lizard's movements slowed.

Reviving, it twisted and threw itself over with a thud that

echoed around the arena. The gladiator released the noose, leaped clear of the massive body and the sandy wave it displaced and jumped again to avoid that sweeping tail. Before the beast could finish recovering, the gladiator whipped free the second rope coil and tied the slavering jaws shut. He caught the noose rope and tightened it again.

The lizard's tail twitched a final time, and stilled.

The audience released a thunderous roar. Arms overhead, the gladiator accepted the adulations with triumphant glee.

A dozen handlers raced onto the sands toward the lizard, carrying more rope coils. They worked like fury to hobble the lizard's legs, and they secured the creature's neck, jaws and tail. Rhyddes presumed the men were preparing to drag the dead beast away, though why they'd hobbled it first, as if it were a grazing horse, she couldn't begin to guess.

The tail lashed.

The motion knocked one man off balance, and he lost his grip upon the rope. He scuttled backward and rolled out of the tail's reach. While he recovered his position, the other handlers gripped their ropes as the beast woke, looked about groggily and heaved to its feet.

The lizard glanced up at the crowd as if it were a seasoned veteran. After a pause, the audience cheered again.

Uttering what sounded like a disgusted snort, the lizard waddled toward the tunnel, flanked by its handlers and followed by the waving gladiator.

"That thing must be a favorite," muttered one of the slaves, in Celtic.

"What?" Rhyddes asked, as surprised by hearing the man speak her tongue as by the strange fight they'd witnessed.

"I'd heard they don't always kill the beasts. Must be true, then." He laughed bitterly. "Two fortnights' worth of that monster's food costs more than any ten of us, I'll wager."

Rhyddes hated to imagine what the handlers might feed such a fearsome creature. The bodies of dead gladiators, mayhap? Disobedient slaves? She shuddered.

The closest guard rapped his spear's butt on the slate floor and barked a word that sounded like "ta-kee-tee." Even if it wasn't the command for silence, Rhyddes and her companion abandoned their conversation.

To do anything else wasn't worth the risk.

With "Obey or die!" echoing in her mind, she resigned herself to silently watching the rest of the matches.

MARCUS STOOD INSIDE the tunnel, adjusting his provocator's helmet, which obscured his face and extended down his chest in a crescent breastplate. Upon completing the adjustment, he repeatedly flexed and relaxed the fist of his sword arm as his opponent entered via the tunnel across the arena floor following the announcer's introduction.

For his final performance, Marcus had requested Iradivus, "Wrath of God," the best of Jamil's gladiators who fought in the middleweight, provocator class.

Typically gladiators did not fight within their class, to produce the most spectator-gratifying results. But for some reason the cross-class custom had never extended to provocators. Marcus had sparred with Iradivus often, but this was the first time he'd chosen him for an arena opponent.

The Wrath of God was not something to challenge carelessly. The fact that Iradivus had painted crackling flames on either side of his black helmet enhanced the notion. Marcus smiled at the private admission of his superstition.

Ruthlessly quelling his nerves, he drew his sword and stalked onto the sands at the announcement of Aquila Britannia, the "Eagle of Britain."

Although Marcus had never troubled to look at a reflection of himself while garbed in his gladiator gear, he hoped the fresh silvering he'd commissioned for the eagle painted on his helmet would impress the audience and, most importantly, his father.

Judging by the audience's booming welcome, he had succeeded, at least partially.

Together he and Iradivus strode toward the governor's box, and together, sword in fist and fist over heart, they bowed to the dignitaries, including Senator Falco and Lady Messiena.

Eleven days of constant contact—smothering contact, in his view—had made Marcus even less enthusiastic about the betrothal. Although he'd done his best to play the dutiful bridegroom-to-be, he honestly couldn't wait for the pair to depart on the morrow, so Marcus could reclaim some semblance of his life.

Even if that semblance would no longer include competing in the arena, he expected it to at least give him an illusion of the freedom that seemed to be slipping from him, grain by inevitable hourglass grain.

Straightening, Marcus realized he'd held the bow longer than Iradivus had done. So be it; the audience, including his family, future wife and her father, were free to interpret the gesture in any manner they pleased.

Waiting for what felt like an aeon for Agricola to begin

the match, he studied his father, who had raised his right hand high overhead. To anyone else, Agricola probably looked like the consummate Roman politician, granite-faced and unreadable. More than two decades of practice revealed to Marcus his father's tension in the way Agricola squinted intently at the combatants as if trying to evaluate which would emerge the victor.

Perhaps that was exactly what Agricola was doing. And, just perhaps, that could be what had prevented Agricola from watching Marcus before.

He resolved, as sincerely as a temple vow, to demolish any doubts his father might harbor about his skills.

Agricola's hand fell, and the match began.

Though the gladiator-slaves had been locked inside the viewing room for all the games, which lasted past sundown, the experience had not been devoid of basic comforts. At frequent intervals, the guards brought beef, bread and ale. Just as frequently, the slaves were escorted to the latrine— a widened section of a stream flowing beneath the amphitheater to sluice away the filth of men and animals— whether the slaves needed such relief or not.

Rhyddes was surprised the first time guard and slave alike turned their backs to offer her a dollop of privacy.

After one such journey, the group returned to find the other guards windmilling their arms to hurry the slaves back into the chamber. Rhyddes felt swept along as if caught in a rain-fed torrent, somehow getting to the front for an unimpeded view through the bars while the other slaves and even the guards pressed around and behind her.

Two men in heavy leg padding, belted loincloths and full-face helmets, hefting shields and wielding swords like the one her owner wanted her to use, were hacking at each other with ferocious abandon. They seemed closely matched in size, strength and speed. The best way to tell them apart was by the markings on their helmets. One's helmet sported golden flames; the other's was adorned with a spread-winged silver eagle.

Despite Rhyddes's limited experience, instinct told her every other match she'd witnessed had been like watching a children's game compared to the performance of these masters.

As if of one voice, the crowd was shouting, "ah-kee-lah, ah-kee-lah, ah-kee-lah!" The noise level inside the viewing cell rose to deafening proportions as the guards and some of the slaves took up the chant.

Not knowing to whom the chant was directed, Rhyddes remained silent, enraptured by the rhythm of the pair's violent dance.

If someone had pressed her to choose a favorite, she'd have identified the eagle-helmed warrior, who moved with more grace and precision. Softly, in the Celtic tongue, she began chanting for him, feeling her admiration surge with every blow, thrust and kick he landed.

Fire-helm deflected Eagle-helm's heel after one such kick. Eagle-helm stumbled backward onto the sand. Ululating, Fire-helm lunged closer, sword extended. It missed Eagle-helm's shoulder by half a finger's breadth as Eagle-helm rolled clear.

Upon regaining his balance, Eagle-helm redoubled his

attack. Fire-helm, on the defensive from the furious rain of blows, blocked them but was driven backward, step by reluctant step. Both warriors' chests were heaving by this time, and sweat mingled with blood from myriad cuts.

Eagle-helm anticipated his opponent's move and thrust out his shield. It collided with Fire-helm's sword hand and knocked the weapon from his grasp. The sword left a trail of gouges where it skittered across the sand.

Fire-helm dropped to one knee, raising his weaponless hand with the first finger extended. Eagle-helm twisted to avoid hitting his downed opponent. He recovered a solid stance and pointed his sword at the expanse of Fire-helm's flesh lying exposed between the bottom of his helmet and the top of his loincloth's wide belt.

They froze in that position long enough for Rhyddes to have sketched their detailed images on the slate wall, had she possessed chalk.

From observing the earlier matches, she had learned to listen to the crowd's chants and watch their hand movements to predict the outcome. If they chanted "mee-sum" with thumbs thrusting upward, both warriors lived. A chant of "ee-oo-goo-lah," while jabbing thumb at neck, resulted in the loser's execution, either by the winner slitting his throat or delivering a thrust angled downward through the upper back.

While the richly attired, gray-haired Roman standing beneath the ivy-twined canopy appeared to be the judge, he had not opposed the crowd's will whenever it had sounded unanimous, as in their verdict regarding this match.

Fire-helm had fought extremely well, and the audience, as Rhyddes had expected, chanted for his dismissal.

The Roman judge's thumb jabbed toward his neck.

In spite of the crowd's disapproving roar, he repeated the gesture several times, vehemently.

Eagle-helm sheathed his sword and yanked off his helmet.

Rhyddes gasped.

The Roman from the slave market! The memory of his hands caressing her breasts weakened her knees. And his enchanting smile...but he wasn't smiling now.

He glared at the judge with naked fury, shouting something she couldn't begin to discern. It yielded no reprieve for Fire-helm, who had removed his helmet to expose his neck and back.

Sorrow enshrouded her heart for the doomed warrior.

As Eagle-helm drew his sword, she squeezed her eyes shut, holding in her tears but not her loathing of the nobleman for failing to sway the judge.

"THIS IS POLITICAL SUICIDE, Father!" Marcus shouted from the arena.

To say nothing of killing their tenuous relationship.

He didn't expect that argument to help when no others had worked, but he refused to give up without trying.

"The people need a reminder of who is in command." A predatory grin split Agricola's lips. "Obey or die, Aquila Britannia."

Messiena shot to her feet, horrified. "Governor, please!"

Falco restrained her with a firm grip on her wrist. "Your bridegroom needs to remember who is in command, too." He pulled her back toward the bench. "As do you, Daughter."

Her chin quivering, Messiena sat. Loreia, seated on Messiena's other side, drew her into an embrace. Messiena buried her face against Loreia's chest, her shoulders shaking. Loreia looked everywhere but toward the arena.

Head in hands, Jamil slumped in abject misery. His pleas on behalf of his finest provocator, as well as his reminder of the monetary penalty Agricola would by law be required to pay, had gone unheeded, too.

Falco and the rest of the spectators leaned forward with merciless expectancy, led by the governor's example.

Obey or die, indeed.

Marcus bent and positioned his sword beneath Iradivus's chin, despising himself for what had to be done but despising his father more for having ordered it. Eyes closed, Iradivus tilted his head back as if welcoming death.

"Walk proudly with the gods, Iradivus," Marcus whispered. "You have earned it tenfold."

A grim smile formed and froze on the warrior's face as Marcus cut a second one across his neck.

Rather than letting the body topple over, Marcus lowered Iradivus to the arena floor, where his blood pumped out to make a hideous paste with the sand. Marcus stood over the body, his head bowed, and raised his gladius's hilt over his heart in the gladiators' salute.

The Eagle of Britannia heard not a sound from the crowd as he flung down the gladius. Leaving his helmet and weapon where they lay, he stormed out of the arena for the last time.

HER CURIOSITY IGNITED by the stadium's eerie stillness, Rhyddes opened her eyes.

Fire-helm's body was being dragged off by the feet, hitched to a mule flanked by a pair of arena attendants wearing disconcerting, dog-headed masks, a bloody smear marking the warrior's final passage. Of Eagle-helm, only his helmet and blood-streaked sword remained.

Obviously, Eagle-helm had dispatched his opponent with what she had learned to recognize as typical, cold-bloodedly despicable Roman efficiency. She wished she had never cheered for him, and she squelched the admiration and…other feelings to which she'd fallen prey.

That man was no better than any of the other Romans she had encountered.

And probably worse.

## 6

R̲HYDDES'S FIRST FORTNIGHT passed in a pain-clouded blur of drills and more drills, each action glued together with a mercilessly bland diet of barley-and-bean porridge. Limbering and strengthening exercises, running, wrestling, weapons training, sparring with other gladiators; usually with little time to eat and drink, and even less time to think.

Following the evening bath and meal, Rhyddes and the other new, non-Roman gladiators spent an hour learning to speak the empire's language, Latin. She resented the lessons at first, but her life as a gladiatrix became less confusing as she grew accustomed to conversing with others in what her tutor called the "common tongue."

Invariably, when Vederi or one of his fellow guards escorted her to her cell each night, after she'd bathed, sometimes enjoying a massage from Materia, and had her injuries tended by the school's physician, she collapsed upon her cot and fell into a dreamless slumber. If Hemaeus drugged the honeyed concoction he made her drink each time she visited him for treatment, she didn't care.

For one being trained to kill for others' pleasure, it was perversely fitting that her sleep emulated death.

Most of the gladiators either tolerated Rhyddes's presence or viewed her with outright disdain. Shrewdly, Jamil paired her with two older men, both volunteer contract gladiators, not slaves, who were short of stature yet skilled in their respective martial arts. Unconcerned with the opinions of their peers, they readily befriended Rhyddes and helped her become accustomed to every aspect of a gladiator's routine.

Exotic-accented Nemo of Iberia taught her to wield a gladius, using the *rudus,* a wooden sword upon which all novice gladiators trained. Although Nemo was old enough to be Rhyddes's father, and the practice sword's name sounded uncomfortably close to Rudd's, Nemo's ready smile put her at ease as if he were one of her brothers. Pleasing Nemo with her performance became like pleasing them, which dulled the razor edge of her grief. She learned quickly under the Iberian's guidance and strove toward the day when she could progress to the blunted iron practice sword designed to imitate the combat gladius in length, balance and weight.

Gordianus, a Carveti Celt from the western end of Hadrian's Wall who in his final contract year was performing as the green-clad "hunter" of the pony-sized lizard named Belua, helped Rhyddes hone her wrestling skills. For, as Jamil had explained when he ordered their pairing, there could come a moment in any match when weapons would lie broken or out of reach, and a gladiator had to know how to wield his body to survive.

Training with Gordianus offered a daily reprieve from having to puzzle out Latin commands and comments, since she conversed with him in the only "common tongue" that mattered to both of them: Celtic.

MARCUS RODE BESIDE the escort tasked with delivering Agricola's penalty for having commanded the death of Jamil's best provocator. No one had asked Marcus to accompany them, and he couldn't have given a plausible reason anyway.

With each clop of his horse's hooves on the cobbled avenue, he relived another blow or lunge or kick of that fateful fight. But nothing could have changed the outcome. His heart felt heavier than the hundred thousand sesterces the soldiers had been ordered to protect.

Jamil met them at Villa Britanniae's gate and waved the soldiers through. One of the school's guards led the men toward the heavily guarded building where the familia's banker stored the funds belonging to the school, gladiators, workers and Jamil's personal wealth.

Marcus, still astride, gazed wistfully through the gates he had never thought to enter again.

Jamil patted the horse's neck and gazed at Marcus earnestly. "Coming inside, lad?"

"Am I welcome?" Marcus asked.

"Iradivus's death wasn't your fault."

"Perhaps not, but if I hadn't chosen him—"

Jamil shook his head. "Quit punishing yourself. Your esteemed father would have executed anyone you'd chosen."

"Then perhaps I shouldn't have chosen anybody." Marcus sawed on the reins to wheel his mount around.

Jamil lunged to catch the bridle. "Now you're talking nonsense." He eased his grip, and the mare tossed her head as if in agreement. "Your sparring partners have been asking about you. Come inside and greet them, at least." Grinning, he led the horse toward the gates, and Marcus didn't resist. "You know where the practice tunics and weapons are kept."

Marcus chuckled. It had been a boring fortnight without his sparring regimen. He dismounted, and Jamil released the bridle. Marcus handed the reins to a guard and asked him to take the mare to the stables. The guard looked to Jamil for confirmation and got a dismissive nod from his employer.

After watching the pair depart, Marcus turned his attention upon the man for whom he'd caused such a terrible loss. "Will you not accept my apology for Iradivus's death?"

Jamil clapped him on the shoulder. "I will, if it eases your mind." He gave Marcus's shoulder a final squeeze before letting go. "But your father's gold is apology enough for me."

No surprise, that. Some things never changed.

Some things, however, did.

A gladiatrix had joined the familia's ranks. Her drill moves appeared in sore need of improvement, but despite her inexperience, her speed and agility showed definite promise.

With her coppery mane subdued in braids and pinned to her head, it took the space of a few breaths for Marcus to recognize the woman for whom he'd tried to outbid Jamil, two weeks earlier. A sweaty sparring tunic and knee-length breeches hid her body, except where the garments molded to her glorious curves, making it difficult to forget the lush treasures that lay beneath.

No, he amended as the memories of fondling her flesh stirred his loins, it was damned impossible.

He smiled as he strode toward the changing area, returning everyone's enthusiastic greetings while musing upon how he could acquire what he desired without paying a fortune to add another slave to his retinue.

A COLLECTIVE SHOUT of "Aquila!" broke Rhyddes's concentration. Nemo and some of the other gladiators halted the sword drill, earning flicks from the overseers' whips.

As Nemo resumed the drill, grinning for a reason Rhyddes couldn't fathom, she wondered who this "Eagle" might be to have caused her partner to risk the lash. But sweat, fatigue and the sun glaring off the sand prevented her from seeing anything beyond her partner's moves.

Until *he* stepped into her field of view. He of the short, wiry locks blacker than a raven's wing. He of the finely chiseled face, hazel eyes, disarming smile and boldly questing hands. He of the rippling muscles that bedecked a tall, powerful frame. He who handled a gladius as masterfully as if he'd been born with the weapon in his fist.

He who murdered worthy warriors.

"Eagle-helm"…Aquila. Of course.

She felt stupid for not making the connection sooner.

He wore a plain, belted sparring tunic no different than that of any gladiator-slave, though the linen had yet to be stained with sweat. As he conversed with Nemo using words that danced beyond her ken, he kept skewing glances her way, glances suggesting he desired a very different form of sparring.

The notion made her vision redden with the image of Fire-helm's bloody corpse being dragged from the arena. Injustice heated Rhyddes's blood and fueled her hate. The battle rage of her Votadini warrior ancestors ignited within her soul.

She tightened her grip upon the rudus's hilt.

Aquila seemed to be requesting a trade of Nemo's rudus for the blunted iron sword Aquila had brought to the training ground.

'Twas the best chance she'd ever get.

"Thrice-cursed Roman murderer!" she yelled in Celtic, brandishing her rudus and aiming for his head.

His surprise lasted but a moment. He spun and brought his weapon up to block her blow. The force nearly jarred the rudus from her grasp. As she cocked her arms for another swing, searing pain tore into her back.

'Twas an all-too-familiar pain.

Knowing she'd be killed if she didn't desist, she dropped the rudus and fell to her knees, gasping, as guards rushed in to restrain her.

She felt someone grasp her tunic's neck and haul her up. Jamil of Tanis glared at her as if he intended to throttle her.

"Why attack him, woman?" he demanded in Celtic, jerking his head toward Aquila, who was looking...remorseful?

Aquila's reaction did not sway her. "Fire-helm should have lived! That one murdered him."

Jamil shook his head as if in confusion. "What?"

She released an exasperated sigh, trying to think of Latin words to convey her accusation. None obeyed her summons.

Jamil drew a sword and held it beneath her throat. "Speak, woman, or die." She felt the blade nip her flesh. "Now!"

Aquila stepped forward to grip Jamil's sword arm. "No, my friend," he said in Latin. The rest of his words remained a mystery to Rhyddes, but his concern for her rang clearly.

Could she have misjudged Aquila?

Her head insisted she had not. Her heart disagreed.

"BE REASONABLE, JAMIL." Marcus couldn't bear the thought of another performer dying because of him and forced Jamil's blade away from the gladiatrix's throat.

Her hatred yielded, reluctantly, to surprise.

"Reasonable?" Jamil leveled his glare at Marcus. "I want to know why this ill-mannered barbarian—" his emphasis conveyed the full measure of the insult "—attacked you."

"That barbarian cost you more than any twenty of those men combined." Marcus swept an arm toward the gladiators who had returned to their drills.

"Don't I know it." Jamil spat. "The hellion is yours, Aquila…for two hundred thousand." Marcus rolled his eyes. "What? I am allowed to recoup my losses, am I not?"

"Recoup your loss, yes," Marcus said. "Double your investment in two weeks' time, no."

No longer in the mood to spar, he stalked toward the training enclosure's guarded gate.

"You sure you wouldn't be interested," Jamil called, "after I have whipped her into submission for you?"

Marcus halted and spun. Guards were hauling her toward the post where the dirt was stained red from the many floggings.

The way she'd dropped at the first few strikes of the lash had wrung Marcus's heart. Better to feel its bite himself than allow her to suffer more pain.

He pelted across the sand, dodging startled gladiator pairs, and caught Jamil with his arm cocked.

"The lash is not necessary, Jamil. She did not hurt me."

The gladiators' owner relaxed his arm and regarded him frankly. "I shall be the judge of what is and isn't necessary regarding my property."

"For me, then." Marcus grinned as a reason presented itself that Jamil couldn't argue with. "As a favor for someone whose performances helped fill your coffers many times over."

"You have me there, you whelp. Very well." To the guards he said, "Take her to an isolation chamber."

As the men unbound her hands from the whipping post, she gazed up at Marcus with wonder. He offered her what he hoped was an encouraging smile. Whether she saw it or not, he had no idea, for the guards were already ushering her from the training grounds. Through the rents in her tunic, blood welled from the lashes she'd sustained.

"You will have her wounds tended." Marcus didn't care that it sounded more like a command than a question.

"Of course." The Egyptian gave Marcus a strange look as if he thought Marcus had taken leave of his senses. "She must remember who is master, but she is of no use to me if she is not fit to drill."

Marcus watched her, striding with quiet dignity in spite of her pain and fear, until he lost sight of her down the co-lonnade leading to the gladiators' barracks. He had never visited Villa Britanniae's isolation cells, but he'd seen gladiators return to training subdued from having spent just a single night inside one.

He prayed the gods would bestow upon the fiery gladiatrix the strength and courage to endure her ordeal.

RHYDDES'S HOPE OF being confined to her sleeping cell became dashed as her guards marched her to the far wing of the gladiators' barracks. They each snatched a torch from a wall sconce and prodded her at spearpoint down a set of steps leading into a pit containing the gods alone knew what. The fetid reek assaulting her nose and the faint, piteous moans reaching her ears suggested a human presence, but she couldn't be certain.

After the Roman named Aquila had flipped her expectations on end, she couldn't feel certain of anything.

Least of all, her emotions toward him.

She had expected him to be furious for her attack; if not furious then at least angry enough to demand her flogging.

Although she had no idea what he'd said, remorse seemed to drive him to save her neck from Jamil's blade. Remorse, mayhap, because he didn't want to watch her die…but why should a wealthy Roman, who could have anything—and anybody—care what befell one rebellious gladiatrix-slave? Espcially a Roman who had killed a gladiator a fortnight ago.

The guards stopped in front of a narrow door and stowed the torches in brackets. In the fitful light she saw the door was fashioned of solid iron, save for a tiny grille near the top. One of the guards opened the door.

Inside, there was barely enough room for her to stand upright…and breathe.

Panic welled with palpable force.

Her only other choice, she realized glumly as the guards backed her into the tomblike chamber, was to impale herself upon their spears.

She seriously considered the option.

The thought of Aquila's remorse upon learning of her death stopped her. To say naught of the fact that she would never again see his charming smile, or feel his arousing touch....

The pain grinding into her back from the rough bricks against her lash wounds wrenched her into reality. For all she knew, her owner had decided to let her rot in this hellish chamber. That seemed to be the general idea as one guard pinned her to the wall with the point of his spear while the other locked her ankles and wrists into manacles.

A Votadini Celt, Rhyddes sternly reminded herself, does not display fear. As the cold iron weighted her flesh, she bit her lower lip to keep from crying out.

Their task complete, the guards withdrew. They slammed the door with a horrific clang and locked it.

As they took the torches with them, darkness engulfed her. She closed her eyes and loosed a trembling sigh.

The image of Aquila's concerned face appeared in her mind's eye. She squeezed her eyes tighter but couldn't stem the burning tears. They streamed down her cheeks unchecked.

Her bonds left her powerless to dash them away.

Countless visions assaulted her in the unrelenting darkness. Visions so real she could smell the sweet aroma of freshly scythed hay...and the gagging stench of the soldiers' lust. She could feel the soft fur of her favorite golden-striped barn cat…and the weight of the rudus in her calloused hands.

Her mouth watered to welcome a juicy bite of hot, roasted pork…and dried when that mouthful transformed into the gladiators' bland porridge. Her muscles quivered with the effort of harvesting Rudd's barley…and of connecting with Aquila's practice sword. Sweat rolled down her back to renew the sting left by Rudd's whip…and Jamil's.

She could hear the croaking of crows as she lay beside Owen on a hillock in the fragrant meadow, a freshening breeze dancing across her cheeks….

"Gladiatrix."

She turned her head toward her brother, confused that he would address her thus, but he was gone. Aquila lay in his place, beaming at her. She reached her hand to caress his face.

"Time to leave, Gladiatrix."

Leave? So soon?

Aquila laughed, but it sounded coarse. She blinked several times. The torchlit features of Vederi wavered into view.

She shook her head and wished she hadn't. Pain throbbed in her temples. She rubbed them with her hands…and realized the wrist manacles had been unlocked.

"Come, Gladiatrix." Vederi slipped a hand under her elbow and pulled her forward. "No one wants to stay here."

She took a step, but her knees buckled and she would have fallen if not for Vederi's support. He eased her from the cell, moved beside her, lifted her arm to rest across his neck and retrieved the torch.

As they shuffled forward, she asked, "Am I to get the lash

now?" She trained her gaze on the floor and willed her legs to keep moving and not cramp.

"Only if you plan to attack someone again." She felt him twist to regard her, and she met his stern gaze. "Do you?"

"No." She expelled a rueful laugh. "That was stupid—I don't know what possessed me." They'd already begun their ascent when she thought to ask, "How long was I in there?"

"Overnight."

She didn't believe him until they emerged into the soft light of dawn bathing the quiet courtyard. The gladiators had departed their cells to begin the day's routine. Jovial sounds of talking and splashing washed toward her from the bathhouse.

Strange…her time in that hellhole had seemed no more than an eyeblink, and yet no less than eternity.

Vederi escorted her to the infirmary, where Hemaeus fussed over her wounds, bathing them in warm water redolent with herbs before binding them with clean linen strips. The physician also offered her a valerian and mint tisane, which Rhyddes gratefully accepted. It tasted more potent than usual.

At some point during Hemaeus's ministrations, Vederi had departed. He returned carrying a fresh tunic to replace the torn one Hemaeus had ordered Rhyddes to strip off. After slipping it over her head and belting it, thankful her back didn't hurt too badly, she nodded her gratitude to both benefactors.

Upon leaving the infirmary, Vederi marched her to the mess hall, where the gladiators had begun filing in from the baths. Rather than allowing her to rejoin them, however, he escorted her to the dais, in front of Jamil. Vederi's employer nodded once, and the guard backed away.

Without giving the men leave to begin their meal, Jamil of Tanis gave Rhyddes a long, severe appraisal.

"What you learn, Gladiatrix?" Jamil asked in Celtic. Loudly, he repeated the question in Latin.

Rhyddes recalled yesterday's failure to communicate with him and chose her words with care, not in Latin but in the tongue of her birth. "I was stupid, Lanista Jamil. I thank you for your mercy. I shall not do that again." She rendered the gladiators' salute as smartly as her sore body would permit. "I will obey or die." She repeated the oath in Latin. It was the first phrase her tutor had taught her.

"Good. Aquila will not save you next time." Jamil regarded her with a closed expression, making her wonder what he was thinking...and what he'd meant.

Was Aquila no longer willing to intervene on her behalf? Or would Jamil refuse to be swayed by the nobleman's arguments?

Either way, she supposed it didn't matter. She'd escaped the death sentence once and probably wouldn't be so lucky again.

"Dismissed," Jamil snapped to her and commanded everyone to sit and begin eating.

The porridge, once she'd taken her usual seat and been given a bowl and a flagon of ale, had never tasted sweeter.

**7**

"HE WATCHES YOU," Nemo said to Rhyddes during their morning sword bout.

Chillier weather heralding the procession from summer to fall prompted the gladiators to wear long-sleeved tunics and, for Rhyddes, thicker breeches, as well.

"Our master?" Rhyddes had become more confident with the Latin tongue but had yet to adopt the practice of publicly referring to Jamil by his given name.

"Lanista Jamil, of course, along with the governor's son, who is sponsoring the autumnal equinox games in honor of his bride-to-be."

She was about to ask Nemo what he meant when she recalled overhearing a gossip snippet about some local nobleman and a Roman senator's daughter. *So,* Rhyddes mused between blows, *this nobleman must be quite wealthy to indulge in sponsoring gladiatorial games.* Not for a moment did she believe she'd be chosen. Although she'd progressed to the iron blade weeks ago, her skills still fell short of arena quality.

Without breaking the drill's rhythm, Nemo maneuvered them in a semicircle. Rhyddes nearly dropped her sword.

"The governor's son" was none other than the Eagle himself, dressed not for sparring but for Rome's Senate floor and hefting a sack of coins in one hand. Aquila made eye contact with her and flashed one of his heart-stopping smiles.

Her emotions roiled in a battlefield of warring factions, led by anger, guilt and, gods help her, desire.

'Twas all she could do to keep breathing.

*This man's people enslaved mine,* she reminded herself. And, oh gods, he had to be that "local nobleman" fated to marry a senator's daughter.

Jamil, beside Aquila, called Rhyddes to the bars. She plunged her sword into the sand and ran to obey. The exertion helped her preserve a neutral countenance.

"The Moridunum troupe has brought a gladiatrix," Jamil said to Rhyddes in Latin. He'd abandoned the Celtic tongue after the last moon's waning. "Tomorrow, you fight your first bout."

She averted her gaze, too shocked for any response—in any language—other than a murmured, "Yes, Lanista."

Jamil reached through the bars to slip a finger under her chin. "This woman has much experience, but I trust you will acquit yourself well."

Words failed her again. He withdrew his hand, and she stepped back a pace to render the gladiators' salute with what she hoped would appear as greater confidence than she felt.

Her gaze met Aquila's. His appraisal of her seemed to delve deeper than an evaluation of her fighting skills. He would have had ample time for that already this day—and every other day since he'd resumed his sparring regimen several weeks earlier. As her pulse quickened, she tried to prevent her breath from keeping pace.

"This is my wager on you, Gladiatrix."

Aquila, a merry glint sparkling in his hazel eyes, dropped his sack onto Jamil's palm. Rhyddes gasped. Even if it contained only brass sesterces, it had to be worth at least four seasons' hire for a farm worker.

Rhyddes longed to quip that he was welcome to throw away his gold wherever he pleased, but held her peace. She cared naught where he wasted his coin. Nor, she suspected, did he.

Yet learning that the games' sponsor and her owner expressed confidence in her abilities gave her spirits, which had plunged upon realizing Aquila was fated to marry someone else, a welcome boost.

MARCUS SURVEYED THE forum's most exclusive dining chamber. Centuries of tradition bound him, as the games' sponsor, to host a dinner party for the wealthiest bettors to mingle with and, more importantly, evaluate the gladiators scheduled to compete on the morrow. The staggering wagers placed in this chamber would establish each pairing's odds.

Normally, the sponsor staged the feast in his home to demonstrate his munificence and power. Yet Agricola would have no part in "this foolish foray into orgiastic overindulgence."

The phrase set Marcus's teeth on edge.

Then again, everything Agricola said to Marcus these days set his teeth on edge.

He stepped into an arched doorway leading to one of the many small chambers that flanked the dining area, as a pair of slaves passed toting a wide bronze dish fastened atop four tall, gracefully curving legs. Several such braziers were being set up around the room to lend a more elegant and cleaner burning source of light than clumsy, smelly torches. Other slaves perched on ladders, hanging swags of brightly colored fabric to enliven the walls or tacking fragrant rose and ivy garlands to the tables. One woman was standing on tiptoe to polish the two silver medallions, each as wide as a man's outstretched arms, depicting the faces of coemperors Marcus Aurelius and Lucius Verus.

Fingering the arch support's cool, tiled surface, the son of the governor of Britannia couldn't help but imagine what he might be doing inside the intimate chamber behind him, after the banquet, with Jamil's gladiatrix.

If she would deign to have him.

Although she had never attacked him after that first day, obtaining her agreement might be problematical at best.

"You wanted to see me, Aquila?"

Marcus heard the impatience, muted by thinly veiled courtesy, and turned to find Jamil standing in the corridor, dressed in the plain if well-crafted style of tunic he wore when overseeing drills. He clutched a muslin-wrapped parcel.

Doubtless the lanista wanted to return to Villa Britanniae to bathe, change and marshal his gladiators—and gladiatrix—for the feast. Marcus resolved not to impose upon Jamil's time any longer than necessary.

He offered his friend an appreciative nod. "Thank you for stopping here, Jamil." Stepping out of the arch, he gestured toward the room. "What do you think?"

Jamil shrugged. "Looks splendid, as always. Do you need anything else?"

An interesting question. "Yes." Marcus sucked in a breath. "What can you tell me about your gladiatrix?"

"Aside from the fact that she attacked you without provocation?" Jamil's perplexed look dawned to comprehension. "You want to bed her, don't you?" Marcus felt heat rise in his cheeks, and Jamil smiled sympathetically. "Lad, you would have an easier time seducing one of the Furies."

"I know." Marcus sighed. "And I would like to know why."

"I doubt I know all the reasons myself." With his free hand Jamil stroked his clean-shaven chin. "Her father mistreated her. Did you see the whip scars on her back, that day she was auctioned?"

"No." If he had, he would have bid high enough to free her from the equally brutal life into which she'd been thrust.

"I thought not," Jamil said. "The next day, she watched your final match. I didn't think anything of it at the time, but I recall her acting withdrawn and unhappy afterward. Angry, even." A thoughtful look creased his scarred features. "I didn't understand why she'd attacked you. I thought I heard her use the Celtic word for 'murder,' but that made no sense to me."

It made perfect sense to Marcus, if she had misunderstood what had occurred in the arena following his bout with Iradivus.

Quelling his guilt, he offered his hand to Jamil. "Many thanks, my friend. Go in peace, and I shall see you and your troupe later this evening."

Jamil completed the arm grip and swiftly departed.

Perhaps it would be easier to seduce the Furies, but Marcus cared only about convincing one furious gladiatrix to think more kindly of him. Seduction might have to wait.

So be it.

SINCE RHYDDES WAS scheduled to compete the next day, her training unit's foreman excused her from the afternoon drills. But instead of being escorted back to her cell to await the start of the evening meal, Vederi took her to the bathhouse. This was not unusual; only severe illness or injury exempted a gladiator from the daily bathing regimen. 'Twas the one time each day Rhyddes reveled in her status as the familia's sole gladiatrix: it afforded her the luxury of bathing unguarded, and today she looked forward to enjoying an extra-long soak.

Vederi assumed his usual position in the courtyard outside the dressing area. Rhyddes beelined for the alcove that had been curtained off for her use, made quick work of stripping off her sweat-drenched practice tunic, breeches and undergarments, swathed her body in a clean towel from one of the niches and collected from an adjacent niche a delicate glass vial filled with lavender oil. She then marched straight for the hottest pool, shed the towel, added the oil and eased into the steaming, aromatic water.

Here, as at no other time in her entire life, she felt like a lady of the manor, for Materia always collected her soiled garments and towels and empty oil vials, and replaced them with fresh supplies. Frequently, Rhyddes would ask Materia to massage her aching muscles, or to anoint her body with oil and scrape it off with the blunt iron tool they called a strigil.

But this day she craved solitude to ponder her match.

The elderly woman seemed to understand her dismissal and bade Rhyddes good fortune before departing the bathing chamber.

The gods were not as understanding as Materia.

"Hurry, Gladiatrix!" called Vederi from his post. "Lanista Jamil does not want you to be late!"

*Late?*

Rhyddes gave a shrug and stood, dripping, to step carefully out of the pool. Disobedience of a direct order meant death. That morning she'd cringed when a new gladiator-slave balked at being commanded to learn the net and trident. He didn't live long enough to finish his protest.

Death neither frightened nor appealed to Rhyddes, but she preferred to meet the gods on her own terms.

Her feet left a trail of wet splotches across the tiles as she padded into the dressing area. To save time—though she couldn't fathom what event she might be late for—she toweled herself dry as she walked.

Rather than the undyed, unadorned, thigh-length tunic worn by gladiator and servant alike, Materia had left a pale green dress folded neatly on the stone bench in Rhyddes's alcove, next to a pair of hammered copper brooches and sandals fashioned from supple calf leather.

Upon holding up the dress, Rhyddes could see her hand shadowed beneath a layer of the flimsy if gorgeous fabric. The gown was meant to be draped double, but her cynicism flared.

Jamil, supposing that she would lose tomorrow in the arena, wanted her to play whore rather than warrior tonight, because he was planning to sell her virginity.

*To Aquila, perhaps...*

She cut off that thought with an exasperated sigh. The man was going to wed a noblewoman.

And yet, she could imagine far worse things, things that had happened to her at the hands of those thrice-cursed Roman soldiers.

She chafed her arms, but nothing could scrub away the horrible memories.

*Obey or die,* she reminded herself.

Fortunately, the plainly styled, hard leather gear worn by Jamil's contract guards did not resemble the soldiers' armor, or Rhyddes would have gone screaming mad during her first week at Villa Britanniae.

She stepped into the dress and pulled it to her shoulders, realizing why she'd been given two brooches. Vederi shouted another admonishment, and she quickly fastened each clasp, tied on the sandals and strode into the courtyard.

Upon beholding his charge, her guard's impatience modulated into a serenade of appreciative whistles.

Rhyddes smiled in spite of herself.

"We must do something about your hair," was Jamil's only response upon meeting them in the colonnade. "Roman women do not sport untamed locks."

"This style suits me perfectly, master." Rhyddes twirled a damp tress between her fingers as she lengthened her stride to match the Egyptian's pace. "I am an untamed Celt."

Jamil laughed. "Too true."

Gordianus, Nemo and the other men slated to fight the next day had formed a neat column, looking like respectable Romans in their grass-green tunics. Only their scars and swaggering manners, and, of course, the guards, revealed the truth.

Jamil waved Rhyddes toward a hole in the front rank of gladiators, and he strolled off to climb into a small, boxy structure with open-air windows, hitching his toga to keep it from catching on the wooden frame. Two house servants, muscular as any gladiator, stood before and behind the structure. At Jamil's hand signal, the servants stooped to grasp a pair of poles, and when they stood, the box rose, swaying slightly. After another signal, the servants marched forward.

Absorbed in watching the odd little ritual, Rhyddes almost didn't step out with her rank when the troupe surged to follow their owner. Trying to keep pace with her shorter legs encumbered by a dress posed a challenge, but she managed.

Once they reached the vast courtyard defined by buildings that housed the market, judicial chambers and offices, Jamil ordered his bearers and gladiators to halt. He climbed out and led them to the tallest building, up three sets of stairs, down an inner hallway, and through a gilded set of double doors.

If the prominence of finely wrought adornments, leathers, embroidery, silks, linens and perfumes was any indication, this chamber boasted the wealthiest men and women in Londinium, perhaps even all Britain.

Including, gods help her, the Eagle himself.

Aquila gazed at her, that charming smile bending his lips.

He saluted her with his goblet, damn him. She contrived to look elsewhere.

A pattern of identical bronze-colored tunics emerged from the confusion of brighter hues. The opposing gladiatorial troupe, Rhyddes realized, was already mingling with the nobility. A tall woman, gowned much like Rhyddes but with her blond hair piled atop her head and graced with ropes of multicolored glass beads in Roman fashion, had attracted several men, although Aquila didn't number among them. Her poise and mannerisms radiated a confidence at odds with the way Rhyddes felt.

The woman's admirers didn't seem to care that her beauty had been marred by a faded scar running the length of one cheek. More scars crossed the rippling muscles of her arms. An arena veteran, indeed.

Rhyddes's gut constricted.

The convivial buzz of conversation died as more guests noticed Jamil's gladiators. Jamil ordered his warriors to line up along one wall. Having no idea what to expect, Rhyddes followed the men, praying that she wouldn't appear foolish in front of her opponent—or Aquila.

Jamil proceeded to introduce the gladiators by name. Each summoned gladiator stepped away from the wall to strike a warlike pose, flex his muscles, make an intimidating face, or some combination of these moves, to the crowd's appreciative claps. Afterward, the gladiator was ushered by a servant to a place at one of the long tables, usually between two of the invited guests, though the married gladiators were permitted to sit with their wives.

Rather than using her given name, Jamil introduced

Rhyddes as "Jamila Nova," the newest member of Familias Jamilus.

Cat-quick she leaped away from the wall, cocking her right arm and extending the left as if to throw a spear, whooping the Votadini battle cry.

Most of the guests flinched backward. A few women gasped. The other gladiatrix laughed, applauding. Jamil's gladiators added their hearty approval. The ovation swelled as the guests recovered their composure and joined in.

Aquila nodded at Rhyddes with unmistakable admiration. She relaxed her stance and offered a deep bow to hide her discomfiture.

Whether by accident or design—most likely the latter—the only place left at the table was beside the Eagle's perch.

She looked for her opponent, but the woman had been seated at a different table. Too bad; Rhyddes had hoped to converse with her about their bout. Apparently that wasn't the purpose of this evening, she concluded as guests seated nearby plied her with all manner of questions about her origins, fighting experience and the weapons she'd been trained to wield.

Jamil, seated opposite Rhyddes, raised a hand. His stern look forestalled any reply she might have made. "Jamila Nova shall answer no questions before her match."

"I would very much like to hear her speak." Aquila raised his goblet to her again, a wistful smile bending his lips. He leaned close, and her nose was assaulted by the sweet yet acrid odor of whatever he was drinking. It made her stomach churn. "If she has mastered the common tongue."

She glared at him. "I know Latin well enough, my lord."

She made a show of scooting her chair to open a gap between them. Although the distance was barely measurable, the victory felt enormous. "Among my people, a maiden need not tolerate unwanted advances."

The table's other occupants laughed raucously. Aquila drained the contents of his goblet, but not before Rhyddes saw, with great satisfaction, the redness coloring his cheeks.

She was thankful when he turned his attention to the noblewoman seated on his other side.

Jamil gave Rhyddes an admonishing look, but she felt no contrition. Nobility or not, games' sponsor or not, that Roman had no right to take liberties with her.

At Aquila's command, the servants bustled in carrying tureens and platters heaped with more food than Rhyddes had seen in a lifetime. Fruits, nuts, cheeses, vegetables, meats, fish, shellfish, eggs, bread, soup: all prepared in a dizzying variety of ways and carefully arranged as if intended to be admired as works of art rather than being eaten.

She was certain it would take all night to sample just one mouthful from every dish.

In fact that seemed to be the general idea. Although the gladiators favored the fish, fowl and meat dishes as a welcome diversion from the barley-and-bean boredom, and Rhyddes felt inclined to agree, the other guests selected tinier portions of a wider variety.

Conversation ebbed and flowed as people either preoccupied themselves with their plates or the drink Jamil told her was called "wine." Feeling self-conscious and very much out of place as the barbarian Celt among these Roman nobles, Rhyddes toyed with more food than she consumed. The wine tasted as sharp, yet sweet, as it smelled.

Another thought made her heart lurch: was she consuming her last meal on this side of the Otherworld?

"Is the fare not to your liking, Jamila Nova?"

Startled, she whipped her head toward Aquila. "No— that is, I do like it, my lord." His concern unnerved her more than his charm did, which drove her to take a long pull of wine.

It didn't help.

"But you aren't eating much. Jamil feeds you that well, then?" He tossed a teasing glance at her owner, who grinned.

She stared at the morsels of roasted beef, lamb, lobster and salmon on her plate. "I have no complaints about my treatment."

"Perhaps this might stimulate your appetite."

Rhyddes glanced up to see Aquila proffering a platter containing a bright green, spearlike vegetable flanked by small, round, black ones. She felt her eyes widen as the pattern's bawdy implication sank in.

"My lord, what—" she swallowed thickly, recalling the soldiers' abuse "—what are those?"

"Asparagus and olives." Aquila gave her an odd look, regarded the dish, and blushed. Using the serving tool, he pushed the vegetables out of their suggestive arrangement before picking up one of the round pieces, which had a hole cut into it. "Surely you know of these little marvels? Much of what we're eating tonight was cooked in oil pressed from olives." He popped it into his mouth, chewed, swallowed and grinned at her. "Tart yet delicious. Try it." With the fork he rolled a few asparagus spears and olives onto her plate.

It sounded too much like a command to refuse. She tried a bite of each and was pleasantly surprised that the asparagus's milder flavor tempered the olives' tartness. She finished the portion, chasing it with a draught of wine. Its taste grew more tolerable by the swallow.

Smiling, and feeling a little giddy, she nodded at Aquila. "I thank you for the suggestion, my lord." And for showing her that a Roman could possess a mote of sensitivity, though she'd die before admitting that to him. "But, please, no more suggestions this night."

Aquila looked disappointed. "Perhaps another time, then."

Rhyddes felt it safest to remain silent. He offered her a tentative smile, and her stomach fluttered. Trying to tell herself it was from the rich food and wine, she gazed beseechingly at her owner.

It took her several moments to attract his attention, for he was exchanging ribald jests with the men on his side of the table. When he finally looked at her, his laughter fled. "What is wrong, woman? Are you ill?"

That was the safest description. She nodded. "May I return to the school now?" With the other feasters showing no signs of finishing, she didn't hold much hope of being excused.

"Of course, Jamila Nova," Aquila said. When she stood, so did he. "I would like to speak privately with your gladiatrix, if I may," he informed Jamil.

"Certainly." Her owner grinned broadly. "If she consents."

Curiosity afire, Rhyddes couldn't refuse. Aquila accompanied her through the chamber's outer door and into the corridor, with Vederi following a pace or two behind them.

With the party's noise only slightly muted, Aquila paused beside a column, bade Vederi to give them some distance, and faced her.

"Gladiatrix, I am sorry for any unseemly behavior this evening."

A nobleman apologizing to a slave? Had the world gone mad?

"My lord?" Surely she hadn't heard him aright.

His gaze intensified. "I am serious. I did not intend to cause you discomfort."

She glanced past him. The braziers were burning bright and warm. The aromas of roasted meat and fish wafted from the dining hall. Her guard kept his gaze trained upon them. As she regarded Aquila, her stomach's fluttering returned.

Mayhap she was the one who'd gone mad.

"My lord, I thank you." Her honor demanded a trade in kind. "I am sorry I raised my sword against you, and I thank you for intervening with Lanista Jamil on my behalf."

He nodded, his expression enigmatic. "I deserved your scorn. You did not deserve to feel the lash for my transgression."

"Your...what?"

"My mistake." He reached his hand toward her, seemed to think better of it and rested it against the column. "You attacked me because I killed a worthy opponent, did you not?"

"Yes, my lord. I—" There could be no remedy other than the truth. "I viewed it as an act of murder. And I despised you for failing to change the sponsor's decision."

"It was murder," he ground out between clenched teeth. "But I was sponsor that day."

"You?" Her jaw slackened. "But why couldn't you—"

"That man was my father." His fist pounded the column with a dull thud. "He ordered me to obey or die." An ocean of anguish washed through his tone.

*That was the governor?* "He used the gladiators' oath against his own son? Oh, gods." Bowing her head and wishing she could offer him a mote of comfort, Rhyddes pressed her fist over her heart. "My lord, I am deeply sorry."

"Please don't be," he whispered.

She felt the warmth of his hand over hers as he pulled it gently away from her chest. Yearning glimmered in his gaze that seemed to transcend mere physical needs, but a yearning for what, she couldn't ken.

Aquila raised her hand to his lips and brushed them lightly across the backs of her fingers. The tingling lasted long after he'd released her hand.

"Rest well tonight, Jamila Nova," he murmured, "and fight well tomorrow."

Rhyddes prayed to every god she could name that Aquila would not have to watch her die on the morrow, too.

# 8

LIKE A GENERAL inspecting his troops, Jamil paced along the column of gladiators ready to commence the traditional parade that originated at Villa Britanniae, progressed down Londinium's broadest avenue, circled the forum and ended at the arena.

His gladiatrix looked gorgeous in her black breastplate and matching leather-fringed kilt, braided fiery hair and blue woad paint anointing her face, arms, legs and right breast. Her scowl—doubtless because Jamil had ordered her to be dressed and decorated like her people's deadliest enemy, except for the exposed breast, which was solely for the benefit of the male spectators—increased her allure.

Inwardly, he smiled. She had come a long way, in bearing as well as martial skills.

And he had invested far too much money in this woman to lose her in her first bout.

He pinched her blue-tinted nipple, feeling it harden between his fingers. She did not flinch, but if lightning bolts could have shot from her eyes, he would have died where he stood.

Good. Igniting her rage could save her life. And, with luck, win back thrice his initial investment.

Jamil stepped away from the column and signaled the standard-bearer. Amid the slap of sandals on cobblestones and the clatter of armor, accompanied by the troupe's musicians, the procession began.

TWO HOURS OF MARCHING through the stinking streets of Londinium, enduring the crowd's stares and jeers, blackened Rhyddes's humor. The fools actually thought that she, a Votadini Celt, was a craven, thieving Pict. Hatred flared toward her owner, who had commanded this supreme insult upon her person.

She felt even more hatred for the empire and her father, who together had authored her deplorable situation.

The longer Rhyddes stayed dressed in the accursed Pictish garb and paint, the more she despised it. And she had all day to seethe, since her bout with the Moridunum gladiatrix was the day's featured match and not scheduled to begin until after the other bouts had finished.

Being locked in a cell facing one of the arena's tunnels, where she could observe the comings and goings of other combatants, did not dilute her rage.

But at the sight of Gordianus being carried past her cell on a leather sheet stretched taut between two long poles, ashen-faced with a set of nasty slashes revealing the blood oozing from his chest, she traded rage for overwhelming concern. She implored the bearers to halt and was surprised when they complied.

"Make it quick, Gladiatrix," the lead man warned.

"Will he be all right?" she whispered.

Gordianus opened his eyes and raised the hand closest to the bars. She reached through to grasp his fingers and squeezed them. "Belua got her claws on me this time, and no mistake," he said in Celtic. "But Hemaeus has patched me up before. I will mend." He returned her grip and switched to Latin to address his bearers. "Let us hurry so I can return to watch Jamila Nova's bout."

Reluctantly, she released Gordianus, and the bearers took him deeper into the tunnel.

Nemo fared better, winning his match handily "with moves so dazzling, they blinded my opponent!" His Iberian habit of outrageous exaggeration reminded her that they shared common ancestors, a score of generations ago, and it earned her smile.

The smile died after Nemo left her to disarm and have his wounds tended. A thousand questions whirling in her brain, she returned to pacing the cell's dirt floor confines, stopping only to eat, drink and marshal her strength.

Would she leave the arena under her own power, be wounded severely enough to warrant litter bearers…or would the mule drag her bloody corpse off the sands?

Another question pestered her, too.

Would the games' sponsor care if her body departed with the mule?

ATTIRED IN HIS FAVORITE crimson-and-gold embroidered toga and matching undertunic, Marcus Calpurnius Aquila took his place inside the governor's box, waving and smiling to the crowd, which greeted him with chants of "Aquila!" Clearly they wished he was a participant and not a spectator. Behind the congeniality, Marcus couldn't help but share their wish.

Selecting the gladiators to fight had been entertaining, but he would have rather lost a hundred matches than be the man responsible for deciding the fate of every match's loser.

For the first time, Marcus understood how Tribune Darius Caepio could perform this duty so efficiently on Agricola's behalf: if Darius possessed a shred of compassion, he must have buried it beneath two decades of military service.

Romans viewed compassion as a sign of weakness. Therefore, it was the only trait the games' sponsor could not afford to demonstrate.

The morning rounds—mock hunts of rare animals—were easy to judge: if both gladiator and animal survived and had fought well, both were spared, for the animals were too expensive to replace. And Marcus didn't have to preside over the executions, which entailed setting legendarily vicious Caledonian bears upon prisoners nailed to ground-level crosses. That task fell to his father, as governor, and Agricola conducted the proceedings with as much zest as he'd shown in ordering Iradivus's death.

Agricola's "obey or die" remark had prevented Marcus from confronting him about what had happened that day, and Marcus's resentment festered. In one sense, he was glad when Agricola had excused himself from the box "to attend more important matters" before the commencement of today's hand-to-hand combat events.

However, what disturbed Marcus most about the sponsor's duties, from his perspective as a former combatant, was being required to judge the worthiness of fallen men.

Or, as in today's final match, women.

Through the tunnel across the arena to his left appeared the starkly beautiful, blond Moridunum gladiatrix. Garbed in silver-and-crimson Roman armor, with a shortened kilt that flashed the curves of her buttocks through silver-studded red fringes, she drove a chariot pulled by two magnificent white mares. As she circled the arena, the announcer introduced her as Hyperosa. She wore a gladius strapped to her left hip, and a whip lay coiled against her right thigh.

The crowd lifted her name unto the heavens.

Hyperosa completed the final turn, halted the chariot in front of the governor's box, and dismounted to beat her shield with her gladius as attendants drove the chariot back into the tunnel. She looked every inch the invincible Roman giantess, and the predominantly Roman audience adored her.

Fervently, Marcus beseeched Jupiter to give Jamila Nova extra measures of strength, courage, cleverness and skill.

Light flared, a loud crack sounded and the tunnel on the right disgorged black smoke. Many spectators, gasping, shifted nervously upon their benches.

Jamil's gladiatrix appeared within the smoke's acrid swirls, armed in midnight leather, her flesh smothered in mysterious blue designs. The effect was that of a Pictish raider having just made a kill, and the slave's severe countenance, sweat-limned muscles and heaving chest enhanced the notion. A gladius hung from her belt, and she gripped a spear in her right fist.

The announcer introduced her as "Ruth, Menace of the North."

A strange expression cascaded over Ruth's face. She regarded the announcer for a moment, as if confused by the sound of her own name, before focusing her attention on her opponent. The crowd booed her supposed Pictish barbarism.

At Marcus's signal, the women faced off in the center of the arena. He sent up another silent prayer on Ruth's behalf and began the match.

Howling to exasperate the dead, Ruth charged with leveled spear and reckless abandon. Hyperosa released her whip and snagged Ruth's spear, to the crowd's thunderous approval. But when she would have wrenched the spear from Ruth's grasp, Ruth twisted it and yanked. The whip's handle went flying. Ruth threw aside both weapons, drew her gladius and closed in. Hyperosa recovered from her astonishment to confront the blue-painted threat.

They met with a clash of arms as fierce as any bout between seasoned men. The veteran Hyperosa landed her blows more accurately, but Ruth was by far the more swift and agile, causing some of her opponent's strikes to fall short. The rest, Ruth blocked with her gladius in an impressive show of strength.

As the match progressed, the crowd warmed to the fiery Pict.

The warmth Marcus felt for her he attributed to an entirely different reason.

He turned toward her owner, who was perched on his usual seat in the governor's box, leaning forward to rest elbows on the rail and chin atop his steepled fingers.

"Name your price, Jamil." His voice felt husky, and he cleared his throat. He wasn't sure how much raw desire he'd managed to bleed from his tone.

Jamil's eyes never left the arena. "You will have to speak with Hyperosa's owner, Aquila." As the women paused for breath after a particularly aggressive exchange, he smiled smugly at Marcus. "Ruth is not for sale."

Not surprising, but worth a try nonetheless.

The bout might have lasted longer, but Ruth risked disengaging to dive for the spear. The whip slithered free of the spear's shaft, and Ruth flung the barbed missile at Hyperosa, who couldn't raise her shield high enough to deflect it. The spearpoint pierced her right shoulder between the fringes.

With a startled outcry, Hyperosa dropped to her knees, releasing her gladius and clawing at the quivering shaft with her left hand. Ruth wasted no time in claiming victory, grabbing a fistful of her opponent's flaxen hair and thrusting her gladius under Hyperosa's chin. In that pose they froze, facing the governor's box.

"Definitely not for sale," Jamil stated.

Marcus had expected the crowd to help him decide this match, but the chants of *"Missum!"* for dismissing the loser, and *"Iugula!"* for the death sentence, sounded equally divided.

Swallowing a sigh born of many reasons, he rose and approached the rail. Though her biceps twitched with the effort of holding her right hand aloft, index finger extended in the sign of surrender and plea for mercy, blood streaming from the wound, Hyperosa had closed her eyes as if resigned to her fate.

Ruth, panting heavily, glared at Marcus with unveiled hatred as if challenging him to give her the order dreaded by every gladiator whose conscience had not been destroyed in the crucible of arena combat.

Did she believe him to be no different than his father?

Probably.

Marcus was unprepared for how profoundly that speculation bothered him, and how strongly he wished to change her opinion.

As he lifted his right arm, fist knotted and thumb extended in the neutral position, a hush stole over the audience. Ruth pulled back on Hyperosa's neck.

Like exotic animals, women performers were too rare; talented women, rarer still. The Moridunum gladiatrix had fought well, and Marcus couldn't help but draw an association between this match and his final bout.

He turned his thumb upward.

Surprise and relief banished the hatred on Ruth's face.

The women stood and saluted Marcus. While medics helped Hyperosa remove the spear, stanch the blood and walk toward the tunnel from which she had emerged, Ruth took a few moments to wave to the crowd, not with a victor's exultant triumph but with contemplative reserve. She sheathed her sword and marched from the arena.

To Marcus she gave not even the tiniest backward glance, and it widened the wound she'd inflicted upon his heart.

UPON HER COT AT Villa Britanniae, Rhyddes had closed her eyes for what seemed like only a moment before she heard the clang of her barred door being opened. Blinking groggily, and aching in more places than Hemaeus's valerian tisane could possibly fix, she sat up as Vederi and another guard stepped inside her cell.

"Come, Gladiatrix Ruth," said the closer of the two, gesturing toward the corridor. Fatigue prevented her from recalling his name. "Lanista Jamil has summoned you."

*Ruth.*

Rhyddes shivered. She had been too exhausted to clean off the Pictish paint after her match.

*Gladiatrix Ruth.* Her ire welled, and she felt warmth rush to her cheeks.

"Are you not well?" asked Vederi. Genuine concern creased his craggy features. "Perhaps you need to visit Physician Hemaeus again, Ruth."

Heartily, she wished she could force them to stop using that thrice-cursed name. "Just cold, sir," she lied.

In silence they traversed the school to a wing she had never been privileged to visit before, remarkable by the opulent luxury of its fountains, mosaics, statuary and furnishings.

The slaves were more finely dressed here, too, hurrying about on any number of missions, some more obvious—such as the women balancing large jugs upon their heads or laundry-heaped baskets on their hips—than others. Every slave quickly and politely deferred to the passage of Rhyddes and her guards.

Nor was she the only combatant present.

Rhyddes's party passed several gladiators apparently

returning from audiences with Jamil. Even the contract gladiators were escorted by guards in this wing.

Nemo, his right shoulder bound with a fresh bandage, gave her a grin and the thumbs-up signal. It pleased her to return it. But it pleased her even further to see Gordianus walking unassisted, if stiffly, with his torso's bandages bulging beneath his tunic. They clasped forearms like free Celtic warriors.

"You honored our gods today," he murmured in their tongue before Vederi tugged Rhyddes away. "Now enjoy the reward."

*Reward?*

Her guards quickened the pace, preventing her from asking Gordianus what he meant.

No matter. She considered it reward enough to have survived the fight.

A servant carrying damp towels draped over his right arm met them at the door of Jamil's chambers. He rendered a deep bow and, upon straightening, led Rhyddes and her guards through a door that opened onto a large indoor pool. Tendrils of steam, scented by the refreshing fragrance she'd learned was called *eucalyptus,* curled across the water's surface, which was broken by the pool's sole occupant.

"Ah, Ruth."

That accursed name again! She clenched her fists.

Jamil didn't seem to notice. He slapped the water invitingly. "Come and wash off your arena paint."

"An order, master?"

"If I must." Jamil's tone hardened.

Rhyddes slipped off her sandals, noted the guards' positions near the water's edge and waded in without bothering to shed her tunic or knee-length breeches. At once, the heat began dissolving her pain, fatigue and ire, as well as her paint. Materia entered from an inner chamber and stooped to give her a nubby hand towel, with which Rhyddes attacked the stubborn woad splotches.

Finally, Rhyddes met Jamil's gaze. "Thank you for this opportunity, master."

After ducking up to her chin in the water, Rhyddes worked the towel under her tunic to scrub the paint from her breast. Gods, but it felt good to get that evil stuff off.

The aging Egyptian's dark eyes narrowed. "Gladiatrix, do you care whether you live or die?"

She stilled her hand. "Lanista Jamil?"

"You won out there today, I'll grant you that. But you took foolish risks." Crossing his arms, he leaned forward, expression intensifying. "That is the mark of someone who has nothing to lose and everything to gain by death. The criminals the governor forces me to take fight in that manner, and I have too many of them in my ranks. If I could, I'd be rid of them in a thrice and count myself fortunate.

"Does that describe you, Freedom, daughter of Red?"

She sucked in a breath. "Master, I…"

Did that describe her? Had she stopped caring whether she lived or died? If so, when had that happened?

And if not, why not?

The only question she could answer was the last one, and that reason she dared not admit, even to herself.

"No, master. It does not describe me."

"I have never seen anyone—man or woman, volunteer, slave or criminal—fight with more passion. What drove you?"

"If I told you, master, you probably would kill me."

The guards, who were obviously trying not to succumb to the temptation of leering at her water-enhanced curves, exchanged a glance and adopted more alert stances.

Jamil chuckled. "I am not in the habit of murdering honesty, woman. I give you leave to speak freely."

"Dressing and painting me like a Pict was bad enough." Studying the blue flecks floating upon the water's surface, she drew a slow breath. "But the worst of it was the name you gave me for the arena."

"Ruth? I chose that as a name the crowd would have an easier time with. And it sounds like your father's name."

She glared at Jamil. "Rudd sold me to pay his debt to this gods-forsaken empire. But even before that, he treated me more like rogue livestock than a daughter." She wasn't sure what had made her blurt out that last bit and felt her cheeks flush. To hide her embarrassment, she rubbed the cloth vigorously across her arms, where a few spots of paint clung.

"I am sorry, Rhyddes." She felt the water current as Jamil waded closer to her. "I had no idea." He stretched his hand toward her arm, seemed to change his mind and drew it back.

"My body belongs to you, master. So, I expect, does the naming of it," she replied stoically.

"Not necessarily." Jamil stepped to the pool's edge and hoisted himself out with a graceful push on muscles scarred and hardened by two decades of military service rippling beneath his wet garment. Servants clustered around to drape him with towels. "In this familia, a gladiator who wins his first bout may choose his persona."

He nodded at one of the male slaves, who disappeared into Jamil's main chamber.

Rhyddes climbed out of the pool to be similarly cloaked with towels.

The slave returned with a wool-wrapped, oblong object in one hand and what could only be a pouch full of coins in the other. He gave them to Jamil, who skirted the pool to present them to Rhyddes.

She unwrapped the wool to reveal the figure of a man surmounted by a black dog's head, with long, alert ears and an even longer muzzle, his clothing and ornaments exquisitely painted in gold and red enamel.

"What manner of animal is this?" She fingered the smooth, tapered snout.

"The head is that of a jackal, a creature of Egypt and other dry lands. Your figure's name is Anubis," Jamil explained. "Lord of death for my people."

The similar masks worn by the arena mule's attendants made sudden, harrowing sense.

Clutching the figure in the fist she laid over her heart, she bowed, the remnants of her anger evaporating. "I am deeply honored, Lanista Jamil."

"It is my custom to present an Anubis figure to my gladiators after their first win." Briefly, the Egyptian's gaze grew distant. "It often seems to bring comfort to them."

That, Rhyddes could imagine. Although she worshipped a different pantheon, she appreciated the sentiment.

The pouch contained, to her astonishment, a hundred

gold pieces, called aureii by the Romans, though until that moment Rhyddes had seen only the most common coin, the brass sestertius. She cradled tenfold what a male farm laborer earned in all the days between one summer and the next; not enough to match her slave-price, but more than she'd ever expected to see in her lifetime.

"You received this for my win?" she asked breathlessly.

"That is but your share, Rhyddes." He folded her hands over the pouch. "You may buy whatever persona you desire."

"I thank you, master." She uttered a rueful laugh. "I desire only what my name, Rhyddes, means: freedom. But since you believe my Celtic name may be too difficult for these Romans' stiff tongues, they shall come to know me as 'Libertas.'"

*Liberty.* A concept as foreign to herself as to her conquered people, but a right that every man, woman and child should enjoy.

Jamil's expression reflected naught but approval.

**9**

RHYDDES COMMISSIONED AN impressive set of bronze-and-leather armor to fit her chosen persona of "Libertas," the fearsome Celtic warrior-woman. Greaves embossed with feline figures intertwined and devouring each other in the Celtic style, matching armbands, a breastplate molded to her curves, a helmet with oversize cheek guards: not a detail went unaddressed. While she refused to fight bare-breasted, she compromised with Jamil by shortening the fringe of her bronze-studded battle kilt.

The end result, Jamil had to admit when she appeared in her next bout during the harvest games, was stunning.

The Londinium crowd took an immediate liking to the small but athletic Libertas, a liking that only deepened as she scored hit after hit upon Alta, her Gallic opponent.

In fact, Libertas fought too well. By the end of the match,

Alta was bleeding profusely and couldn't rise from the sand, even to display the signal for requesting clemency.

"Iugula!" clamored the spectators as if already scenting her death. "Iugula!"

Jamil spared a glance for Aquila. The lad let slip a flash of consternation as he yielded to the crowd's will. Libertas glared at Aquila before bending to obey the order.

After she finished, she greeted the crowd as Jamil had taught her, but her smiles and gestures lacked enthusiasm. To the thunderous chants of "Libertas! Libertas!" she stalked off.

Aquila faced the arena long after Libertas had departed. When the Anubis-masked attendants led out the mule and hitched it to Alta's body, he turned away with a sigh.

"Compassion befits poets and physicians, Aquila." Jamil reached up to clap the powerful shoulder that no longer rippled under the strain of combat. "But not politicians."

The governor's son grunted, shrugging off Jamil's hand. "I did my duty." His gaze grew distant. "And she did hers." He regarded Jamil sharply. "Romans despise weakness, and you seem to have taught Libertas that point well. Congratulations."

As the lad left the governor's box, Jamil couldn't shake the sense that he had betrayed both Aquila and Libertas.


"YOU FOUGHT WELL today, Libertas," said Vederi as they strode from the bathhouse to the gladiators' cells.

The lavender Rhyddes had chosen to scent her bath curled around her in heady, soothing waves. "Thank you, sir."

In her mind, "fighting well" and "wholesale slaughter"

didn't equate. But the afternoon's exertion—emotional as well as physical—had fatigued her too deeply to take issue with a kindly soul who was only trying to pay her a compliment.

They rounded the final corner, and Vederi smiled. "I like the name Libertas. It fits you well. Much better than Ruth."

That wrenched a rueful laugh from her throat. "'Ruth' was Lanista Jamil's choice." She returned his smile, thankful for the diversion from her match. "'Libertas' was mine."

"Well, I approve. I think the crowd did, too."

"I appreciate that, Vederi." By this time they'd reached her cell. He opened the door. She stepped inside and turned to face him. "In fact, I appreciate all you've done for me."

He barked a laugh. "Even when it's not pleasant?"

She shrugged. "We all must obey or die, yes?"

"True enough." His look became earnest. "You didn't visit Hemaeus this evening. Are you sure I can't bring you something? A valerian tisane, perhaps, to help you sleep?"

"That's very kind of you to offer, but no." She glanced at her Anubis figure standing on the table beside her cot, sharing the space with a lit lamp and a lump of chalk. Her limbs felt leaden. "Tonight I shall sleep like one of this god's charges."

Vederi nodded, swung the door closed, and locked it. Rhyddes had long since become accustomed to the clang and click. "Sleep well, then, Libertas. You have earned it."

Humming a drinking song, he strode away.

She left the lamp lit and gratefully fell back onto her cot, trying to ignore the creaking ropes, the mattress straw prickling through the canvas cover, the woolen blanket's musty smell and itchiness, and the mounting ache in her muscles.

Sleep deserted her.

Huddled on one side and staring at the lamp's low flame, she contemplated whether to shout after Vederi. But no tisane could heal the wound rending her soul.

With her arena armor and weapons locked in the armory, her combat winnings ensconced with the familia's banker, and garments, footgear, lamps and oil, bedding, eating implements and other necessary items supplied by Jamil, her remaining worldly possessions consisted of the jackal-headed Anubis figure and chalk to record the results of her bouts. One day, while being escorted through the cell block on the way to drills, Nemo had shown her the many methods gladiators used, from gouging tick marks in the slate walls to drawing elaborate scenes.

Her first fight, even when clad and named in a manner that had infuriated her, Rhyddes didn't mind depicting in detail. Hyperosa's worthy performance had saved her life, so Rhyddes had honored her with as fine a sketch as she could muster.

This day's match was best forgotten, though Rhyddes knew she would always remember Alta's final look: fearful yet resigned. Rhyddes had despised killing the woman, yet her gladiator's oath forbade disobedience. Briefly she had considered refusing. But the certain knowledge that she and Alta would have shared the same fate had driven her to comply.

Rhyddes sat up and threw the blanket aside, struck by a discomfiting realization: Jamil had been right.

When she'd first come to Villa Britanniae, she hadn't cared whether she lived or died. Three moons ago, she'd have defied Aquila and welcomed death.

As she turned the chalk between her fingers, its dust

whitening her hands, she failed to identify any single event that had altered her outlook. She couldn't have given a wagonload of cow dung for her winnings—coins couldn't buy her what she most wanted. The crowd's adulation and Vederi's compliments pleased her, but those couldn't buy her freedom, either.

Her thoughts drifted to Nemo and Gordianus, and how she had come to regard them as brothers.

Alta must have had brothers, too. If not by birth, then surely by the shared blood of arena combat. Brothers who would never enjoy her company again.

Intense longing to see Owen and the rest of the clan pierced Rhyddes's gut like a gladius blade.

Hot tears blurred her vision, but she dashed them away. She couldn't let herself cry. Jamil might happen past her door, since he often inspected the cell blocks of an evening before retiring.

The blue-gray slate wall beside her cot seemed to dare her to leave it blank. The more Rhyddes pondered her match, the less right it seemed to let Alta go unremembered. Yet she couldn't represent the truth without dishonoring the fallen.

The fallen one had dishonored herself.

Uttering a low growl, she smashed the chalk into the wall amidst an explosion of dust and shards.

"Libertas?"

As Rhyddes hastened to stand, Jamil instructed Vederi to open her cell.

"What in Lady Maat's name are you doing?" he asked Rhyddes as he entered, waving a dismissal at the guard.

For a moment it appeared as if Vederi, concern etched

into the weathered lines of his face, would refuse the order. At last he complied and backed out of sight.

"Recording the results of my bout, master," she answered truthfully, if acerbically.

Jamil maneuvered within the close confines to view her first drawing, on the opposite wall. "Quite different from this one."

"I felt differently about the match, sir."

Jamil faced about. "Why? Because the sponsor ordered you to kill your opponent?" He planted his hands on his hips. "This is the way of the games. Become accustomed to it."

She jutted her chin. "On my Da's farm, I had to end a sick or wounded animal's suffering many a time. But today—" Tears threatened again, and she choked off the words with a quavering sigh as she stared at the rush-strewn, chalk-littered ground.

Her owner moved closer, and she felt his fingers slip beneath her chin and pull upward. When she met his gaze, she found no reproach there, as she had expected, only compassion.

"Tell me, Libertas. What happened today?" he asked softly.

"I—I couldn't…" She sucked a breath through her gritted teeth, willing herself to continue. "I had to pretend Alta was a suffering animal." Shame branded her cheeks, and more tears slipped free.

Jamil enfolded her into an embrace. She muffled her sobs against his chest, and he held her, stroking her hair and back, until they had run their course. Rhyddes couldn't help but wonder what her life might have been like had this man been her father.

"Every gladiator does what he must to obey the order, Libertas. I see no shame in your actions."

How she longed to agree! She pulled back to regard him frankly, wiping her eyes and nose with her tunic sleeve. "People are not animals, master."

"No." Jamil bent over her cot and ran a finger through the expression of her frustration. "That is why you should craft some other memorial for Alta than this ugly splotch."

Indeed.

Rhyddes ventured a smile. "An order, Lanista Jamil?"

"Must I make it one?" He shared her smile.

She shook her head. "But I have used all my chalk."

Jamil chuckled. "I'll have Vederi bring you all you wish."

"Thank you, sir," she said as he turned to summon Vederi to be let out. "For everything."

He acknowledged her with a nod and strode briskly from the cell. Vederi gave her a sympathetic look as he secured the door.

"I could do with that valerian tisane, now. If your offer still stands," she said hopefully.

"Of course, Libertas." Vederi grinned. "My pleasure."

Later, as Rhyddes sipped the steaming drink Hemaeus had sweetened with honey and mint, she vowed to carry out Jamil's suggestion.

But she resolved to leave the splotch as a reminder that she harbored no intention of turning into what many of her gladiator-brethren had become: an emotionless killing-tool.

WORD OF LONDINIUM'S gorgeous and talented gladiatrix spread like a brush fire through southern Britannia, thanks in no small part to the visiting Roman military officers who had witnessed her bouts. At least, that was what Jamil presumed when in November he began receiving invitations for her to entertain the legions stationed at towns as far away as Isca Silurum, Glevum and Camulodunum.

Jamil accepted the invitations upon the condition that he would be permitted to bring other gladiators, as well. The garrison commanders agreed with pleasing alacrity.

The substantial fees accompanying the couriers pleased him even more.

He ordered Vederi to escort Libertas to his private workroom so he could inform her of the news, hoping she would welcome a change in venue, as gladiators usually did.

However, the mercurial Libertas was far from being a typical gladiator.

THE FIRST TIME RHYDDES had been escorted to her owner's wing, she had marveled at the exotic furnishings, statuary, painted wall decorations and floor mosaics. The murals featured comely, black-haired people drawn in an oddly angular style, performing tasks ranging from the mundane, such as scything and weaving, to the sacred. Creatures with animals' heads and human bodies graced the latter scenes, some sporting wings, making Rhyddes wonder just what sort of gods Egyptians honored.

Then again, perhaps these beings were not so very different from the Celts' great horned god, Cernunos, lord of every living creature.

Jamil interrupted her reverie to divulge his plans for her immediate future.

"Isca Silurum in late December?" Rhyddes pulled her cloak tightly about her, in spite of the heated floor that warmed the room, as if winter had already invaded the villa. "Glevum in mid-February, Camulodunum in March?"

"I know that seems like a heavy schedule, Libertas, when most gladiators fight no more than thrice in a year. But I am trying to establish your career."

Her career, indeed. She rolled her eyes. "Establishing your preeminence among the other lanistae would be closer to the truth," she muttered.

A gladiator could be killed for such insubordination, and well Rhyddes knew it. But she possessed a fair idea of just how valuable she had become to this man.

Jamil slapped his palms on the tabletop with a resounding thwack and stood, a scowl darkening his olive-skinned face.

"Woman, you shall fight in Tartarus if the games' financiers demand it."

"At least I would not be cold," she shot back. "Master."

Abrupt laughter shook Jamil's frame. "That much is certain." Affection warmed his expression. "But I, for one, would miss you, Libertas."

"As would I."

Pulse quickening, Rhyddes whirled to the sound of the familiar voice. Aquila stood in the doorway, wreathed in torchlight. Sweat had pasted his wavy black hair to his head and molded his sparring tunic to his broad chest. In that attire, it was easy for Rhyddes to imagine the governor's son was just another gladiator-slave.

Aquila favored her with an appreciative look that intensified as their gazes met and held. Rhyddes fought the racing of her heart to maintain a neutral countenance but couldn't deny his magnetism.

She broke the spell with a shake of her head. "Please forgive me for staring, Lord Aquila. I intended no offense."

"None taken, Libertas."

The lilting sound of her arena name on his lips sent an unexpected thrill through her soul.

She bowed to hide her reaction and turned toward Jamil. "If I may have your leave, master, I suspect the two of you have important business to discuss."

"Indeed." Smiling enigmatically, Jamil gave her a nod and looked past her to address Aquila. "So important that it couldn't wait for you to become properly clothed?"

Aquila squared his shoulders. The action flexed his chest alluringly. Rhyddes knotted her fist and dug it into her thigh to prevent herself from reaching out to stroke it.

"I noticed Libertas being escorted to your private wing and I want you both to hear what I have to say." His expression's frankness proclaimed his honesty, but the desire smoldering in his gaze hinted at more.

Jamil's raised eyebrow invited him to continue.

"My father celebrates his natal day on the calends of April, and he asked me to stage games in his honor. I know," Aquila said, raising both hands. "I was just as surprised as you, Jamil. But he wants this for the people of Londinium, and he wants your best, including Libertas." Aquila slid a glance and a smile at Rhyddes, making her stomach feel like a home for a flock of waking bats. "Especially Libertas."

Jamil crossed his arms. "Then please convey my respectful regrets to the governor, Aquila. I have committed Libertas to an ambitious tour of several legionary fortresses. By April, she will have earned a long rest."

"Which fortresses?" Concern colored Aquila's tone.

By the time Jamil finished enumerating the schedule, Aquila looked aghast. "Ambitious? I would call it suicidal."

"Does that matter so much?" Rhyddes dared to ask him.

He took her hand into his much larger one and pressed it. The tingling sensation lingered long after he had let go. "It does to me," he murmured.

His face dipped closer, and she closed her eyes, certain of what would happen next. Against all rational thought, and in spite of her head's ruthless reminder of who this man was and what he represented, she stood ready to welcome the moist warmth of his lips upon hers.

The touch she craved never came.

The noisy rumbling of Jamil clearing his throat made them step hastily apart.

And it revived her better judgment. Aquila's people had murdered many of hers and enslaved the rest, his father had caused her enslavement with his crushing taxes, and she possessed no good reason to consort with the governor's son.

Her heart vehemently disagreed.

"Libertas, you are dismissed," her owner said sternly.

Rhyddes, relieved, gave Jamil an apologetic nod. As she moved to join Vederi in the outer chamber, her eyes were drawn once again to Aquila's gaze. Passion smoked in his hazel eyes. She felt her cheeks heat. Her knees weakened, as if they had become molten wax.

Reluctantly, she broke eye contact, bowed to Aquila, and fled the workroom.

"Aquila," she heard Jamil say before the door swung to, "you and I have much to discuss, indeed."

MARCUS WATCHED LIBERTAS'S exit, an ache throbbing deep inside his chest, until long after the door had clicked shut.

"Name your price, Jamil," he whispered.

"She is not for sale." The warning thrum in Jamil's tone caused Marcus to face him. "Nor ever shall be."

He drew a deep breath. The ache deepened and plunged lower. "Just one night...even one hour—"

"I sell my gladiators' arena skills," Jamil snapped. "Not their bedchamber talents."

"Hah." Marcus folded his arms. "I've nearly been trampled by the legions of women who frequent this school. Your men are far from celibate. Don't try to tell me that you do not profit from the liaisons with their adoring admirers."

The Egyptian grinned, his teeth sparkling in contrast to his olive skin. "Very well, then, I won't."

Jamil stepped from behind his worktable, snatched a cloak off a nearby wall peg and tossed it to Marcus, who caught it deftly. While the wool's welcome warmth settled about Marcus's shoulders, Jamil moved in front of the window that overlooked the training yard and threw open the wooden shutters. A chilly November breeze swooped in, rattling the parchment lying on the tabletop.

He stood beside Jamil at the window and was rewarded with the sight of Libertas rejoining her sparring partner, Nemo of Iberia, among the controlled melee. Even in drills, Libertas moved with a level of agility and grace that made her a sheer joy to behold.

His craving escalated.

"Every gladiator—and gladiatrix—of Familias Jamilus

must obey me in all matters relating to the arena," Jamil continued. "But the choice of bed partners remains theirs."

Marcus gave the Egyptian a sharp look, as if he had begun babbling in his native tongue. "With the contract gladiators I can understand. But your gladiator-slaves have a choice, too?"

Jamil regarded him without apology. "With a few exceptions, yes. They do."

"The exceptions being…?" It probably was too much to hope that Jamil would number Libertas among the exceptions.

"Condemned criminals do not enjoy this privilege," Jamil answered, which came as no surprise to Marcus. "And no one in this school—guard, servant, craftsman or gladiator—is permitted to touch Libertas."

Marcus noted Jamil's choice of words. "You exempt yourself?"

Jamil gave him a pointed look before turning back toward the window.

On the training ground, the gladiators had begun their afternoon rest period. Most sheathed their weapons to sit on the sand. A few hobbled off, some of them under guard, presumably to seek medical attention.

Men and women servants hurried into the caged expanse bearing platters of small, flat barley cakes, baskets of empty, pitch-sealed leather flagons and urns of what Marcus knew from experience was watered ale. Social rank made no difference when partaking of the fare offered within the walls of Villa Britanniae.

Libertas ate a barley cake, washed it down with a swig of ale, wiped her mouth with her hand and gazed toward Jamil's window. The fading afternoon sun lit her coppery tresses with an unworldly glow. Any sculptor would have gladly used her flawless face and body to craft his greatest creation.

With a terse nod, Jamil pulled the shutters closed.

"You haven't answered my question," Marcus reminded him, in part to hide his disappointment at being unable to continue watching Libertas.

Jamil's chuckle sounded wistful. "Aquila, my interest in Libertas lies in…other directions."

Again Marcus noted the unusual choice of words, but his most pressing issue demanded resolution. "Is she fated to remain a virgin? Or will you exempt an aristocrat?"

Jamil clapped Marcus's shoulder and tugged off the cloak. "Bathe, but don't make yourself look like an aristocrat, lad, and I shall see what I can arrange."

## 10

As Jamil closed his window's shutters, Rhyddes looked down with a sigh.

Nothing could shutter the image of Aquila's handsome face, surmounting that irresistible body, from her mind's eye. Moreover, as a former competitor, he understood the life she'd been forced to lead. What she wouldn't give to be held, even once, in his strong arms. To be kissed, cherished, loved…

A hiss-thump caught her attention. In the sand between her feet quivered a blunted practice knife. Nemo loomed above her, holding out a hand and grinning triumphantly, as if he'd caught a naughty child.

"Come, Libertas," he said with a peremptory flick of his hand. "Rest period is over."

Grabbing the knife with her left hand, she accepted his assistance to haul herself to her feet. Nemo drew another knife from the sheath swinging from his belt. Rhyddes shifted onto the defensive, and they began circling each other in mock wariness, amidst the score of gladiator pairs performing the same drill.

Rhyddes tried to banish the memory of Aquila's smile to focus on the task at hand.

She saw an opening and lunged. Nemo responded with a chop to her shoulder; not hard enough to hurt too badly, but it caught her off balance and sent her sprawling, face-first, in the sand.

"Concentrate!" he admonished her. "You haven't erred that badly in weeks. In the arena, such a mistake could be your last."

She needed no reminder; that mistake had cost Alta her life.

But Rhyddes had never felt so attracted to—and distracted by—a man before. A Roman man, a conqueror of her people, a spoiled, soon-to-be-wed nobleman likely more interested in gratifying his lust than in sharing his heart.

That thought propelled her off the sand and back into the drill, where she acquitted herself passably well for a few moves. But as she whirled to make another strike, she caught sight of Aquila, damp-haired and dressed in a clean sparring tunic, strolling along the colonnade. Nemo dumped her unceremoniously onto the ground.

She closed her eyes, chastising herself.

Footsteps crunched in the sand nearby, and she presumed that Nemo had approached to help her rise. Without looking, she lifted her arm and connected with another hand.

What she didn't expect was for her owner and chief trainer to be attached to it.

"Walk with me, Libertas," Jamil said as she rose.

Ashamed by her poor practice session, which he surely could not have missed, she sketched a hasty bow. "My humblest apologies, master. I assure you that I shall try harder."

His pox-scarred face folded into an expression she couldn't read. "I'm sure you will." He set a course away from Aquila, rather than toward him as Rhyddes had hoped.

She had no choice but to follow, quickening her pace to match his stride. They exited the training area and headed toward the bathhouse, which seemed an odd choice until she recalled the building would be empty at this hour.

No guards accompanied them, which also seemed odd.

Jamil motioned her into the building and veered toward her curtained alcove in the changing room. Although tiny compared with the rest of the chamber, it featured its own tiled bench, pegs protruding from the walls, niches stuffed with fresh towels, unguent vials and other bathing implements, and empty niches suitable for stowing her tunic, breeches, undergarments, belt and sandals.

Curiosity afire, she sat beside him upon the bench.

"Lord Aquila wishes to pay you a great honor," Jamil said. "He has asked for you to share his bed."

A tide of conflicting emotions ebbed and flowed within her heart. She desired the man, without question, but to act upon that desire seemed a betrayal of everything she held dear, because of who he was and what he represented.

She had no wish to become Aquila's whore, used for a season and then cast aside, no matter how pleasurable that season might promise to be.

Yet her oath as a gladiatrix-slave bound her to obey or die.

Rhyddes bowed her head, sighing. "Yes, master."

"You give your consent?"

"Consent?" She twisted to regard her owner quizzically. "I thought gladiator-slaves had no such privilege."

He patted her shoulder, smiling in a fatherly fashion. "In matters of the heart, mine do." His expression turned earnest. "So, shall I tell him to return after supper?"

She propped her elbows on her knees and rested her chin on her hands, staring at the blue-gray dolphins frolicking across the mosaic beneath her feet. "No."

"Tomorrow, then? He seems quite eager."

Rhyddes swallowed hard. "Never."

"What? But you and he, in my workroom…" Jamil gripped her arm, and she met his gaze. "I thought you liked him."

"I do." She let another sigh escape.

"Then why the reluctance? Villa Britanniae has chambers where you two would be very comfortable. By all reports Aquila is an excellent lover—"

"He is Roman. His people brutally conquered mine, and I have no right to feel anything for him other than contempt." Into Jamil's surprised silence, she continued, "I would think that you, an Egyptian, would understand that, master."

Jamil's laugh bore an undercurrent of bitterness Rhyddes couldn't fathom. "I am a pragmatist first, and a Roman citizen second." He rose, and so did she. He gave her a slight nod. "But I respect your convictions, Libertas."

In silence, they left the bathhouse. Aquila was waiting on the top step leading to the building's column-flanked entrance. His beaming smile almost made her change her mind.

Almost.

She shook her head, and his expression collapsed into profound disappointment.

Sighing, she looked away and continued walking, as much to hide her emotions as to shield herself from his.

But her convictions could not stem the ache cresting within her. Although her head claimed she had made the right choice, her heart condemned her for a fool.

LIBERTAS'S SILENT REFUSAL reverberated in Marcus's head as loudly as if she had shouted it.

Occasionally women refused his invitations, but never had a rejection made him feel as if his heart had been wrenched from his chest.

Clenching his fists, he took a step after Libertas.

And collided with Jamil's stiffened arm.

"Leave her be, Aquila." As Marcus shifted to move around Jamil, the Egyptian grasped him by both biceps, not gently. "I said, leave her be."

"But she—that is, I must—" Marcus broke off as Libertas disappeared into a walkway intersecting the colonnade. Jamil released his arms. He regarded Jamil squarely. "I have done something to displease her, haven't I?" The Egyptian's upraised eyebrows confirmed Marcus's suspicions. "What can I do to make amends?"

Jamil draped his arm companionably across Marcus's shoulders, and they set a course toward the school's main entrance. "Aside from changing the past or your ancestry, my friend, nothing."

Marcus halted. "What do you mean?"

"If you wore a sparring tunic by necessity rather than by

choice, it might be different with her. But her mind's eye sees a highly ranked member of the race who subjugated her people and caused her enslavement."

Marcus jerked away and stalked toward the gate. "I had nothing to do with any of that."

Jamil charged past him to bar his way. "Only you, Aquila, can convince her otherwise."

"If I so choose," Marcus snapped, surging forward. In response to his glare, the guards moved with alacrity to swing open the gate.

"Indeed, the choice is yours," Jamil said to his back as the gate clanged shut behind him. "But if this incident affects Libertas's performance any worse than it already has, I shall send you a bill."

Bemused, Marcus swiveled about to determine whether Jamil had been jesting, but he had already withdrawn from sight.

Marcus snorted. Jamil, who worshipped money more ardently than he worshipped any deity, probably was being serious.

Did he, Marcus Calpurnius Aquila, really want to win Libertas's heart? He made his way back toward the praetorium in the swiftly retreating twilight. With each greeting he bestowed upon soldiers, merchants and passersby, seeing instead the shimmer of Libertas's hair, the sparkle of her eyes and the tantalizing fullness of her lips, his heart returned the same answer.

Marcus could no sooner change his ancestors or their bloodthirsty predilection for world domination than he could grow a third arm. Spending time with Libertas might convince her to look upon him more favorably, but only the gladiators' drill sessions afforded him such opportunities, and Marcus couldn't fathom how that would help his cause.

Worse yet, if Agricola learned his son had become infatuated with a gladiatrix-slave, the gods alone knew what the consequences would be—beginning, most likely, with being banned from Villa Britanniae. And there'd be no end of trouble if Senator Falco and Lady Messiena found out.

But it all paled against the fact that Jamil would be taking Libertas away from Londinium soon, perhaps, gods forbid, never to return.

*No!*

The pair of guards flanking the praetorium's front gate straightened at his approach. The gods alone knew what they'd been doing; perhaps they'd been late in arriving to their posts following the evening meal. The men saluted smartly with their spears, probably silently thanking Mars that Agricola hadn't witnessed their transgression. Marcus considered reprimanding them on behalf of his father, but that duty belonged to the guard captain...

An idea occurred, one that surely even Agricola would approve.

Grinning, Marcus gave the guards hearty greetings and bounded up the marble steps three at a time. By the time he reached the dining chamber, he'd worked up a sizable appetite—and a plan to slake a hunger of an entirely different sort.

His mother softly but firmly admonished his tardiness, and he gave her an apologetic bow before claiming his vacant couch and falling upon the platter heaped with finger-sized pieces of honeyed chicken, steamed mussels and herb-crusted salmon.

"Although you honor your promise not to fight in the arena, Son," Loreia began, pointing a nod at his attire, "your father and I think you spend too much time at the gladiatorial school."

Marcus saluted his parents with his wine goblet and took a long swallow. "I agree, Mother." He smiled at her surprise and turned toward his father. "Appoint me as a tribune and send me to inspect the legions for you."

Agricola nearly choked on his wine. A servant ran forward to slap his back. Spluttering and coughing, Agricola took several deep breaths. "Inspect the legions?" he rasped, and cleared his throat.

"Why? To help you, of course, Father."

"Indeed." Agricola finished his wine and demanded more. "You have never demonstrated any interest in military affairs before, Marcus. Why now?"

"Why not now?" Marcus shrugged and scooped a spoonful of spiced pear slices onto his platter. "What better time to test the legions' readiness than when they would least expect such a visit?"

"That is not what I asked." Agricola scowled.

"Oh come now, Sextus, the answer is obvious." Loreia patted her husband's arm. "Our son stands ready at last to take his rightful place at your side." Briefly she beamed at Marcus before regarding Agricola. "Why must you be so suspicious?"

"It is a father's duty to be suspicious," Agricola muttered. "Although I must admit the idea has merit." His expression adopted a stern cast. "But is it just that, Marcus—an idea? Or have you developed an itinerary and list of provisions, or given thought to the size of escort you'll need?"

"A cavalry turma should suffice as escort. I have a fair idea of the provisions we would require, though I haven't had time to create a list yet. As for itinerary—" Marcus rubbed the stubble on his upper lip to mask his smile "—what say you to Isca Silurum, Glevum and Camulodunum?"

Agricola nodded grudging approval. "An ambitious journey, Son, especially if you tour the smaller installations in between, as well." He contemplated his refilled goblet for a long moment before taking another swallow. "I still want to know why you have proposed this plan."

Propped on one elbow, Marcus gestured toward Loreia with his free hand. "It's as Mother said—I wish to take my rightful place." He let his parents assume which place he meant.

Their silence caused him to launch into the litany he'd rehearsed: "The projects to design and raise funds for building the northern lighthouses consume much of your time, Father. I don't know lighthouses, but I have lived around soldiers my entire life." Recalling the incident at the gate, he allowed his smile to show. "I think I can distinguish an ill-prepared unit from a combat-ready one." His smile faded as a concern presented itself. "If you trust me."

"Of course he trusts you." Loreia shot Agricola a warning glance. "Don't you, my love?"

Agricola surrendered with a sigh. "You do seem to have thought this through, Son. When do you propose to depart?"

Marcus shifted on the triclinium, considering his words. "I would like to reach Isca Silurum before Saturnalia—"

Slapping his thigh, Agricola chortled. "Ah, the truth comes out. You want to see how folk in other parts of the province conduct their reveling."

"And why not?" Marcus countered, grinning. "Don't I deserve at least that much reward for performing this service for you?"

Fingering his chin, Agricola regarded Marcus so long that Marcus became convinced his father was going to refuse. Finally, Agricola said, "I shall look forward to receiving your reports. Weekly, at a minimum."

"Agreed." Marcus nodded solemnly, fighting to hold his elation at bay.

"And I shall look forward to seeing you in time for your father's natal day on the calends of April," Loreia added, her tone carrying a mild but clear warning.

Marcus grasped her hand. "I have no intention of missing those festivities, Mother."

Especially since the festivities would feature a performance by the gorgeous gladiatrix who had enslaved his heart.

PUGIONIS DISTRUSTED ANY man who insisted upon meeting in a public place to discuss less-than-public business.

*Bugger that,* he mused, peering through the sweat pouring off his brow; he distrusted nigh unto everyone.

Especially politicians.

Hitching the towel more securely about his loins, and keeping a tight grip upon his caution, he stalked deeper into the steam chamber, one of many inside Rome's vast Baths of Agrippa.

At this hour, the traditional rest period between luncheon

and the resumption of afternoon business activities, Pugionis should have been dodging a dozen bathers. But today only one man lounged upon the tiled bench that ran the length of the back wall. An array of towels failed to cover his flabby bulk, and sweat plastered his gray hair to his balding head. Heavy jowls flanking a jutting chin proclaimed a lifetime of oration and of lofty goals aggressively sought. Bushy eyebrows surmounted narrowly set eyes that remained, for the moment, closed.

He must have bribed the bathhouse attendants to reserve this chamber. Typical politician.

One of the attendants staggered in toting a basket of hot stones. The senator didn't react as the young man dumped his load to freshen the steam and gathered the cooling stones into his basket. After bowing to the chamber's occupants, the slave pushed open the door with one shoulder and lugged the basket from the chamber.

"You came," said the senator.

"Your message intrigued me." The cryptic note had referred to an unspecified recruitment job. "Who, exactly, do you need me to recruit?"

Pugionis sat on the bench and propped his shoulders against the corner so he could watch both doors.

"Gladiators." The senator swung around to face Pugionis and regarded him intently. His dark, darting eyes reminded Pugionis of the hunting bird of the senator's cognomen. "Rome's gladiatorial schools stand at half strength. I need another thousand gladiators, the best in the empire."

The request for gladiators made perfect sense; Pugionis

and his associates were well-known in the Colosseum's highest wagering circles. They would have become wealthy enough to own their own gladiatorial school if they hadn't been swindled by another bettor, a fact that, a decade later, still rankled so bitterly that only the Egyptian's blood would repay the debt.

The quantity of gladiators specified by the senator, however, was ludicrous. But Pugionis wasn't yet willing to refuse what promised to be a lucrative job.

"An ambitious task, my lord. And extremely expensive. They will need food and other supplies, and a huge escort. At least five cohorts, since the gladiators will have to be sent back in groups no larger than a hundred apiece." Pugionis squinted at the senator through the mist, scrutinizing him for any reaction but seeing none.

"Ah, yes, escorts. Seek out former Praetorian guardsmen. You won't have any trouble with them heading the escorts' ranks."

"Should I find any wishing to participate in this venture, how do I release them from their postings?"

"I shall execute a document you can present to their commanders." He rubbed his chin slowly as if lost in thought. "If you happen across any former Praetorian Guard prefects, send them to me immediately."

"When do you need the gladiators?"

"The full contingent must be in Rome, ready to fight, by the nones of August."

Pugionis's eyebrows shot up. "Less than ten months hence?" He sharpened his stare. "That will double the cost."

The senator gave a bored wave. "All expenses shall be

covered, never fear." He narrowed his eyes. "All *legitimate* expenses."

"And the payment, over and above—" Pugionis coughed behind his hand "—legitimate expenses?"

"Your profit shall be quite substantial *if* you deliver the thousandth man on time." The senator's menacing expression sent a chill up Pugionis's spine in spite of the steam. "Otherwise, you get nothing."

"Fair enough, my lord." Besides, expenses could be "legitimately" padded to ensure profit even if delaying delivery became a necessity. However, one detail puzzled him. "What is so auspicious about the nones of August?"

"You should pull your head out of the betting dens once in a while." The senator chuckled, low and harsh, prickling the hair on Pugionis's arms. "It is the natal day of Commodus, our esteemed emperor's son, who on that day shall be—" he tapped his chin again "—five years old. At the height of the festivities, the emperor plans to confer the title of Caesar upon the prince."

Pugionis noted the slightly mocking emphasis placed on the word *esteemed* but let it pass without comment. He also dared not comment upon the ridiculousness of calling a child "Caesar."

"Two thousand gladiators will make quite a spectacle," he said, giving the senator a subtle opportunity to reveal his intentions but not expecting him to rise to the bait.

"Indeed." A coy smile seeped across the senator's face. "That is one way of describing it."

## II

RHYDDES COULDN'T BELIEVE IT.

Not only did Aquila haunt her nightly dreams, but by day she saw him more often than ever on the practice grounds. Always there, always watching, as if he expected her at any moment to change her mind and leap into his bed.

Instead she leaped into drills with frenzied abandon to prevent Aquila's expectations from becoming reality.

Finally, the day arrived when Rhyddes and six of Jamil's best and most trustworthy gladiators packed their gear, climbed into enclosed wagons—stuffed with pillows and furs for comfort yet strengthened with steel bands to reduce the likelihood of their escape—and embarked upon their legion tour.

Rhyddes relished the respite, albeit temporarily, from the Roman who had besieged her heart.

Her wagon rumbled through Londinium and she caught

glimpses of the receding town through the slit between the two leather flaps covering the wagon's rear. Mayhap if she were lucky, she mused, Aquila might become infatuated with someone else in her absence.

"Hail, Jamil!"

So much for luck.

Rhyddes flung aside the pillow she'd been clutching and crawled over to peer between the flaps, ignoring her breath clouds and the guards who glared at her over their horses' heads.

Jamil had elected to ride between her wagon and the one behind it. Although he wore unadorned if well-made riding leathers, his spear-straight posture and firm yet easy control of his mount reminded her that he had once held high rank in the personal service of an emperor.

Next to him, trailed by a column of twenty mounted soldiers, rode the man she had both hoped and dreaded to see.

Attired in silver-and-red leather battle gear, a plume of crimson feathers billowing from his helmet that matched the silver-trimmed crimson cloak flowing from his shoulders onto his horse's flanks, Aquila looked more the conqueror than any Roman Rhyddes had ever seen. And yet, when his gaze locked with hers, his smile banished the disconcerting notion.

Her head and heart instantly resumed their war.

She retreated behind her wagon's curtain, thankful that Jamil had assigned Vederi to ride beside her wagon, rather than inside with her. With her fist she thumped the wagon's floor. The oak planks were real; her burgeoning feelings toward the governor's son couldn't possibly be.

*Could they?*

She crawled as close to the parted flaps as she could without thrusting her head through. So she could learn Aquila's plans and therefore be better prepared, she told herself, though with the next breath she chided herself for the lie. But Aquila and Jamil rode too far back for their words to reach her over the cacophony of creaking wagons, jingling tack and clopping hooves.

As the miles passed, and Aquila and his unit showed no signs of turning onto a different road, Rhyddes began to suspect the worst. Sharing the same encampment, outside the Atrebati tribal capital of Calleva, confirmed her suspicions.

Jamil left her with no time to dwell upon them, however. While the guards set up camp, the gladiators paired off to engage in their normal drills. As the seventh person, Rhyddes headed to the nearest fence post and focused her concentration inward to execute the solo routine Jamil had taught her.

"May I join you, Libertas?"

Aquila had exchanged his ceremonial armor for a gladiator-slave's belted sparring tunic and practice sword.

If only he could exchange his identity as easily.

She bowed to hide her unease. "As you wish, my lord."

As the sun blazed toward its evening rest and cooking fires perfumed the air with delectable aromas, Aquila and Rhyddes saluted each other with their swords and began the drill.

Soldiers and gladiators alike were required to kill, but gladiators were trained first and foremost to entertain while inflicting minimal injury upon the opponent. Maiming and death occurred upon occasion, but typical gladiatorial combat involved complex lunges, kicks, rolls and jumps designed to impress an audience rather than fell an enemy.

Although Rhyddes had watched Aquila compete, and had noticed him practicing with other gladiators, she'd always been too busy sparring with her partners to closely evaluate Aquila's fighting skills. Never had she been afforded the opportunity to experience his strength and cunning firsthand.

This spoiled son of a Roman nobleman could lunge, kick, roll and jump with the best.

Exhilarated as with no other sparring partner, Rhyddes used her speed to dart in and around his guard like a dragonfly, but she felt his superior strength each time his sword connected with hers. Sweat poured from her brow and her breath shortened as she found herself struggling to keep up, yet she didn't want the match to end.

When she missed a parry and his blunted blade grazed painfully off her wrist, she raised it to signal a halt.

His face, which had been a frozen mask of concentration, melted into concern.

"I didn't hurt you, did I?"

The sharp scent of his sweat, the shifting of his chest as he steadied his breath, his very presence threatened to throw her off balance.

Fighting to retain some semblance of control, Rhyddes loosened the laces of her leather wrist guard and tugged it off. Rubbing the sore but intact flesh and sensing no broken bones, she shook her head. "Nothing permanent, my lord."

"Good." His relief bordered on the comical. But there was nothing comical about the way his kiss upon the injured spot seemed to erase the pain. If only it could erase her pride-bound convictions. "Otherwise, Jamil would have my head."

"No, my friend." Grinning broadly, Jamil approached to clap them both on the shoulder. "Only the weight of it in gold aureii." To Rhyddes, Jamil whispered, "Don't forget to acknowledge your audience."

*Audience?*

While she and Aquila had been sparring, the troupe had drawn many curious folk from Calleva, Celt and Roman alike—although here in the tamed south of Britain, Rhyddes found it difficult to distinguish the two peoples except by the occasional shock of red hair. And by the wistful expressions of those who must have glimpsed in Rhyddes a type of freedom they could never attain: the freedom to fight on even footing with their Roman over-lords, if only in pretense.

As Jamil passed an upturned helmet through the crowd to collect donations, and the aroma of roasting meats reminded Rhyddes of her overdue meal, she postured and waved as she had been taught, to the crowd's obvious delight. Aquila, too, comported himself like the arena veteran he was, before departing to attend his troops.

More than Jamil's approval, the crowd's praise or her share of the earnings, even more than the chance to win her freedom, Rhyddes wished with all her being that she could one day accompany Aquila, not as his slave but as his equal.

Bathed in the fading twilight's glow, she resolved to live for the hope that her impossible wish might somehow come to pass.

SHE HAUNTED HIM.

In the music of the hunting wolf he heard her voice. In the chilly December breeze he felt the refreshing coolness of her flesh. In the tangy pine smoke of the campfires he smelled her maddening nearness.

Neither his dreams nor his waking thoughts provided sanctuary from the ruthlessly relentless yet gentle specter....

Marcus, stretched upon his bedroll, stared up at the canvas apex of the tent he shared with the turma's decurion and shook his head as if that could clear it.

Whom was he trying to fool? The fiery little Celt who called herself Libertas had been anything but gentle during their match. He had lost track of how many times she had surprised him with her strength, agility, speed, courage and tenacity.

And there she went again, haunting his thoughts.

Better by far to have her haunt him in the flesh.

Carefully, to avoid disturbing his tentmate, he donned his footgear, flung his cloak about his shoulders and emerged from the tent's warmth into the chilly, starlit night. The nearest sentry noticed him and gave a nod, perhaps assuming Marcus needed to obey nature's call.

It wasn't far from the truth.

A stiff breeze kicked up as Marcus strode toward Jamil's side of the encampment, and he pulled his cloak closer about him. The gladiators' guards gave him only a token challenge. The flickering firelight revealed their knowing smiles as they pointed the way, at his request, toward Libertas's wagon.

Seldom had Marcus reason to revel in his status as the governor's son. Tonight, he did.

A stool had been left at the wagon's rear, allowing him to part the flaps and peer in without disturbing the wagon's occupant. Though the gloom prevented him from distinguishing her features, the soft, rhythmic sigh of her breathing tantalized and aroused him.

And yet, standing on the verge of bringing his desire to fruition, he felt as if a hand were holding him back. A ghostly hand, the recollection of her decision all those weeks ago to refuse his invitation.

As an aristocrat of the world's most powerful nation, he had been raised from infancy to take what he wanted. Any consequences that befell him could always be overcome by Roman might.

*Not this time,* Marcus realized. "Roman might" could conquer a body but never a heart.

As his vision adjusted to the darkness, her petite yet powerful form came into focus, partially obscured by the furs. Ignoring the wind that wrestled with the edges of his cloak, he allowed his gaze to caress her where his hands could not, knowing that he must leave and yet lacking the volition to move his feet.

At last, he closed the flaps, dismounted from the stool and turned to leave.

"Wise choice, Aquila." Jamil, hooded in a dark cloak, stepped from behind the wagon to drop a hand onto Marcus's shoulder.

Marcus shrugged Jamil off and stared eastward, where the sky met the horizon in a gray band heralding the advent of dawn. "Here's another wise choice for you—this morning, my squad and yours part company."

As if in agreement, the winds calmed.

Marcus couldn't see Jamil's surprise but heard it in the Egyptian's swift intake of breath. "I thought you wanted—"

"What I want and what I can have seem destined to tread diverging roads." Marcus's laugh sounded bitter to his own ears. "There is no wisdom in torturing myself." *Or her.* Though to judge from Libertas's behavior, Marcus believed she would not feel tortured whether he left or stayed.

He headed back toward his men's encampment, Jamil keeping pace beside him until they reached the sentry.

"I thought you had planned to accompany us to Isca Silurum. Where will you go now?" Jamil asked.

"Dorcastrum, first." When Jamil lowered his eyebrows, Marcus explained, "I had planned to visit that fort on my way back to Londinium. But I have decided to reverse my circuit."

"Will we see you at any of the legion forts?" The men of both camps were starting to stir, and Jamil no longer made an effort to keep his voice low.

"If the gods so will it." Marcus stared at the lightening heavens, questing for answers but finding only more questions. He regarded Jamil levelly. "Please tell Libertas…"

*Tell her what?* That he regretted his people had overpowered the world, her tribe included? That he was sorry she had been sold into slavery to become a gladiatrix, and even sorrier that he was powerless to help her? That he couldn't bear to be so near to her, and yet so far away?

That, if he could, he'd renounce his betrothal, his family and even his citizenship to spend a single, blessed moment in her embrace?

He bowed his head under reality's crushing weight. "Please convey to Libertas my thanks for the sparring session, and my wishes for her good fortune in her upcoming bouts."

Jamil nodded sympathetically, and Marcus trudged back to his men, an inferno of unfulfilled desire consuming his heart.

AWAKENED BY VOICES and by the pressure in her vitals, Rhyddes roused herself and emerged from the wagon to see Aquila's form receding into the dawn-lit distance. Jamil ordered her to break fast and then help break camp.

The unspoken explanation came when Aquila's party turned onto the north road at the fork while Jamil and his troupe pressed westward.

Rhyddes's heart turned north, as well.

The previous day formed the pattern for the journey. Cunetio, Verlucio, Aquae Sulis, Abona: each day, Jamil timed their progress to arrive at a town by midafternoon, and ordered his gladiators to perform their sparring drills while the guards made camp.

Jamil watched Rhyddes closely, almost suspiciously, often choosing to spar with her himself. She practiced with all her might, caring not whether her performance pleased her owner, trying desperately to rid herself of the Roman who had invaded her thoughts.

The scenery sloped from hilly farmland to windswept

plains to dank moors, but neither rugged coastline nor soaring mountains could purge Aquila's image from her mind. Finally, she gave up trying. Having him as a constant companion to her thoughts seemed a poor second choice, but 'twas far better than having naught.

The morning of the eighth day after they'd set out from Londinium found Jamil and his troupe shivering on the docks of the Sabrina River ferry as a strong, cold wind attacked them from the sea. Huddled in her cloak, Rhyddes watched Jamil speak in earnest tones, using even more earnest gestures, with the ferry captain for passage across. The river, several miles wide at this crossing, presented their final obstacle prior to arriving at the headquarters of Legio II Augusta, Isca Silurum. And clearly the boat's captain preferred the snug warmth of his thick-walled cottage to braving the fickle and oft perilous December winds.

At last they quit their haggling. Jamil dropped a sizable purse into the other man's outstretched hand. Twirling it by its leather thong, the bandy-legged captain swaggered off, calling in a lilting Celtic dialect to rouse his crew. Rhyddes heard the man's elation above the wind's howls. Although she knew not the exact contents of the purse, Jamil's scowl, darker than the snow-laden clouds amassing overhead, gave her a fair idea of how dearly this leg of the journey had cost him.

"Lanista Jamil?" she asked him as he approached. "Is there anything I—"

"Get back into the wagon." Jamil brushed past her with hardly a glance. "Enjoy the ride." His tone snapped as coldly as the wind.

The river, whipped to froth by the tide and winds, proved anything but enjoyable. Rhyddes alternated between clutching the wagon's handholds and her stomach. If she didn't know better, she'd have sworn she had been stricken with bairn-sickness.

After what seemed like an eternity, the ferry made land on the opposite bank, near the mouth of the Isca River. Her wagon rumbled down the massive gangplank over to a cluster of warehouses, where Vederi and the other guards who'd accompanied her set up a perimeter.

Not that she intended to go anywhere: her nausea didn't abate until long after the rest of Jamil's troupe had caught up and the procession had gotten underway again.

By midafternoon, chatter from the guards riding beside her wagon caught her attention, and she presumed their destination had been sighted. Since her view from the wagon revealed only where they had come from, she would have to wait until the next rest period to slake her curiosity.

The other towns had left Rhyddes with the discomfiting impression that the Romans had razed existing buildings to erect their fortresses wherever they chose. But the imposing defensive structure at Isca Silurum appeared as if the town had sprouted around it.

Granite walls, abristle with soldiers, soared high above the dozens of squalid wattle-and-daub huts that seemed to cower to either side. An imposing gatehouse jutted from the wall, surmounted by a huge bronze disc bearing the legion's symbol, a goat leaping toward a winged horse, the creatures separated by a goblet inscribed with the Romans' strange markings.

Inbound wheeled and mounted traffic moved sluggishly through the gatehouse as soldiers questioned each driver and horseman about his business at the fort. No such restriction was imposed on outbound traffic, but having to make way for an exiting vehicle slowed the entering wagons, carts and chariots. Folk on foot, also forced to endure the guards' scrutiny, passed through a narrow entrance to the right of the main gate, while people departed the fort through a similar door on the left.

Another, far smaller fort stood beyond the settlement to the right of Isca Silurum. Some of the traffic turned off the road to head there directly, though not enough to relieve the congestion. Behind it all towered the jaggedly beautiful, snowcapped Cambrian Mountains.

As Vederi ordered Rhyddes to climb back into the wagon, she wondered where the amphitheater lay.

She found out when Jamil's troupe bypassed the main fortress for the fortlet, which served as barracks for visiting gladiators and their guards and entourages. The amphitheater stood beside the Isca River to take advantage of the natural drainage. Unlike Londinium's structure, this arena was much smaller, and its base had been constructed entirely of turf, bisected by eight stone tunnels that opened onto the combat floor.

An army of carpenters swarmed over a lattice of wooden benches that crowned the turf mounds in an unbroken ring, shoring it up in anticipation of large crowds. Rhyddes wondered at this until she recalled the games had been scheduled to coincide with the Roman Saturnalia festivities.

By contrast, the dressed-stone dignitaries' box, which

reminded Rhyddes of the towers crowning Isca Silurum's walls, perched atop the amphitheater's main entrance. As she contemplated the structure, which during the games would be festooned with brightly colored linen and holly swags, she couldn't suppress a pang of regret for the man who would not be present.

Just as well that Aquila was occupied elsewhere, she realized several days later while the fort's physician bound her ribs and she gritted her teeth through the searing pain.

He would have watched her lose.

## 12

As the physician finished binding Rhyddes's torso, Jamil stormed into the ward. She'd seen thunderheads less ominous. Jamil's toga, rumpled from several hours of sitting in the stands, bore sharp creases on the outside of each knee, mayhap because he'd hitched it up to make better time.

In his left fist he carried a coiled whip. The other hand curled and flexed in a slow, steady rhythm, as if he was debating whether to use the whip first, or his fist.

Though the physician's oath to the legion did not obligate him to answer to Jamil, and he appeared husky enough to defend his charges, one glance at her owner convinced the man to busy himself with another patient. He chose a soldier lying safely on the opposite side of the ward with a bandaged thigh.

Rhyddes pulled the tunic over her head, eased it past her aching ribs, tugged it into place and mentally girded herself for the worst.

"In all my years of owning gladiators, woman—no, strike that, in my entire *life,* your bout today was the worst I've ever seen!"

She bowed her head. "Yes, master."

Muted cheers from the amphitheater seeped through the building's thick stone walls. The Saturnalia featured a reversal of roles, when slaves became the masters for a sennight. Upon completion of the day's scheduled games, of which Rhyddes's match was the last at the headquarters of Legio II Augusta, the winning gladiators were invited into the dignitaries' box to watch mock contests between legion officers. Some remote part of her wondered how her gladiator-brethren were enjoying the spectacle from the stadium's best seats.

No such role-reversal existed within the hospital, of course. The patients remained in need of care, and no slaves took the place of the trained staff.

And an observer could harbor no doubt, regarding Rhyddes and Jamil, as to which was the slave and which the owner.

"Thanks be to the gods I'd insisted in advance that these legion matches not be fought to the death. Otherwise, I'd have no gladiatrix to bring back to Londinium." Jamil's scowl deepened as he bent to thrust his face closer to hers. "Explain yourself, woman."

"Lanista Jamil, I—" As she drew a breath, her ribs ached sharply, and she winced. "I am sorry for my poor performance. I have no excuse for it."

"I don't want excuses." He shook the whip's coils in her face. Its tail slipped free to flick against her cheek, softly, like an adder tasting its prey before striking. "I want a bona fide reason why I shouldn't use this on you."

Misery from such treatment at her father's hands roiled up within her, and she sighed heavily. Since that disastrous day when she'd attacked Aquila, she had convinced herself Jamil was different from Rudd. Tears stung her eyes at the realization that he wasn't.

She blinked hard. "My master is free to deal with me as he sees fit."

"You're damned right about that, woman."

The hand not clutching the whip latched on to her wrist and hauled her off the cot. Jamil, with Rhyddes in tow, set a blistering pace toward the ward's door. The physician, who had moved to a feverish patient, looked up, registering concern that one of his charges was being forced to leave. He rose, glaring at Jamil, then seemed to think better of it and returned to his bedside seat with a shake of the head.

Even during Saturnalia, the will of a gladiator's owner was law.

By this time the mock games had ended, and revelers from all social classes streamed from the amphitheater. The crowd reeked of sweat, cheap perfume and even cheaper ale.

Prostitutes, their breasts fairly bursting from the necklines of their gowns and their legs bared to the knee, posed seductively inside the doorways to several huts, enticing men to sample their wares. Even the ugliest of these women didn't seem to want for clients. Though they seemed eager enough today, their chosen occupation made them infamia in the eyes of Roman society, just as being a gladiatrix branded Rhyddes for all time. She couldn't help but shudder at the association.

Between her shameful loss and the reminder of her position in the Romans' world, her dream of one day becoming Aquila's equal had never seemed so remote.

Soldiers, exempt from Saturnalia's chaotic switch, stood posted at close intervals to funnel the crowd toward the civilian settlements, intervening as need be to halt brawls. Several passersby, the ones sober enough to notice Jamil and Rhyddes but too drunk to spot his whip, pointed and made sniggering predictions about what was about to transpire between the pair.

Ignoring the drunkards and giving only the tersest of greetings to the barracks guards, Jamil dragged her into the set of rooms at the end of the block. While fivefold larger than the chamber to which Rhyddes had been assigned, its furnishings displayed the same level of plain yet sturdy craftsmanship.

However, her quarters lacked the iron ring bolted to the wall.

She was mildly surprised he hadn't taken her to one of the oaken posts standing in the practice yard so he could make a public example of her. Her surprise ratcheted up several notches when she realized he was not going to use the manacles, dangling menacingly by their chains from a nearby peg, to secure her to the wall.

"Grasp the ring," he ordered.

The stretch, because of her height, was made more painful by her bruised ribs, but she obeyed. To do anything less would, according to the gladiators' oath, invite death.

Although the chamber was warmer than the outside air, the iron felt burningly cold to her sword-callused palms.

Jamil grabbed the back of her tunic. The linen yielded

with a sickening rip. Hanging on to the ring as if it were a lifeline, Rhyddes shut her eyes, clenched her teeth and tensed her body for the first blow.

LIBERTAS'S OLDER WHIP scars gave Jamil pause. The soldiers who had taken her into custody half a year ago had not inflicted them, he recalled, nor had the slaver.

Had her father punished her for disobedience, dereliction of duty or some other legitimate cause? Or had he merely sought to assuage his wounded pride upon her body?

Although Libertas possessed an unconquerable spirit, and often a mouth to match, never had she wittingly disobeyed a command, whether Jamil's or those of his foremen and guards.

Nor had she disobeyed today.

Her performance, against a heavily muscled local woman who made up in brute strength what she lacked in skill, had been fraught with missed openings, strikes that fell short and ill-timed kicks. If Libertas had fought that badly in her first bout, Jamil would have sold her to Aquila at a heavy loss and considered himself well rid of her.

But this afternoon she had not seemed unwilling to fight, just acutely distracted, often glancing toward the dignitaries' box when she should have been concentrating on the match. During the last of those inattentive moments, her opponent launched a mighty swing. Libertas managed to dodge the blade, but her opponent's gloved fist, weighted by the sword's hilt, smashed into her side, knocking her down and possibly fracturing a few ribs.

That blow had ended the match, and it was nothing short of miraculous that it hadn't ended Libertas's life.

Worse than the twenty thousand sesterces Jamil had for-feited to Libertas's ineptitude was the acute embarrassment he'd suffered among his peers. As he uncoiled the whip, its tail slithered to the floor slates with a hiss. He backed up and cocked his arm.

Her muscles tightened, and she braced her forehead against her left shoulder. Her hands, extended so high above her head that her biceps quivered, gripped the ring with white-knuckled tenacity, but she made no protest.

From his position across the room her scars disappeared, but their implications didn't. If Libertas had served her father with the same faithful, if sometimes flawed determination she had shown Jamil, she should never have received those stripes.

Did she deserve more punishment today?

Libertas turned her head to one side and drew a sharp breath, as a swimmer fights for air. Quickly she hid her face again—but not before Jamil saw the trickling tear. Abruptly he fathomed the source of her arena distraction.

Lashes would effect a solution only until the pain abated, leaving her unfit to fight in the meantime. And while the sting of her wounds would fade, the pain in her heart would return as surely as Lord Ra emerged from the netherworld to illuminate the east each morning.

Jamil could no sooner punish Libertas for being in love than he could punish Lord Ra for plunging the earth into darkness.

Lady Isis help him, he was getting soft.

He slapped the whip's handle onto the nearby desktop with a loud crack and stalked from the room, slamming the heavy oaken door behind him.

JAMIL'S DEPARTURE PUZZLED Rhyddes, but she dared not release the ring. He had probably decided to make a public example of her after all.

How like Rudd, she thought bitterly.

But Jamil had left her unguarded. Mayhap she should slip away. She didn't expect to get far, with more soldiers buzzing about than flies on carrion, but an escape attempt would give Jamil a reason to execute her. And give her the ultimate means of escape from all who would use her for their own gain.

Everyone except Aquila. He had nothing to gain from associating with an infamia gladiatrix-slave, and a lofty reputation to lose. And yet he seemed to crave an association with her…although not so much so that he had followed her here, as she had fully expected of him.

He hadn't made any promises; indeed, he parted from her without so much as a word that day on the road, but since he had been present at all her previous bouts, his absence today felt like a betrayal.

The ache in her heart caused her to clutch the ring in spite of the ache in her arms and ribs. Letting go before Jamil returned would make her a dead woman. She wanted to live at least long enough to confront Aquila on her own terms, not his, or Jamil's or anyone else's.

After what seemed like an aeon, the door opened quietly. The cold air raised gooseflesh on her exposed back, and she flinched. The tread of approaching footsteps sounded tentative and so foreign to what Rhyddes had expected that she questioned whether she'd heard aright.

But the warmth of wool enveloping her shoulders certainly felt real enough, as did the lanolin's musky scent.

"Let go, Libertas, and turn around." Jamil's voice lacked its earlier anger.

Gratefully she complied, shaking the ache from her biceps and flexing her stiff fingers. As she adjusted the cloak, the neckline of her torn tunic slipped forward. She fixed the tunic as best she could—no one would accuse her of looking like a whore if she had any say—and pulled the cloak's edges closed.

Across Jamil's upturned palms lay a fresh tunic.

Cynicism gripped her anew with the thought that he intended to clothe her simply to parade her in front of the gladiators and rip the tunic off before inflicting the rest of her punishment.

"Put it on."

As she grasped the crisp, undyed linen, her eyebrows quirked upward. This garment, though of the same plain weave and cut to which she'd become accustomed as Jamil's slave, was not merely freshly laundered. It had come from the wagon containing new supplies.

She nodded her acceptance of his unspoken apology and set aside the cloak to shed the rent tunic and don the new one, slowly, to avoid aggravating the bruised ribs.

When she had clothed herself, she found him regarding her with stern intensity.

"I have chosen not to leave you with a reminder of your performance, Libertas. I presume it will not be necessary."

"No, Lanista Jamil." She felt thankful beyond measure he had rejected the path her father had so often trodden.

"However, I have posted messages to the legion commanders at Glevum and Camulodunum, reversing my request to exempt you from fights to the death." His eyes narrowed, glittering like twin obsidian flames. "I trust that will help you to better focus upon your upcoming bouts."

She bowed in acknowledgment. "May the gods look favorably upon my master's wisdom."

THOSE MESSAGES OF which Jamil had spoken weren't the only ones he had sent.

On the final day of Saturnalia, Rhyddes looked up from the floor of Isca Silurum's arena, her foot pinning her prone opponent to the ground following a hard-fought match, to find Aquila sitting in the dignitaries' box between the legion commander and a local Silurian Celt who'd been chosen by popular acclaim to preside as king of the Saturnalia festivities. The governor's son outshone his peer and pseudo-peer, bearing his silver-and-crimson ceremonial armor as if he'd been born to the uniform.

Born to conquer, as those soldiers had conquered her the night of her sale, she reminded herself sternly.

Visceral loathing vied with unbridled desire in Ryddes's heart. Upon peering beyond the revulsion for what Aquila represented, however, she had to admit she derived more satisfaction from his smile than from the Saturnalia king's approval of her victory.

That satisfaction lasted only until Aquila tossed a holly bough, replete with ripe berries, to the sand at her feet. Whether he had intended the association or not, she interpreted the offering as a tacit invitation to a more intimate form of Saturnalia sport.

Not wishing to appear ungracious in front of five thousand spectators, she collected the holly, brandished it at the crowd, saluted and marched off the field. She cast it aside the moment the tunnel's shadows closed about her, and stomped, under guard, back to her cell.

She had no time to begin stripping off her armor before Vederi appeared at her cell's door with a summons to report to Jamil's quarters.

She had expected Aquila to be there when she arrived. What she didn't expect was that he would be alone.

He had not changed out of his armor. Her heart redoubled its assault on her head.

Aquila gave Vederi a curiously long appraisal before dismissing him. Gruffly, Rhyddes thought, which also seemed odd. After the guard had closed the chamber's outer door behind him, Aquila bade her wait while he ducked into the inner room. She averted her gaze from the iron ring and manacles to study the pattern of chisel marks in the floor's slates.

He returned a few moments later with one hand hidden behind his back. A silly grin splitting his face, he brought the hand forth to reveal a wreath of plaited fir boughs, a common Saturnalia gift among Romans.

She crossed her arms. "Have I your permission to speak freely, my lord?"

He arched an eyebrow. "During Saturnalia, you don't need my permission."

"It is your custom, my lord. Roman custom." She didn't bother to bleed the disapproval from her tone. "Not mine."

"Very well." He set the wreath on a side table, his gaze lingering upon it with muted sadness mingled with…regret?

Surely not.

"Why are you hunting me, Lord Aquila?"

"Hunting?"

She ticked the events on her fingers. "Bidding upon me in the slave market. Accosting me at every opportunity in Villa Britanniae and at banquets. Watching my matches and practice sessions. Following us on the road. Leaving for a time, long enough for me to believe you had lost interest in me…" She sighed but pressed on. "And now, on the eve of our departure, I find you here again. Why?"

"I thought the answer would have been obvious, Libertas." After dipping his head and pointing another glance at the wreath, he stepped toward the door.

She scurried around him to block his path, feet planted solidly and fists on hips. "No, you don't. Not without answering me. My lord."

In a swift, fluid move worthy of an ex-gladiator, he latched on to her shoulders, bent forward and fastened his lips to hers, hungry and insistent. Her mouth, in league with her traitorous heart, welcomed him ravenously. Her desire surged with each stroke and thrust of his tongue twining with hers.

Gods, but she'd never felt so loved, so free!

Then she remembered who and—more to the point—what he was. She broke contact and cocked her fist but hesitated in confusion. Did she wish to strike him because she didn't like the liberty he had taken with her…or because she did?

He seized the advantage of her pause to entrap her fist in his and guide it back to her side. "I love you, Libertas," he whispered.

"Hah. You love the challenge I represent."

"That's not true—"

With a disbelieving grunt she turned and paced away. Gazing at the door, she yearned to bolt for freedom, but the attempt would be pointless.

Her victories had earned her thrice the sesterces required to buy title to her freedom, even after subtracting the penalty Jamil had imposed following her loss. But in an empire where citizenship stood paramount, where she would always be considered infamia for having fought in the arena—no better than the whores plying their trade among the men outside this fort's gates—that option also seemed pointless.

"You Romans are all alike."

She heard the muted creak of leather and metal as he drew near, but she didn't move. That, too, would be pointless.

Slowly, as if she were a skittish mare, his arms came up to encircle her waist, where the flesh lay bare between her breastplate and battle kilt. His skin felt cool upon hers, but his breath puffed warmly against her neck.

"No, Libertas, we are not all alike."

"Indeed, my lord?" She turned, annoyed, but did not break his embrace. "Your actions betray you. Romans see what they want and take it. Whether by guile or by force, the end result is the same. That kiss was your inbred Roman nature forcing its way to the fore."

He cupped her face. "My nature as a man—not a Roman—exerts itself in your presence." His thumbs lightly stroked her cheeks, tempting her.

Determined to remain stoic, she dismissed his assertion with a derisive snort, and he lowered his hands. "You play the role of the conqueror convincingly enough."

He glanced down at his armor and gave her a lopsided grin. "Point taken." With his index finger, he traced the finely tooled curves of her breastplate. "You play at being a warrior, too. We make a well-matched pair."

"*We?* How can there ever be a 'we' when you remain fated to marry another woman?"

His brow furrowed. "You know about Messiena?"

Not the woman's name; Rhyddes hadn't heeded the gossip that closely. But the fact of her existence she knew well enough.

"You weren't planning to tell me about her? What do you take me for, some whore to spread her legs for the first pair of breeches to saunter by?" She blew a riff with her lips. "Not all infamiae are alike, my lord."

"Indeed."

Recovering his grin, he sidled closer, but she stepped back and flinched when her shoulder bumped the door's frame.

"I don't understand, my lord. You would defile a union sanctified by your gods?"

"My betrothal was forged for political reasons, Libertas. Only unions between Roman priests and priestesses are sanctified and inviolate. Roman law gives all other husbands perfect freedom to take whatever lovers they desire, male or female."

Rhyddes felt herself gape at him. "And you call us the barbarians?"

Shrugging, he said, "It's worked for hundreds of years."

"For the men, no doubt, but what say have your women in this abominable custom?" She branded him with her glare.

He spread his hands in a conciliatory gesture and flashed

that charming smile of his. "Besides, what union could be truly sanctified without even one spark of love?"

'Twas a valid point she had no intention of conceding.

Rhyddes expelled an exasperated sigh. "Why can you not leave me alone, my lord? Do your maidservants not please you anymore?"

"I sold them the day I met you." His tone sounded oddly subdued, his gaze distant.

Still, she couldn't resist quipping, "You used and discarded those virgins that quickly, then?"

"I didn't…use…any of them, Libertas."

She had no idea what to make of that remark. "But surely there must be many women who would be happy to relieve your lust."

His head jerked as if she'd slapped him. "Lust? Is that all you think I feel toward you?"

"Is it not?"

He briefly closed his eyes with a sigh. When he opened them, they revealed a pain and wistfulness that tugged at her heart.

"From the moment I saw you in the slave market, I knew you were special. Lust drove my bidding that day, I admit. But after I watched your first match, I found myself wanting to know every aspect of the woman beneath—" he tapped a neatly trimmed fingernail against her breastplate "—this." Stepping back a pace, he placed his right fist over his heart and bowed to her in a gladiator's salute. "But if it is your wish that I leave you alone, you have my word I shall never pursue you again."

Although he sounded sincere, he looked lost and forlorn.

As a fortress made of sand succumbs to the invading ocean waves, so her resolve toppled. She closed the distance, lifting her hand to touch his cheek, his temple, his short, wiry, laurel-scented black hair.

"No, my lord, that is not my wish," she whispered. "But I need time."

When she would have let her hand fall to her side, he caught it. "Time? Why?"

Even his touch chipped away at her resistance. Displaying a rueful smile, she withdrew her hand before he could inflict more damage.

"In you, I see a man I desire and a man I loathe. Your armor…" She shut her eyes against the brutal memories. It only intensified them.

"Libertas, what is wrong?"

Sighing, she opened her eyes and looked away. "My lord, I…your armor reminds me of the soldiers who—" she shuddered "—the soldiers who took me." She felt his fingers slip beneath her chin to turn it back, and she didn't resist. Gazing wistfully at him and feeling her eyes moisten in response to his concern, she prayed for his understanding. "I must purge myself of the man I loathe before I can claim the man I desire."

"I'm sorry, Libertas. I had no idea they raped you."

She shook her head. "My da sold a virgin, and so by your laws a virgin had to be delivered to the slave market." Her stomach writhed at the painful recollection. "The soldiers' sport took…other forms."

"I am so, so sorry." He clutched his sword's pommel, knuckles whitening. "I would gut them myself if I knew who they were." Aquila's gaze unfocused for a moment before he regarded her earnestly. "I would never hurt you, or force you to do anything against your will. That I swear before all the gods." Again he saluted her. "I also swear to do all within my power to find and punish the soldiers who abused you."

Rhyddes gasped. "You would punish your fellow Romans for me, a Celtic gladiatrix-slave…an infamia nobody?"

"No." Aquila relaxed his fist and held his hand toward her, palm up. "But I would gladly do it for the woman I love."

Her head refused to accept his implied promise. She gazed at the floor, her cheeks heating with the recollection of the fort's whores, and dropped her voice to a whisper. "How can you, a pampered aristocrat, possibly love the likes of me?"

"Because, Libertas, you understand the likes of me."

She looked up. "What do you mean?"

His gaze seemed distant again. "That night, after your first banquet…" He regarded her frankly. "When we spoke in the corridor, after you vented your anger over what I'd done to Iradivus, you gave me two priceless gifts—forgiveness and acceptance. I cannot tell you how much that meant to me." Smiling, he extended his hand. "But I can show you, with your permission."

As she stared at his hand, her heart surged stronger and faster. *Freedom*, its beat urged. *Freedom, freedom, freedom!*

Against such a vibrant refrain her head couldn't possibly compete.

Rhyddes grasped his hand and entered into his embrace. Slowly his head bent toward hers. He slid his hands down her back, leaving a trail of tingles in their wake, as his heady and altogether male scent enveloped her. His lips brushed hers, sparking her desire. She stretched to reach her hands behind his head, glorying in the feel of his hair, which was far softer than it looked, and pulled him closer. Their tongues entwined, deepening the kiss and freeing her soul to soar with her eagle, if only for a short while.

Aquila had vowed to find and punish the soldiers who'd harmed her. With that kiss he could have sealed a hundred vows.

A GUST WRESTLED with the workroom's shutters, and Agricola scooted his chair closer to the brazier, but not so near that a stray spark might ignite his parchment sheaf. An honor though this governorship might be, the bleak Britannia winter was proving to be a formidable drawback.

He missed Rome in all its splendor and squalor: the magnificent view from his mansion on the Esquiline, the exotic goods from all over the empire and the equally exotic peoples who bartered them and the endless days of sunshine and warmth. Especially the warmth.

Turning the missive to better catch the light, Agricola found himself acutely missing his friends in the Senate, and, gods help him, even his enemies. And the intrigue that was every politician's stock-in-trade.

Although he'd been obliged to sell his sumptuous estate before moving to this freezing capital of the empire's hinterlands, he congratulated himself on possessing the foresight to retain a network of agents to keep him apprised of developments in the Eternal City. And this particular report, as innocuous as it might seem at first blush, stank of intrigue like mackerel left a week past market day.

Senator Falco had commissioned the purchase of a thousand gladiators to bring Rome's four schools to full complement prior to the commencement of thirty days of arena games in celebration of Prince Commodus's fifth natal day and elevation to the rank of Caesar. But why would Falco also recruit ninety mercenary soldiers? The number, equivalent to a typical legion century, made no sense. Unless Falco had received a threat that had prompted him to double the size of his estate's guard, he had to be planning something other than Prince Commodus's natal-day festivities.

Agricola locked the dispatch in the chest reserved for his most important documents as he pondered the troubling report he had read earlier that morning. Jamil's gladiatrix was becoming popular. Perhaps dangerously so. Every gladiatorial school across the empire still employed extra guards and fortified defenses, imposed minimal contact between gladiators, and took other precautions mandated in the wake of Spartacus's revolt, two hundred years earlier.

A warrior-woman like Libertas could have a galvanizing effect on the fractious local population.

Agricola grasped his ivory-hilted knife and sharpened a quill. Contemplatively, he rubbed a thumb over his personal seal etched into the hilt, recalling with a brief smile the natal day Loreia had presented it to him.

His immediate problem vanquished the pleasant memory. The gods alone knew how he would convince Jamil to part with his gladiatrix, whose victories no doubt lined his purse handsomely, but perhaps the gods might part with an idea.

He laid aside the knife and inked an order on the parchment: find Falco's associates and convince them prime gladiators resided in Britannia, including one exceptionally talented female…if she survived until their arrival.

After sealing, addressing and setting aside the dispatch, he reached for another parchment leaf to pen the next letter. For once, he just might enjoy the games commemorating his own natal day.

Agricola had not won Britannia's governorship by leaving significant matters in the hands of the Fates.

**13**

Jamil knelt before the pair of wings, woven of peacock tail feathers, fastened to the wall inside the tiny chamber devoted to the goddess Maat in his private wing at Villa Britanniae. Frankincense tendrils spiced the air, and oil lamps bathed the statues and altar in a golden glow.

Blessed Maat, it felt good to return at last. The homecoming had been sweetened by the gladiators' excellent performances, relatively few injuries, the profitable side betting and an uneventful journey.

Not entirely uneventful, he reminded himself, with a silent apology to the goddess. Aquila, for all that he'd been about the governor's business, inspecting troops at far more military installations than the gladiators had toured, had contrived to view most of Libertas's bouts. Why the lad hadn't sought to visit her at either Glevum or Camulodunum, however, Jamil couldn't fathom, and he knew better than to pry.

Whatever the two had said—or done—to each other at Isca Silurum had resulted in improved performances from Libertas. That was the only thing that mattered to Jamil. That, and how many sesterces she won for him.

Sighing, he apologized to Lady Maat again. The prospect of Libertas being killed at Isca Silurum had frightened Jamil badly, and not, he realized with a jolt, because of the investment he'd have lost.

He rose, bowed to the winged image of Maat, snuffed the lamps and incense burners and turned to leave. One of the gate guards met him outside the chamber with a message sealed with a waxen eagle clutching in each talon a sheaf of wheat: Governor Agricola's seal.

Jamil's gut gave an uneasy twist, but he waited until he reached the sanctity of his workroom before breaking the seal. The message proved to be a terse summons, at Jamil's "convenience"—which was a peculiarly Roman way of saying immediately. No topic was disclosed.

The governor had made no secret of his aversion to gladiatorial combat, especially since Aquila's fateful bout with Iradivus; therefore, whatever Agricola wished to discuss with Jamil most likely wouldn't be positive.

He could lose another of his best gladiators.

Summons in hand, he headed for his chambers. "At his convenience" didn't mean arriving in the plain tunic, breeches and cloak he preferred to wear while overseeing the gladiators' training sessions. Lady Maat probably didn't care what her devotees wore, but the governor of Britannia surely would.

He called servants to assist him with shedding his garments and donning fresh ones. For this meeting he selected a dark blue tunic with sleeves and neckline bordered in silver, and his finest toga. While one manservant helped him with the toga's draping, Jamil ordered another to fetch the wide silver collar studded with turquoise stones.

It couldn't hurt to remind the governor of his Roman citizenship, his Egyptian heritage and his legitimately earned wealth. A pity he couldn't emphasize his past association with the Praetorian Guard, but weapons were not permitted inside the praetorium, and for excellent reason.

He thought a moment before reaching to strap on his newest pair of calf-leather sandals. The air carried a chill, but Jamil decided the praetorium's hypocausts would keep the floors sufficiently warm. A lamb's wool cloak, dyed dark blue like the tunic, completed the attire.

He sent a servant ahead to bring his sedan chair and bearers from the stables to the front of the villa, and strode past the practice enclosure toward the main gate.

Libertas was there, wrestling with Gordianus under the foreman's critical eye. Apparently satisfied with their form, the overseer moved on to scrutinize the next pair of wrestlers. For the thousandth time, Jamil marveled that so small a woman could hold her own against a man twice her weight.

Of course, Gordianus wasn't trying to kill her.

Jamil passed the area where the retiarii were practicing throws with their nets. Piscator, stout but possessing great agility, accuracy and strength, made a series of excellent casts at the post. Although it hadn't happened to Libertas yet, Jamil had seen women compete against men, and he couldn't shake the thought that a warrior with Piscator's talents would pose her a lot of difficulty in the arena.

Jamil's gut writhed.

Even full Praetorian battle gear wouldn't have helped him feel less nervous for the governor's audience.

The sedan chair's bearers carried him to the praetorium's gates without incident. When Jamil gave his name to the guards and showed the summons, they admitted him readily, directing his bearers to leave him at the foot of the building's marble steps and wait for their master in the stables.

He stepped down from the chair, mounted the steps and again displayed the summons to the soldiers flanking the massive, oaken door carved with the seal of Britannia. Rather than wheat sheaves, this eagle clutched a spike-haired warrior in each talon. The guards opened the doors, where two more soldiers met Jamil to escort him to the governor.

They led him into a spacious, vaulted chamber lit by glazed windows set higher up the walls than three men could stand upon each other's shoulders. The heated floor provided more than enough warmth for Jamil, as well as for the profusion of potted ferns, figs, dwarf flowering almond trees and other plants lining the walls.

Governor Agricola was reclining on a couch in the midst of this fragrant jungle, contentedly chewing on a fresh fig. Though he had to be approaching threescore years, as his graying hair attested, his body retained a warrior's lean, muscular build. Power radiated from his intense gaze.

A short, tile-topped table stood near the governor's couch, bearing a pitcher of wine and a platter laden with honeyed dates, halved pomegranates and more figs.

Jamil rarely opted to import such expensive treats. He clamped his lips together before his mouth started watering.

"Ah, Citizen Jamilus, welcome." The governor waved a hand, and a servant brought out a chair. Not a couch, Jamil observed wryly as he bowed and sat. "Please refresh yourself while we discuss the games to be staged in honor of my natal day."

Jamil suspected the conversation wouldn't be quite so simple, but he waited for the governor to initiate it.

At Agricola's nod, the servant poured Jamil a goblet of wine and offered him the platter of fruit. The governor might judge him based on every choice he made, no matter how small; so be it. Unhappy the man who let others' opinions dictate his decisions. Jamil chose a fig.

What Agricola had to say nearly made him choke on it:

"I want your Libertas to fight a man disguised as a woman."

Jamil coughed behind his fist while he sought a tactful response. Losing his stomach for the governor's hospitality, he abandoned the fig's remains on the table. "My lord, she has just survived a grueling schedule—"

"Injured?"

"Nothing that won't heal before your natal day, but—"

"I want her to compete against…who is the best retiarius you can think of who's not one of yours?"

"Hamus," Jamil supplied glumly. "Of Moridunum."

"Libertas versus Hamus, yes, though of course he'll have to be called 'Hama' as part of his female disguise."

"The net and trident is all Hamus knows, and Libertas is no secutrix." The protest sounded ineffectual to Jamil's ears.

Agricola gave a dismissive wave. "Gallic arms or British, it'll make no difference to the spectators. One Celt looks much like any other. The people only clamor to see two half-naked women fighting."

The governor leaned forward on his couch, grinning ferally. At the snap of his fingers, a servant entered, his arms wrapped around a bulging sack, which at the governor's command he deposited at Jamil's feet. It settled to the ground with a muted ringing.

"This shall ensure that Hamus—that is, *Hama* wins."

"I'm sorry, my lord, but I must refuse. What you propose is nothing short of murder. Libertas is too valuable to risk in this manner." To say nothing of how suspicious it would look if Jamil did not wager on her.

The governor seemed unperturbed. "Look in the sack, Lanista, and then give me your final decision."

Jamil looked. Unwilling to believe his eyes' report, he delved deep to bring forth a fistful of coins.

Newly minted aureii, every one. The heads of emperors Marcus Aurelius and Lucius Verus gleamed in sharp relief, even to their cheekbones and locks of hair.

He let the coins slip, jingling, through his fingers and into the sack in a mesmerizing golden cascade.

"Fifty thousand sesterces," Agricola said. "Another fifty shall be yours after Libertas loses. That is the customary penalty if she should die, as I recall."

"Yes, but…" Jamil swallowed thickly, unwilling to bare his soul to this man yet sensing his choices disappearing like

water spilled in the desert. "I do not want her to die."
Neither would the governor's son, but he didn't dare broach
that issue.

"You would walk away from a hundred thousand sesterces to protect a slave?" Agricola's tone bore incredulity
and disdain in equal measure.

Jamil squared his shoulders and jutted his chin. "For one
who has become like a daughter to me, yes, my lord. I
would."

The governor sat up and stroked his clean-shaven chin.
"That is most unfortunate, Citizen."

"Why, Governor, do you seem bent on seeing Libertas lose?"

Agricola glared at Jamil. "She is a warrior and a Celt. Her
popularity soars, even among my soldiers. This land is
infested with Celts itching for the chance to strike back at
Rome for that Boudicca debacle, and Libertas's fame poses
a distinct threat. The citizens I have sworn to protect stand
in grave danger."

"What if I retire her from the arena?"

"Not good enough. She would retire as a popular winner
and could still pose a threat should she choose to wield her
fame to foment rebellion."

Jamil could scarcely believe what he was hearing. "I could
take her away from Britannia. Gaul, perhaps—or, better yet,
back to my home in Egypt."

"Egypt, indeed. Where Pugionis, Rodo and Furcifer
would find you in half a heartbeat, and make short work of
you both." Agricola's grin turned triumphant. "Yes, I do
favor that scenario. I thank you for suggesting it."

Jamil's eyes rounded. "How do you know—?"

"About those three warts and their relationship to you?" Agricola chuckled. "I like to keep informed about the citizens I govern. And backwater Britannia is a perfect place to escape one's sordid past. Wouldn't you agree...Kalil Al-Omar?"

Jamil swallowed hard. If Agricola knew that much about his past, it was a safe wager he also knew the whereabouts of Pugionis and his associates. And that was not a risk Jamil—or Kalil Al-Omar—wished to take.

He reached for the sack, though it was cold comfort when faced with the prospect of losing Libertas.

As Jamil stood, so did the governor. "I have your word that you shall keep silent on this matter, Citizen Kalilus?"

The owner of the gladiatrix slated to be sacrificed to appease Roman security concerns bowed stiffly, heartsick. "Of course, Governor Agricola."

Keeping silent would be the easy part.

To act in front of Libertas and Aquila as if nothing were amiss would require assistance of divine proportions.

MESSIENA, DAUGHTER OF one of the most influential senators in Rome, reclined on the couch the servants had angled to put the morning sun at her back. The spring air bore a refreshing coolness that would yield to the day's warmth soon enough, even up here, on the brow of the Esquiline, the hill reserved for the city's wealthiest residents, with the exception of the emperors, whose vast palace complex sprawled across the Palatine, complete with a private tunnel leading to the Circus Maximus imperial box.

Affluence could purchase only so much elevation above this pulsating city, whose million inhabitants rushed madly about their business far below, like ants on spilled honey. Messiena seldom tired of the vista from this balcony, with Rome's marbled splendor spread at her feet, framed by the winding blue ribbon of the Tiber, dotted with boats. Most of the vessels belonged to fishermen, couriers and merchants of jewelry and other lightweight goods, since the river's shallowness prevented ships with larger drafts from sailing any closer than Ostia.

Messiena returned her attention to the project on the easel before her, a rectangular slab of beige slate. She had been laboring over the image for months, first sketching with charcoal, then applying oil-based pigments. Without the live subject, the task left her with more doubts than satisfaction. Not that she would ever forget what Marcus Calpurnius Aquila looked like; the picture of him, beaming at her in triumph as he stood over his vanquished opponent in Londinium's amphitheater—not the second time but the first—would remain indelibly etched in her memory.

She doubted her skills would do her beloved justice.

Love had inspired this project as a means of passing the time until their wedding, the date for which had not yet been set. She suppressed her ire with a sigh and dipped her brush in the rugged bronze color she was using to shade his muscles.

Messiena had given up on arguing with her father about the wedding. Every time she mentioned the subject, Falco invariably put her off with vague assurances that the date would be established "soon." Her favorite retort was that she would die a maiden.

An abrupt chill raised gooseflesh on her arms, and she chafed them.

Messiena had no idea what Falco awaited beyond his insistence that an undisclosed business transaction had to be concluded before she could wed, a transaction Falco claimed would leave them all very well off indeed. So well off that he might consider selling this mansion to move to a finer one.

The memory of her father's boast brought a smile to her lips. The only mansion finer than the one in which they resided belonged to the two men who ruled the world.

Thoughtfully she traced the outline of Marcus's face. Even a palace would seem a dreary cave without her beloved.

The sound of someone clearing his throat made her glance up. Falco's steward, Porticus, was standing a respectful distance away. He advanced at her nod and gave a slight bow.

"I crave your pardon, Lady Messiena, but your esteemed father requires your presence."

She replaced the terra-cotta lids on each open pot of paint and wrapped her brush in a cloth to keep it moist. After unfurling a larger piece of linen, she lovingly draped it over the slate. "What about?"

Porticus shrugged. "If my lady would please follow me?"

Messiena accompanied the steward off the balcony, down the stairs, through the central courtyard and gardens, which were redolent with chamomile and sage, and along the far colonnade to Falco's audience chamber.

As she stepped into the vaulted chamber, its formal grandeur designed to impress the senator's peers rather than inspire familial camaraderie, she envied Marcus and the easy relationship he seemed to enjoy with his mother.

Messiena's mother, Lady Antonia, had died four years ago. The memory of losing her closest confidante gave Messiena a sad twinge.

"Come, Daughter," Falco boomed from his ornately carved reception chair across the chamber. His echo bounced off the frescoed walls, making it seem as if the marble busts of her ancestors were summoning her, too.

She hated the unruly sound of her sandals slapping the floor and lightened her tread. Approaching her father, she donned what she hoped was a demure smile. "Have you decided upon a wedding date at last?" she dared to ask.

"I have, Pulla." Falco gave her the same indulgent grin he'd used whenever he resorted to her childhood nickname, which had been far too seldom these past several months. "What say you to the calends of September?"

Messiena felt a frown pull at the corners of her mouth. "So late?"

Falco spread his hands as if in supplication, though she knew better. Her father wouldn't make supplication to anyone, even the gods, if he thought he could get away with it. "My business transactions are progressing well, and the timing couldn't be more perfect."

"As you will, Papa." She hoped her smile masked her disappointment.

"Another thing, Messiena," Falco said as she turned to go. "Please write to Governor Agricola and extend an invitation for him, Lady Loreia and Aquila to join us in advance of your nuptials. I would write to them myself, but my investments are keeping me quite busy."

She murmured her acquiescence, bid him a pleasant day

and departed, fighting the urge to run. Outside the chamber, she cornered the nearest servant and ordered her to bring parchment, ink, quill and sealing wax to her workroom.

After Messiena settled into the cushioned chair behind her desk, Agna returned with the writing implements, including a lit oil lamp for melting the wax, neatly arranged atop a gilt mahogany tray. Messiena dismissed the woman with thanks and picked up the freshly sharpened quill, eager to begin the task her father had assigned.

Falco had neglected to specify when the Calpurniae ought to arrive. She let slip the grin she had hidden from her father.

Surely there could be no harm in inviting them sooner than the customary fortnight prior to the wedding. Perhaps the action might even convince both fathers to hold the nuptials earlier.

And if her impulse vexed her father, then so be it.

SOMETHING WAS WRONG.

Rhyddes had sensed it from the day after the touring troupe had returned to Londinium. She tried to tell herself she was imagining things, but every time Jamil visited the practice sessions, he seemed to avoid her gaze.

Could he have incurred debt from financing their expedition that the winnings didn't cover? Had something happened to one of the other gladiators in their absence, or to the school? Had he received bad news from afar, mayhap the death of a family member?

Was he planning to sell her?

Her status prevented her from asking Jamil outright, but

neither could she bridle her concern, especially as his gauntness grew more alarming and circles darkened under his eyes.

On the eve of her performance, while staring at the lamplit, whitewashed monotony of her cell's ceiling—because it seemed more productive than staring at the black monotony of her eyelids as sleep evaded her—a different explanation presented itself.

Perhaps her owner's trouble had to do with the man he had avoided the day he'd purchased her from the slaver. Rhyddes had thrust that unpleasant day out of her mind. Now its memory clamored with urgent persistence.

Closing her eyes, she tried to recall the chaotic market scene, but she had no better idea of who had been the focus of Jamil's fear than when the incident had occurred. And if she couldn't ask him about any of those other issues, she certainly couldn't press him on this one.

Sleep, when it finally came, was fitful and fraught with confusing dream fragments that flitted away with the dawn.

The most helpful thing she could do for Jamil—truly, the only course lying within her power—was to fight this day's match to the best of her ability.

Which might prove to be harder than anticipated, she mused as Vederi delivered her armor and stayed to help her don it. Rhyddes had never fought against someone wielding a net and trident before; the only retiarii she knew were men, and she never sparred with them. But she was slated to combat a retiaria named Hama.

Of Hama's origin and experience, Rhyddes knew nothing. "Vederi, what does 'hama' mean?"

"It's the bucket a fisherman uses for his catch," he said while cinching the buckles holding her breastplate in place.

The term was apt for a warrior who fought, like a fisherman, with net and trident.

After he finished and stepped back, she flexed and swung her arms experimentally. Judging it a sound fit, she nodded her approval. Vederi squatted to repeat the process with her leg armor.

She strapped on her sword belt, snatched her helmet from the cot, and followed Vederi from the cell to join the procession to the arena. Before she took her place in the rank, Vederi clasped her forearm.

"May Fortuna smile upon you, Libertas." His grip tightened. "Fight with honor, and she surely will."

Rhyddes bowed her thanks and stepped into line.

The moment she set foot upon the arena sands for her bout, she received a fearsome shock. The Romans' goddess Fortuna not only wasn't smiling, she had to be downright scowling at Rhyddes.

Thickly applied face paint, blond braids, and a light leather harness padded to suggest female breasts might fool spectators from afar. But standing close enough to smell the sweat and count the chest hairs, Rhyddes could not mistake the fact that Hama was male.

As she mentally girded herself to face this opponent, she made the mental shift to the masculine form of the name, Hamus.

Jamil's strange behavior made sudden, terrible sense.

Somebody wanted Rhyddes dead.

As she and Hamus circled warily, she spared a glance for

the dignitaries' box, where Governor Agricola was watching the bout intently beside his son. A flash of insight revealed who had ordered this match.

Rage flooded her soul. Uttering the ancient battle ululation of her people, she charged her opponent's defenses.

MARCUS HAD NEVER seen Libertas close upon her opponent with such reckless abandon. The retiaria didn't stand a chance.

Except the retiaria seemed unperturbed by the attack. She swung her net in a sweeping arc, the weights spraying sand as they grazed the arena floor. Libertas leaped, but not quite high enough. Her left foot became entangled in the net. The retiaria yanked, and Libertas fell heavily on her hip.

Before Hama could bring her trident to bear, Libertas slashed at the net with her sword, freeing her foot. She rolled clear of the net half a second before the retiaria jammed the trident into the ground. Libertas leaped to her feet as Hama freed the trident and cocked her arm for the next blow.

Instead of staying on the defensive and waiting for a better opportunity, Libertas thrust her sword between the trident's tines and twisted. If she had thought to wrench the weapon from her opponent's grasp, however, she miscalculated. Hama backed up and caught Libertas under the chin with the trident's butt to send her sprawling.

But Marcus's favorite gladiatrix wasn't finished yet. As she landed, she snatched the torn net and rolled to her feet, swinging it around to snare the retiaria with her own weapon. Hama jerked the trident free, rending the net in an incredible burst of strength.

Perhaps too incredible, for a woman.

As the combatants' battle took them closer to the dignitaries' box, Marcus scrutinized Hama. The woman's muscles bulged suspiciously like a man's. And Hama didn't appear to be tiring as quickly as Libertas, who was bleeding from several places where the tines had pricked her. Yet she had failed to score a single strike on her opponent's body.

The fickle crowd began chanting for the retiaria to win.

A brutal thrust to the midsection took Libertas down, where she lay pinned on her back, gasping for breath and writhing in obvious pain beneath Hama's trident. Blood welled forth in an ominous pool.

The chant for Hama became Libertas's death sentence.

Agricola, smiling broadly, rose to carry out his people's wishes.

**14**

"FATHER, WAIT!" Marcus laid a hand on Agricola's outstretched arm and pushed it down.

Agricola glared at him murderously.

Without offering an explanation, or apology, Marcus stripped off his toga. Caring little that he was clad only in his belted tunic and loincloth, he planted a hand on the cold marble rail and vaulted onto the arena floor, landing in a crouch. Guards raced toward him from the tunnels, but he stood and brandished his aristocratic rank.

"Remove Hama's belt," Marcus ordered one of the guards.

Hama's triumphant smirk faded to dread. Libertas, eyes shut, seemed to be suffering too much pain to follow the proceedings, if the blood clotting the sand was any indication. Marcus's heart went out to her, though he dared not show it.

A guard unbuckled the belt, and Marcus jerked off the cloth binding Hama's loins.

A collective gasp rose from the spectators.

Marcus commanded the gladiator to step away from Libertas and turn a full circle to show everyone the unmasked deception.

"Good people, as you can see, this was not a fair combat." Marcus pitched his voice to carry to the highest seat, as he had learned from the military commanders while inspecting their troops. "Libertas fought hard and well. She does not deserve death for failing to defeat a man under false pretenses."

He tossed the retiarius his loincloth and ordered him to cover up as spectators' mutterings skittered about the arena. Agricola, hands braced against the box's rail, surveyed the crowd, undoubtedly waiting for one opinion to dominate. Marcus bowed his head, fearing he had failed to make a convincing case and cursing himself for not being a better orator.

It was the Iradivus fight all over again, and the sick pit in his gut prophesied the outcome.

Upon raising his head, he chanced to notice a girl, not more than eight, standing on the front-row bench, clutching a clay doll made in the likeness of Libertas, armed and poised for combat. Tears streaked the girl's cheeks. Over and over, she mouthed, "Libertas." If she was speaking above a whisper, Marcus couldn't hear it.

But the child's actions gave him an idea.

"Libertas!" Marcus repeatedly lifted his arms to encourage the crowd. "Libertas!"

Nor did they disappoint him. Although Marcus heard a few votes for her death, the bulk of public opinion swung the other way, thanks be to all the gods.

And thanks to one young girl who refused to give up on her favorite warrior. Marcus gave the child a big grin, which she returned, unabashedly displaying the prominent gap where two lower front teeth had fallen out.

Marcus returned his gaze to his father, who seemed reluctant to signal Libertas's dismissal. Agricola's chief aide, Darius, leaned over to whisper something in the governor's ear; a reminder about the dangers of bucking public opinion, Marcus fervently hoped. Agricola never listened to his son in such matters.

Whatever Darius said proved effective, and Agricola, looking none too pleased, gave Libertas her life.

As medics ran into the arena and Libertas's opponent collected his weapons and swaggered off, Marcus helped Libertas to her feet. She pressed her fingers over a trio of gashes in her abdomen left by the trident's barbed tines. Her pallor attested to the loss of blood, but her wounds appeared superficial. Marcus stepped back to permit the medics to perform their work. They bound her worst wounds and steadied her so she could wave limply but gratefully to the crowd.

When she turned and beheld Marcus, her bearing stiffened, though whether from a fresh bolt of pain or some other cause, he couldn't be certain. Arm in arm, the medics assisted her out of the arena. At least she was moving under her own power, if only partially—a wager Marcus would not have made five minutes earlier.

He wished he could be helping her, too, but to do anything more would betray how deeply he cared for her.

Occasionally acting like an infamia by fighting in the

arena was one thing; openly consorting with one, especially while trapped in betrothal to an influential senator's daughter, was another matter altogether.

Suppressing a sigh, he followed them into the tunnel, at present more concerned with assuring himself of Libertas's welfare than confronting his father, who had seemed far too eager to command her death.

Hidden from public view, Libertas permitted the medics to lay her onto a litter. One man grasped the poles nearest her head, the other manned the poles at her feet, and at some unspoken signal they hoisted her between them to bear her to the infirmary.

Marcus paced beside them, but she kept her eyes closed.

Since the infirmary occupied a small building adjacent to the arena, they had to pass through a knot of curious on-lookers before reaching the door.

"Hree-dthes!" shouted a young man with red hair and familiar facial features who tried to part the crowd and step closer. Another cry of "Hree-dthes!" was followed by a string of unintelligible, presumably Celtic words.

By the breadth of his shoulders, rippling biceps, homespun tunic and sturdy footgear, Marcus judged him to be a farm laborer. His wild auburn hair, ruddy complexion and the swath of multicolored wool slung jauntily across his chest and shoulder marked him as a northern Celt.

Libertas's eyes snapped open, but when she would have twisted toward the Celt, the medics forced her back onto the litter. As they carried her into the infirmary, she gazed beseechingly at Marcus, mouthing the word, *"Frater."*

*Brother.*

Marcus nodded and waded into the crowd to find the man, which was a child's game compared with convincing him, without benefit of the common tongue, to accompany Marcus.

Glaring, her brother pulled free of Marcus's grasp, fists forming. Marcus backed away, both hands raised, casting about for some way to make him understand.

An idea presented itself: "Libertas…hree-dthes?"

The Celt's expression brightened and he nodded vigorously. Recognition lighting his green eyes, he offered Marcus a deep bow. When Marcus beckoned, Libertas's brother eagerly followed him into the infirmary.

The guards stationed inside didn't give Marcus trouble, since he had frequented this establishment after particularly hard-fought arena bouts. They would have refused entry to the Celt, however, until Marcus explained who he was.

It scarcely proved necessary once Libertas, who had been transferred to a cot against the far wall, acknowledged the man's arrival with a whoop.

Not wishing to intrude, Marcus retreated outside.

IN SPITE OF THE PAIN, Rhyddes favored Owen with a lingering hug. He smelled of the fields, and it sharpened her longing for home. "You don't know how glad I am to see you, dear brother."

"And I you. The clan called me daft, but I held the hope of finding you in Londinium. But I had no idea they'd put you into the arena." Owen scowled fiercely. "Show me the brute who almost killed you, Rhyddes, and I'll show you a corpse."

He stepped aside to allow Hemaeus to stitch her gash, first sluicing it with cheap wine. She winced at the stinging, and gritted her teeth as the needle repeatedly pierced her flesh.

"I hold no malice toward the gladiator," she said when the worst of the pain had subsided. "He was only obeying orders, as was I. For us, disobedience is a death sentence."

Owen shook his head, clearly mystified. "Why would they pit a woman against a man?"

Why, indeed. "I know not." She cast a glance toward the exit Aquila had taken. "Ask the Roman who brought you here. He commanded this day's pairings." Bitterness corroded her tone.

Owen's eyes rounded. "Him? Surely he couldn't have arranged your match. He seemed just as surprised as everyone else. And doggedly determined to save your life. I was cheering for him just as hard as I'd cheered for you."

Rhyddes growled her disbelief. Aquila probably had staged the event as a macabre drama for his father's titillation, a drama that had forced her to death's brink and called into question everything Aquila had promised her.

"I survived," she acknowledged. "Leave it at that."

Hemaeus finished stitching the wound, poured more wine over it, gently blotted the excess, and applied salve and a fresh bandage. But the ache of her wound was nothing compared to the ache of Aquila's betrayal.

"Aye, you survived." Owen sighed and sat heavily on the unoccupied, adjacent cot. "'Tis more than can be said of Da."

*What? Rudd, dead?* "How? When?"

Owen uttered a regret-laden chuckle. "During the harvest. After you left, the brunt of his wrath fell upon me."

"Owen, I'm so sorry—"

He waved dismissively. "One day, when Da thought I wasn't working hard enough, he made as if to whip me, gave a great gasp, turned crimson and blue and collapsed. He was dead afore he hit the ground."

Rhyddes's mouth dropped open. "Oh, Owen." She stretched her hands toward him. He grasped them and squeezed. "How terrible that must have been for you."

"Aye," he admitted quietly. He pulled free of her grasp. "But I'd be a liar if I said I missed him overmuch."

Rhyddes felt the same way, although the prospect of never reconciling with Rudd in this lifetime grieved her more than she could have imagined.

"And you came all this way just to tell me? How did you know where to find me?"

"In truth, I had no idea the gods would grant me this great good fortune. The clan will be glad to hear tidings of you."

"So, if not for me, then why did you journey to Londinium? Have you something special to sell?"

"Aye." He grinned, flexing his right arm. "I want to become a gladiator."

"What? Nay, Owen, don't!"

He wrinkled his brow. "Why? Men volunteer all the time. You don't think I'm good enough, strong enough? Brave enough?"

She sighed, shaking her head. "Never that, dear brother." Memories of her fights crowded her brain, too many to decide which to relate first. Sighing again, she swept a hand across her abdomen. "Look at me, Owen. Take a good, hard look. Remember what you saw today, how easily I could have been killed, and then tell me this is the lifestyle you want for yourself."

"Not for myself," he murmured, "but for the clan. Roman taxes don't stop for the death of any man."

Rhyddes could well understand his resentment. These self-proclaimed saviors of the world were slowly but surely squeezing the lifeblood from it.

"But I thought my sale would have settled Da's tax debt for a half-score of moons to come."

"Not even close. The harvest was barely sold afore they came to collect more coin, spouting some nonsense about building manned coastal signal towers to ward off the Picts." He snorted. "Not even the divine glare from Lugh's silver arm could keep those bastards at bay."

By "those bastards," she presumed he meant the Picts— although the Romans were doing a hefty amount of pillaging, too, just in more subtle ways they labeled legal.

"Don't become a gladiator, Owen. I can supply all the coin the clan will ever need." She paused a moment, tapping her chin. "In fact, I can give you enough out of my winnings to hire a goodly escort to take you home, pay the clan's taxes until the harvest after next and have plenty left over to buy a fine dress and jewelry for each of our brothers' wives."

He gave her shoulder a playful cuff. "What? Not enough to feast the entire village, too? Then mayhap being a gladiator won't be worth my time after all." They shared the laugh. Expression sobering, Owen continued, "And what of you, Rhyddes? Will you be coming home with me?"

"Nay," she whispered, averting her gaze.

"Surely you've earned enough coin to buy back your freedom, have you not?"

"I can afford my slave-price, if that is what you mean." A draft chilled her arms, and she rubbed them. "I'm not sure I know the meaning of freedom anymore."

"Now you're not making one whit of sense." He rapped her head. "Did that gladiator knock your brains loose?"

Grinning briefly, she swatted his hand away. "Owen, you came to this town fully prepared to sell your body to the arena, aye?" He nodded. "Then I propose that you return home, with my gold, while I stay here to continue earning coin for the clan. I shall arrange it with the gladiators' banker and ask my owner to let you visit me whenever you come to Londinium."

Jamil owed her that much for this day's travesty, at least. What Aquila owed her for his involvement, she couldn't begin to contemplate.

Owen's frown blared doubt and concern.

"I have grown accustomed to this life. I shall be all right. This match was an oddity. Usually I fight other women, and usually I win." Fortunately, that seemed to satisfy her brother. He helped her rise and gave her a hug, mindful of the stitched and bandaged gash. "And you, Owen? Have you a place to sleep? I could ask my owner—"

He held up a hand. "No need, Rhyddes. I found lodging as soon as I arrived." His short laugh sounded wry. "In this town, one doesn't need to know the Romans' tongue to speak with coin."

"True enough."

Together they walked toward the infirmary's door.

Noticing her improved condition, Hemaeus called for city guards to escort her back to Villa Britanniae. As the soldiers formed a box around her, she bid her brother farewell until the morrow, when he was to come to the school to collect Rhyddes's winnings.

Watching Owen disappear down the street revived dreadful memories of the day the tax collectors had carried her off. But Rudd's death failed to diminish the resentment she felt toward his decision that day, resentment now fated never to find resolution.

She suspected that facing Aquila and Jamil would prove just as difficult.

MARCUS LEANED AGAINST the infirmary's wall, arms crossed, as he counted passing pedestrians in an attempt to keep the afternoon's events from replaying in his mind ad infinitum. It didn't help.

At last Libertas's brother emerged from the infirmary, waved and smiled to Marcus, and veered away from the amphitheater, probably in search of lodging, since dusk had begun to advance. Marcus would have offered assistance, in spite of the language barrier, but the Celt seemed sure of his bearings.

He felt a pang of regret that he hadn't learned her brother's name.

Absently, he pulled the cloak he'd borrowed from the physician closer about him as he pondered the problem.

Two soldiers left the infirmary, followed by Libertas and two more soldiers. Marcus bade them to halt. The soldiers obliged and stepped aside to offer Libertas and Marcus a modicum of privacy.

Smiling, Marcus approached Libertas. "It gladdens me to see your color much improved. Are you feeling better?"

"I am, no thanks to you," she whispered acerbically. "My lord."

He felt his smile sour. "Surely you cannot believe I had anything to do with that abominable ruse."

She folded her arms. "I know not what to believe. You staged the games in honor of your father, did you not?"

"You were slated to fight a rematch against the woman who defeated you at Isca Silurum." He ran his fingers through his hair, questing for the right words. "I never would have ordered you to fight a man disguised as a woman."

She stared at him for a long moment; searching for what, he hadn't a clue. "You didn't betray me for the sake of entertaining the crowd?"

"Gods! The way I leaped into the arena, revealed the deception and argued to spare your life—you thought that was all an act for the benefit of the audience?"

"They certainly seemed to enjoy the spectacle," she retorted.

"No doubt, most did." He ached to fold her into an embrace but restricted himself to grasping her shoulders, which were tense as twin tree stumps. Kneading them didn't seem to help. "Libertas, what I did—all of it—I did only out of concern for you. I cared nothing for what anybody else thought. All I could see was—" he couldn't suppress a shudder, and he lowered his hands "—your death. I simply acted to prevent it."

She chuckled softly. "I wouldn't have called your actions 'simple.'" Her expression grew earnest. "I apologize for my outburst, my lord, and I thank you for saving my life."

She reached up, pulled his face closer to hers and expressed her gratitude with a kiss that, by necessity, had to be far too brief. But Marcus didn't savor the moist warmth of her lips any less.

In fact, it made him all the more ready to confront his father regarding how the switch of a fake gladiatrix for the true one had been made—and, more importantly, why Agricola had seemed so keen to see Libertas die.

## 15

JAMIL LEFT ORDERS with Villa Britanniae's guards to usher Libertas into his presence as soon as she returned from the infirmary. They fulfilled their directive during his evening meal. He asked a servant to bring in another couch and invited Libertas to join him.

Bruised, scratched, bandaged, bloody, reeking of the arena and looking utterly fatigued and famished, she still refused.

Jamil couldn't blame her.

"Sit, woman, before you collapse on the floor." He motioned toward the empty couch, and she complied, moving warily.

He couldn't blame her for that, either.

Hefting a silver goblet, he swirled its blood-red contents contemplatively before taking a swig. The excellent vintage turned rancid in his mouth.

"Libertas, I owe you an apology."

She looked as if the shock might make her faint, but she pressed a hand to her forehead and shook it off. "Master?"

"I mean it. I never should have allowed you to be paired with Hamus today."

The focus of her gaze sharpened. "Did you have a choice?"

Jamil grimaced. "Not one I could live with." *Literally.*

"I thought as much," she muttered at the goddess Maat, whose winged likeness dominated the floor mosaic.

"You're not angry?" He studied her carefully.

"Would it help me?" Shrugging, she sighed. "I am oath-bound to perform whatever I am commanded to do. Gladiator-slaves do not have the luxury of expressing anger."

"Except in the arena," he reminded her. "If you had fought any less fiercely, Aquila's impassioned pleas could not have saved you."

"Lord Aquila..."

"Today was not his fault, if that's what you're thinking."

"I know, Lanista Jamil. We spoke outside the infirmary." Again she assailed him with that sharply focused gaze. "If I were to ask you who arranged my bout today, would you tell me?"

"No." Although Jamil suspected she had guessed already.

"What about future matches?"

An excellent question. If Agricola wanted her dead before, then today's events probably had done nothing to alleviate his concerns.

"You don't have to fight anymore, Libertas."

"Bought freedom means nothing for one such as me."

"You don't have to buy what I would freely give you."

She uttered a soft gasp. "You would just...let me go?"

"And make sure you had the means to get home safely."
*And disappear where Agricola would never find you,* he silently
urged her. He smiled at her wide-eyed astonishment. "Yes,
I would do this for you."

Her mouth opened and closed convulsively, like a fish. "If
I had but known…no. Master, I am grateful for your
generous offer. But as much as it tempts me, I cannot accept
it. If I leave the arena, my brother will enlist. For his sake,
and my clan's, I cannot permit him to do this. My family
needs coin, but not at the expense of suffering two infamiae
in our midst."

"Your brother?" Jamil gestured toward the platter heaped
with fruit, cheese and fragrant bread. With a thankful smile,
she selected a crisp pear slice and finished it in two bites.
"How do you know this?"

"He saw my bout today. Lord Aquila arranged for him to
visit me in the infirmary. My fa—" She regarded some point
beyond Jamil's shoulder for a few moments, blinked and
gave a slight shake of the head. "My family stands in greater
need of coin than when I was sold. In fact, I would like to
have a document drawn up entitling my brother, Owen map
Rudd, to withdraw most of my funds. I told him to come
here in the morning. With your permission, of course,
Lanista Jamil."

"Of course. I shall inform the guards."

With Jamil's assent, Libertas reached for the cheese and
bread but held the slices for a long moment. "Owen may
wish to know when I shall be competing next."

"The next games aren't until July, to celebrate the
governor's return from a journey he's planning to take to

northern Britannia." Jamil leaned forward to underscore the earnestness of his next statement. "But you have more than earned the right not to participate in those games, and I shall do everything in my power to keep you out. Unless your family would need those winnings, too?"

"The purse I will give Owen tomorrow should suffice for quite some time." She offered him a rueful grin. "Unless you are faced with another choice you cannot live with?"

Jamil had been pondering that issue ever since his audience with the governor. Gazing at this lovely, fearless woman's face, he reached a decision.

"No, Libertas. On that day, they will have to trample my corpse before they could bring any harm to you."

The problem with such a pronouncement, he realized with chagrin as the words escaped his mouth, was the gods too often took special delight in bringing it to pass.

BY THE TIME MARCUS reached the praetorium, his father had adjourned to the bathhouse. That seemed like a fine idea, since Marcus, having left his toga at the arena, wasn't adequately attired to beard the proverbial lion.

He wondered whether any amount of scrubbing could remove the stench left by the day's events.

He found Agricola soaking in the calederium. His father nodded a terse welcome. Marcus shed cloak, sandals and tunic, and eased himself into the steaming water.

"I want to thank you for a most memorable natal day, Marcus." Sarcasm dripped from his tone. "That was quite a spectacle you staged."

"It wouldn't have been half as dramatic without your help, Father." No lie, that.

"Me?" Pine-scented water splashed, some of it hitting Marcus, as Agricola moved his hand to his chest. "Why, I was merely another spectator."

"The only spectator wielding the power of life and death over the combatants."

"Ah, that. Now I understand why my peers become obsessed with the games. The outcome can be rather—" Agricola's grin turned wolfish "—exhilarating."

"Would it have been exhilarating to watch Libertas's execution?"

"You can't possibly imagine," his father replied dryly.

"And a gladiatrix-slave can't possibly mean so much to you that you should care whether she lives or dies."

Agricola raised an admonishing finger. "That is where you err, Son. This woman is popular, she is a warrior and she's a Celt. People of her ilk have been inciting mayhem from time immemorial."

"Libertas is not dangerous in that sense."

"Son, your unflagging admiration for this woman blinds you to the truth about her." Agricola gave him a pointed look. "Has your admiration transferred to the bedchamber?"

"No, sir." *Not yet.*

"Excellent. I wouldn't want you to give my future daughter-in-law cause for complaint."

"Nor I," Marcus dutifully replied.

This time his father's smile seemed sincere. "Since you did such a commendable job with the legions, you shall accompany me to Hadrian's Wall to inspect the reinforcement efforts."

That came as no surprise. "When do we leave?" Marcus tried not to sound glum.

"TOMORROW, MY LORD?" Rhyddes bit her lip. "And how long do you expect to be gone? If I may be so bold to ask."

Earlier that morning, she had received permission to be excused from drills to complete the financial arrangements for Owen. After bidding him a reluctant farewell, she had returned to the practice yard with a heavy spirit that lightened only with Aquila's arrival, nigh unto sundown. He had sparred until the gladiators were called in for their evening meal, and he lingered to speak with Rhyddes.

Now she wished he hadn't come.

Aquila spared a glance for Vederi, who followed them at a discreet distance as they strolled the colonnade outside the practice yard's iron fence. "I love your boldness," he whispered. "We return in late June."

He may as well have said *never.*

*And I might never get another chance to show him what he means to me.*

She halted and gazed at his face, desire mounting with each heartbeat. Desire that conquered her revulsion for the wrongs his people had done to hers. Desire that revived and quelled memories of the harm those brutal soldiers had inflicted upon her. Desire that made her forget he was betrothed.

Desire she dared not act upon in a public setting.

"My lord, is your…invitation…still valid?"

His eyebrows knit in obvious puzzlement. "My—" At once his expression cleared. "Ah. Yes." The barest of smiles bent his lips. "Yes, it is, Libertas." His eyes smoldered with passion and a hint of…rebellion?

Her mind conjured the moment, many moons ago, when Jamil had presented Aquila's bedchamber invitation to her.

*Villa Britanniae has chambers where you two would be very comfortable….*

Comfortable and private, no doubt. No one need ever know, save Jamil and mayhap a guard or two. Gaining access to those chambers, however, would require her owner's permission.

Stepping aside, Rhyddes beckoned to the guard. "Vederi, we must speak to Lanista Jamil."

Skepticism wrinkled Vederi's brow. "Lord Aquila?"

Gazing intently at Rhyddes, Aquila nodded. "Conduct us to him at once, please."

"He won't like being interrupted," Vederi warned Rhyddes.

"I know. The interruption will be brief," she promised.

As Vederi wheeled about to lead them toward Jamil's private wing, Rhyddes and Aquila exchanged a secret smile.

Upon their arrival inside Jamil's workroom, Rhyddes offered her owner a smart salute. "Lanista Jamil, I—" A dozen fears assailed her tongue. Yet if she allowed those vile soldiers to conquer her all over again, she might never find a mote of pleasure with Aquila…or any other man. She glanced at him to draw upon his strength. He gave her a subtle but no less encouraging nod. With her right fist still pressed against her heart, she forged on, "My apologies for disturbing you, master, but we—that is, Lord Aquila and I—"

Jamil, who had been gazing at them with dark, measuring eyes, lifted a hand. Gratefully, Rhyddes fell silent.

"No apologies necessary, Libertas. I can guess why you have come." His grin confirmed it.

Jamil rose from behind his desk and crossed to a stack of shelves bearing loose parchment leaves, elaborately-decorated incense pots and Egyptian figurines. From atop the highest shelf, he brought down a wooden chest inlaid with attractive blue-green stones and studded with copper bosses. He set it upon the desk, produced a tiny key from the pouch at his belt and opened the chest. She could not see inside, but the chest had to contain coins, to judge by the metallic scraping as Jamil pawed through them.

The shining disc he produced was no coin.

Rhyddes gasped in painful recognition.

'Twas the brass tag the slaver had made her wear, which had identified her as a virgin. After stepping from behind the desk, Jamil picked up Rhyddes's hand, pressed the cold tag into her palm, and closed her fingers around it. He grasped Aquila's closest hand and placed it over hers.

"Master? Why do you give this to me?" she whispered. "I must continue earning gold for my family."

"And so you shall. I keep these tags as additional proof, along with the bills of sale, of my slaves'…physical attributes." Jamil smiled. "I expect your tag soon shall not serve its purpose anymore, Libertas. You are free to do with it whatever you wish." His smile deepened, and he winked. "Enjoy your evening. Both of you. Vederi, show them to the Alexandria Room."

The guard led them deeper into the maze of Jamil's wing, echoing to Aquila and Rhyddes the wish of a pleasant evening when they arrived at the ornately carved door to the chambers in question.

Vederi followed them inside only long enough to light the oil lamps and show them the chests where spare clothing, towels and other amenities were stored. After she and Aquila declined Vederi's offer of food and drink, he repeated his benediction and departed, firmly closing the door behind him.

Rhyddes had glimpsed what she assumed were people and gods from Jamil's homeland during previous forays into his private domain. But nowhere did the Egyptian influence blossom as profusely as inside this chamber. Painted murals smothered the walls, depicting the angular images of Egyptian people at work and play, weaving, scribing, planting, building, fashioning jewelry and sculptures of great beauty. Gray-veined marble spanned the floor. The chests and other furnishings were crafted of a wood so richly dark, it seemed black.

An enormous bed, made of the same brownish black wood and partially obscured by a gauze curtain, dominated the inner chamber. Here, the murals displayed men and women engaging in intimate poses.

Her memories intensified. She drew a breath, willing them to stop tormenting her, willing herself to stop imagining the soldiers' leers on the faces of the painted Egyptian men. She became acutely aware of Aquila's quickening breaths behind her, and she fought to keep her own under control. With his male essence filling her nostrils, reminding her of the soldiers' lust, 'twas by no means an easy battle.

He gently grasped her arm and turned her to face him. High color suffused his cheeks. His hair, uncombed following his sparring session, framed his finely chiseled face in an unruly shock. His sparring tunic molded to his muscular chest. In that garb she could almost forget who Aquila was and what he represented. Never had he appeared more ruggedly handsome, or more acutely desirable.

Instinctively she knew that to purge the evil men and their lurid acts from her mind, she had to conquer her fear of the conqueror standing before her.

She reached for Aquila's cheek, and he nestled into her touch.

A fluttery feeling invaded her stomach, akin to what she often felt in the predawn hours before combat. But she also felt an exquisite ache, lower and sharper, that had nothing to do with nervousness.

Her lips felt dry. Slowly she licked them as his head descended toward hers.

Their mouths met in a torrent of mutual passion. As his tongue probed, his hands cupped her buttocks to pull her closer. She felt his quickening response, and her aching intensified. The slave-tag slipped from her fingers to clatter onto the floor.

Almost without thinking, she reached down to stroke him in the manner the soldiers had commanded of her. His soft grunt brought her back to the moment, and she stopped.

"I like that," he said huskily. Supporting her with his left arm, he brought the other hand up to caress her breasts, tracing light spirals from the nipples outward. "Don't stop."

It sounded like a command. But her body was too firmly

imprisoned within these breathtaking new pleasures to care. She began tracing patterns of her own devising upon him.

"Why," he whispered between feathering kisses down her neck, as his fingers slipped beneath her tunic and spiraled closer to their final target, "have you changed your mind?"

His tantalizing touch sent shivers of delight through her soul. "My reasons aren't important."

The spiraling ceased. He gripped her shoulders, his gaze insistent. "They are to me, Libertas."

She drew a shuddering breath and pulled away from him. "Why? I am a slave, not your peer. An infamia gladiatrix-slave, a classless resident of the Roman Empire."

He stepped closer, beaming that infuriatingly charming smile of his. "If your reasons matter to you, then they matter to me, and I would like to know what they are." Reaching out, he tucked a stray wisp of hair behind her ear.

She marveled at how simple a gesture could chip away at her resolve.

"As you wish." After sweeping aside the curtain, she sat on the luxuriously cushioned bed. The linens smelled of lavender. "Yesterday's bout brutally reminded me that my life can end at any time, at the whim of my owner—or whomever he answers to." She gave him a shrewd look, but he shrugged blandly. "While everyone else was clamoring for my blood, you proved you aren't like them. Yesterday, I failed to express my thanks for that."

Patting the blanket, she invited him to join her on the bed and wriggled out of her tunic.

He hesitated, staring toward the tunic where it puddled on the floor at her feet. "Lord Aquila?"

"My father does not approve of my sexual liaisons."

She chortled. "With anyone? Or just me?"

"He doesn't want me to upset my future bride."

Typical politician's son; he'd evaded the question. But she let it pass, asking instead, "Do you love her?"

"I love you, Libertas." He sank to his knees. His hands, powerful and sure, kneaded her thighs as they inched toward the cloth binding her loins. "And only you."

With his thumb he pressed the source of her ache, deepening it. She arched back, gasping, and he rose from his knees to wrap his other arm around her. His mouth covered hers, his tongue slowly thrusting to the rhythm of his thumb.

The soldiers had touched her thus, but clumsily, their movements governed by drink-soaked lust. Aquila's hands didn't err as he untied her breast band and loincloth, teasing her with light, arousing strokes. Her body felt afire, and she parted her lips, panting softly.

He gathered her in his arms, shifted her farther onto the bed, shed his tunic and loincloth and stretched beside her, cradling her head in his hands.

"Are you sure this is what you want, Libertas?"

"What *I* want?" She searched his face, seeing for the first time not a Roman but merely a man she desired to the core of her soul. Yet her head demanded one final assurance. "Does it matter so much what I want? After all, I am only—"

He stopped her with a long, wet kiss. "You are a strong, talented, gorgeous, incredible woman. And I am only a man." He shifted down to nibble one nipple, then the other. When she tipped her head back, he kissed her neck, sending shivers of delight racing through her body.

With one arm wrapped around his neck, she reached the other hand down to stroke him, smiling as he groaned his pleasure. "I do want you, more than anything," she murmured. "Even more than my freedom."

He gazed at her earnestly. "I don't mean to hurt you, Libertas. But I might…and I'm not talking about only this." Gently he traced the folds of the one item he had not removed: the linen binding the trident wounds. She had forgotten them in her escalating desire. "There are other ways to give pleasure—"

It was her turn to interrupt him with a kiss, hard. "I live with pain every day. Pain is nothing to me," she insisted, tugging him closer.

He shifted between her legs, and his lips sunk upon hers as he descended into her depths. Pain splintered into a thousand exquisite needles that melted in the furnace of passion.

It was the most liberating choice she'd ever made.

He seemed content to let her set the rhythm of their dance. Her body seemed to act of its own volition, undulating faster and harder by no command of hers save primal need…the need to feel him free her very soul.

When he gripped her buttocks to thrust even deeper, his gasps mingling with hers behind their united lips, she rejoiced to know she had freed his soul, as well.

After their lovemaking, as she pillowed her head against his chest, feeling the steady thrum of his heartbeat, only one thought troubled her.

She couldn't dismiss the notion that after this night, she would never see him again.

**16**

THE ACT OF FULFILLING a promise made enforced separation from Libertas a mote easier for Marcus to bear. Before leaving Londinium, he'd inquired about the slaver who had sold her to Jamil. The Fates kindly allowed the man to be present in the slave market; no small boon, since that occupation took him to all corners of Britannia, and probably farther afield.

Although the slaver didn't know the names of the soldiers from whom he had acquired Libertas, the bill of sale bore their unit's designation, Ala Petriana, a cavalry troop stationed at Coriosopitum, near Hadrian's Wall.

And since Agricola had planned to inspect troops and military facilities en route, in addition to overseeing the completion of the Hadrian's Wall refit, Coriosopitum ranked highly on the list of fortifications to visit.

In the ensuing weeks of travel, punctuated by visits to the seemingly endless parade of fortresses, forts and fortlets along the road that connected Londinium with northeastern Britannia, Marcus did not forget these divine boons.

Gratitude for them, and for the Roman military habit of chronicling each soldier's orders in turgid detail, prompted Marcus to donate fifty aureii in Coriosopitum's temple honoring his namesake, the war god Mars. As the priest took the gold, Marcus silently vowed to double the amount if Mars would deign to grant him success.

But, since the god refused to give Marcus a private conversation with the fort's commander, he had no choice but to broach the issue while he and Agricola were seated in the legate's workroom, reviewing the soldiers' performance following the next morning's inspection.

When Agricola asked whether Marcus had anything to add, he sucked in a swift breath, nodded and hoped for the best.

The legate, a combat-grizzled veteran who appeared to have survived a decade past the compulsory twenty years, inclined his head politely toward Marcus in an attitude of feigned interest.

Any other time, that wouldn't have aggravated Marcus. But, any other time, he wouldn't have been defending a lover.

"Legate Domitian," Marcus began, "a serious complaint has been lodged against a turma attached to Ala Petriana."

That commanded his attention, as well as Agricola's. He raised a hand to forestall the legate's response. "Since when have people started bringing complaints to you, Son?" Agricola's tone conveyed confusion and sarcasm in equal measures.

"The source of the complaint isn't important." Not to any other man in the room, anyway. "Its nature is."

"What is this complaint?" Domitian asked gruffly.

Marcus pumped disgust into his glare. "Those soldiers brutally abused a woman in their custody."

Agricola's face flushed livid. "That accursed gladiatrix put you up to this, Marcus, didn't she?" He turned toward Domitian, hands spread in a gesture of conciliation. "My apologies, Legate Domitian. My son must be mistaken—"

The memory of Marcus's failure to save Iradivus's life smote him; failing Libertas was not an option.

"I am not mistaken, Father, and she never encouraged me to take action. I raise this issue of my own choosing." To Domitian, Marcus said, "I cannot offer proof. But whatever these men did to her, she was so shaken she refused to describe it."

Domitian lowered his eyebrows. "'Abuse' is a vague accusation. Do you have any details?"

"She was sold as a virgin slave."

"These soldiers broke the law?" Agricola asked sharply. To Romans, misrepresenting merchandise in a sale was deemed just as reprehensible as the act of damaging it.

"No, sir," Marcus admitted, "but they bent it out of recognition."

The legate, who had been stroking his finger along a gnarled scar marring his right cheek, nodded. "I know who you are referring to." He glanced apologetically at Agricola. "I've received other complaints of this nature."

"And you have done nothing?" the governor bellowed.

Marcus's eyebrows shot up.

"I have tried, Governor. But floggings, latrine duty and reduced pay don't seem to cool these men's lusts."

"Castration and dishonorable discharge should," Agricola stated.

Marcus couldn't have agreed more. But, "Why the change, Father? Because Libertas's abuse isn't an isolated incident?"

"Precisely," said Agricola. "Just because we Romans can take what we want doesn't excuse us from breaking the law—or mangling it, in this case. I am striving to fend off the Picts. I don't need their Celtic neighbors wreaking havoc, as well." Agricola regarded a grim Domitian. "Castration and dishonorable discharge, Legate. If these men want to lodge a complaint, I will be happy to listen to them."

The legate's lips thinned. "It shall be done as you command, my lord." He used an iron stylus to make notations in the wax of the tablet lying on the table before him.

"After the sentence is carried out," Marcus added, "I would like a report sent to Gladiatrix Libertas via Lanista Jamilus of Villa Britanniae, in Londinium." He would have preferred penning the letter personally, but he knew she couldn't read, and what he yearned to say he couldn't risk sharing with anyone else.

"Yes, Lord Aquila." Domitian made more notes on the tablet.

Marcus expressed his thanks to the legate.

Agricola shoved his chair back with a noisy scrape and rose, causing Marcus and Domitian to do the same. "Legate, we shall join you for dinner this evening. Bring your report of the punishment." The look Agricola directed at Marcus was more severe. "Son, come with me."

His father stalked out the door. When a soldier stationed

in the corridor shut it behind them, he whirled on Marcus, Jupiter's thunderbolts collecting in his gaze.

"That is the second time you have countermanded me in public. If you ever do that again, Son, I will have your head on a plate."

The soldiers standing on either side of the legate's door snapped to attention, their gazes fixed to the opposite wall.

"Indeed, Father?" Marcus's anger boiled up past caring what he said or who heard it. "I know you wouldn't deign to sully your hands with the task. Would you order me to do it for you? Again?"

"*Again?* What in Tartarus are you talking about?"

"Iradivus."

Comprehension banished Agricola's confusion. "Ah, yes. Iradivus." His expression hardened. "He could have killed you."

Marcus released exasperation on a noisy sigh. "If you had bothered to attend the games more often than just when you wanted to execute someone—" thinking of Libertas, he aimed an accusatory glare at his father, who refused to react "—you would have known I was never in any real danger."

Closing his eyes, Agricola exhaled slowly. "That wasn't how it looked from my seat."

"That was the point, Father! I wanted to present a good, entertaining match for the crowd." He studied the floor slates. "And for you."

"There is nothing entertaining about believing your only child is about to be killed." The whisper's vast sadness prompted Marcus to look up. Unshed tears moistened his father's eyes.

Marcus bowed his head, shame branding his cheeks. "I am sorry, Father. If I'd but known, I would have selected an easier opponent." One who wouldn't have caused so great a loss to Jamil. He sighed again. "I apologize for my disrespectful conduct in front of the legate, and I thank you for your forbearance." Looking up, Marcus ventured a tentative grin. "I am sure Libertas will want to thank you, too."

"Libertas!" Agricola's compassion evaporated, and he strode toward the headquarters building's main entrance. "That damned gladiatrix can thank me by dying in the arena." He paused and tossed a triumphant grin back at Marcus. "Or by getting herself carted off to Rome."

Marcus wasn't sure which disturbed him more profoundly: the strangeness of the remark, or the certainty with which his father had uttered it.

Shouted orders, even louder acknowledgment and the overhead thud of running feet dragged Pugionis from a doze. His companions, the lanky Furcifer and stout Rodo, were beginning to stir, as well.

Furcifer swiped a hand across his bleary eyes and glanced about. "We there yet?"

Rodo glanced up at the open hatch. "That'd be my guess. Ship's not moving forward."

Quite the contrary, in fact. The cargo vessel, hauling everything from Mediterranean olives and spices to fine Samian glassware packed in sawdust-filled crates, was sidling sideways in odd little lurches as if against her will.

The grating of the gangplank being deployed encouraged the three companions to grab their belongings and emerge, blinking into the pale northern sunlight, from the cabin that scarcely had been large enough to accommodate one man, to say nothing of three. Even the senator's gold couldn't compete with such lucrative cargo as pleasantly fragrant but outrageously expensive Lebanese cedar.

Said logs, some as thick as a man was tall, were being winched out of the aft hatch, rolled ponderously across the deck and maneuvered down the gangplank to the workers waiting dockside to transfer them onto specially designed wagons. Every crewman not occupied with securing the rigging or other shipboard tasks was helping with the leviathan lumber.

Rodo, Furcifer and Pugionis stayed well clear. They edged over to a portside section of rail to wait for their turn to disembark.

In the previous eight months, the trio had scoured the Roman world, from Asia Minor to Alexandria, Italia to Iberia, Galatia to Gaul and countless points in between, purchasing the best gladiators they could find and hiring armed escort for sending the acquisitions back to Rome. They had almost fulfilled the senator's commission, in fact, when Pugionis received an invitation from the governor of this remote province, indicating the presence of many prime candidates.

But the boast failed to intrigue Pugionis as much as the governor's second statement: that someone of "supreme interest" to the trio resided within Londinium.

While Furcifer and Rodo exchanged bawdy gestures with women onshore, whose immodest attire and mannerisms marked them as sailors' whores, Pugionis watched the proceedings occurring upriver from their mooring place, the Londinium slave market.

Not that Pugionis expected this person of "supreme interest" to make such a costly mistake as to appear, unguarded, in public. But time dulled even the wariest man's caution.

The first order of business would be to seek lodging in a district near the amphitheater and gladiatorial school. After establishing their base of operations, the trio could scout the alleys, derelict structures and other likely places to lay an ambush, and monitor their target's movements.

Crew gossip had focused upon an apparent falling-out between the governor and the lanista Pugionis and his associates sought; perhaps someone on the governor's staff, or even the governor himself, might provide assistance in this operation.

With any luck, the trio wouldn't have to expend the senator's gold to acquire the last of the gladiators required to fulfill their commission. It would leave more funds for getting them back to Rome, and yield a higher profit margin.

Pugionis licked his lips and indulged in a private grin.

IN THE ABSENCE OF the man she loved, life became a dreary routine for Rhyddes. Rise at dawn, run, eat, drill, eat, drill again, followed by another run before supper, bathing, then falling into a dreamless slumber just to begin the cycle all over again. Rain, drought, heat, cold, snow, frost, wind, illness and injury provided only minor variances. It was, she realized mirthlessly, the same routine that had been forced upon her from the day Jamil had bought her in the slave market.

Only now her days were devoid of the expectation of

seeing Aquila drilling and supping with the other gladiators, or watching them to select combatants for the next round of games. She had all but forgotten the pleasure she had derived in working harder because she could feel his gaze trained upon her.

And, oh gods, the exquisite pleasure of his lips, his hands, his...

"Gladiatrix Libertas."

From behind her, a hand clasped her shoulder.

Rhyddes dropped the wooden spoon she'd been holding. It fell into her bowl of barley porridge, spattering her tunic. Embarrassed, she brushed at the lumpy splotches and looked up. The other gladiators seemed too busy wolfing down their own meals to pay her any heed.

She turned around to see who had addressed her.

Vederi, who often escorted her back to her cell of an evening, had arrived early. His comrades-at-arms were positioned at intervals along the mess hall's walls, staring impassively, if a bit impatiently, at their charges. The guards never ate until after the gladiators were locked into their cells for the night.

Was that why Vederi had approached her now? She arched an eyebrow at him.

"Lanista Jamil wishes to see you," was all Vederi would divulge.

Rhyddes downed her ale, leaving the porridge, and rose to follow him. Without Aquila to lend joy to her days, food had lost its appeal, but ale blunted her heartache for a wee time.

Vederi quick-marched her to the armory, where Jamil and

the familia's clerk seemed too engrossed in conducting an inventory of the weapons and armor to notice their arrival. Rhyddes and Vederi stood a respectful distance away from the proceedings, which followed a simple pattern. Jamil would press his opposite thumb into the small box he was holding, smudge a streak of black powder, mayhap coal, onto an object, identify it aloud, and the clerk would jot something onto the wax tablet he balanced in the crook of his left arm. Usually it was a single mark, but sometimes he made a long string of mysterious scratches.

After the pair had finished with the helmets and prepared to start on the shields, Vederi loudly cleared his throat.

Jamil and the clerk turned toward them. Jamil set his box on the floor beneath the last item he had marked, dismissed the clerk to the mess hall, ordered Vederi to stay by the doorway and beckoned Rhyddes into the armory, ushering her to the corner farthest from the guard.

Eyebrows lowered, he placed his fists on his hips, making her wonder what she had done to earn his displeasure. Although she missed Aquila terribly, the events at Isca Silurum had taught her not to let lovesickness interfere with her training.

"I knew your father had hurt you," he said in a harsh whisper, "but you never told me the tax collectors had, too."

She quipped, "You never asked, master." His scowl deepened, and her gut gave an uneasy twist. "I'm sorry, I meant no disrespect. It's just not a matter I feel comfortable revealing to anyone."

The corners of his mouth quirked upward. "But you did reveal it to someone. Lord Aquila."

"Partially." She studied the gray floor slates. The mention of his name sent a wave of longing coursing through her soul. "But I couldn't bear to give him the details. And I pray you won't press me for them." She blinked to stem the tears.

Warm fingers slipped under her chin. "The only detail I wish to know is whether those soldiers…harmed your ability to enjoy another man's company."

It took Rhyddes a moment to puzzle out what he meant. His wink helped. She offered a tentative smile. "No, Lanista Jamil. They did not." Then something else occurred which puzzled her even more. "But why would you care about that?"

His dark eyes flashed a wounded look. "I care about all my gladiators." He gave a bitter chuckle. "Most of them, anyway." Jamil pressed her hand between his. "And I care about you above all. In case you haven't noticed." After giving her hand a squeeze, he released it.

"Master, I thank you for your concern," she murmured. "But how did you find out?"

"I received an interesting dispatch today. Or, rather, you received it, since it was addressed to you."

"A dispatch—as in, a military report?" She couldn't fathom who would have sent such a thing to her, a lowly infamia.

"Just so. From the commander at Fort Coriosopitum." Her furrowed eyebrows must have prompted him to add, "Headquarters of the troop guarding the section of Hadrian's Wall south of your family's farm. The legate wrote to report that your malefactors have been punished and shall not harm anyone like that again."

She snorted her disbelief. "Men of that ilk aren't so easily parted from their lust."

"These men were." Jamil grimaced. "Permanently."

"They were executed?"

"Worse." His grimace deepened.

"What could possibly be worse than—oh." Rhyddes searched her feelings for a mote of compassion but found only relief. "Lord Aquila must have arranged it." She stared at her distorted reflection in one of the shields hanging on the wall. Relief yielded to wonderment that anyone, never mind the son of her homeland's Roman governor, would go to such lengths to fulfill a promise to her.

Her pining for Aquila sharpened into a visceral ache.

She turned to address her owner, who was regarding her with amused affection. "Lanista Jamil, I would like to send two messages, both expressions of thanks. One to the fort's commander, and the other to Lord Aquila. I have more than enough of my winnings left to hire a scribe and a courier." She felt her cheeks heat. "With your permission, of course."

Jamil chuckled. "Of course, Libertas. Consider it done."

Rhyddes's only regret was that she couldn't deliver the messages—especially a certain one—in person.

AT DAWN OF THE DAY after getting settled into their chamber in the tenement building near the amphitheater—if the tiny, minimally furnished, vermin-ridden room could bear such a grandiose title—Pugionis sent Furcifer and Rodo to scout the area. Since there existed a chance of encountering their target, they went out cloaked and hooded, in spite of the promise of another warm mid-June day.

Pugionis extracted his toga from where it lay buried in his duffel and gave it a shake, wishing he had unearthed it the night before. Appearing before the governor in such a rumpled state wouldn't help his cause, but, then, he had traveling to use as an excuse. He shrugged into the unwieldy garment as best he could, strapped on his sandals and donned his cloak. A quick check of his purse, containing the governor's letter and a few gold, silver and brass coins—the vast balance of their traveling funds they'd left on deposit at a nearby bank the day before—and he was on his way.

The street vendors had already set up shop. The competing aromas of beef, mutton and pork made his stomach gurgle. A brass sestertius paid for a generous helping of roasted beef on a skewer, interspersed with onion wedges. By the time Pugionis reached the public stables, the meal was a pleasant memory and the skewer had long since been cast away, carried off by a scruffy mongrel.

At the stables, eight silver denarii bought him the hire of a sedan chair and two bearers for the day. Before stepping into the chair, Pugionis shed his uncomfortably warm cloak. The sedan chair would provide cover in case they happened across Kalil en route to the praetorium, but Pugionis hoped Rodo and Furcifer, on foot, would not become similarly tempted.

Preserving the element of surprise was vital to the success of this operation.

The governor's letter should have gained Pugionis entrance into the praetorium, but not, according to the perimeter sentries, while Agricola was occupied on business elsewhere in Britannia.

As Pugionis stood arguing about the necessity to see the governor's chief of staff, a mounted troop emerged from behind the building complex and trotted toward the gate. The guards motioned Pugionis and the sedan chair aside. The bearers complied, but Pugionis did not.

The troop's leader, a dour veteran whose hair, what Pugionis could see of it beneath the helmet, shone as silver as the expensive armor he wore, called a halt. He gave Pugionis a long appraisal, probably evaluating his wealth by the presence of the sedan chair, before inquiring about the nature of the difficulty.

"I have been invited by Governor Agricola. I know he is not due back for another week, but my business cannot wait that long. I need to see his chief of staff."

The troop leader's eyebrows disappeared under his helmet. "You see him right now. I am Tribune Darius Caepio."

A memory stirred. "The Darius Caepio who commanded the Praetorian Guard under Emperor Antoninus Pius?"

A flash of pleasure, quickly squelched, stole across the man's bearing. "The same, sir. And you are Citizen…"

"Pugionis," he supplied, quelling his rising excitement.

"Yes, sir. The governor mentioned that you might arrive before he returned." Darius dismounted, handed the reins to a troop member with an order to return the horse to the stables, and appointed another soldier to take command of the unit, admonishing the man to report back by sundown. To Pugionis, he said, "Your bearers can take the chair to the stables while we discuss why you have come."

As Darius strode briskly past the courtyard's fountain toward the wide marble steps leading up to the praetorium's main entrance, Pugionis allowed himself a smile.

The governor's absence might prove quite fortuitous—and profitable—indeed.

## 17

THE REFURBISHMENT OF Hadrian's Wall and its companion forts from Cilurnum to Vindobala culminated in the ceremonial placement of a commemorative altar, flanked by life-size statues depicting coemperors Lucius Verus and Marcus Aurelius, inside Coriosopitum's legionary chapel. This solemn act triggered a week-long festival staged with all the considerable splendor the army could muster. While civilians and soldiers purchased food, drink, animals and goods from local and visiting merchants, the amphitheater hosted an impressive array of military demonstrations, athletic contests, horse and chariot races, plays, battle reenactments and, of course, gladiatorial games, one of the bouts even featuring women.

Marcus couldn't watch the combatants without acutely missing the gladiatrix he loved.

"Lord Aquila?"

Marcus had been sitting hunched over, bracing his hands against the cool marble ledge of the dignitaries' box while below him, a murmillo, his left foot and leg padded to protect against injury by his tall rectangular shield, traded blows with a thraex bearing a small, square shield, a wickedly curved sword and far more padding. Not recognizing the voice, Marcus straightened and turned toward the man who had addressed him.

By his travel-stained riding leathers and cloak, dusty smell and weary countenance, Marcus judged the man to be a courier. For a fleeting moment he indulged in the fantasy that the man had brought another letter from Libertas. Quite properly, she had confined her first message to a simple if heartfelt expression of thanks, but it touched Marcus every time he thought of the trouble she'd taken to arrange to have it written and sent.

But this courier's tan, of a depth impossible to achieve in Britannia's perpetual damp, announced that he hailed from somewhere far to the south. Rome, most likely.

If he had traveled from Rome to Britannia, Marcus could easily guess who had sent him.

The muscular blond man identified himself in a thick Gallic accent as Velox of Ostia, the port that served Rome. Marcus accepted the parchment and bade him rest. Velox saluted and sank onto the marble bench beside Marcus, swiftly becoming engrossed in the gladiatorial combat, while Marcus studied the message.

He didn't need to read past the salutation to confirm his guess. Swallowing a groan, he finished the message. Lady Messiena had invited him and his parents to Rome to complete the wedding preparations, indicating that Senator Falco had established the nuptials to coincide with the calends of September.

Marcus knew this day would dawn eventually. He just hadn't foreseen his love for another woman making his commitment to Messiena so much more difficult to fulfill.

Yet duty left him with no choice.

He folded the parchment and tucked it into his belt. When Velox would have risen to accompany him, Marcus gave him the option of remaining to watch the rest of the games on this, the final day of the wall rededication festival. Unless the governor had an urgent message to send back to Rome, Marcus expected Velox to be traveling with them.

The governor's son envied the man, who wouldn't be riding to meet an unwanted destiny.

LORD RA PRESIDED OVER the first day of summer, ushering in a gloriously painted dawn fairly bursting with promise that reminded Jamil of the day he had acquired Libertas, a scant eleven months earlier. For many reasons, she had proven to be the best investment he'd ever made.

With that auspicious association buoying his spirits, he set a jaunty pace toward Londinium's slave market in high hopes of finding yet another stellar gladiatrix, to give Libertas a proper sparring partner.

Jamil arrived at the viewing area while the chained queues of naked slaves still stretched toward the perimeter walls. The three burliest men already had been purchased and were standing near a clothing vendor as their new owner haggled over the price of tunics. Jamil overcame the sting of disappointment by heading to the platform where a muscular woman was being displayed for potential customers.

He never made it.

As with last year, his gut clenched as he thought he saw one of his longtime creditors, standing apart from the crowd as if surveying the proceedings.

This year, however, Jamil's gut was right.

Though Pugionis had gained considerable flesh in a decade, and the hair at his temples had grayed, there could be no mistaking the closely set, furtive eyes and the aggressive chin that bore a scar courtesy of Jamil's dagger. Jamil didn't see the other two, but they wouldn't be far, perhaps manning an ambush.

Heart hammering, Jamil ducked behind the aromatic cart of a bread vendor and sucked in a breath while he decided how best to return to Villa Britanniae. The training of a Praetorian guardsman concentrated upon defending someone else from attack. The protection of oneself was deemed secondary.

A knife fight, the preferred modus of Jamil's pursuers, tended to favor those with the most agility and ruthlessness, regardless of experience with other weapons. Although Jamil regularly trained with his best gladiators and felt as fit as his five and a half decades would allow, he would not have wagered upon himself to overcome three younger men lusting for both his blood and his money.

One thing his elite training had bestowed upon him was the ability to formulate escape routes. The primary duty of a Praetorian guardsman was to keep the emperor safe at all times, which often meant spiriting him away from danger, rather than making a stand to confront the threat. Against lopsided odds, it was the only sensible choice.

If Lady Maat chose to be kind, she would grant Jamil safe passage to implement the escape plan he had designed against such an evil day as this.

If not, then the man who once had been known throughout the empire as Kalil Al-Omar would be dead.

PUGIONIS LICKED HIS lips and pretended not to notice the man edging away from the slave market. Half the fun lay in watching the target panic. Panic bred mistakes, and mistakes made the target that much easier to trap.

He gave Kalil to the count of ten before sauntering after him, making sure Kalil knew he was following.

THE MAIN PROBLEM WITH Londinium, Jamil realized as he wove as tangled a path as he could to elude pursuit, was that, excepting the avenues leading to the praetorium, fort, amphitheater and forum, its streets formed a maze of narrow, twisting, slop-sluiced alleys. And they all looked alike.

After the third time passing the same group of children, who were using sticks to keep a tall wooden hoop rolling back and forth between them, he knew he was in trouble.

Panting, he ducked into a shadowed doorway and admonished himself to calm down and think. With any luck, his pursuers were as lost as he was.

No, he chided himself. He wasn't lost. He'd lived in this bloody town for a decade; he couldn't possibly be lost. Only temporarily disoriented.

But he had no prayer of reorienting himself unless he could see the sun, which hadn't reached its zenith yet, although, by the way Jamil was sweating, it wouldn't be long before the full heat of the day came to bear.

Cautiously, he stepped out of the doorway to peer around the corner.

A fist connected with his jaw in a hard uppercut. His teeth felt as if they'd been jammed into his brain. Pinpoints of light exploded across his vision, and he could make out nothing more than vague silhouettes. He stumbled backward into the alley, fumbling for his dagger. Three shapes lunged after him.

He managed to keep them at bay by slashing his dagger in sweeping arcs. But his head felt like dough, and he couldn't see well enough to land any blows. His attackers, who reeked of sweat, ale, beef and onions, closed in, pinned him against the wall, and pummeled him with more head-jarring blows. Jamil didn't need his sight to tell him at least one of them had drawn a dagger—he felt its cold blade pressed against his throat.

"If you kill me, you get nothing," he rasped. "My will bequeaths my property to my family in Tanis, except my gladiator-slaves, who shall be freed."

"We shall see about that. Drop your weapon, Kalil." Pugionis pressed harder with the dagger, and Jamil felt it bite into his neck. Reluctantly, he complied, and Pugionis kicked it aside. "Time seems to have taught you how to be cooperative."

As Pugionis backed away, Rodo and Furcifer stepped forward to grasp Jamil's arms. Jamil swayed and would have fallen if not for their assistance. The three men laughed harshly.

Pugionis moved in close and pricked Jamil's side with the dagger. "Now, we shall go somewhere private to finish this discussion. If you so much as look askance at a city guard, I swear it will be the last action you ever take." Another prick convinced Jamil of his creditor's sincerity, and a blow between the shoulder blades sent him staggering, flanked by Furcifer and Rodo, into the street.

As they neared Villa Britanniae, Pugionis pricked Jamil again. "You will tell your guards you are drunk," he grated into Jamil's ear. "You fell and need our assistance."

The gate guards looked alarmed and would have rushed forward to help, but Jamil waved them off and gave the expected lie, prodded by Pugionis's concealed dagger.

"But, Lanista Jamil, you need to get to the infirmary."

"Stay at your post, Bonacies. My friends—" Jamil all but choked on the word, and his hesitation earned him another subtle poke "—can get me there."

They entered the school and proceeded, at Jamil's stumbling pace, toward the infirmary. Once they had moved beyond the guards' sight, Pugionis ordered Jamil to change course toward his workroom. Jamil chose a less direct route that did not take them past the training enclosure. He couldn't bear the thought of his gladiators seeing him. Even though most would attack his captors at his command, it would take too long for guards to unlock the fence's gates. Jamil would never live to see the first blow struck.

Ten years of running had exhausted him past worrying about the outcome of this whole bloody business. He only wanted it to be done, to settle his debt and accept the consequences like the descendant of ancient Egyptian nobility that he was. To behave honorably, as he should have done a decade ago, instead of letting greed blind him to the stupidity of his choices.

To face the gods' judgment like a man.

Oddly, he found himself caring less about what was going to happen to him than to his gladiators, one in particular.

Libertas, Jamil thought with a sharp pang of regret as they approached his workroom, should have accepted her freedom when he had offered it. Now the gods alone knew what would befall her.

Before crossing the threshold, he offered a final, heartfelt prayer to whichever divine eye might be watching him that he would survive this encounter and find a way to deliver Libertas from these men. For, at the hands of Pugionis and his companions, her life would become nothing less than a hell on earth…if they chose to let her live.

AFTER CLIMBING A SET of stairs and traversing half the length of a corridor, Kalil halted for a long moment in front of a door that looked no different than any of the others they'd passed. Thinking it might be a trap, Pugionis commanded Kalil to enter first. The Egyptian complied and stood in the center of the tiled floor, arms outspread, to indicate he was alone. Pugionis ordered his accomplices to keep watch outside and cautiously followed Kalil into the chamber.

Even though it belonged to a man of means, it was the simplest workroom Pugionis had ever seen. No, not simple, exactly. There was nothing simple about the fragrant mahogany desk and chairs, or the latticed shelves stacked with parchment leaves and scrolls that lined every square inch of wall space, with the exception of the large picture of a winged Egyptian woman painted onto the wall opposite the desk.

Except for the painting, flanked by unlit candles, Pugionis would have called the chamber austere. Not a cushion or a curtain in sight. Not even a weapon, as he'd expected. Kalil probably kept the opulent items in his private chambers rather than a workroom to which everyone had access.

The Egyptian's most prized treasures stood sweating and whacking at one another inside the enclosure beneath this workroom's lone window.

Pugionis gazed at them for a few admiring moments before pulling the shutters closed. He wasn't here to gawk at Kalil's possessions, but to take possession of them himself.

Gesturing with his dagger, he directed Kalil to light the oil lamps, retrieve writing supplies and sit behind the desk.

"And what am I to write?" Kalil, his quill poised over the parchment and dripping ink, sounded more fatigued than fearful. Too bad.

"First, write to your banker, authorizing the transfer of all your funds to me. Then draft a bill of sale—this school and its contents for the price of one denarius."

"Feeling generous, are you?"

Pugionis rewarded him with a punch to his already bruised and swollen face. "Less talking, more writing."

After scribbling a few words, Kalil glanced up. "You mean to take the gladiators, too?"

Pugionis leaned across the table, sneering. "Especially the gladiators. How many do you have?"

"A hundred, more or less. Forty-four contract gladiators, fifty-one slaves. The criminal contingent varies, but I usually have around ten."

"How many of the volunteer gladiators have contracts extending past the nones of August?"

Kalil shrugged. "Most of them, probably. I would have to confer with my records keeper—"

"Do not trouble yourself, Kalil." The fewer who knew of this transaction, the better.

"What of the guards, armorers, physicians and other workers?"

Pugionis gave a sharp laugh. "Your gold will continue to pay them if they choose to come with us."

Kalil looked confused. "You are not staying here to run the school?"

In answer, Pugionis spat on the floor. "*That* for this armpit of a province and your insignificant school. I see no reason not to tell you that your—*my* troupe shall travel to Rome." Again motioning with the dagger, he directed Kalil to stand and hand over the documents, which the latter did with an air of resignation. "Now we will proceed to the training enclosure, where you shall announce the transfer of ownership and introduce us to the gladiators."

Pugionis wasn't sure which he enjoyed more: the shock on Kalil's bloodied face, or the dismay.

WHEN THE FOREMAN called an early halt to the afternoon drills, it didn't take much mental power to guess that something momentous had happened. Rhyddes could read it in the dejected slump of Jamil's shoulders, the extent of his injuries, and in the triumphant leers of the three men accompanying him.

The fattest man pushed Jamil forward.

Jamil coughed and cleared his throat. "Gladiators, I have sold Villa Britanniae and everything in it to these men. You guards, other workers and volunteer gladiators whose contracts expire before the nones of August may leave now. Your contracts were not included in the transaction." He surveyed the gladiators but refused to make eye contact with Rhyddes. Her gut tightened uneasily. "The rest of you belong to them."

He turned and trudged away without bidding farewell. All that talk about her having been his favorite, and he departed without giving her so much as a single glance. He may as well have stabbed her in the stomach.

"Kalil, wait," the fat one called to him.

Jamil responded to that name as readily as if he'd been born to it. Certain other actions began making sense.

"You have neglected to introduce us to your—that is, *our* gladiators," crooned the fat man.

Jamil—Kalil?—introduced the stocky, weasel-faced man as Rodo. The giant, who made up in muscle what he appeared to lack in wit, Jamil called Furcifer. Their third new owner, the fat one who seemed to be the trio's leader, Jamil named Pugionis. Jamil made as if to leave again when Pugionis reached into a pouch dangling from his flabby neck, withdrew something, and flipped it at Jamil. It hit the ground and rolled away from him before falling onto a paving stone with a muted clatter. At first he looked as if he was going to pass it by, seemed to think better of it, and stooped to snatch it from the ground. Villa Britanniae's new owners laughed.

Rhyddes despised them.

And she felt a wagonload of reproach toward Jamil, who had sold everything he owned to these vermin.

She was given no time to explore that thought, however, for Pugionis delivered his first pronouncement as the new co-owner, and her second shock of the afternoon:

"Gladiators, return to your cells and pack your gear. On the morrow, every bondsman—and woman—of Villa Britanniae departs for Rome."

The gladiators shuffled away, some, like Gordianus, to leave. Those lucky few were freed of their arena obligations if not of the stigma of having competed, while the rest were fated to begin a new journey known only to the gods.

And the gods alone knew whether Rhyddes would ever be able to buy her freedom from her new owners. The pang in her stomach, born of her refusal of Jamil's offer, made her doubt it.

THE FOLLOWING MORNING, clad in a tunic fit for a banquet, Gordianus stopped by Rhyddes's cell. Vederi, who had chosen to remain in the new owners' employ, unlocked it for him.

She was sitting on the cot, which had already been stripped of bedding, tracing the engravings on her slave-tag in a vain attempt to conjure a happier time.

Her arena armor and weapons had been packed with the rest of the armory inventory. The canvas sack she'd been given for personal effects wasn't very large, but it more than sufficed.

Gordianus glanced around, retrieved an object from the floor and sank beside her onto the straw-stuffed pallet. "Forgetting something?" he asked softly, in Celtic.

Rhyddes dropped the slave-tag into the sack and reached for the object he proffered. Caressing its long snout, as she'd done so often in the past, brought tears to her eyes.

"Why?" she whispered to the jackal-headed god. "Why didn't he order us to fight?" She regarded Gordianus expectantly. "I would have, Gordi."

"As would I." His smile turned rueful. "Who knows these things? Lanista Jamil must have had his reasons."

"Reasons, aye." Reproach boiled up within her, and she flung the figure against the back wall. It hit with a resounding crack but didn't break. "That, for his reasons. His cowardice."

"Rhyddes, you cannot mean it." He stared aghast at her.

"I know not what else to believe, Gordi." Blinking back the tears, she regarded her wrestling mentor. "What shall you and Belua do now?"

"She and the other animals have been sold to the legion at Camulodunum." Gordianus's expression became wistful. "I'm getting too old to perform, but I am going with her to petition the legate to employ me as a trainer."

Sadly Rhyddes noticed he did not speak of returning to the home of his birth; no gladiator, even a freed one, could ever hope to recapture his former way of life.

Rather than drawing attention to that Roman-inflicted curse, she said, "A thousand blessings upon you, Gordi, whatever road you tread." She smiled faintly. "Belua, too."

Rhyddes wanted to extend their conversation, fearing it would be the last time she'd hear the tongue of her homeland. But her heart's heaviness weighted her spirit past words.

He wrapped his arms around her in a brotherly embrace. "Walk with honor, Rhyddes ferch Rudd, and fight with honor."

'Twas mayhap the last time she would hear the name bestowed upon her at birth, too. After reluctantly breaking the embrace, she closed the sack, slung it over her shoulder and stood. She left the Anubis figurine where it lay.

She turned a slow circle, rendering the gladiators' salute to the images of each of her opponents, loser and victor, living and dead. With Gordianus and Vederi to flank her, she departed her cell for the last time.

The foreboding she'd experienced in her lover's arms had come to pass. The only reason she hadn't left the slave-tag with Anubis was to preserve a reminder of that night's fragile happiness.

For in the clutches of these vile new Romans, she never expected to see Aquila—or happiness—again.

## 18

AFTER SPENDING THE last several weeks either in tents beside the road, inns whose best beds featured creaking frames and lumpy mattresses—the vermin-infested ones having been reserved for less wealthy clientele—or hard military cots, Marcus's bed at home felt like heaven. It would feel even more heavenly with Libertas to share it.

A vain wish, with his wedding to Messiena lurching closer by the day, but a pleasant fantasy nonetheless.

Marcus resolved to visit Libertas as often as he could before he left. But that would have to wait until the morrow. Tonight, his and Agricola's return to Londinium was being celebrated during a special feast.

Loreia had spared no expense, obvious in the abundant flowers and garlands perfuming the dining chamber, the richly embroidered table linens, the proliferation of musicians, acrobats, jugglers and other entertainers, and the vast numbers of Agricola's top officers and Londinium's wealthiest men and their wives in attendance.

And, of course, the dizzying array of sumptuous foods. Salmon steeped in tangy fermented garum, the highly prized fish sauce imported from Iberia; thinly sliced beef stewed in wine hailing from the rich valleys of Gaul; pickled African flamingo tongue lying upon a bed of lettuce surrounded by pink feathers; steamed mussels and oysters by the bucketful; even a roasted peacock, browned to perfection. The peacock's magnificent tail feathers had been arranged as if he were fanning for peahens.

If not for the servants, garbed in new tunics and dresses for the occasion, constantly circulating among the tables to replenish food and drink at each diner's place, Marcus would scarcely have known what to try first.

"My dear Loreia, you have simply outdone yourself."

Agricola, no doubt feeling expansive after having quaffed his fifth goblet of excellent Setian wine, placed a lavish kiss on his wife's cheek. She blushed like a maid.

"This is, in part, a prenuptial celebration, too," she said, smiling at Marcus.

"Thank you, Mother." Marcus hoped he sounded more grateful than he felt.

Loreia directed her attention to Agricola, who had taken the opportunity to exchange a few words with Pronavis, the owner of Londinium's commercial shipping fleet, and Claudia, his wife. "When do we depart, Sextus?"

"For Rome?" Agricola gave a toss of his head. Excusing himself from the shipping magnate, he regarded Loreia and

Marcus. "I'm not sure. It seems odd that the invitation didn't come directly from Senator Falco."

"Perhaps he was too busy for such niceties," Loreia whispered with acerbity. "You men love to flatter yourselves so."

"Point taken, but—"

"But are you sure you want to risk offending your future daughter-in-law? Lady Antonia's passing put her daughter in charge of Falco's household several years ago. Surely Messiena would not have extended the invitation without Falco's approval," Loreia said.

Agricola splayed his hands. "You are probably right, Loreia. We shall leave as soon as it is practical to do so. How much time do you need to prepare?"

*A month, at least,* Marcus silently pleaded with whatever gods had deigned to grace this gathering.

"I knew the time for this journey would come soon." Loreia favored her husband with a triumphant smile. "So I ordered the servants to lay up stores and begin packing while you and Marcus were cavorting across Britannia. The remaining preparations shouldn't take more than a week."

Agricola stroked his chin thoughtfully. "And that should leave me more than enough time to ensure Darius has all he needs to continue governing the province in my absence." He clapped Marcus on the shoulder. "On the calends of July, then, we shall be off to reunite you with your bride."

Marcus retained the good sense not to groan. Still, one week with Libertas was better than none.

Pronavis, whose gaunt countenance attested to a lifetime of worrying which ships would make it to their destinations, extended a hand toward Agricola, while Claudia and Loreia returned to their animated chatter about wedding garments, food, wine and decorations. "At Lady Loreia's request, I have reserved my best passenger ship and crew for you and your entourage. She's not as fast as some vessels, but she's large and steady, and should meet your party's needs in every detail."

"I'm sure she shall, my friend," said Agricola. "I'm sure she shall."

Marcus wished heartily that everyone was not so enthusiastic about commencing his exile.

His father, however, was forgetting one thing. "What of the games that were to be held in honor of our return to Londinium?" Marcus asked.

"Canceled," Agricola said, and went back to discussing travel plans with Pronavis.

Marcus cocked a questioning eyebrow at his mother.

She and Lady Claudia donned tragic faces. "Poor Citizen Jamilus," Loreia crooned, "losing his home and livelihood to creditors like that."

Marcus felt his pulse quicken. Jamil losing his livelihood meant… "He lost the gladiators?"

Claudia nodded gravely. "The entire school. They say he wanders the alleys near the amphitheater, poor man, drunk half the time and raving the other half."

Marcus modulated his tone to sound only politely interested. "Villa Britanniae had several good sparring partners. Have you heard whether any of them are for sale?"

Loreia's look turned to one of knowing sympathy. "They're gone, dear. Every last one."

He had to find Jamil as soon as he could decently disengage himself—pleading discomfort from having consumed too many rich foods—from the dinner party.

On his way out of the praetorium, he stopped by the barracks to request a mounted detachment to assist him in his search. After leading the men to the amphitheater district and giving them Jamil's description—a muscular man nearing sixty with a pox-ravaged face, most likely drunk—the unit fanned out to implement Marcus's orders.

The decurion rejoined Marcus after what seemed like hours, while he and another soldier were conducting a fruitless house-to-house inquiry.

"We believe we have him, sir, three lanes down." Decurion Idoneus pointed the way.

"You believe?"

"You'll understand when you see him, Lord Aquila," was all the officer would divulge.

"Very well, show me."

Marcus thanked the merchant with whom he had been conversing, mounted, ordered his escort to do the same, and together they followed Decurion Idoneus down the lane to the cross street, where they turned left, passed two alleys and turned left again.

Huddled on the ground against a derelict residence, swathed in a tattered cloak, Jamil would have been all but invisible if not for the ring of soldiers, some bearing torches illuminating his pathetic state. He sat with his knees drawn up and head down, swaying slightly. A broken glass bottle lay nearby, and he clutched a jagged shard in his bloodied hand. As Marcus rode nearer and dismounted, giving the reins to Idoneus, the stench of urine, vomit and cheap wine wafted even stronger than that of the horses.

Ignoring it, Marcus squatted beside his friend and pried the shard from his grasp. "What happened, Jamil?"

"Who wan'st'know?" came the muffled response. Jamil didn't bother to raise his head.

"It's me. Aquila." Marcus tried to rein in his growing impatience.

"Eagle? No mor'eagles. All flownaway. Never comin' back." The last words sounded more like a moan than a sentence.

Marcus dug his fingers into the back of Jamil's hood, making sure to grab some hair with it, and yanked to lift his face. The flourish of bruises gave Marcus pause but stiffened his resolve. "Sober up, Jamil, and talk to me!"

That won a crooked grin. "Talk's free, yer lor'ship. I c'n talk. All th'talk ya want." He exhaled a throaty laugh, and his breath reeked of onions, making Marcus's stomach churn.

"Libertas, man! Where is she?"

Jamil's countenance fell. "Gone. Gone, gone, gone! Over land, over sea, with Anubis she shall be."

Marcus's heart twisted. "She's dead?" he whispered.

But Jamil kept repeating that stupid lyric, and Marcus couldn't get another lucid word out of him. Disgusted, but unwilling to surrender hope, he stood to address the decurion, who had been watching the proceedings with mild interest.

"Idoneus, get this man back to barracks. Give him a cot and clothes, and tend his wounds. For gods' sakes, get him cleaned up, but have one of your men accompany him in the baths to make sure he doesn't drown. Feed him all he wants, but don't let him near strong drink. In the morning, get him up with the rest of the unit and send him to me."

"Yes, my lord."

Decurion Idoneus thumped fist to chest and ordered his men to load Jamil onto one of the horses. Jamil put up only a token resistance. They wrapped him in his cloak, pinning his arms beneath the fabric, and hoisted him facedown across the back of a horse like an overstuffed sack of wheat. Someone produced a length of rope, and they lashed him to the saddle and set off, at a jolting walk, to the praetorium's barracks. The action made Jamil vomit, and the mare shied, but the soldier leading her soon had her calmed and walking steadily.

Marcus spent a few moments watching them depart before mounting his horse for the return ride, wondering why in the name of all the gods Jamil had allowed himself to descend to such a shameful state.

And he tried his best to reject the notion that Libertas had joined Egypt's dreaded lord of death.

SENATOR PUBLIUS MESSIENUS Falco presented the emperor's invitation, which included admittance for the other occupant of the carriage, with a bored air. These soldiers might not know the man Falco was bringing to the imperial palace, but they had seen Falco often enough, and surely they knew of the imperative need for the skills Falco's friend had to offer.

After the ranking guard examined the invitation, and peered through the window, he greeted Falco with a salute and waved the carriage through the tall, gilt bronze gates.

Falco had visited this residence too often to bother noting the exquisite statues that adorned each bubbling fountain, the impeccably trimmed hedges, some shaped like animals and people, and the aromatic profusion of flowering plants, shrubs and trees. Falco's companion, however, spent the entire trip gazing out the window, craning his head this way and that, no doubt exercising the powers of observation critical to his trade.

Of Rome's three imperial residences, this, the Palace of Tiberius, was the smallest and least imposing. It was lavish enough compared to other aristocratic residences, and its public wing boasted plenty of workrooms for the hundreds of magistrates and clerks who labored to address the needs of the palace, city and empire. But Falco would have chosen Domitian's palace, Domus Augustiana, constructed like a temple to remind visitors of the emperor's supreme position and divine authority.

Falco moistened his lips in anticipation of the dwelling he would build for himself, using Domus Augustiana as a model and expanding upon it.

At the entrance to the palace's domed public basilica, they disembarked and were met by a detachment of Praetorian guardsmen, distinctive in their black armor, cloaks and crow-plumed helmets, who ushered them into the presence of Emperor Marcus Aurelius.

One look at the gaunt man, robed in a simple if finely woven purple toga bearing a wide gold border, reminded Falco of why Marcus Aurelius and Lucius Aurelius Verus had chosen to live in Domus Tiberiana. The brothers Aurelii subscribed to the Greek Stoic philosophy, which disdained the pleasures of the flesh in favor of nourishing the soul. With Lucius Verus off fighting the Parthian war, it was a wonder that Marcus Aurelius, the more austere of the two, hadn't opted for a one-room cell.

The emperor nodded once, approving Falco's approach. He subtly motioned Falco's companion to join him. Six Praetorian guardsmen kept pace without crowding the visitors.

Falco and his companion bowed deeply. "Hail, mighty and victorious Emperor Marcus Aurelius." Decades of public service had taught Falco the fine art of delivering unpalatable speeches. "I am honored to present to your exalted majesty the most highly skilled physician in the empire, Galen of Pergamum."

Galen didn't blush at Falco's description of his talents; it was quite simply the truth, and Falco had never seen Galen wallow in false modesty. Anyone who could keep Falco's gout under control, in spite of the culinary excesses in which Falco loved to indulge, deserved a peerless reputation.

The physician gracefully dropped to one knee and bowed his head. "I am at your majesty's complete disposal." His confident tone was tinged with a lilting accent that revealed his Trojan origin.

"Rise, Galen of Pergamum," intoned the emperor, "and walk with me."

Since Marcus Aurelius had not given orders to the contrary, Falco took that as his cue to accompany them. With the ubiquitous Praetorian guardsmen in tow, they left the basilica via a heavily guarded rear exit that gave access to the palace's private wings. They crossed a large courtyard

laced with an inviting series of reflective ponds, adorned
with more statuary and sculpted hedges, and entered the
central wing, trooped up a wide set of silvery veined black
marble stairs, and joined the parade of people scurrying in
and out of a certain chamber. The servants were carrying all
manner of linens, vials, implements, food and drink,
bringing fresh supplies in and soiled or discarded items out.

At the emperor's approach, the parade halted and
everyone bowed until he had passed. Falco imagined the day
when such folk would be bowing for him.

Soon, he hoped.

Arranged neatly on the shelves built against opposite
walls of the chamber sat hundreds of miniature clay horses
and soldiers, and wooden engines of war. A model fortress,
fashioned of twigs and stones lashed together, sprawled
across a table in one corner, with defenders manning the
walls and four infantry divisions forming the siege. Another
table held a scale model of the Colosseum, complete with
tiny clay replicas of the dozens of statues, and a pair of gladiators poised to hack at each other on the sand-dusted
board representing the arena floor.

Their young owner lay on the bed, thrashing and moaning,
his body covered in raised red welts he was trying to scratch
in his delirium. Servants attempted to calm him and hold his
hands, and his mother, Empress Faustina, sat beside him,
swabbing his brow with a lavender-scented cloth.

Marcus Aurelius turned toward Galen, all pretense of
formality stripped away by anxiety. "My son, Prince Commodus. My only son. He has been suffering this rash and
fever since last night, and no one seems to know why. Cure

him, Galen of Pergamum, and you may name your price, unto half my personal wealth."

Another man might have displayed an avaricious grin; this physician thinned his lips and nodded once. Marcus Aurelius drew Falco aside while Galen began his examination of the boy.

"If this Trojan cures my son, be assured I shall reward you, too, for bringing him to us."

Falco's smile masked his concern at the implications in the event of Galen's failure. In fact, that risk had almost prevented Falco from becoming involved in this crisis of the imperial family. But he had to see for himself how the emperor was reacting to his heir's illness and was pleased to note it would factor into his plans quite nicely indeed.

"Your majesty is most kind. But to see Prince Commodus fully recovered and enjoying the gladiatorial games to be staged in his honor next month shall be reward enough for me, my lord."

The aftermath of the games would yield the real reward.

Galen finished conversing with the empress and the other physicians, and joined Falco and the emperor, whom he greeted with respectful nods. "My lord, your son suffers from a pox that typically strikes children, but it presents no grave danger. His high fever, however, is unusual and must be tended carefully. And it is imperative that his hands be gloved to prevent him from scratching his rash. Otherwise, he could scar himself. Today's welts should disappear in a few days, but more may appear until this pox runs its course. I have left treatment instructions with your majesty's physicians to deal with the fever, the rash's itching and scar prevention. Also, he must be kept clean, with the hottest water he can stand, and confined to this room, with minimal contact with others, until the rash disappears completely. If he suffers any change for the worse, I implore your majesty to summon me at once."

The emperor, gazing fondly at his son, sighed with palpable relief. He returned his sharp scrutiny to Galen. "And your price, good physician?"

"A thousand sesterces, if it pleases your majesty."

Falco resisted the urge to gape.

Marcus Aurelius offered a rare smile. "Surely you know you could have requested ten times that amount, Galen of Pergamum, and I never would have questioned it."

Inclining his head, Galen returned the smile. "Some men accumulate wealth and power, my lord. I remain content to accumulate medical knowledge."

Foolish Greek. Wealth and power were the only things worth accumulating in the Roman Empire.

IF RHYDDES'S LIFE without Aquila had seemed dismal before, in the hands of her new owners it had become downright miserable.

Miserable enough to crave death to escape from the torture called sea travel, which made that Sabrina River crossing seem like a child's game of hop-square in comparison. Escape, too, from the torture inflicted by her owners' lewd looks and even lewder fondling of her at every opportunity.

At least the stench of her seasickness held them at bay for the seemingly endless crossing from Britain to the southwestern coast of Gaul at the neck of the Iberian Peninsula.

Seasickness wasn't the only peril she braved; midway through the crossing, the vessel became ensnared by a storm. The contract gladiators were helping the crew secure the sails when a mammoth wave broadsided the ship, sweeping a few men overboard. One of the lost, she later learned, for she'd been locked with the other slaves below deck during the storm, was her friend and weapons mentor, Nemo.

"Show me where it happened," she implored of Vederi, who had borne the news.

Her guard gave her a dubious look. "Are you sure? The seas are still quite high."

"Am I forbidden to go above?"

He shook his head. "But you look—"

If she looked anything like the way her stomach felt, she could understand his hesitation. But this couldn't wait until her recovery. "Please, Vederi."

He grunted his assent and bade her to follow him up the ladder leading out of the hold, stooping to assist her onto the slick deck. The tangy air—a welcome relief from the fetid vomit and offal below—helped quell her sickness.

With a hand cupping her elbow, Vederi guided her to a spot along the rail. A strip of a gladiator's tunic had snagged on a splinter; whose it had belonged to was anyone's guess, since volunteer and slave dressed alike. Rhyddes chose to believe it had torn from Nemo's tunic, and she carefully worked it loose.

After finishing that task, she gazed out over the waters and uttered a bitter laugh.

Nemo had perished within sight of land. And death at sea had robbed him of the funeral for which he'd paid out of his winnings, a practice in which most gladiators engaged.

Grief smote Rhyddes as sharply as on that gods-forsaken day the Pictish raiders had murdered Ian and Gwydion. Clutching the linen scrap over her heart, she closed her eyes, tipped back her head and uttered the ulu-lating dirge of her people, caring naught for who heard her or what they thought.

It fell far short of the memorial Nemo deserved, for she possessed no lamps, oil, food or incense, but she poured her soul into the music.

After her notes trailed into wavering silence, she felt a warm hand clasp her shoulder. "Nemo might have survived, Libertas," Vederi said softly. "He was a strong swimmer."

She'd never known Vederi to lie, but her heart's ache warned his words had been birthed of wishful thinking.

Fervently she prayed Nemo had found ultimate freedom.

And silently, though no less fervently, she cursed her gods for refusing to take her, and she cursed herself for not being worthy of the honor.

THE FOLLOWING EVENING they disembarked at the port of Burdigala, and a staggeringly drunk Rodo caught Rhyddes in a rare moment alone behind one of the newly pur-chased supply wagons. He ripped her tunic to expose her right breast.

As he leaned forward, licking his lips, she slapped him hard, raking his cheek with her nails. Uttering a startled yelp, he reeled backward and fell in the horses' muck.

"You're dead, you rotting whore!" Rodo screamed. He leaped from the stinking mire as if it had burned him, and charged toward Rhyddes, fist cocked to kill.

Calmly she closed her eyes and waited—nay, prayed for the blow that would propel her to final freedom.

It never fell.

She opened her eyes to find Rodo struggling in Pugionis's grasp and sighed.

"She is not dead," the fat man said to his companion. "And you will not provoke her like that ever again. Understood?" Pugionis gave Rodo's arm a savage twist. "We still have weeks of travel ahead, and we need to get every last one of our surviving gladiators back to Rome before the nones, or there's no commission for us."

Pugionis had to be referring to August. But Rhyddes viewed the mystery with only detached interest; with any luck, she would create an opportunity to end her wretched life. And if her death could hurt the men who had hurt Jamil, so much the better.

Thinking of her former owner in those terms helped ease the pain of his apparent betrayal, and the grief of losing a man she had begun to love with a daughter's devotion.

And she'd gladly sacrifice her soul for just one more of Aquila's kisses....

Pressure from her nipple being pinched startled her from her reverie. She tried to yank free, but Pugionis squeezed harder, making her gasp in pain. Like a stooping falcon, he dropped his mouth onto hers, thrusting his tongue deep and grinding his hips against hers in a matching rhythm.

Rhyddes raised her knee to his vulnerable spot. He blocked her with his thigh but let her go.

"Remember who is the master and who is the slave, woman." He chuckled in his ugly, irritating manner and strolled away.

Vederi joined her as she was trying to tie the remnants of her torn tunic for modesty. He gave her a head-to-foot appraisal, followed by a low whistle. "Are you all right, Libertas? What happened?"

She tossed her head. "My owners were exercising their rights."

"I'm sorry I wasn't here to prevent it." She believed him. "Furcifer sent me on an errand that took longer than I expected."

"No doubt a ploy to leave me unguarded. It wasn't your fault, Vederi." She climbed into the supply wagon, found the trunk containing the new tunics and took two.

After she emerged from the wagon and stepped down, he noted her break from the rules but said nothing, except, "I could have fetched those for you."

She smiled briefly. "The most important thing you can do for me, until I am safely lodged in the gladiators' school at Rome, is to make sure I am never alone again."

Vederi nodded. "I shall tell the other guards." He grinned at her in a brotherly fashion, making her ache to see Owen and her other brothers, especially Gwydion and Ian. "Don't worry, Libertas, I will personally see that you remain well guarded from this moment onward." His grin widened. "I don't want to risk earning Lord Aquila's wrath."

Rhyddes couldn't help but smile at the mention of the man she loved, but Vederi's well-intentioned remark drove yet another pike into her wounded soul.

For, surely, marriage to the daughter of a senator would cause Aquila to forget his tryst with a gladiatrix-slave.

## 19

WHEN DECURION IDONEUS reported to Marcus, the morning after they'd found Jamil in the streets, that the Egyptian was sleeping heavily, Marcus allowed Jamil to recover in his own way. Which galled him, but he knew he wasn't going to get the answers he craved any more quickly if he tried to force the issue.

And since he felt underfoot around the servants tasked to pack his belongings for the journey to Rome, and he ached to do something—anything—to put him in closer proximity to Libertas, even if only in spirit, he took a horse from the praetorium's stables and rode to Villa Britanniae.

With the gladiators, staff and guards gone, Marcus expected the complex to be deserted and was surprised to find the perimeter vigilantly patrolled by guardsmen he knew well, who explained they had been retained by the school's new owners to discourage thieves and squatters. While one guard held Marcus's horse, their leader, Crebro, unlocked the gates and volunteered to conduct Marcus to the cell Libertas had occupied.

It felt ungodly strange to tread the familiar path down the colonnade that ran the length of the central exercise yard, with no sound to relieve the eerie silence save for the slap of their sandals against the paving stones. Marcus fancied he could hear the cracks and clanks of practice weapons clashing, along with the gladiators' shouts and their overseers' commands.

But he couldn't conjure Libertas's voice among the ghostly din, and it saddened him beyond measure.

Crebro turned down the same corridor Marcus had seen Libertas use. It connected the building housing the gladiatorial school's public rooms and Jamil's wing, grouped in a rectangle around the exercise yard, with a second rectangle containing the gladiators' and guards' barracks, separated by the baths.

Marcus often had used the baths after sparring, and once after trysting with Libertas. That night's memory made his loins ache, but he gritted his teeth and kept walking past the pool where they had enjoyed each other's bodies for the final time—now a dry tomb for dead leaves and bugs—and on to the rear door where Vederi had forced Marcus to bid her farewell.

An uneasy thought gave him pause. "Where is Vederi?" he asked as casually as he could manage.

"He went with the gladiators." If Crebro thought Marcus's question odd, he didn't show it as he selected a key from the collection dangling from his belt, unlocked the door and held it open for Marcus to step through.

Jealousy smote him with palpable force. The gods had allowed Vederi to be with Libertas while he, Marcus Calpurnius Aquila, faced an unwanted marriage. Marcus barked a bitter laugh.

"My lord, is something wrong?" Crebro asked.

Slaying the inner demon with a shake of his head, Marcus briskly strode forward.

Little daylight penetrated the cell blocks. Windows were weaknesses to be exploited in an escape, and the only ones gracing this building were located in common-rooms and fitted with thick bars.

Crebro withdrew flint and tinder from the pouch hanging next to his keys and lit a torch from a nearby sconce. The guttering flames threw restless shadows against the walls, making it seem as if the cells were occupied.

Marcus wouldn't have been surprised to meet the ghost of a dead gladiator.

Perhaps the same prospect made Crebro quicken his pace. When they stopped in front of a cell, Marcus relieved Crebro of the torch and stepped across the threshold. He picked up a figurine shaped like a jackal-headed man, obviously a gift from Jamil, whose gods appeared in such fanciful combinations. The ebony wood was finely carved and polished to a silky sheen. With his thumb he slowly stroked the narrow ridges of the figure's ankle-length, red enameled kilt.

*Over land, over sea, with Anubis she shall be.*

The lyric wouldn't leave his head. Yet Libertas was gone, and the Anubis figurine was here. He interpreted it as a positive omen.

Why had she left it behind? Perhaps her departure had

been so precipitous she'd had no choice. But if that were the case, she'd have left more effects. Other than the straw mattress and the Anubis figurine, the cell stood forlornly empty.

Resolving to keep the figurine safe for the day he would see her again, he paced to the wall where she had recorded amazingly lifelike renditions of her fights, even the loss. He longed to trace the images that represented her, but he refrained to keep from smudging the chalk.

One drawing attracted his attention with its sharp lines and a blotch beside it. That had to be the fight where he had ordered her to kill her opponent. As he braced against the cool, smooth slate, carefully avoiding her handiwork, he could almost hear her raging against the injustice. For the first time since returning to Londinium, he smiled, heartened by the fact that she seemed no more enamored of killing than he. He would have to ask her if his supposition was correct—if he ever saw her again.

AGRICOLA STOOD IN THE arched doorway leading into the praetorium's military chapel, hands clasped behind his back and gazing at the pedestal that had been enlarged to accommodate statues of two emperors, rather than the customary one. The standards of the Second, Sixth and Twentieth Legions stretched taut against the wall behind the statues. These were framed by two shield-sized silver medallions, each embossed with the Eagle of Rome. The one on the right, representing the emperors, wore a laurel crown, and a wreath encircled its neck. The other eagle, symbolizing Britannia's conquest, clutched a spike-haired Celtic warrior in each talon.

In front of the pedestal, which was paneled with an alabaster relief detailing Marcus Aurelius's elevation to the purple and his petition of the Senate to approve his brother as coemperor, soldiers labored to haul trunks filled with aureii from the vault guarded by the emperors' likenesses.

After offering yet another round of silent thanks to the man responsible for posting him to this position, Agricola turned his thanksgiving to the goddess Fortuna, who had contrived to rid this land of a potential troublemaker: one tiny but tenacious and extremely popular young woman.

The sound of footsteps echoing behind him alerted him to another presence, and he turned to see Tribune Darius Caepio, his chief of staff, standing inside the chapel's main entrance, accompanied by his second-in-command. That in itself wasn't odd. Darius's attire, a plain belted tunic and breeches, swathed by a floor-length and decidedly nonmilitary hooded cloak, was.

"You are out of uniform, Tribune," Agricola admonished.

Squaring his shoulders and jutting his chin, Darius strode forward, brandishing a scroll. "My request for retirement, sir."

Agricola took the scroll and unrolled it. The document, no doubt crafted by one of the praetorium's scribes, appeared in perfect order. All it lacked was the gubernatorial seal.

After carefully rolling it up, he tapped one of its smooth wooden finials to his chin. "Darius, the gods know—as do I—that you have earned this thrice over. Years of distinguished combat service and a stint as prefect of the Praetorian Guard under Antoninus Pius, to say nothing of the outstanding way you have served the empire while commanding my staff here in Britannia." Agricola returned the scroll. "But the timing of this request is not the best. I need you now more than ever. See me again after I return from Rome."

As he turned back toward the emperors' statues in tacit dismissal, he felt a hand clamp onto his arm. Agricola whirled, an angry reprimand forming on his tongue.

The sheer desperation on Darius's face prevented him from uttering it.

"My lord, please forgive me. If there were any way to delay this, the gods know I would, but I must retire immediately." He motioned his second-in-command to step forward, which the latter did without hesitation. "I've made sure Centurion Oranius knows everything."

Agricola raised an open hand. "What can be so urgent that you must retire now? Family troubles?" He squinted at Darius, recalling the report of another citizen whose illicit past had thrust him into financial difficulty. "A debt you cannot repay? If that is the case, perhaps I can assist you."

Darius shook his head. "A business venture, my lord, which requires me to leave Britannia at once."

The governor scrutinized his top officers. Oranius had proven invaluable during Agricola's expedition to Hadrian's Wall, according to Darius's report, overseeing the receipt of revenues from the province's tax districts. Agricola had never known Darius to exaggerate, but now he couldn't be sure.

The young soldiers, struggling under the combined weight of trunks packed so tightly with coins that scarcely any jingling could be heard from within, breathlessly but politely asked to pass. Agricola, Darius and Oranius obliged without hesitation.

It gave the governor an idea. Perhaps the time had indeed come for Darius to step aside in favor of younger blood.

The question remained whether younger blood would prove capable of administering the entire province, not just the relatively straightforward office of tax collection.

Agricola regarded Darius. "You have a ship to catch, then? You cannot wait for another?"

"Yes, my lord, and no. If I delay, I shall forfeit this lucrative opportunity."

"Then I shall not be the one to bring that ill fortune upon you." Agricola extended his hand to accept the scroll, and they made final obeisance to the emperors before exiting the chapel. "Come with me to my workroom. My supplies are either still unpacked from the last journey or in the process of being packed for the next one, but I'm sure I can find my seal and some wax." As they strode the colonnade's length, an idea occurred. "Your retirement entitles you to a land grant. Would you like the equivalent amount bestowed in sesterces instead?"

Darius stroked his clean-shaven chin. "Many thanks for your generosity, Governor, but no. Where I am going, the added weight may prove more of a burden than it's worth." They stopped outside Agricola's workroom, and Darius offered a rare, if cryptic smile. "Once this business venture ripens to fruition, I shall become very well off indeed."

Mindful of the soon-to-retire officer's need to hurry, Agricola crossed the threshold carrying the scroll, laid it flat on the table, grabbed the seal and a finger of red wax, heated the wax in the oil lamp already burning upon the table, dripped a splotch onto the parchment and impressed it with his crest. Darius, expressing effluent thanks, barely allowed the wax to harden before he rolled the scroll. Agricola dismissed him with a heartfelt wish for good fortune, but bade Oranius to stay.

Britannia's governor settled into his tall chair behind the desk, folding his fingers while his new chief of staff stood spear-straight before him. "Now, *Tribune* Oranius, you and I have much to discuss for the next three days."

THE GODS ALONE knew with what vile brew Jamil had been poisoning his body, but it took three days before he was willing to talk. While Agricola remained closeted with his new chief of staff, making sure the man knew all the procedures and, more importantly, which people to depend upon for running the province while the governor traveled abroad, Marcus invited Jamil to the family's bathhouse.

"I may never be able to repay you for rescuing me from the streets, Aquila." The last words sounded garbled as Jamil sank up to his chin in the steaming water.

"Think nothing of it." Marcus joined him in the heated pool, which had been scented with the piney essence of juniper berries. "You'd have done the same for me."

After they exited the pool, toweled and retired to lie atop marble platforms, each with a slave ministering to his needs, Marcus uttered the question that had been consuming him for days:

"What happened to Libertas?"

Jamil sighed heavily. "She fell victim to my evil past."

"Meaning?"

"Meaning I no longer own her. To recover an old debt, with compounded interest, my creditors seized my funds and property, including the gladiators." Jamil turned his head to gaze levelly at Marcus for the first time since becoming his guest. "They seemed keenly interested in the gladiators." He rested his forehead upon his crossed arms. "Lady Maat only knows why."

"They are bound for Rome?"

Jamil grunted his assent. "Probably to perform for the emperor."

Marcus doubted it. One of the reasons Agricola had found high favor with Emperor Marcus Aurelius was a mutual distaste for blood sports.

His groan caused the slave to stop the massage. While bidding the man to continue, he mentally reviewed his options, which were growing more complicated by the moment. If Libertas would not be performing inside the city of Rome, the area boasted several other amphitheaters within a day's travel. Locating a gladiatrix at one of the Eternal City's four gladiatorial schools would be difficult enough; having to scour Italia's countryside, while juggling obligations relating to his nuptials, promised to be nigh unto impossible.

"What is to become of me once you marry?" Jamil asked. "I cannot remain attached to your household. An old soldier serves no useful purpose." Bitterness marred the Egyptian's tone.

"You shall serve an extremely useful purpose, Jamil. You are coming with me to Rome, to be my eyes, ears and feet in finding Libertas."

Jamil eyed him dubiously. "Your esteemed father would never approve."

He didn't have to say what, undoubtedly, they were both thinking: Agricola wanted to see Libertas dead. Marcus could read the thought in Jamil's frown.

"My esteemed father knows you are my friend. By the sacred laws of hospitality, he cannot refuse my request to continue assisting you, and he should become too busy to heed your actions once we reach Rome."

Jamil bade his attendant to stop and bring more towels. When the slave returned, Jamil sat up and swung his legs over the table's side, gazing at the whitewashed, arched ceiling. Marcus sat up, too, grateful for the heated towels the slave draped over his shoulders as the final stage before dressing.

He couldn't understand Jamil's hesitation. "Are you afraid your creditors might try to finish the job they started?"

"You mean by killing me?" Jamil snorted. "I would deserve it. I was stupid to run from that debt, and even stupider to wallow in despair after my creditors caught me. No, what bothers me most is what Libertas might say. She must believe I betrayed her." He looked away, but Marcus glimpsed the Egyptian's eyes moistening. "And I wouldn't disagree."

Marcus laid a hand on Jamil's shoulder. "You have no chance of setting things right with her if you do not try."

Jamil cocked his head and grinned. "You're right, you whelp. Very well, I shall accompany you to Rome and look for Libertas." He lifted his arms as if in supplication and uttered a phrase Marcus couldn't understand, presumably Egyptian. "May all the gods—" Jamil switched back to the common tongue "—grant us success with our quest."

THE MORE AGRICOLA THOUGHT about Darius's retirement, the less he liked it. Not that he harbored any doubts about Oranius's ability to oversee Britannia's affairs in Agricola's absence; the seasoned officer seemed blessed with a quick wit, a discerning eye and a sensible head. The governor was glad Darius had suggested Oranius and foresaw no trouble from that quarter.

When casual inquiries among the men turned up no concrete answers regarding their former commander's retirement plans, Agricola began to wonder if something from Darius's past had asserted a hold upon him.

"Come to bed, Sextus," called Loreia from the inner chamber. "We've a long journey before us, and I don't wish to share it with someone cross from lack of sleep."

He smiled at that; she knew him too well. "In a moment, my love."

It had been only a few days since Darius's departure. Surely it wouldn't be too difficult to find out where he had gone. Agricola penned a hasty note on a scrap of parchment, folded it, stamped his seal over the outside edges, stepped into the main corridor to summon a guard and charged the man with finding a courier to deliver it immediately to Londinium's shipping magnate, Pronavis.

The answer, when it arrived the next morning as Agricola and his family were preparing to board the luxuriously appointed ship that would convey them to Rome, was simple but no less puzzling:

Darius had gone to Rome on the fastest ship of Londinium's merchant fleet.

The revelation spawned far more questions than it answered.

Why had Darius been in such a rush to leave Britannia, when he surely knew he would have been welcome to travel with the governor's party? How could he have afforded to hire passage on Pronavis's swiftest vessel?

What sort of business venture could be so lucrative that Darius had spurned receiving his due as a twenty-three-year combat veteran?

As Agricola watched Britannia's receding coastline from the ship's deck, while Marcus settled a nauseated Loreia in their quarters below, his mind dwelled upon the idea that Darius had spent part of his military career as prefect of the Praetorian Guard. These elite, powerful men had a disconcerting habit of shaping the empire's future based on which politician could promise them the most gain.

Had someone harboring overweening ambition lured Darius into an intrigue to overthrow the current order? If so, how? More to the point, why? What could a retired officer, who probably had no contacts within the current Praetorian Corps, possibly contribute to such a cause?

"Good day, Governor."

Agricola interrupted his musings to watch the latest addition to his son's entourage troop past. It seemed odd to see Lanista Jamil—rather, Citizen Kalil Al-Omar—bedecked in the trappings of a contract soldier until Agricola recalled the Egyptian had earned Roman citizenship through army service…including a stint in the Praetorian Guard.

It gave him an idea.

"Good day to you, Citizen Kalilus." In spite of how he felt about any man who profited from others' deaths in the name of "entertainment," Agricola forced a smile. "Have you a moment?"

Kalil's surprise looked comical as he halted abruptly and saluted. "Of course, my lord. How may I serve you?"

"How long ago were you assigned to the Praetorian Guard?"

"It's been fifteen years, sir."

Agricola's hopes fell, although he refused to let it show. "Then you would not have served with my former chief of staff, Darius Caepio."

"Briefly. He joined the Praetorian Corps a few weeks before I was transferred to Judea."

"Ah, so you do know him."

Kalil shrugged. "He's an acquaintance." His expression turned quizzical. "Sir, did you say he's your *former* chief of staff?"

"Darius retired this week," was all the information Agricola felt inclined to volunteer. His eyes narrowed. "You wouldn't happen to know why he would refuse his retirement grant and take the first ship bound for Rome, would you?"

The Egyptian uttered a low whistle. "No sane man would refuse his retirement bonus. As for Rome…" He regarded Agricola, the corners of his mouth twitching upward. "I still have contacts there. Would my lord like me to see what I can learn?"

Agricola nodded. "We shall speak of this when we arrive."

As Kalil saluted and strode aft, Agricola's mind turned toward who might attempt a coup. Doubtless every senator cherished fantasies of wearing the imperial purple. Agricola often thought about how he would solve some problem or another if he could hold the reins of power.

But who would be bold enough, wealthy enough, influential enough and hated emperors Marcus Aurelius and Lucius Verus enough to put a coup into motion? Probably many men, but only one of import had visited Britannia in recent memory.

And if that man caught even a whiff of Agricola's suspicions, it could buy a world of trouble for Marcus, Loreia, Agricola and their entire party.

The writhing in Agricola's gut had less to do with the rolling seas than the subtly undulating political landscape.

Without bothering to seek out the vessel's chapel, he pulled a fistful of sesterces from the pouch hanging from his belt and flung them into the frothy waters. After promising a much larger donation once they reached a proper temple, the governor of Britannia offered an earnest petition that he wasn't leading his family into a trap.

**20**

TRUE TO HIS word, Vederi alerted the rest of the guards to be extra vigilant around Rhyddes as the troupe traveled through the verdant wine country between Burdigala and Narbo, flanked on the right by the spear-sharp Pyrenaei Mountains. Even the volunteer gladiators made strategic appearances when Furcifer, Pugionis or Rodo got too close to her. Against their solidarity, Rhyddes's owners didn't stand a chance.

Or so she thought.

She'd adopted the routine of being the last person to use the latrines, for the modicum of privacy it afforded. She had just hitched up her breeches, looking forward to retreating to her wagon for the night, when a hand clamped over her mouth. It stank of the latrines and made her gag. Another hand locked around her wrist and yanked her arm behind her back with a cruel twist. She tried to kick and buck her captor off, but he seemed to anticipate her every move and held her fast.

With her outcries sounding no louder than sleep mumblings, he half dragged, half carried her toward a copse of pine trees outside the camp's perimeter.

Guards and gladiators lay sprawled about as if they'd been drugged. Queasiness attacked her stomach. Even if she broke her captor's grasp, her protectors would be too slow to rouse to her call.

Arena bouts had taught her to bide her time for the best opportunity to strike. She relaxed, feigning resignation.

Inside the circle of pines, facing their approach, Rodo and Pugionis sat beside a small fire. Their lustful faces looked demonic in the shifting light.

Which meant her captor had to be…

Furcifer spun her around and fastened his rancid mouth to hers, his hands groping her body in ways that made her flesh crawl. His actions left her fists free to pummel him with all her strength, but the stupid lout didn't seem to care.

She landed a blow to his gut that made him release her, doubled over and gasping. The other men laughed raucously. Furcifer straightened, scowling murderously and backhanded her across the face.

Her head throbbing, she reeled backward and would have fallen, but he grabbed her and ripped off her tunic. Her breeches came next. The clothing lay at her feet in a ruined heap.

Battle rage welled up within Rhyddes, and she stood, naked save for the cloths binding her breasts and loins, fists on hips in a defiant pose before her smirking owners.

There comes a moment in every fight when the losing combatant realizes victory cannot be achieved. 'Tis the moment of crucial decision: yield and hope for clemency, or continue fighting to the death.

Rhyddes ferch Rudd would not yield.

But the arena—nay, *Jamil* had taught her that most fights were won with cunning rather than brute strength. She prayed for the right opportunity.

Grunting, Pugionis levered himself to his feet, waving Furcifer back, and sauntered up to Rhyddes. "Woman, you cause more trouble than any slave I've ever known." He untied her bands and began fondling her bare breasts.

She dug in her heels and resisted the urge to flinch. "My masters forget I am a trained warrior."

"Ah, yes. A warrior oath-bound to obey or die." Pugionis grinned wickedly. "So much the better."

She gritted her teeth as his hands removed her loincloth. He caressed the gateway to her core gently, as Aquila had done…aroused by the memory, she felt the moist rush and fought for control. "I am prepared to die," she grated out.

He hooted in disbelief. "Your body tells me otherwise." He slid his fingers deeper.

She spat in his face. He shoved her to the ground and hitched up his tunic. The other two, cackling with lustful glee, closed in, each pinning one of her arms over her head.

"I am a virgin," she lied. "I can make it worth your while to keep me that way."

"I don't think so." Pugionis heaved his bulk on top of her, stealing her breath and forcing her legs apart.

"It's true, master." She wasn't sure whether her gasp came

from lack of air, desperation or both. Probably both. "Riding horses on my father's farm broke my maidenhead. If you don't believe me, ask my former owner."

She prayed her owners had not confiscated Jamil's chest containing the slave-tags. If they had, they might have already realized hers didn't number among the others.

"Kalil isn't here, woman." Pugionis began grinding his hips against hers. "And he couldn't help you even if he were."

With a surge of strength, she broke the hold on her wrists, braced her hands against Pugionis's shoulders and pushed for all she was worth, as much simply to breathe as to free herself. "When I said I could make it worth your while, I wasn't referring to Jamil."

Mercifully, he stilled his hips. "Who, then?"

"I know an aristocrat who would pay—" she cast about for an amount that surely would ignite Pugionis's greed "—half a million sesterces to buy me for his bed. That's what he tried to offer for me at the slave market, but Jamil outbid him." Her slave-price had been only a fifth that much, but these men had no way of verifying her claim. She hoped. "But you know aristocrats never purchase used goods."

"Which aristocrat would be stupid enough to waste half a million on the likes of you?" Pugionis sneered grotesquely.

The remark stung, but Rhyddes refused to let it show. "Marcus Calpurnius Aquila, son of the governor of Britannia." Confidence rang from every syllable. Somehow it made her feel better, as if his name were a shield.

Pugionis made a rude noise with his lips, spraying spittle on her face. "Nice try, woman. He's not here, either."

The grind began again. She could feel him quicken against her thigh. Despair enveloped her heart.

"Aquila's the one slated to marry Senator Falco's daughter," Rodo said.

For some reason Rhyddes couldn't fathom, Rodo's statement gave Pugionis pause. He rolled off her into a sitting position to regard his companion expectantly. Rhyddes could have kissed the little rat of a man. "Word is he's traveling to Rome, with the governor, to prepare for his nuptials. If Libertas's claim is true, we'd know soon enough."

"It had better be true, woman." Pugionis leaned over to renew his assault with his fingers. "If it isn't, we shall have our sport with you, and then kill you."

He tangled his fingers in her short hair and yanked hard, forcing her to arch up, a cry escaping from her throat. He covered her mouth with his, giving another yank in rhythm with each thrust of his tongue. Tears streamed from her eyes, as much from the pain as from the vile taste of his mouth and the stench of his breath. But she refused to beg for him to stop.

Finally, he did. Her pain and humiliation didn't. Nor did the urge to see him skewered and turning over a blazing fire, his fat dripping down to make the flames leap higher.

"That is but a taste of what we will do to you, woman," he said. "I hope you enjoy it, because I guarantee your execution will be slow and far more painful."

Not if Rhyddes ferch Rudd, a farmer's daughter whose ancestry boasted countless proud and fearless Votadini warriors, had any say in the matter.

PRONAVIS HADN'T BEEN exaggerating about the passenger ship's speed; or rather, the lack of it. If Marcus had thought it would have helped, he'd have jumped overboard and pushed the boat.

Actually, that wasn't entirely fair, he reminded himself as he stood at the port rail, watching the Iberian mountains loom nearer as if to swallow the ship whole. Every time they put in to port to take on additional supplies—the gods forbid that the ship's galley run short of garum sauce or pickled flamingo tongue—Marcus's mother took an entourage ashore for a shopping expedition.

Usually, Loreia insisted that Marcus accompany her.

"Coming, dear heart?"

As was the case today. Marcus had yet to find a gift for his bride, and Loreia never wasted an opportunity to remind him.

"The captain says Olisipo is a large port with many rich merchants selling a variety of fine wares," his mother said. "Surely you should find something nice for Messiena here."

Marcus answered with a noncommittal grunt and followed his mother down the gangplank, trailed by their strongest servants. Invariably Loreia bought several huge amphorae of wine, wheels of the cheeses, sweetmeats, fruit, game and other local delicacies, armloads of silks and brocades and embroidered linens, finely wrought glasswork and pottery and enough jewelry to armor a legion soldier.

Small wonder the ship was sailing so slowly.

This excursion, as they wandered the maze of market stalls, was proving no different. Loreia sent a pair of slaves back to the ship hauling an elaborately carved, leather-padded, double-seated couch. "For the newlyweds to share intimate talks," she told Marcus with a wink.

Smiling wanly, he turned his attention to the jewelers' stalls. The gods alone knew what Agricola thought of Loreia's expenditures, though he did forbid the purchase of livestock, since animals would pose too much trouble on a ship designed for the comfort of people.

Which was too bad, Marcus thought as he watched a trader leading the sleekest pair of black chariot horses he had ever seen. But regardless of Agricola's stricture against livestock, Marcus had no idea whether Messiena even liked horses.

Libertas probably did. Growing up on a farm, she likely had experience riding and training horses, perhaps choosing the best stock to breed or harness to the plow. Watching the chariot horses parade with their owner to the far side of the market, Marcus conjured an image of Libertas riding in a chariot drawn by the ebony beauties, a spear clutched in one fist, her gladius flashing in the other, a battle cry on her lips, and her hair streaming in a coppery wave as if her head was afire.

Gods, but he missed her!

The horses became eclipsed by the jostling crowd, and he sighed, returning to the task at hand. If he didn't find a gift for Messiena soon, his mother was going to drive him mad by dragging him ashore at every port from here to Rome.

Lost in the sea of gold, silver and copper adornments, much of it cleverly wrought with vividly colored enamel, glass, pearls and gems, he almost missed the unassuming stall containing the most unusual jewelry he had yet seen. The stones ranged from clear to the color of burning embers, many of them embedded with what could only be, strangely enough, insects.

He hefted a large pendant, expecting it to be heavy. To his astonishment, the gold chain from which it swung weighed far more. He peered at the stone from all angles but learned no useful answers.

"A lovely piece, my lord," crooned the merchant, stepping forward, "for a lovely lady."

"Is this a trick?" Marcus ran a fingertip over the warm, smooth orange surface. "How do you trap the insect inside the stone?" He lowered his eyebrows. "Why would you?"

The man, all smiles, shrugged. "No trick, my lord. I sell amber, which is not a stone but the hardened sap of ancient trees. As for why these creatures became entombed thus, you must ask the gods." The merchant gave Marcus a measuring look. "If cunning craftsmanship is what you seek, then please permit me to show you this item."

He reached toward a side table and pulled up another pendant, shaped in the form of a slim cylinder. The bottom end was rounded, the top flat. Its hue, shot through with dark veins, reminded Marcus of Libertas's hair.

With a quick twist, the merchant opened the pendant to reveal a small chamber. "Just large enough for your lover to hold your words of endearment against her heart," he suggested.

Although Marcus wasn't sure what he would do with the piece, he hated to walk away from such a clever thing. He couldn't give it to Messiena because it reminded him of another woman, and it wouldn't be right to buy it for his lover before finding a gift for his bride.

That could be remedied easily enough.

To the merchant's obvious pleasure, Marcus selected a second piece. Not the pendant that had first caught his attention, for he wasn't sure how Messiena would react to the prospect of having a dead bug gracing her throat, but a long necklace crafted of tumbled amber beads shaded in yellow hues.

Pleased with his selections, Marcus didn't haggle with the merchant as much as he should have, daydreaming instead of how he would find Libertas and present his gift to her. He did, however, retain enough presence of mind to insist the two pieces be wrapped separately, which won a sly grin from the merchant.

Marcus interpreted it as a sign that he would be able to give the chambered pendant to the woman he loved so she would possess a tangible reminder of him, no matter what happened.

It became his most persistent prayer.

By EARLY AUGUST, Pugionis's troupe found themselves trundling toward the port city of Forum Iulii, remarkable for the immense amphitheater dominating the main road into town, surrounded by dozens of cemeteries. Rhyddes gawked in slack-mouthed awe as the building, all arches and columns and statues, loomed closer.

"The Flavian Amphitheater of Rome is twice as large," Rodo said from the back of his horse, which he held to the pace of Rhyddes's wagon. "Biggest in the empire."

At the head of the column, Pugionis gave the signal to make way for the procession of gladiators emerging from the city's gates.

Rhyddes, staring at the amphitheater as her wagon's driver complied with the order, couldn't imagine a larger structure. She had trouble assimilating what her eyes reported. How many thousands—nay, tens of thousands of men it must have taken to place the massive blocks and pillars lay far beyond her ken.

But she forgot the marvel as the local gladiators trooped into view, clad in gleaming armor, each one's helmet tucked under his or her left arm. Most of the men and women presented fearless faces, some painted to resemble Picts and Celts, waving the victory sign with their free hands and inciting the crowd to higher levels of excitement.

A few warriors looked as if they wished to be anywhere else. With these souls Rhyddes made an extra effort at eye contact, offering a smile she hoped would encourage them.

A dispirited gladiator soon became a dead one.

Ever since that awful night in the pines, Rodo had been the most approachable of her three owners. Rhyddes drew a swift breath, hoping he felt in a magnanimous mood this day.

"May I watch the games, Master Rodo?"

"Why? You know none of the combatants."

*Why, indeed.* She shrugged. "Just once I would like to view the bouts as a true spectator."

Rodo laughed, though not unkindly. "View's a lot better from the arena floor, woman. Slaves must sit in the highest seats."

She craned her neck, assessing the height, before regarding her owner again. "That doesn't matter to me, master. I wish to experience what it's like." Rhyddes inclined her head. "With your permission, of course."

"Very well." Rodo turned toward her guard. "Vederi, we sail to Ostia on this evening's tide. Have Libertas aboard before the sun touches the horizon."

After rendering Rodo a smart salute, Vederi helped Rhyddes down from the wagon, and they set a brisk pace toward the amphitheater in the gladiators' dusty wake.

"FATHER, WE'RE IN LUCK!" Marcus, watching the gladiatorial procession from the ship's rail as the crew secured the mooring lines, felt like a child in a toymaker's shop. "They're staging games today."

"You go ahead, Son." Agricola patted Loreia's hand, which was resting atop his. "Given a choice between gladiatorial games and shopping, I'll select shopping any day." He gave his wife a smile, which she returned. "Although the games are usually less fatal to my finances."

Gasping in mock dismay, she slapped his shoulder but couldn't suppress a giggle.

His parents' decision suited Marcus perfectly. The closer they came to Rome, the more frayed his nerves felt. Spending time alone, surrounded by thousands of strangers to whom he owed nothing, seemed a fine way to take his mind off the final curtailment of his freedom.

He couldn't leave the ship fast enough.

As with every amphitheater, the arena at Forum Iulii provided a special entrance for the aristocracy. This one was distinguished by gold-leaf endowed statues of Atlas and Hercules. City soldiers stood posted everywhere to maintain order, but the nobles' entrance also featured a clerk sitting behind a table, quizzing some of the people as they approached and waving others through with a hearty greeting.

The wizened man with the beetling eyebrows surmounting bulging eyes, whose flesh and toga appeared to sag in equal measures, seemed more likely to have stepped out of a child's nightmare than an office in the city's forum.

Still, Loreia had drilled into Marcus the concept that much could be accomplished if he treated people with respect. He nodded politely at the clerk.

"Your name, young sir?" The man's high-pitched, nasal voice grated on Marcus's ears.

"Marcus Calpurnius Aquila, son of Sextus Calpurnius Agricola, governor of Britannia province."

The wild, white eyebrows hitched up a notch. "Agricola I have heard of." He squinted at Marcus. "Have you proof?"

Smiling, Marcus reached into the pouch concealed by a fold of his toga and produced the token he'd borrowed from his father for this occasion, stretching forth his hand, palm up.

"The seal of Britannia, eh? That will do, my lord." As Marcus stowed the signet, the clerk's face adopted a hopeful cast. "Will your esteemed father join us today?"

Divining the purpose of the clerk's question and not wishing to disappoint him, Marcus gave a noncommittal shrug. "Perhaps, after he finishes escorting my lady mother at the forum."

Uttering a sympathetic grunt, the clerk beckoned to a soldier, who stepped smartly forward. "Centurion Iustus will escort you to the dignitaries' box, Lord Aquila, and introduce you to the games' sponsor, the prefect of Forum Iulii. Prefect Stator shall be delighted to make your acquaintance."

Marcus fought down a groan, wishing he had used any entrance but this one. All he wanted was a seat reasonably close to the arena floor with the rest of the nobles, not special recognition.

He supposed, with a silent sigh, that he ought to begin getting accustomed to it. After marrying the daughter of one of Rome's most powerful senators, recognition probably would become his constant companion.

## 21

TWELVE FLIGHTS LATER, Rhyddes was huffing and blowing, and yearning to massage her aching calf muscles. Vederi, who exercised with the other guards, didn't seem much better off. As they found room on a crowded pine bench, obliging the other slaves to shift closer together, they exchanged a grateful glance. Rhyddes would have preferred a bench of sharpened spikes to one more set of steps.

Before leaving their caravan, Vederi had procured a full wineskin for each of them, explaining that the swill typically sold inside any stadium, costing half a day's wage, could poison an ox. Food he didn't bother with, though, since their cold travel rations couldn't begin to compare with freshly roasted meats. He bought Rhyddes a lamb skewer from a passing vendor, while selecting beef for himself, and they settled in with their purchases for a welcome diversion.

Rodo was right, however. The view of the arena floor

from this height was scarcely worth the effort. She and Vederi had arrived in time to witness a part of the proceedings she'd never seen: the nonbloody entertainment. Jugglers, acrobats and musicians strutted across the sands, appearing as fleas hopping about a mongrel's back. Still, Rhyddes laughed and clapped along with everyone else, for this vantage offered her something she had not felt in far too long.

The illusion of freedom.

From her lofty seat, higher than most birds flew, she could fancy touching the clouds. The fabulous vista overlooking the island-dotted sea promised an ocean of possibilities.

"…introduce a special guest this afternoon…"

The announcer's voice, powerful when heard upon the arena's floor, sounded thin and remote. Up here, even the crowd seemed less deafening; in fact, if she closed her eyes and invoked her gladiator's concentration skills, she could ignore the noise, wrapping herself in a cocoon of blessed silence, freed for a few precious moments from the horror that had become her life.

"…Britannia province, the governor's son and an expert gladiator himself, Marcus Calpurnius Aquila."

"What?" Rhyddes yelled over the crowd's cheers. She jostled Vederi's arm. "Lord Aquila is here?"

Vederi nodded, grinning. "Down in the dignitaries' box." He pointed toward the canopied structure on the opposite side of the arena, which was decorated with white flowers Rhyddes couldn't identify. "Can you see him waving?"

Barely. If not for the announcement, she wouldn't have

given the dignitaries' box a second thought. But what her eyes couldn't discern, her heart more than compensated for in its response.

Unfortunately, Aquila had no way of knowing she was here. Not yet.

She offered her guard what she hoped was her most charming smile. "Vederi, I have a huge favor to ask of you."

MARCUS COULDN'T CONCENTRATE on the games with the florid, balding prefect of Forum Iulii constantly quizzing him about life in Britannia. Not that he could blame the man, since Stator probably would never travel there.

The son of Britannia's governor wondered whether he would ever see those shores again, or a certain gorgeous, feisty Celt who had ensnared his heart.

"I crave your pardon, Lord Aquila," said another voice.

Marcus glanced from Prefect Stator to find Centurion Iustus had returned to the dignitaries' box.

The centurion thumped fist to chest. "Please forgive the interruption, my lord, but a certain contract guard insists upon speaking with you. He claims you know him."

The only men of that profession with whom Marcus was acquainted worked at Villa Britanniae. Could one of them have followed Agricola all this distance, hoping to secure a position on the governor's staff? Is so, then why wait so long before seeking an audience? And why here, of all places?

"Let him approach," said Marcus, intrigued.

The man responding to the command possessed a rugged face, graying thatch of hair and solid build Marcus knew well.

Hope ignited.

"Vederi, this is a welcome surprise." Marcus smiled an apology at his host, who was viewing the guard's intrusion with mild distaste. "Please excuse me, Prefect Stator. This good man is indeed an acquaintance of mine, and he must have an important message if he's gone to such lengths to seek me out here."

"Yes, my lord," Vederi said. "It's from—"

Marcus held up a hand and continued addressing the prefect. "Is there someplace he and I may go for privacy? I shall return soon, I assure you."

Mollified, the prefect addressed Centurion Iustus. "Show them to the Caesar Room."

Marcus probably could have found the chamber unassisted. Romans tended to use the same plans in every city, modifying the scale and materials as availability, finances and public sentiment dictated. Every amphitheater, even those built with wooden seating, as at legion outposts, featured a set of meeting chambers positioned near the dignitaries' box for the sponsor and his guests. Invariably the best one was named after Julius Caesar. Activities conducted inside the chambers varied from business transactions to sexual liaisons, and Marcus had participated in both ends of the spectrum at Londinium's arena.

But, in deference to the prefect's command, he allowed Iustus to lead the way.

This Caesar Room proved remarkable for the profusion of light cascading in from its many high, glazed windows. Beams streamed upon the low table and tall, cushioned bench seats that formed the three-sided, oaken triclinium. Although designed for diners to recline while eating, the triclinium's benches were just as comfortable if one chose to sit upright.

Murals depicting scenes from the life of Julius Caesar, the city's patron, adorned the walls. The tiled floor mosaic featured satyrs and nymphs cavorting around the god Bacchus, complete with affable smile, grapevine crown and eternally full goblet.

The aromas from a meat vendor wafted into the room, prompting Marcus's stomach to rumble. Centurion Iustus inquired whether he should arrange for refreshments, but Marcus politely declined. If Vederi's message fulfilled his hopes, he soon would be supping upon an entirely different sort of refreshment, one that had been sorely missed.

After Iustus saluted and left, shutting the door behind him, Marcus could contain his curiosity no longer. "Is she here?"

Vederi smiled. "Yes, my lord. She asked me to arrange an audience with you, if you would."

"Of course I would!" He gripped the guard's shoulder and propelled him toward the door. "Bring her here inside of ten minutes, and I'll match your salary for a month."

Vederi yanked open the door and broke into a sprint.

Marcus felt his pulse rise and his blood heat as if he were the one running.

As the minutes dragged, Rhyddes felt tempted to break her promise and try to meet Vederi farther down in the stands. But he had been adamant about her staying put, and duty would require him to report her disobedience to her owners.

Not to mention the fact that she would get herself quite lost in a thrice.

The performers disappeared through one of the arena floor's many trapdoors. Other openings appeared in the sand as men chained to posts were raised up, their faces and bodies bearing dark smears that could only be blood. Once they were set into place, rattling their chains in desperate but futile attempts to free themselves, sleek tigers charged into the arena from the tunnels. The crowd's reaction drowned out the animals' roars and the condemned men's screams.

This was another aspect of a typical day at the arena Rhyddes had never witnessed, but she couldn't watch for more than a few moments. Whatever crimes these men had committed, surely they didn't warrant being mauled to death for the viewing pleasure of forty thousand bloodthirsty Romans.

Although Rhyddes contrived to look everywhere other than the amphitheater's floor, merely imagining what must be happening to the helpless men caused the roast lamb to sour in her stomach.

A hand dropped onto her shoulder, and she jumped.

"That involved with the executions, are you?" Vederi's grin radiated pure mischief.

She rolled her eyes. "Lord Aquila…is he…I mean, does he—"

"He is, and he does." Vederi offered her a hand. "This way, Libertas. Hurry!"

Rhyddes did not need to be told twice. Nor did she heed the annoyed looks and rude remarks of other slaves as she stood and pushed past them toward the aisle.

Following Vederi's example, she bolted down the stairs

two at a time. On the level supporting the lowest seating tier, he exited the staircase, exchanged a word with a soldier who seemed to be expecting them and led Rhyddes into a wide, arched promenade that encircled the amphitheater.

In contrast to the overcrowded slaves' seating, this level boasted plenty of room. It also boasted plenty of muraled arches, carved columns and gilt trim. The refreshing tanginess of pine incense masked the stench of death wafting from the arena sands. Here men in elaborately draped togas escorted women in gaily colored gowns, though some of the women looked pale and shaken, as if the executions had violated their delicate sensibilities.

Rhyddes couldn't blame them.

And yet she found herself fantasizing about the demise of three particular Romans in the tigers' jaws.

Vederi slowed, but Rhyddes still had to stretch her stride to keep up. Seeing so many beautiful gowns, brooches, strands of pearls and elegant hairstyles made Rhyddes regret her slave's tunic and braids, and that she was not free to appear before her lover in a manner of her choosing.

Besides, what if—she chewed her lip—what if Aquila had commanded her presence only to tell her he could never see her again? Vederi's demeanor didn't indicate that possibility, but mayhap Aquila had not revealed his intentions. He would soon wed a woman worthy of his rank. In that woman's place, Rhyddes would not want her husband to bring a lover into her household, even if that lover was a slave.

Judging from the disdainful looks Rhyddes earned from the noblewomen, she could not imagine any self-respecting Roman woman tolerating such behavior in her husband, no matter how much power Roman law permitted men to wield over their families.

Dread weighted Rhyddes's feet.

Vederi glanced back, frowning. "Come, Libertas, it's not much farther."

Easy for him to say, she thought glumly as she resumed a brisker pace. He didn't have devastating news waiting for him.

HEAD IN HANDS, Marcus sat on the triclinium's center bench, staring at the mosaic tiles beneath his feet. Eighty-seven, shaded from tan to ochre, comprised Bacchus's curly hair. Octagonal purple tiles represented the grapes of his crown, thirty in all. Another fifty-two formed the god's golden goblet, with seven dark red tiles suggesting the level of wine within.

Eyes, teeth, face, hands, sandals, feet: Marcus had more than enough time to count everything thrice over, except the folds in Bacchus's voluminous white toga. He kept losing his place halfway across the god's expansive torso.

If Libertas didn't arrive soon, Marcus was going to go mad.

Resisting the urge to get down on hands and knees to better examine the mosaic, he stood and paced to one of the wall murals, a battle scene. But rather than admire the mural in its entirety, boredom drove him to inventory the details.

Ten mounted soldiers comprised Julius Caesar's personal guard; all but one wore the white sash twined around the sword belt that indicated distinguished service in prior combat. That struck Marcus as odd. Was the tenth man's lack of a sash a deliberate omission on the artist's part, or accidental?

Pounding rattled the door, startling him. Turning, he began to speak, but his throat felt dust-dry. He cleared it.

"Enter."

The door swung open. Vederi, hand on the handle, flattened himself against the door to reveal Libertas, who had been standing behind him.

Marcus drank in the glorious sight of her as a parched man quenches his thirst at a desert oasis.

Light from the promenade glinted off her coppery hair and glowing skin. Her chest was rising and falling rapidly, her full lips parted in an incredibly alluring manner.

Marcus paid Vederi with a fistful of aureii from his pouch and bade the guard to wait outside while he motioned Libertas into the chamber. Vederi, shaking the gold coins in a grateful gesture, nodded and closed the door behind him.

Shoulders slumped and gaze averted, Libertas looked like a condemned criminal, and it wrenched his heart.

AQUILA APPROACHED RHYDDES, slipped his fingers under her chin and pulled up. His compassion forced tears to her eyes, but she blinked hard.

"What is wrong?" he whispered.

"You tell me, my lord." She jerked her chin free, girding herself for the awful truth. "It's why you agreed to meet me here, isn't it?"

Aquila's eyebrows lowered. "I don't know what you mean."

"Don't you?" She folded her arms to resist the temptation to touch him and shatter her resolve. "What is going to happen to you after you reach Rome?"

"Marriage." Comprehension dawned across his face. "And you must believe I had intended to tell you that I never wanted to see you again." He stepped closer and encircled her with his arms. Tingling erupted where his flesh touched hers, and his musty scent reminded her of the wonderful night they'd shared. "My dearest Libertas," he whispered huskily, "nothing could be further from the truth."

He bent to cover her mouth with his, and she gladly welcomed his moist warmth. Inwardly she smiled upon recognizing the taste of roasted lamb—the same meal she had enjoyed only minutes before—and it ignited hunger of a wholly different sort, hunger too long unslaked. Shifting closer, she molded her body to his as their kisses escalated in fervency, and she began stroking him in the manner she knew he enjoyed.

However, before she could allow events to proceed to the conclusion they craved, a certain boast had to be resolved; otherwise, she might as well cast her lot with her sisters in the infamia class, those who brandished their bodies in bed rather than in the arena.

When Aquila left her mouth to trickle kisses across her throat, she released him and stepped back. "Will you buy me for your household?"

"What, now?" He seemed genuinely confused by her request.

"Yes! Now! My new owners are beasts!" She shook her head, fighting to regain control. "A Votadini Celt never begs, my lord. But I will tell you that if you do not buy me soon, they will—" a sigh escaped, and she couldn't quell the tremor in her chin "—they will do terrible things to me."

Grasping her chin, Aquila gazed into her eyes. "I shall not let them hurt you, Libertas." Concern and assurance radiated from him. "This I swear on the ashes of all my ancestors."

"But you won't buy me." So much for boasts. Back upon Pugionis's ship, she would be a dead woman. Unless, "You could sell me to a gladiatorial school in Rome. I wouldn't be a member of your household, but we could see each other."

Chagrin and regret twisted Aquila's expression, strangling her hopes. "My father would never allow you aboard our ship."

"Then bribe my guard to look the other way while I disappear into the crowd. Vederi could seek employment at the school here—otherwise, Pugionis and his companions would surely kill him for letting me escape. Once they leave port, I could enlist..."

And be thrust into the same sort of life all over again. What a choice. She averted her gaze.

Aquila caught her hands. "Do you know how much they would be willing to take for you?"

She uttered a rueful laugh. If he thought her slave-price had been too expensive before... "I told them you'd pay five hundred thousand."

"What! Five hun—"

"They were going to rape me! All three of them." She yanked her hands from his and wrapped her arms about herself, shivering as she gazed at nothing, powerless to prevent those awful memories from reasserting their grip. "I never expected to see you again, so I picked a ridiculously high number, one I knew their greed would hear."

Aquila enfolded her into an embrace, and she felt her heart's wild thrumming grow calmer. "It's not ridiculous, Libertas. You are priceless to me."

A fine sentiment, to be sure, but mere words couldn't solve her problem.

She regarded him frankly. "You don't have that much money, do you?"

He gave her a lopsided grin. "When I was packing for this journey, I didn't plan for acquiring the empire's best and most beautiful gladiatrix along the way."

Words, again. Fie on words! She needed action. And Aquila didn't seem willing to help her.

He may as well have cleaved her heart in twain.

Mayhap her head had been right. Mayhap he viewed her merely as the latest of his conquests. Or mayhap, her heart relentlessly asserted, she stood on the brink of committing the biggest folly of her life.

But the magnitude of Aquila's betrayal could not be ignored. Or forgiven.

"Hah. If you take me for some tavern strumpet to be pacified by a dollop of flattery, Marcus Calpurnius Aquila, then I suggest you think again." Consternation dominated his expression, but her glare granted him no quarter. "My lord."

"But, Libertas, I intended no such thing—"

"Keep your lies." She made a chopping motion with her hand. "What you don't intend to do is help me."

He expelled a noisy sigh. "I can't purchase you, if that's what you mean. But there are other ways to—"

She rolled her eyes. "Let me make myself clear. The men who own me would as soon rape and kill me as look at me. If you don't love me enough to rescue me from them, then we have nothing more to discuss."

A horrified look stole across his features. Regret almost made her change her mind.

Squaring her shoulders, she turned toward the door.

Aquila latched on to her arm and spun her around. She reared back in his grasp, but he held her firmly.

"Listen to me, Libertas. I am constrained by forces I cannot control. It is not that I don't love you enough."

"Isn't it?" she growled. "If you truly loved me, no power in heaven or earth could stop you from coming to my aid. Since that's not the case, I must conclude that I am merely a plaything to satisfy your lust."

He released her abruptly.

His silence thrust another sword into her heart. She didn't believe it could have hurt any more.

How wrong she'd been. About everything.

As Marcus watched Libertas march toward the door, obviously determined to face whatever fate awaited her, he had never felt more powerless in his life.

Could she be right? Was he using his father and his lack of funds as excuses because he did not love her in the truest, most meaningful sense?

She tugged on the heavy oaken door, struggling to open it. One voice in his head urged him to prevent her from leaving. The part of him that felt wounded by her accusation wanted to help her go. After all, that voice argued, it would be grossly unfair to his bride to enter into their marriage encumbered by emotions for another woman, however shallow those emotions might be.

At last Libertas succeeded in opening the door. After exchanging a few terse words with her guard, she left without a backward glance. The door thumped shut with lonesome finality.

If she was right, and Marcus didn't love her any more deeply than a tavern whore, then why did her departure—with another man whose concern for her had been emblazoned across his face—hurt so damned much?

**22**

RHYDDES SET A blistering pace away from that accursed chamber, pumping her arms and legs in furious rhythm as if the action could somehow erase what had happened. Whether Vederi kept up or not, she scarcely noticed. Or cared.

What a fool she was for thinking a spoiled Roman nobleman might deign to help her, a gladiatrix-slave, a dregs-of-society nobody. An utter fool.

She was worse than a fool, for she'd allowed his kisses to give her hope. Hope, and a sense that she loved him.

Gods, how futile it had been.

Not knowing whether to cry or scream, she did neither, but maintained the litany of her mental self-castigation.

After she depleted her supply of epithets for herself, she turned her attention to the gods, unleashing a stream of silent curses for allowing her to be duped by Aquila's charms.

They were no doubt enjoying a grand laugh at her expense, damn them.

Worst of all, they wouldn't let her banish his face from her mind. The flash of his smile, the music of his laughter, the enticing ruggedness of his scent, the arousing tenderness of his touch, the mind-liberating pleasures...

Gritting her teeth, she balled her hands into fists and increased her pace, veering toward the first exit not restricted to nobility. She dashed down the stairs.

"Libertas, where are you going?" asked Vederi behind her. "Don't you want to see more of the games?"

She didn't bother to look back. "I've had a bellyful of games this day. I'm returning to my wagon."

In the street, their progress was hampered by the crowds surging this way and that around the amphitheater. Vederi latched onto her arm, mayhap to keep them from becoming separated. When he halted and spun her to face him, she forced down her ire to regard him questioningly.

"Did you and Lord Aquila have a disagreement?"

The question wrenched a brittle laugh from her throat. "That would be one way to describe it." She turned to resume her course, but he wouldn't budge. "Please, Vederi. I need to get away from here."

"What's wrong, Libertas?" Concern colored his tone.

"Wrong? Oh, I don't know. Let me think." She held up a fist to count the points on her fingers. "My Da sold me into slavery, against my will. My first master trained and equipped me for arena combat, against my will. Then he sold me to other men, against my will. They assaulted me sexually, against my will, and now are dragging me off to the gods alone know where, to do the gods alone know what, against my will."

She heaved a sigh, knotting her fingers and lowering the fist. "And I fell in love, against my will, with a man who doesn't care whether I live or die," she whispered at the dusty ground.

If she cursed the gods fiercely enough, surely one of them would take umbrage and release her from this joyless existence.

Not entirely joyless. She had to admit being with Aquila had suffused her with unsurpassable contentment, however fleeting.

But it made his betrayal hurt that much worse.

"I think Lord Aquila does care about you," Vederi said. He pivoted her toward the amphitheater. "Look."

Not wanting to, but lacking the volition to refuse, she raised her head.

Pugionis, Rodo and Furcifer had emerged from the exit nearest the nobility's portal to be cornered by a glowering Aquila. Their customary smug demeanors evaporated. Whatever he was saying to them, which distance and crowd noise rendered impossible for Rhyddes to overhear, it was obvious from their nervous twitches and solicitous bows that they believed him.

Cynicism urged her not to hope he might be ordering them to leave her alone. Her pathetic heart refused to believe otherwise.

"I've seen enough, Vederi."

"You should at least speak to Lord Aquila first. Perhaps whatever transpired between you two in there—" he jerked a thumb over his shoulder, toward the arena "—was a misunderstanding."

"I misunderstood nothing." Vederi was still gripping her arm, and she placed her opposite hand atop his. "I like you, Vederi. But I would prefer it if you would confine yourself to guarding me, and stay clear of my personal affairs." She removed his hand from her arm.

He inclined his head. "As you wish." They began threading through the crowd heading out of the city. "All I know is that I've seen you happy with Lord Aquila before, and I was hoping he might make you happy again today. The gods know you have precious little happiness in your life."

The gods knew, indeed, and they cared naught for her plight. But her heart clung tenaciously to the fragile hope that she and Aquila might find happiness together someday. Cynicism condemned her for harboring the vain fantasy, and on some level she agreed. Aquila would marry the senator's daughter and become a high-and-mighty politician, and Rhyddes one day would falter in combat and be executed. End of story.

Yet the grain of hope refused to die.

MARCUS GRASPED THE rigging and rested his cheek against his forearm, bracing his other hand on the ship's rail, even though the past few weeks had bequeathed him with sturdy sea legs. Facing portside, he could glimpse the vessel carrying Libertas and the other gladiators who once had belonged to Jamil as it nosed into the harbor on the evening tide, blessed with a fair following breeze.

Agricola's ship wasn't scheduled to leave until the morning. Finding Libertas in or near Rome would become more difficult as the gap between their arrivals widened.

Earnestly Marcus hoped he'd done the right thing for her. Gods, he hoped it would be enough.

"Come below for supper, dear."

"I'm not hungry, Mother."

Loreia, approaching him from behind, claimed a place at the rail to his right. The sun had slipped behind the hills facing them, and as the sunlight faded, bright pinpoints from torches and braziers winked on throughout the town. The amphitheater became a veritable beacon as slaves lit thousands of torches for the benefit of spectators and gladiators alike. Now and then a roaring cheer went up, doubtless because someone had struck a worthy blow.

"It's not like you to return early from the games."

Marcus grunted, unwilling to either affirm or deny her observation.

"Such a lovely view from here," Loreia said.

Indeed. But it would be lovelier with someone else gracing his line of sight. Someone who seemed to want nothing more to do with him.

"What?"

Marcus looked at his mother and grimaced. Had he uttered his thoughts aloud? He had no earthly idea. "I'm sorry, Mother. I have…something else on my mind."

She smiled the maddeningly knowing smile that seemed to be the special province of motherhood. "Some*one* else, you mean." Her expression sobered. "And it's not your bride."

Experience had taught him that he might deceive his father, but never his mother. He sighed, closing his eyes, and conjured an image that couldn't go away. Nor did he wish it would. "Libertas."

"I thought as much." Lightly she touched his arm, and he looked at her. "You love this woman, don't you?" It sounded less like a question than a statement of fact. A fact that didn't seem to upset his mother, as he'd fully expected it to, which puzzled him.

"I don't know. She claims I don't, but—"

"Why would she say that, Son? What did you do to her?"

He laughed mirthlessly. "It's what I didn't do that seemed to infuriate her." His mother's arched eyebrow invited him to continue. "Libertas wanted me to buy her, but I knew you and Father and Messiena and Falco would be wroth with me. So I refused."

Loreia nodded once, whether in agreement with Marcus's assessment or not, he couldn't be certain. "Why would she insist that you purchase her? Is she that enamored of you? Or did she see you as a means to escape the arena, perhaps?"

"No. Maybe." He shook his head, feeling more confused—gods, downright lost—than ever. "I don't know. She doesn't like her new owners. She says they are…" He sifted his vocabulary for a word that wouldn't offend his mother. "They are unkind to her."

"They abuse her—sexually, no doubt—and you wouldn't remove her from that deplorable situation?" Although Loreia kept her voice low, her disapproval rang clear. "Perhaps she's right—you mustn't love her very much."

"But I do!"

Marcus clamped his jaw shut. He'd never intended to reveal even half that much. But it was no use reprimanding himself; his mother had always possessed a knack for worming information out of whomever she chose. It was a wonder Agricola never used her as an interrogator.

Too late to withhold anything else, he decided to relate the entire story, concluding with, "I did arrange for her owners to leave her alone."

"Bribery?"

"In a manner of speaking." Marcus grinned, reveling in the satisfying memory. "I made it worth their while, but I also made certain they understood what I would do to them if they renege on their end of the deal. Libertas should be safe."

"Does she know what you've done for her?"

Marcus shrugged. "I thought I saw her and her guard in the crowd outside the amphitheater, but by the time I reached their position, they were gone." Ruthlessly he suppressed the frustration that threatened to erupt anew. "Does it matter so much whether she knows?"

Loreia gracefully twitched one shoulder in response. "Not if she truly loves you. What do you plan to do once we reach Rome?"

"My head wants to do what is right and honorable for Messiena. Father would see my head on a pike if I don't." Marcus's breath caught in his throat, and he swallowed hard. "But my heart feels like a quagmire. I'm being sucked in, and struggling only makes me sink that much faster."

Loreia's light laugh tinkled like wind chimes. "Cupid will do that to a person, Son."

"Then you're not angry with me? If I were to renounce all that wealth and power—"

"Every mother wants what is best for her children. And I do enjoy the wealth and status that marriage to your father gives me." Marcus noted her substitution of "status" for "power" but made no comment. "But sometimes what is best cannot be measured on a banker's scales. A sack of gold makes for a poor bed companion." Loreia sighed, and he wondered what she was thinking. Before he could voice the question, she regarded him shrewdly. "I could be angry with you, Son, if you think that would help."

He only partially appreciated the jest. "Mother, I honestly don't know what would help anymore."

"Find Libertas. Talk to her. Resolve the misunderstanding that lies between you. Then see where your heart leads." She gave a conspiratorial smile. "Just, for the gods' sakes, don't tell your father."

"No worries there, Mother." He gave her a thankful peck on the cheek. The aroma of grilled swordfish wafted up from the galley, and his stomach complained. "I do believe I'm ready for supper now."

RHYDDES THOUGHT THE sea travel she'd already endured would have hardened her stomach, but as soon as the vessel encountered the swells outside Forum Iulii's harbor, her seasickness returned with a vengeance. So did her moon-courses.

Mayhap, she mused grimly between colliding waves of nausea and cramps, this was the gods' way of punishing her blasphemy without granting her the favor of death.

But if they sought her repentance, she wasn't about to yield it to them. Not while producing more vile-smelling bodily matter than any person decently ought to possess.

The advantage to her wretched state was that everyone avoided her, especially her owners, which would have been unprecedented luxury had she felt well enough to appreciate it. The chief disadvantage, physical discomfort aside, lay in the frustrating fact that she couldn't stop thinking about Aquila.

The harder she tried, the more persistently his memory intruded.

It had to be another facet of the gods' punishment.

She didn't mind reliving their argument, for it kindled her anger, and anger held her symptoms at bay. But as the symptoms subsided, her mind, no doubt encouraged by her heart, slipped back to the pleasurable moments she and Aquila had shared. Not just their lovemaking, but the times they had sparred with blunted weapons rather than words.

Even the banquet she'd attended before her first match, when she'd felt more nervous than a fat mouse among a clowder of starving cats, had become a cherished memory.

Facedown on her narrow bunk, head pillowed on her arm and running a fingertip slowly across the roughly hewn planks of the bunk's frame, she marveled at that. She recalled her unease at being thrust into close proximity with so many Roman nobles, the banquet's host in particular, as if it had occurred only yesterday.

And yet she wouldn't have traded that memory for anything, even her freedom.

She shook her head, trying to tell herself the welling tears stemmed from the onset of another cramp.

Her heart decried the lie.

SENATOR FALCO SOAKED in the lavender-scented waters of his bathhouse, reviewing the status of his plans. Most of the newly purchased gladiators already had been spread through-out the city's four gladiatorial schools. That was the good news.

The bad news was that, thus far, no Praetorian Guard prefects had been recruited to the cause. Falco could hire other men for this facet of his plan, but it would severely diminish his chances for success. Praetorian prefects—even just one man—would guarantee it.

Sighing, he closed his eyes and submerged all but his face.

"Good day, Falco."

The water covering Falco's ears distorted the other man's voice, but Falco recognized it and raised his head to greet his guest.

"I thank you for coming, Ferox."

The wiry little man with cunning eyes and an aggressive chin shed his towels to step into the pool. "And I thank you for inviting me." His smile turned pointed. "What favor do you desire from your greatest political rival?"

Falco gave a mock death cough, tapping his fist to his chest. "Can I not simply invite my neighbor into my home as a gesture of friendship?"

Ferox laughed. "There is nothing simple about you." His eyes narrowed as he leaned closer to Falco. "And some men would use the term 'friendship' euphemistically for 'support.' So, what cause would you like me to consider supporting this time?"

"Cutting straight to the heart of the matter, as ever," Falco said. "I shouldn't have expected any less from you."

Ferox thinned his lips in the barest of smiles. "And the cause?" he pressed.

Falco watched the ripples radiating outward from his shrug. "First let us chat about our emperors' decision to divert more money toward foreign wars than domestic affairs."

"What's to discuss? Rome needs to secure her borders and interests. Marcus Aurelius and Lucius Verus are doing all they can to secure both."

"Ah, but is it enough, do you think?"

"It shall have to be," Ferox replied. "They are the only emperors we have."

Not necessarily, Falco thought. "You cannot tell me you don't harbor dreams of wearing the purple."

"I have no imperial aspirations, Falco. Having to deal with you and the other senators gives me more than enough headaches." Though Ferox's smile seemed engineered to remove the harshness from his words, Falco heard it anyway.

Swallowing his umbrage, he asked, "What if someone else could be proven to be a better leader?"

Ferox fixed him with a level stare. "Who would be idiotic enough to challenge men appointed and ordained by the gods?"

Falco forced a laugh. "No one I know," he lied. Silently thanking those same gods for confirming a potential enemy, he extended a hand. "Come, neighbor. Let us take the cold plunge."

In an attempt to lull Ferox into forgetting what they'd discussed, though not expecting the tactic to work, Falco turned the conversation toward benign matters. After they had finished in the frigidarium, dressed and Ferox took his leave, Falco was strolling back toward the main house when one of his guards approached him and saluted.

"Senator, a man awaits you in your study, Darius Caepio by name. He claims you invited him."

Odd; Falco couldn't recall extending that particular invitation. Unless…

"Tell him I'll be there presently."

As the guard departed, Falco smiled to himself. If this Darius Caepio proved to be who Falco suspected he was, his day had just taken a turn for the better.

He proceeded through the redolent gardens to his study. The man who jumped to his feet in response to Falco's arrival sported more gray hair than Falco would have preferred, but his muscular body and taut bearing lent credence to Falco's guess.

"Darius Caepio. A prefect of the Praetorian Guard, I presume?"

The man gave a sharp nod. "Ten years ago, my lord."

"How long have you served in the army?"

"Twenty-three years."

Falco didn't permit his disappointment to show. If this man was whom the gods had sent, he would have to make the best of their boon. "Then you must be retired."

"Only a few weeks ago, my lord, just before I left Britannia to travel here."

"Britannia? Did you command the Twentieth Legion?"

"No, sir. I was the tribune appointed as Governor Agricola's chief of staff."

Of course. Falco remembered him now. And his presence offered an interesting development.

"I think you might be useful to me. I am prepared to give you a sum I believe you will find more than adequate, but only upon fulfillment of certain conditions." He bade the former Praetorian Guard prefect to be seated. After Falco made himself comfortable in his cushioned chair, he propped his elbows on his desktop and pressed his palms together. "Now, then, Darius, as a Praetorian guardsman, I presume you were called upon to perform assassinations?"

Darius seemed taken aback by the question but quickly recovered his composure. "Yes, my lord, though an oath of secrecy binds me—"

Falco waved him into silence. "I don't care who was involved. I only require you to prove how much of this training you recall." He selected a quill and dipped it in the ink pot. On a scrap of parchment he scratched the letter *M* and held it up for Darius to see. "I will give you this much now, and you can collect ten times that amount upon completing your test to my satisfaction."

"And how much do you intend to pay me for the next assignment, my lord?"

The man's daring won him a smile. "If you succeed with that task, we shall conclude these negotiations." Falco quenched the smile. "If you fail, then you shall have no further need of money. Do I make myself clear?"

"Perfectly, my lord."

It took all of Falco's willpower not to stare agape at the man. Darius had to possess balls of iron not to appear disturbed by Falco's implied threat—but, then, Praetorian guardsmen were selected for their fortitude.

After his latest recruit departed, the emperor-to-be luxuriated in a long moment of private rejoicing.

## 23

By MORNING OF the third day at sea, the vessel's rolling motion eased. Rhyddes woke to the clamor of feet pounding across the deck above, accompanied by the shouted commands and responses she'd learned to associate with the ship entering a harbor. She rolled over and sat up, assessing her condition. Her nausea and cramps had abated, and she blessed the unknown crewman who'd swabbed the filth from her quarters as she slept.

Two days of being confined to a bunk, barely able to hold down watered wine, had left her unsteady on her feet but doubly determined to reenter the land of the living. She donned clean undergarments, a tunic, breeches and sandals. Feeling almost human again, though obliged to support herself against bulkheads, rails and her brother gladiators, who greeted her warmly, she made her tottering way topside.

She found Vederi gazing toward the sprawling port

heaving into view before them. He favored her with a welcoming smile.

"My, don't you look like the pile of bones left over from Cerberus's lunch," he teased.

"And you must have been his dinner," she shot back.

With a nod and a chuckle, he broke a sizable piece from a crusty loaf. "It helps to settle the stomach." After she accepted the offering, he patted the bloated wineskin dangling from a leather thong looped over his shoulder. "Especially when you chase a mouthful of bread with a swig of this."

To her amazement, she felt hungry enough to devour the deck timbers. When sniffing the bread didn't make her stomach balk, she gnawed off a piece, chewed, swallowed and waited. Satisfied she wasn't going to see it again, she took a long drink. Though watered to half its potency, the wine tasted refreshingly cool and tart.

"Ostia?" she asked Vederi, swiping crumbs from her mouth and gesturing toward the port.

He gave a grunt Rhyddes took as *aye*. "I hear tell this city is far cleaner and more affluent than Rome because of the rich merchants living there."

Rhyddes could well believe it, judging from the immense barges headed into or away from the man-made octagonal harbor, pushed by fleets of tiny boats and laden with the gods alone knew what manner of goods, livestock or slaves. The vessel upon which she sailed—no runt because it had to bear a hundred gladiators, their guards, trainers, physicians, cooks, drudges and owners, and all the attendant baggage, wagons, beasts and supplies, in addition to the crew—seemed hopelessly dwarfed in comparison.

Swifter craft, flying the imperial standard indicating they carried diplomats or couriers, darted between the giants and sped toward the docks. Military ships, easily identified by their double or triple sets of oars, in addition to the soldiers bristling across the decks, plied the open seas outside the harbor's mouth, challenging all who would approach the port servicing the mightiest city of the mightiest empire on earth.

In spite of how Rhyddes felt about that empire, she couldn't wait to disembark.

Due to the long line of arrivals, however, workmen walking briskly along the canal's banks easily outpaced the vessels. With the sun beating ceaselessly upon her, their exertion made Rhyddes sweat just watching them. She found a shaded spot between two stacks of crates, with Vederi lingering nearby, and settled in for the duration.

FALCO COULDN'T BELIEVE what he was reading. "What's the meaning of this?" He rattled the parchment leaf.

The messenger bowed deeply. "I am but a hired courier, my lord. I know nothing of the contents of what I am commissioned to deliver."

Grunting, Falco reached for parchment, ink and quill. "Wait outside, then, while I write a response for you to take back."

"I think that would be rather difficult, Papa."

Falco glanced up as Messiena sailed into his study, looking every inch like her dear mother in beauty and bearing. Tendrils of Antonia's favorite gardenia-scented perfume wafted toward him, and he had to remind himself to stay angry.

"What do you know of this? Last I heard, messages between citizens were private." He glared at his daughter.

"They still are, Papa." Messiena advanced close enough to plant a kiss on Falco's cheek. "When I heard that good Velox—" she aimed a smile in the courier's direction "—had arrived from Ostia, I made a guess about the message he carried." She backed away and turned a graceful circle, showing off her lovely green gown that fairly dripped with ropes of seed pearls. "Do you think Marcus will like this?"

"Any man would be a fool not to," Falco had to admit. "But how did you know about—"

"Don't you remember, Papa? I invited my bridegroom and his parents at your request. You just never specified when they ought to arrive."

"You what?" Falco snapped. Velox, looking decidedly uncomfortable, began inching toward the door. Falco dismissed the courier with an impatient nod. The door thudded shut behind him. "Explain yourself, Daughter."

"My wedding is less than a month away! Or had you forgotten?" For a moment it looked as if she would burst into tears, but she clenched her jaw. "If I hadn't taken the initiative to ask the Calpurniae to come at once—as was my right as mistress of this household—they would still be in Britannia, and there wouldn't be a wedding next month. You've been so busy I doubt you've paid attention to anyone other than your business and Senate associates."

During her tirade, Falco wondered when his daughter had reached womanhood. Ire transformed most women into harpies; Messiena looked radiant. And she was right. He had been so intent on shepherding his plans into reality that he had not attended to any other issues, her wedding included.

Especially her wedding.

And yet she was his only child, his dearest treasure ever since the day Antonia departed this world to join the gods. As Messiena stood, aglow with innocence and hope, Falco found it impossible to remain angry. His daughter's well-intentioned but bothersome action could be mitigated easily enough. He dipped the quill into the ink pot and tapped the excess against the rim.

"Very well. Agricola and his family are welcome to stay at our villa outside Ostia until your wedding day." The last thing he needed was future in-laws underfoot before certain events could transpire. "They shall be well cared for, never fear."

"Why, when we can care for them just as well here?" she cried, waving her arms about like a gale-stricken cypress. "Everything is in perfect readiness for them."

He couldn't argue with that. No wonder Messiena had seemed so obsessive about the appearance of their home, ordering new draperies, table linens and other furnishings, commanding that the marble floors, columns and statuary should be buffed to glistening perfection, bedecking the slaves in new clothing and decorating with flowers and greenery everything that didn't move.

"Be reasonable, Daughter. In Ostia your betrothed and his parents shall enjoy every convenience, every comfort—"

She lowered her hands to grip the edges of his desk. "No, I ask you to be reasonable, Papa. I have not seen my bridegroom in a year. We must become better acquainted before we wed. We cannot accomplish that from two different cities."

"And I am trying to safeguard your virtue."

"My virtue!" Her eyes glittered coldly. "Does my esteemed father believe his daughter to be no better than a whore?"

Falco sighed. "No, Pulla." His use of her childhood nickname pulled his lips into a sad smile upon realizing he ought never to call her that once she became a proper matron. "But every father worries about his children." He rose to take her into his arms, remembering a time not so long ago when he would have picked her up to embrace her thus. "We especially worry about our daughters."

"No Ostia, then, Papa?" She grinned mischievously.

How women learned to manipulate men so easily, Falco would never fathom. They probably passed the secret from mother to daughter. He kissed the top of Messiena's raven head. "No Ostia," he affirmed against his better judgment.

"That's fortunate," she murmured, "because I've received a message from Lady Loreia. Their party shall arrive within the hour."

If Falco didn't love his daughter so much, he'd have throttled her then and there.

Though he wasn't a religious man, he offered a hasty but heartfelt petition that everything would proceed as planned.

After all, he boldly reminded the gods, his beloved Messiena and her beloved Marcus—as well as the entire empire—stood to benefit from Falco's success.

THE SUN HAD REACHED its merciless zenith by the time Rhyddes's ship slid into its berth. The ship's master ordered the crew to start unloading everything, which seemed odd because Rhyddes couldn't see much hope of them completing the task before nightfall.

Pugionis, Furcifer and Rodo were too busy overseeing the proceedings to pay Rhyddes any heed, nor did she feel inclined to attract their attention. After she retrieved her meager sack of possessions from her bunk, she located Vederi to ask him what was happening.

"Our arrival was timed so we can drive our wagons straight to the gladiatorial school. Rome is so crowded, wheeled traffic is permitted only after sundown," he replied. "I overheard the ship's master speaking to Pugionis, who was worried until the captain assured him they were on schedule."

Rhyddes stroked her chin. "Why would my owner care when we arrived in Rome? He never seemed concerned before."

Vederi chuckled. "He doesn't complain to the gladiators."

"But what's the hurry? Is there some event scheduled that I haven't heard about?"

He gave her a surprised look. "Pugionis and his companions have been scouring the empire for a year. Word is that Jamil's gladiators represent the last of the thousand they were commissioned to acquire. All of you, along with another thousand, are slated to compete in a month-long series of games in honor of Emperor Marcus Aurelius's son, Commodus, commencing on the prince's natal day, the nones of August."

A high honor indeed. But... "That's in, what? A week?"

Vederi shook his head. "Travel has distorted your time sense, Libertas. The games start two days hence."

She shouldered her sack and took her place in line behind the other gladiators trudging toward the gangplank and the wagons awaiting them beyond the docks.

*Two days.*

Small wonder Pugionis had expressed concern. Rhyddes wasn't the only warrior to fall prey to sea-induced illness, and 'twould be a miracle if she and her gladiator-brethren recovered sufficiently to perform at their best for the empire's most exalted sponsor.

Her gut's twisting had naught to do with seasickness.

THE PROCESSION WOUND its way through the bustling streets of Rome: three litters, each with one occupant and four bearers, plus guards and servants ranging ahead, around and behind to ensure the crowds didn't press too closely.

Marcus felt ridiculous, jolting along inside the third litter like an old aristocrat grown too fat to remember how to use his legs. If Londinium was remote, it had the virtue of being compact, and Marcus had disdained litter travel in favor of foot or horse.

But the city at the heart of the world's greatest nation sprawled forever in all directions, and visitors had no choice but to sojourn through the poorest districts to reach the most affluent ones, praying no one tried to molest them along the way.

Some streets were safer than others, and the local litter bearers Agricola had hired kept to a course that led through more public areas than apartment blocks. Still, Marcus had to wonder how his mother, riding in the middle litter, felt about traveling among the poorest of the poor, such as those souls relegated to a life of burying the dead or hauling off the city's mountains of refuse. She gave no clues, for her litter's red-and-yellow-striped canvas curtains remained closed.

Marcus's curiosity prompted him to observe the sur-roundings: people strolling into shops and staggering out under loads of parcels, children and animals scurrying about seemingly at random, holy men prophesying from street corners, musicians plying their trade for passersby, vendors dispensing all manner of aromatic food and drink from their handcarts, and a legion of beggars suffering from a wide array of ills, whether real or feigned.

"I wish I could do something for them," he said to Jamil, who held his mount to the pace of Marcus's litter as they passed what appeared to be four generations of a family eking out an existence on the street.

"If you give to one, all will expect something," Jamil replied. "It is no different here than in Egypt."

Perhaps following his father to become a politician wouldn't be such a bad idea, Marcus mused, for then he might be able to effect lasting changes in the plight of these unfortunate people. His alliance, through marriage, with one of Rome's most influential senators would be a critical step in attaining this goal.

But he couldn't escape the fact that he didn't want a woman who could bestow earthly power. He wanted the one woman who could empower his soul.

The intersection of the road that ran past Circus Maximus gave Marcus an idea, and he beckoned Jamil closer.

"Find her," Marcus said.

Jamil thumped fist to chest and wheeled his mount out of the formation.

The view grew more genteel as they climbed Esquiline Hill toward Falco's estate. The reeking apartment complexes that had defined the lower city gave way to tidy single-family homes which became steadily larger and more opulently decorated with the increasing altitude, culminating in the majestic Temple of Venus and Rome. Stone-pine trees, famous for their cones' fragrance when burned for incense and especially popular for masking the stench of blood inside temples and amphitheaters, shaded the cobbled avenue with their wide, flat canopies.

Stone pines, perhaps imported from this very district, ringed Londinium's amphitheater. These distinctive trees reminded Marcus of Libertas.

Gods, how he missed her!

With no small effort he submerged those feelings, for the time to greet his bride was finally at hand.

·He felt like a condemned criminal greeting his cross but quickly shook off that sensation. Messiena had done nothing to deserve it. Perhaps, in time, affection would come.

And perhaps he would sprout wings and fly back to Britannia.

MESSIENA HARBORED A FLOCK of butterflies in her stomach. It had to be true; she could feel their wings beating as surely as if she'd swallowed each one whole. Her maids' tittering and giggling, as they freshened her face paint and tugged her stola this way and that to improve the drape, didn't help.

Marcus had finally arrived.

Would he like the way she looked? The way the mansion and grounds looked? Would he like the gift she had made for him, stroke by loving brushstroke?

Would he like her?

Messiena felt so nervous she wanted to spew.

When she could tolerate her maids' attentions no longer, she halted the proceedings with two sharp claps. The women with other assigned duties curtsied and scurried off. Messiena commanded Agna to pick up Marcus's gift, carefully swathed in linen to protect it from unappreciative eyes as much as from the unforgiving sun. Messiena ordered the other women to accompany her, too, as she forced herself to adopt the stately pace her mother had taught her.

They stepped outside and wound their way through the maze of garden paths, Messiena's heart cavorting with the swallows swooping and diving overhead.

Past the cypress hedge, she saw her Adonis, who was every inch as handsome as she'd remembered, and more. His toga scarcely concealed his broad chest and powerful arms. Her lips went dry, and she moistened them, loathe to let him see her at anything less than her best.

His mother was seated on the shaded side of the fountain's edge, trailing a hand in the pool and attracting the curious carp while the men stood upwind of the spray, chatting amicably.

Before anyone noticed Messiena's presence, she hushed her attendants and paused to study her father. Falco seemed to have taken the arrival of the Calpurniae with his customary aplomb, which heartened her. He might not have agreed with her decision to invite them when she did, but surely he had to recognize the rightness of it.

Swallowing thickly, and schooling her face into a welcoming smile, she glided forward, trailed by her maids. Their giggling drew everyone's attention.

The governor and his wife greeted Messiena warmly, but

she had eyes only for her bridegroom. As she approached him, extending her hand for him to grasp, his smile seemed distant and tinted with a hint of...*regret?*

She discreetly tossed her head to dispel the disturbing notion. Surely he was only fatigued from such a long journey.

Marcus bowed over her hand and kissed it, sending her heart into throes of delight. It was all she could do to keep from collapsing into a dithering puddle at his feet.

"Welcome to our home, Marcus," she murmured. With effort she tore her gaze from his alluring form to address his parents. "And of course you, as well, Governor Agricola and Lady Loreia. I have instructed the staff to meet your every need." She couldn't resist fluttering her lashes at her bridegroom. "And desire."

Marcus colored and cleared his throat, straightening to his full height. "I have brought you a gift, Messiena." He signaled one of their slaves to step forward.

"Mine first." She ordered Agna to unwrap the parcel.

The painted image of Marcus as a gladiator stood before them in all his bronzed, muscular glory.

"Oh, my," Loreia said. "What an amazing likeness. And all without having the subject to pose for you. Well done, my dear."

"Indeed," Falco stated approvingly. "I never realized my daughter was so talented."

She flashed him a grateful smile before addressing Marcus. "Do you like it, my betrothed?"

Again regret stole across his face, though he tried to mask it with a bow, fist to chest. "My wife-to-be bestows upon me great honor. I hope I shall prove worthy of it."

Before she could question his strange statement, he ordered his slave to present her with a small box fashioned of aromatic cedar and tied with a sun-colored ribbon. She slipped off the ribbon to open the smoothly planed box. Inside lay a necklace of the same hue as the ribbon, warmly translucent and peppered with black flecks.

"I love it!" She looped a finger through the strand and held it up for all to admire, marveling at its lightness. "Marcus, would you please fasten it around my neck?"

Nodding, he took it from her, unhitched the clasp, stepped behind her and laid the necklace gently in place. When he was finished closing the clasp, he leaned closer to whisper, "A beautiful necklace for a beautiful lady."

More than anything Messiena wanted to believe in the sincerity of his flattering words, but a nagging voice cautioned her that all might not be as it seemed with her betrothed.

However, she wasn't a senator's daughter for naught. If Marcus was harboring a secret, she would use every resource at her disposal to uncover it, as much for his sake as hers.

**24**

JAMIL HUNKERED OVER his mediocre wine in the smoky tavern's darkest corner, observing the influx of customers but not expecting any to be of use to him. His backside ached as if he'd ridden over every square inch of this infernal city, which he damn near had done, to no avail. He'd stabled his mount at Falco's estate and ended his futile journey at this establishment near the Praetorian Corps barracks.

Ownership had passed from father to son during Jamil's absence, the painted murals appeared as worn as Jamil felt, and the greasy food and sour drink hadn't improved, but apparently the tavern was still a favorite among guardsmen.

Even when a man was garbed in a plain tunic and equally plain sandals, Jamil could pick a guardsman out of the crowd by the square jaw and shoulders, closely cropped hair, rigid posture and alert demeanor bordering on the suspicious.

Many fit that description here, but none came close to being the man he sought.

A ten-year absence had made Jamil all but a stranger to this city. He could make his way around easily enough; the monuments, temples, baths, forums and other public buildings had aged noticeably but hadn't moved. The people Jamil had known here, however, had—either away from the city, or on to the afterlife.

The old tavern keeper headed the list, and Jamil was surprised to find himself missing him acutely. He'd hoped to pump Bacifer for information, as on many a past occasion, but the man had joined his ancestors several years earlier. Bacifer's son, Vilicus, had eyed Jamil with open curiosity, perhaps recalling Jamil's frequent visits to the tavern when Vilicus was a boy. But Vilicus had been unable or, more likely, unwilling to further Jamil's present cause.

Jamil took another swig. The wine burned all the way down, a fitting tribute to the shambles of his life.

What a fool he had been for allowing himself to grow so soft, so far removed from his earlier training. So useless. If his fellow guardsmen could see him today, they'd laugh him into the street.

One fleeting glimpse of Libertas would set his world to rights again, yet the gods had seen fit to deny him even that modest boon.

Earlier today, claiming to represent a wealthy patron looking for warrior-women to participate in a private combat event, Jamil had convinced the lanistae at each of Rome's four gladiatorial schools to parade their female performers before him.

None had come remotely close to Libertas in poise, skill or beauty.

Jamil did manage to extract a promise from each lanista to inform him, at Senator Falco's mansion, if new women arrived within the next few days, especially any answering to the name "Libertas," but he didn't hold much hope. The buzz in the streets centered upon the two thousand gladiators set to compete in the thirty-day celebration of Prince Commodus's natal day, commencing two days hence, and as far as anyone knew, all the combatants had arrived already.

"Libertas, where are you?" he whispered into his cup. Jamil had quit asking the gods. They probably had grown deaf from his constant petitions.

Or perhaps they were just slow in answering. Jamil looked toward the door to see a face that had become combat-furrowed in a decade, but the eyes' sharp blue sparkle hadn't dimmed.

"Hail, Caesius!" As the officer glanced about, Jamil waved.

Caesius stared, blinked, stared again, grinned and strode to Jamil's table. "Good to see you again, sir!"

Jamil shook his head in mild protest but couldn't help feeling pleased that habits among soldiers died hard. Caesius had been a recruit under Jamil's command in Judea, too many years ago to count. Jamil motioned to the empty seat.

"And look at you." Smiling proudly, Jamil eyed Caesius's black uniform, with its distinctive red sash, as Caesius sat. "Prefect of the Praetorian Guard, no less. Who would have thought a rawboned pup could have risen so high, so fast?"

Concern creased Caesius's brow. "Take the post if you want it, Kalil."

Jamil lowered his voice. "Trouble?"

"Payroll has been delayed," he whispered, "again."

"Why? Has his majesty been distracted?"

"Prince Commodus lay gravely ill last month. But he seems to have made a full recovery." Caesius scratched his cleft chin and shrugged. "Our pay was diverted to the front, or so we were told. Morale is plummeting. It'll sink even further if I must forbid my men from visiting places such as this until the emperor decides we're important enough to pay, too."

Jamil's eyes widened at Caesius's dangerous but desperate words. "Your duty lies with the gods-ordained men you have sworn to protect," he admonished, as if lecturing the recruit.

Caesius sighed and dropped his gaze to the tabletop stained by decades of spilled food, drink and blood. "I know, sir." When he lifted his head, Jamil saw the plea. "My sword, my heart and my soul belong to Emperors Marcus Aurelius and Lucius Verus." Jamil believed him. "But I don't know how long that will remain true for my men."

"If you're so worried about them, why are you here and not at the barracks?"

"That is precisely what brings me here. Trying to make sure they stay out of…trouble." Trouble in more forms than could usually be had inside a tavern, if Jamil correctly read Caesius's grimace. The prefect returned his attention to the tavern's door, which had opened to admit more customers, mostly of the Praetorian variety. Several cast guarded glances at Caesius before choosing the farthest available seats. "By the way, Kalil, you're not the only retired guardsman to have appeared here in the past few days."

Jamil sharpened his interest while trying not to seem too interested. "Indeed. Anyone I might know?"

"Darius Caepio. I don't know if you knew him."

"Our postings overlapped by a month or two," Jamil said blandly to mask his rising excitement. "But an acquaintance is still an acquaintance, and this seems to be my night for renewing them." He hoped.

"May Fortuna bless you, then, Kalil Al-Omar." Caesius rose, and so did Jamil. As they gripped forearms, the prefect leaned closer. "If you see or hear anything interesting, sir, would you mind letting me know? My presence may discourage certain activities, but yours won't."

"Of course, Caesius. As long as it doesn't conflict with my duties."

Caesius smiled and left the tavern. Jamil could have sworn the conversations between other customers doubled in volume the moment the door swung shut behind the prefect.

Duties to Agricola, Aquila, Libertas…and now his former subordinate. Jamil sat again, wondering when his life had become so complicated.

He had drained the dregs of his wine and was preparing to leave when the tapestry of his life knotted again.

"Kalil? You old Egyptian jackal, can that really be you?"

Inwardly, Jamil cringed but disciplined his face into a wary smile as he glanced up.

Kynthos, a Greek-born former Praetorian guardsman who'd earned his retirement and citizenship at the same time as Jamil, grinned in that ingratiating and faintly insincere way Jamil remembered so well. Of all the people he'd known, Kynthos was the last man he'd have ever sought out.

"Oh, come now." Uninvited, and cheerfully oblivious to the fact, Kynthos grasped the chair Caesius had occupied, turned it backward and straddled the seat, folding tanned forearms across the chair's back. Jamil noticed with an envious twinge that although Kynthos's obsidian hair had faded to pepper-gray, his body appeared trim and fit. "You cannot still be steaming over that harmless jest I pulled on you all those years ago."

"Which one?" Jamil muttered. He tipped the last drops of wine into his mouth. To deal with Kynthos, he needed all the fortification he could muster.

"The stables, of course."

Jamil grunted humorlessly. "If you call getting pushed into the manure pit moments before inspection was due to begin 'harmless,' then spare me your definition of harmful." He flexed his shoulders, feeling the skin stretch around the old flogging scars. Their unit's centurion had refused to believe that Jamil didn't provoke the incident, choosing instead to punish both men.

If Kynthos recalled the painful consequences, he didn't show it. The Greek laughed, signaling for service. An attractive and very pregnant young woman, probably Vilicus's wife, stepped over from an adjacent table. To Jamil, Kynthos said, "Please permit me to make it up to you, my friend," and proceeded to order a pitcher of the house's best wine. He produced a newly minted denarius from his pouch and pressed it into the woman's hand.

She bowed, smiling—as well she ought, for the payment was five times the usual amount—and hurried off as fast as her advanced condition would allow.

"The house's best, eh?" Jamil didn't bother to lower his voice. "You never could afford that before. Or to be so generous a patron."

Again Kynthos bared his teeth in that ingratiating grin. "I'd never been blessed with the right opportunity."

A warning bell clanged in Jamil's brain. "The right opportunity?"

Kynthos opened his mouth as if to speak, but the woman bustled back to the table carrying a brimming pitcher and a cup. She poured a small measure and handed the cup to Kynthos. He sipped, savored it on his tongue, swallowed and announced his approval. The woman filled both men's cups, exchanged the full pitcher for Jamil's empty one, bowed again and left.

"A decent vintage," Jamil agreed after swallowing a mouthful. It certainly outclassed the vinegar he'd been swilling. He saluted Kynthos with his cup. "I thank you." He refrained from mentioning that he could not have afforded even this modest pleasure without imposing upon Aquila's generosity.

"What brings you back, Kalil?" Kynthos drained his cup and refilled it. "You must have repaid that hideous debt."

Jamil grunted, nodding. "And what about you? I'd have thought some soldier would have slit your throat for one of your 'harmless' pranks by now."

Kynthos slapped Jamil's shoulder. "That's my friend Kalil. Always the teaser." Seriousness dropped over his face like a veil, and he scooted his chair close enough that Jamil could smell wine, lamb and onions on his breath. "I have been commissioned to perform a task for someone who walks in exalted circles, and he's looking for more men like me—and you."

"Me?" Jamil wondered if he looked as skeptical as he felt.

"Indeed," Kynthos whispered. "Our esteemed emperors have overextended themselves with these endless frontier wars. Marcus Aurelius has presumed heavily upon his guardsmen's loyalty and has delayed payroll distribution indefinitely. Disaffection is swelling. My patron is recruiting former guardsmen to circulate among them at places such as this and—you may have trouble believing me, but I swear it's the truth—reminisce about what life in the corps used to be like."

Since he'd heard the story's obverse from Caesius, believing Kynthos was not the issue. But, "Reminisce?" Jamil shook his head in bewilderment. "For what purpose? Surely that can only make the situation worse."

"Not if my patron gains power enough to implement changes."

"Bah. For that he would need to be…" Jamil's tongue stilled as the implications set in. Shifting to make sure no one else could see his face, he mouthed the question, "Emperor?"

Kynthos nodded. "You're welcome to join the new regime if the prospect of earning fast cash interests you."

"How much?" Jamil almost didn't want to know. *Treason* had never been a word in his vocabulary, and he harbored no intention of adding it.

Kynthos passed his pouch to Jamil beneath the table.

Surreptitiously, Jamil hefted it, feeling his amazement grow as he mutely speculated about its value. If the pouch contained denarii such as the one Kynthos had given the serving woman, then he was holding at least two hundred.

Jamil passed it back to its owner and reached for his cup, his head reeling from far more than the wine he'd imbibed.

"If you join," Kynthos murmured, shifting on his seat to stow the pouch, "you'll receive this much every day."

Jamil nearly sprayed out the wine. He swallowed the mouthful hard, gulped another, swallowed that and poured more. With considerable effort, he strove to keep his voice low. The din inside the tavern had risen, but the churning in his gut warned him this conversation had become too risky to be overheard. "Who in the name of Anubis wants to waste money on old soldiers' tales?"

Finger to lips, Kynthos shook his head. "Come to the rear of the Temple of Venus and Rome three hours after dusk if you wish to find out, but only if you decide to participate." He grinned. "Otherwise, I shall have to kill you."

If Kynthos had intended the remark as a joke, he failed miserably. Even without knowing the identity of Kynthos's patron, Jamil already had learned too much. And if Kynthos discovered Jamil's renewed association with Caesius, Jamil and his onetime subordinate would have all eternity to become fully reacquainted.

Pushing aside his uneasiness, he resolved to make the most of the unexpected opportunity. "Who else has been recruited?"

The Greek twitched a shoulder. "You may not know him. He joined the guard corps at about the time we were reassigned."

"Try me."

"Darius Caepio."

Jamil buried his reaction by taking a long draught. "You have my deepest gratitude, friend Kynthos," he said at last. The tavern's doors opened yet again to admit customers, allowing shafts of harsh sunset to slice the gloom. "I would like to talk more, but other business awaits me." Business with Governor Agricola, though Kynthos didn't need to know it. "Do I look for you tonight?"

Kynthos shook his head. "My evening's work begins soon. I don't get paid for regaling retired guardsmen with my tales. Look for my patron's agent."

"How will I know him?"

Kynthos displayed an enigmatic smile. "Don't worry, my friend. You will know him."

Jamil clasped forearms with his benefactor and strode for the exit. For the first time in far too long, he felt as if Lady Maat had seen fit to bless his efforts. But he tempered his prayer of thanksgiving with a petition for safety and success.

A man wealthy enough to purchase the loyalty of even a handful of retired guardsmen was not a man to cross.

And just because a guardsman was retired didn't mean his assassination skills had to retire with him.

UNLIKE RHYDDES'S BELOVED, verdant Britain, or even the lush, grape-laden country of her earlier travels, this land called Italia seemed perpetually sunbaked and dusty. The splotches of dark green cloaking the hills appeared impossibly distant through the wavering haze.

Two hours of sitting squeezed among too many gladiators and guards in an overfull wagon had left her tunic drenched and her hair pasted to her head. Mercifully, her nose had become inured to the reek of her sweat mingled with everyone else's.

Though she disdained most Roman customs, she'd have killed a score of men to climb into a warm bath. She'd have killed another score for the privilege of soaking all night.

The long shadows of afternoon had yielded to the advancing dusk by the time the gladiators' wagons approached Rome's outer wall. After the procession rumbled to a halt that stretched into several minutes, Rhyddes pressed her face to the bars but saw only a lengthy queue of carts and wagons. It reminded her of what Vederi told her about wheeled traffic being restricted to certain hours within the city, and she settled back for the wait.

When they finally rolled through the massive gatehouse to emerge on the other side, it was as if they'd entered a cemetery for giants.

Limned in starlight, buildings loomed everywhere, crowning the city's hills and crowding the streets. As Rhyddes's wagon passed one, the vista opened upon another half-dozen. Though lights flickered from the windows of some, where the silhouettes of people flitted past, most of the buildings lay dark.

From what she could tell with her limited view, the wheeled queue that had formed outside the gatehouse dissipated rapidly as the traffic fanned out through the city, each driver in pursuit of his own business. Some folk were still abroad on foot, many of whom appeared to be living in the streets.

Too many. What manner of race could conquer the world

and yet fail to provide basic shelter and food for its own people? She shuddered; such a travesty was unthinkable among her clan.

No one gave the gladiators a second glance. Even the whores ignored the whistles and hoots. Without armor, and stuffed into what amounted to cages on wheels, Rhyddes and her sword-brethren must have appeared like every other collection of common slaves.

She snorted softly. In spite of their uncommon occupation, they were naught but common slaves.

Here she sat, clattering through the city that had birthed such an abominable system. And these Romans had the arrogance to call her people barbarians. She snorted again and pillowed her head on her folded arms, closing her eyes for only a moment.

Or so she thought.

The sudden shifting of bodies jostled her awake. She glanced foggily around to see her fellow gladiators leaning toward one side of the wagon, craning for a better view of the massive building they were passing.

"The Flavian Amphitheater," Vederi responded to her query. "Biggest one in the empire. Residents call it simply the Colosseum."

The huge, rounded structure bedecked with hundreds of arches and statues glowed in the light of torches as numerous as the stars. Rhyddes could see how it had earned its title of "colossal place."

"Must be an interesting place to fight," she said.

"With trapdoors in the arena floor, each one fitted with a lift for men, scenery and beasts, I'd say 'interesting' barely begins to describe it," Vederi said. "It's not even a hundred years old yet, and I hear tell it's already seen the deaths of a million men and animals."

Even discounting half that number to exaggeration, Rhyddes shuddered in spite of the lingering heat.

The wagons halted at a smaller building complex, encircled by a tall iron fence, near the Colosseum, and the guards ordered everyone out. Rhyddes obeyed stiffly, flexing joints and muscles that had gone too long without exercise. The guards formed their charges into a single-file line.

Behind the gate, a pair of braziers flanked the building's recessed entrance, lighting a table and chair on the top step. The place was crawling with guards. Most carried whips, coiled and tucked in their belts, in addition to swords or spears.

The gods alone knew what awaited her past the gladiatorial school's portal.

Rhyddes shoved aside her fears of the future and shuffled forward with the rest of the line.

"Name," demanded the guard seated behind the table, without looking up from his notations.

"Rhy—" She checked herself, swallowing the dry lump in her throat. Jamil might remember her given name, but to these Romans it held no meaning. Nor ever would. "Libertas."

The guard's head snapped up. "Libertas, you said?"

"Yes, sir."

He eyed her curiously for a long time. Finally, with a grunt, he returned to his work, pressing marks into the soft clay tablet with the same type of slim iron tool she'd seen Jamil wield. The man made more marks with quill and ink on a scrap of parchment, folded it once, scrawled something on the outer flap, and handed it to one of the guards, who saluted and rushed away.

Though she hadn't forgiven Jamil for selling her without bidding her farewell, a wave of longing smote her. Once she entered these gates, her chances of returning to Britain and her loved ones would vanish.

Vederi spoke with the man about the possibility of employment, with no success. As she gazed at Vederi, words of farewell sticking in her throat, she tried to recall when he had transitioned from being merely keeper of her person to keeper of her sanity. She gave up with a sigh.

"May Fortuna smile upon you, Libertas." An undercurrent of sadness flowed through his tone. "I shall look for you in the arena. Acquit yourself well, as I know you will."

She nodded, blinking to keep the tears at bay. "Thank you, Vederi. For everything."

They gripped forearms in warrior fashion. Before one of the school's guards pried them apart, she felt Vederi give her arm an extra squeeze.

She clung to the memory of that sensation as the guard escorted her into the school. The breaking of Vederi's grip broke the last link to her former life.

Her heart broke with it, though she'd be thrice-cursed before she let any of these Romans see how she felt.

JAMIL FOUND AGRICOLA as the governor and his family exited the dining chamber with Senator Falco and Lady Messiena. Aquila appeared cheerful as he escorted his bride-to-be, Lady Loreia trailing contemplatively in their wake. Jamil gave his friend a sympathetic glance. Aquila responded with the barest of nods.

Agricola and the senator had lagged behind, discussing something in tones too low for Jamil to hear. Nor did he wish to know. He had enough on his mind already.

Jamil stiffened his posture and coughed mildly to attract the governor's attention.

"Citizen Kalilus, well met. Have you something to report?" Agricola asked. When Jamil nodded, the governor turned toward his host. "Have you a chamber where I might conduct a private audience, Falco?"

"Of course." The senator extended an arm toward the adjacent corridor. "Follow me."

Falco led them to a room remarkable for the shelves lining its walls, built in a diamond pattern and stuffed with hundreds of scrolls. One wall featured a door flanked by tall windows offering a view into the garden. In each corner sat a thickly cushioned chair beneath a cluster of oil lamps suspended from the ceiling. Another, larger cluster hung down over the center of the chamber. Falco ordered a passing servant to light the lamps, and bade Agricola and Jamil to be comfortable and take as much time as they needed.

After Agricola thanked his host, and the door swung shut behind the senator, he signaled Jamil to check the room for peepholes. It took several minutes to peer behind all the scrolls, even with both of them looking.

At one point, a scrap dislodged and fluttered to the floor, but Jamil paid it no heed and continued his search.

He didn't find any suspicious holes or cracks, and apparently Agricola hadn't, either. But rather than choosing one of the corner chairs, the governor beckoned Jamil into the center of the room.

Jamil restrained his voice to a thin whisper. "Darius is involved in setting the groundwork for a coup, my lord."

Agricola didn't look surprised. "Who is planning it?"

Jamil shrugged. "The plan involves the Praetorian Guard. I might learn more in a few hours. I met an old acquaintance who invited me to join what he called the 'new regime.' He instructed me to meet his patron's agent at a temple near this mansion."

"Go, and report to me whatever you learn."

"Yes, my lord."

As Jamil saluted and took his leave, he tried not to dwell upon the infinitesimal odds that the visiting governor of Britannia could thwart a coup staged by the Praetorian Guard and financed by one of Rome's wealthiest men.

In the colonnade on his way to the guest chambers, one of Senator Falco's guards stopped him.

"Sir, this arrived for you." The soldier offered a folded parchment leaf. "It's from the lanista at Ludus Maximus."

Jamil thanked the guard, gave him a sestertius for his trouble, and dismissed him. He had a fair idea of the message's contents.

Curiosity forced him to look anyway.

"Libertas is here." He whispered the written words reverently, feeling his heart lighten with each repetition of the wonderful phrase.

This night had become very busy indeed.

## 25

MESSIENA STROLLED BESIDE Marcus through the moonlit garden, heading toward her favorite spot: the fountain where they'd met that morning. A voice in her head scolded her for not letting him retire to his quarters for the evening.

But she had to learn why his smiles weren't directed at her.

He had to be exhausted from the long journey, the voice argued. But certainly not so tired that he couldn't pay his betrothed the courtesy she was due, she silently argued back. The voice cautioned her to leave well enough alone.

She paid it no heed.

"Thank you for indulging my request, Marcus."

"My pleasure, Messiena."

He did sound tired. Perhaps she was imagining things.

They reached the fountain, and he offered his hand to help her sit, avoiding the light spray. With a firm tug, she drew him down beside her.

Debating whether to pursue a more serious topic, she elected to start with an easy one. "I hope you and your parents have found everything to your liking here."

"We have, thank you. You run a fine household. Your father must be very proud of you."

That wrenched a rueful chuckle from her throat. "I don't know. He never shows it."

"He should."

"Thank you. I'll tell him you said that." She sidled closer to him, not caring that the cement of the fountain's lip tugged at her dress. "And what of my husband-to-be? Is he proud of me, too?"

"Of course." He wrapped an arm around her shoulders to punctuate his response.

Nestling into the warmth of his embrace, she dared to ask, "Does he like me?"

She felt his lips brush the top of her head, sending a tingle rushing down her spine. "Yes."

Her inner voice screamed at her to stop. Again, she ignored it. "And what of...love?"

His sigh ruffled her hair, and she felt his posture tense. "Messiena, I—"

She twisted around to look at him, but his face was smothered in shadow. Panic strangled her resolve. "No, don't, Marcus. If your heart belongs to another woman, I don't want to know."

Tears stinging her eyes, Messiena rose to leave. He caught her hand and would not let her pull away.

"I must be honest with you. You deserve at least that much. Will you please hear me out?" he asked.

She sat, though not as close as before.

"There have been many women in my life. One has affected me more than the others…" He inhaled a deep breath and regarded her steadily. "But even were I not betrothed to you, Messiena, she and I could never marry. I swear I shall strive to be the best husband I can be, and I truly am fond of you, but please understand that love may take time to grow."

*Fondness.* She looked toward her hand, trapped within his much larger one, and wanted to spit upon his fondness. And yet, her voice argued, it was a start. A feeble start, but a start nonetheless.

"Are you offering me your fidelity?" A Roman wife could never force her husband to give up his other bed partners, female or otherwise, but a promise freely offered became a sacred bond in the eyes of the gods.

He gazed at her for so long it sparked the fear that he intended to refuse. "After we are wed, Messiena, I shall not dally with anyone else."

She couldn't overlook his choice of words but had to content herself with his promise of a promise. To be brutally honest, it was better than she had expected.

Besides, she possessed certain resources for enforcing his promise. She was, after all, her father's daughter.

While Messiena smiled her acceptance, she mulled how best she could bring those resources to bear.

"I crave your pardon, Lady Messiena, Lord Aquila."

Messiena stood and turned to find an aging man with a pox-scarred face, dressed in the armor of a bodyguard, standing a discreet distance away. Marcus rose, too. The man surreptitiously balled the fingers of his right hand into a fist, the thumb pointed upward.

Marcus gave the bodyguard a sharp nod, his face starkly expressionless. The man relaxed his fist and adopted an alert stance.

She felt Marcus slip his hand under her elbow. "Jamil and I have a private matter to discuss, but may I escort you inside first?"

Even if he didn't love her, at least he was making a decent effort to be considerate. "Thank you, Marcus, but no."

"Until tomorrow, then." Hand to chest, he bowed deeply. "Sleep well, Messiena."

She bade him a pleasant evening and strolled toward the house. When she was certain Marcus could no longer see her, she veered off the path.

And nearly collided with one of her maidservants. She suppressed the urge to curse.

"Ah, Lady Messiena. Lady Loreia sent me to find you. She has a few questions, if you have a moment."

"Of course, Agna." So much for attempting to learn what Marcus's bodyguard had to say.

Then again, if it concerned news about the woman her bridegroom loved, Messiena wasn't sure she wanted to hear it.

MARCUS WATCHED MESSIENA until well after the path's shadows had obscured her form.

Not trusting anything to chance, he motioned Jamil to the far side of the fountain. "You found her?" he whispered.

"Ludus Maximus." Jamil must have sensed Marcus's

puzzlement, even in the darkness, for he added, "One of the gladiatorial schools near the Colosseum."

"It's too late to visit tonight."

Jamil's teeth flashed in the moonlight. "Not for someone of your means."

Marcus shook his head. "Go without me, Jamil. And, please, take whatever you think necessary for bribing the guards. I…" He gazed in the direction of his betrothed's departure. "I have much to think about."

"What shall I tell Libertas?"

"I will attempt to see her tomorrow. That's the best I can promise."

And Marcus would have two women angry with him, rather than one. No, strike that. They were both angry already. He could read that much in Messiena's demeanor. Yet he couldn't withhold the truth to spare her feelings. It wouldn't have been fair to her.

Jamil clapped Marcus's shoulder. "As you wish. I must hurry."

"Why? Have you some tryst I don't know about?"

"Let's call it an errand for your esteemed father, and leave it at that."

Jamil took his leave and returned to the mansion. Watching his friend depart, Marcus wondered what sort of errand would require Jamil to be abroad at this hour, when most people were already asleep. He resolved to ask his father later.

Beset by the battle between love and duty, Marcus stepped through a dense, aromatic rosemary hedge and sank to the base of an olive tree.

That he loved Libertas, there remained no question,

despite the anger driving their last words. The mere mention of her name had set his pulse to pounding. And yet he couldn't rush off to meet her so soon after that disastrous conversation with his betrothed. Even though he and Messiena were not yet wed, it didn't seem right to seek a reunion with the woman who owned his heart.

If she would deign to have him.

Drawing knees to chin and wrapping his arms about his shins, he gazed heavenward through the olive branches. Duty, obedience, honor: which excuse could justify his refusal to rescue her from her owners? Could he ever make right that failure in her eyes?

Would she give him the opportunity to try?

The slap of sandals on the cobbled path attracted his attention. A warning prickled along his spine. Carefully shifting as close to the tree as possible, he sharpened his senses, thankful for the darkness and the tall hedge.

"This is far enough."

The sandals' patter stopped a body length from Marcus's position. In trying to see the newcomers through the rosemary fronds, his hand crunched onto dried leaves, releasing a burst of scent that almost made him sneeze.

"What was that?"

Marcus pinched his nose, willing the tickle to pass.

"Nothing. A hunting fox, or perhaps the prey."

"You sure it's safe to talk here?"

"I know my own estate. My daughter and our guests are abed. The household servants are not, but the garden staff is."

"And what of your esteemed guests? Do they know anything?"

"If they did, I would be negotiating for an altogether different service."

The senator's companion uttered a rasping sound, halfway between a cough and a laugh. "You mean, as with Ferox?"

Marcus felt his eyes widen. According to servants' gossip he'd overheard on the way to dinner, Senator Ferox, a neighbor of Falco's, had been found murdered in his bed this morning, his throat neatly slit, the bedding drenched in blood.

The urge to sneeze had passed, but Marcus fought to keep his breathing steady and silent.

"The fool got what he deserved for having no faith in the new regime. Give me your report."

"We've brought the last of the gladiators. Tomorrow everyone will receive their orders, as will the guard and others. Should be a hell of a spectacle."

Although Marcus couldn't identify the second speaker, he sensed that he knew the other man. He dared not turn his head and risk betraying his position, but from the corner of his eye he made out a flabby profile that seemed familiar.

"Lie low for a week after the event, and then return for the balance of your payment."

"But, my lord—"

"You dare to challenge me, you miserable weasel's flea?" Through the harsh whisper, menace pulsed palpably.

"No, my lord," the other man replied, his tone sullen.

"Will the guard be ready?"

The rustle of fabric suggested that the senator's companion had shrugged. "My associate meets a new recruit in an hour. With that man's help, they should be."

"See to it, then." With a swirl of his toga, Falco prepared to leave, seemed to think better of it, and paused. "Loyalty shall be rewarded. Make sure the men understand that. The same applies to you and your associates."

"My lord is most magnanimous." The second figure bowed deeply and followed the senator back toward the mansion.

Marcus gave them plenty of time before venturing from the thicket.

Too much time, apparently; he found the house doors locked. And under no circumstances was he about to attract a servant's attention. The last thing he needed was for Falco to suspect he and his coconspirator hadn't been alone.

Aided by moonlight, Marcus eased away from the main doors in search of one that might be open. His persistence was rewarded when he jiggled another handle and the latch yielded.

He slipped inside what appeared to be a small library containing dozens of shelves bearing scrolls and flat parchment leaves bound between leather-wrapped boards. From what he could tell in the gloom, the chamber seemed tidy, except for a parchment scrap that had slid underneath a bottom shelf.

Marcus retrieved the scrap and walked back to the window where the moonlight shone brightest.

And regretted having touched the accursed thing.

The parchment contained a list of names, some with lines drawn through them and others not. Three names bore lines and an *X* beside them. Marcus recognized many as prominent politicians, but he could conjure significant details for only two. Both were marred by a single line. The second had an *X*.

Agricola, and Ferox.

IT TOOK EVERY SESTERTIUS of the hundred Jamil had borrowed from Aquila to bribe his way into Ludus Maximus and be conducted to Libertas's cell. His escort believed Jamil sought a sexual encounter, and Jamil didn't disabuse the notion, expecting the implication to buy him privacy without his having to dip into his meager reserves.

Jamil silently vowed to pay Aquila back, as he strode briskly beside the guard past the torchlit cell blocks; not only tonight's hundred, but his daily stipend, too, as soon as his fortunes reversed. Even though Aquila considered the funds to be a gift rather than a loan, experience had taught Jamil to never become beholden to any man again.

They turned into a corridor where the cells contained women. Most were sleeping, or at least making an attempt upon the narrow, hard cots. A few were entertaining visitors, as the moans and motions attested.

Jamil kept his gaze trained upon the far end of the corridor, and he almost bumped into the guard when the man halted in front of Libertas's cell. Unsure what sort of reception she would give him, Jamil felt his pulse quicken.

"Libertas!" With his keys, the guard clanged the iron bars of her cell, creating a din fit to resurrect Lord Ra hours before the god's appointed time. The commotion caused other women to stir, but Libertas remained prone on her cot, her back facing them. "You have a visitor."

Again no response from her. Not that it surprised Jamil. She didn't seem ill or injured, but he couldn't begin to imagine the horrors she must have endured at the hands of Pugionis, Rodo and Furcifer, and it had been entirely Jamil's fault.

If she never forgave him, he would understand.

The guard thrust his torch into an empty sconce, unlocked the cell door and swung it open for Jamil to enter. "Shout when you're ready to be let out again," he instructed, and winked. "Enjoy yourself."

Right.

Jamil thanked the guard, who locked the cell and left.

Closer inspection revealed that Libertas was sleeping soundly, not choosing to ignore Jamil as he'd suspected. Closer inspection also showed him she had lost weight. Kneeling beside her cot, he longed to gather her into his arms and carry her away from this evil life.

The crushing weight of reality forced him to bow his head. He had no right to touch her. "I am so sorry, Libertas."

"I AM SO VERY, very sorry."

The whispered words sounded real, and profoundly sincere, yet Rhyddes knew she had to be dreaming. Jamil couldn't possibly be here in this gods-forsaken cell.

A breeze stirred at her back, carrying the tang of cheap wine, and she heard the rustling of fabric.

Such things didn't happen in dreams.

She opened her eyes and rolled over.

Jamil was standing at her cell's door, his back to her and hand lifted, preparing to signal a guard.

"You're going to leave me without saying goodbye... again?"

The pain creasing his face, when he turned to regard her, made her regret the outburst. She sat up and swung her legs over the edge of the cot.

He spread his hands in a gesture of supplication. "If I had

revealed how I felt toward you, Pugionis and his companions would have made your life much worse."

"Hah. I cannot imagine how." Staring at the floor slates, she was powerless to prevent memory upon wretched memory from assaulting her.

"Libertas." Jamil knelt and grasped her hands. "My dear Libertas, I was such a fool, and my folly wrought evil upon you." His dark eyes glistened and his voice, scarcely above a whisper, wavered. "Can you possibly forgive me?"

"Did you have a choice—or did greed motivate you, as usual?"

Jamil snorted. "I deserved that." He rocked off his knees to sit on the rough, cold floor. "I did have a choice, if you can call it that. I could either give up my gladiators to settle an old debt, or die. They'd have taken you either way."

"What?" She felt her eyebrows knit.

"Oh, yes. I am quite ruined. And fortunate to be alive. If not for Aquila's kindness and generosity, I'd have drunk my last denarius in a Londinium alley and killed myself weeks ago, to save everyone else the trouble." He barked a mirthless laugh. "I did drink my last denarius, but Aquila found me before I could sober up long enough to slit my throat with a bottle shard."

Compassion flooded her soul, and she reached for his hands to grip them hard. "Please forgive me, Jamil. I—I had no idea…" She couldn't defeat the tremor in her chin, and tears streaked her cheeks. "In my anger at you I left Anubis behind!"

Jamil rose to sit beside her on the cot and drew her into an embrace. His affection shattered her defenses. She buried her head against his chest. Sobs too long suppressed erupted with startling force.

"My dear Libertas," Jamil whispered, rubbing her back. "It is I who must beg forgiveness of you. I should have insisted that you accept your freedom, all those months ago." His voice thickened, and he cleared his throat. "I never intended any of this to happen to the daughter of my pectus."

Sniffing, she lifted her head. "Your...what?"

"*Pectus* means heart, soul and spirit." He wiped the tears from her face and smiled. "You are that special a daughter to me."

*Daughter.* Rhyddes had never hoped to hear that word spoken to her in love, and Jamil's pronouncement left her quite unprepared for the barrage of overwhelming gratitude.

"I thank you...Father." She grinned at his delighted expression. "This means more to me than you can possibly know."

His gaze grew earnest. "I shall get you back, Libertas. I promise."

"How? You said you have no money."

"True, but I have a patron now. Lord Aquila—"

"Will never purchase me." She couldn't prevent bitterness from eroding her tone. "Don't bother to ask him. I already did."

"Please don't judge him too harshly. Duty and love tear at him like a pair of rabid jackals."

*Words, again!* She rolled her eyes. "If he loves me so much, why isn't he here?"

Jamil shrugged. "He plans to try visiting you tomorrow."

As if that could make everything right again.

She sighed. "Please tell him not to anger his betrothed on my account." Upon rising, she strode to the cell door and shouted for the guard.

Jamil stood. "Libertas, surely you want to see Aquila one more time?"

More than anything! Even more than her freedom.

As the guard approached, whistling, she kept her voice low. "Would seeing him again alter the fact that he must marry another? Would it truly change anything between us?"

Jamil had no answer other than the obvious, heartrending one, which Libertas seemed to know already. He gave her a lingering embrace, savoring her warmth as if she were the daughter of his flesh, and stepped into the corridor after the guard had opened the cell.

As the lock clicked shut, Jamil felt compelled to leave her with an Egyptian proverb:

"Treasure the love that blooms in adversity, Daughter, for it is the most beautiful and fragrant blossom of all."

For Aquila's sake as well as hers, Jamil hoped it would be enough.

MARCUS HAD NO SOONER left the library than he heard footsteps echoing from the far end of the corridor. He stuffed the parchment scrap into his tunic and continued on his course as if nothing were amiss.

"Aquila!" boomed Falco.

Heart hammering, Marcus stopped, turned and slowly approached the man slated to become his father by marriage—if Marcus survived to see that day. "How may I serve you, sir?"

"I was wondering what you were doing abroad at this hour, when everyone else is abed."

Marcus grinned. "Everyone except yourself, sir."

The senator laughed, clapping a hand on Marcus's shoulder. Beneath his tunic's fabric, the parchment shifted. Resisting the urge to flinch, Marcus prayed Falco wouldn't hear the crinkling. He feigned a cough, and Falco removed his hand.

"What were you doing, Aquila?" The laughter had yielded to quiet menace.

Marcus drew a breath. "I couldn't sleep and thought perhaps some food might help. Am I close to the kitchens?"

Falco swung about and pointed in the direction he'd come. "That way." He brushed past Marcus as if to enter the library.

"What is all the fuss, Papa? I heard you bellowing from my chambers."

Messiena, wrapped in a wide, gold-brocaded crimson shawl over her gown to ward off the night's chill, glided toward them from the opposite end of the corridor—the end to which Marcus had been headed, though he'd had no idea where her quarters were situated. No wonder Falco had been suspicious. Marcus wanted to laugh in sheer relief.

She stepped between them and twined an arm through each of theirs.

"Your husband-to-be claims he's hungry. It seems he cannot wait for your wedding to satisfy that hunger."

Messiena beamed at Marcus. He felt his cheeks heat; a small price to pay for throwing Falco off the scent. "I'm sorry, sir. This shall not happen again, I swear."

"Oh, Papa, don't be a beast. Marcus and I had a bit of a tiff this evening. I'm sure he was only coming to apologize. Weren't you, beloved?"

Marcus nodded, hating the lie but seeing no other recourse. "I'm sorry, Messiena. I never intended to upset you." That much, at least, was true.

"Upset—how?" demanded Falco.

"It's not important, Papa." Tugging on their arms, she began walking toward the kitchens. "I believe we could all do with a goblet of warm, honeyed wine."

With the incriminating parchment itching his skin, Marcus cast about for a plausible excuse to escape. As they approached the corridor leading to his quarters, he yawned expansively.

Patting Messiena's hand atop his arm, he said, "I think the travel is catching up with me. Would you mind terribly, dearest, if I took the wine in my chamber?"

"Alone, of course," added Falco.

Marcus smiled apologetically at Messiena. "You heard your father. I must not disobey his will."

After glancing murderously at Falco, Messiena softened her gaze upon Marcus. "Of course, my beloved. I shall have someone bring you the wine at once."

Marcus murmured his thanks and quit their company, fighting the urge to run.

Only after he had entered his chamber and bolted the door did he pull the parchment from his tunic. He wasn't sure how the list factored into Falco's plans, but the fact that at least one of the men had been murdered didn't bode well for the others whose names had been crossed off, including Agricola.

A loud knock on the door disturbed Marcus's ponderings. He stuffed the parchment under the closest chair cushion and crossed the room to unbolt and open the door. A man-servant was waiting in the corridor, carrying a tray laden with a silver goblet and matching pitcher. Steam curling from the pitcher bore the aroma of wine spiced with cloves, orange peel, honey and cinnamon.

Marcus invited the servant to enter and, not willing to take any chances, he sat on the chair hiding the parchment. The servant placed the tray on the table, poured a measure and handed the goblet to Marcus. After taking an apprecia-tive sip, feeling the sweet warmth soothe his throat, Marcus dismissed the servant with thanks. The man bowed and stepped toward the door.

"Wait," Marcus said. The servant turned to regard him ex-pectantly. "I require parchment, ink and quills. Please bring them at once."

"Yes, my lord."

After the servant departed, Marcus retrieved the parch-ment from beneath his seat and held it to a lamp, tilting it for closer inspection. The handwriting appeared bold and assured. Not too ornate and, Marcus hoped, not too diffi-cult to copy.

**26**

JAMIL ENTERED LUDUS MAXIMUS'S outer guardroom, where he'd been forced to leave the sword he carried as Marcus's bodyguard.

"Done so soon?" the guard on duty asked.

Annoyed, Jamil ignored the remark. He snatched the sword belt and sheathed weapon from the man.

"Of course," continued the guard, "with a right fair piece of female flesh like that, I'd probably be done before I ever laid a hand on her."

"Libertas is my daughter," Jamil growled. It was the only truth this swine in armor needed to know. He donned his sword belt with practiced ease and fastened the clasp with a loud click. "If you or anyone else in this hellhole so much as looks at her askance, you shall have the governor of Britannia to answer to, in addition to myself." Never mind that the governor had tried to kill her, and might again. The guard didn't need to know that, either. Grinning, Jamil modulated his voice to mimic the man's conversational tone. "Understood?"

"Perfectly, sir." One would have thought the man had been addressing the legions' commander-in-chief.

"Good. Carry on." It hurt nothing to reinforce the illusion of authority.

The striped hour-candle sitting atop the guardroom's table mutely reminded Jamil to hurry. Satisfied for having performed a small service for Libertas, he allowed himself to swagger as he left the chamber.

Outside Ludus Maximus's imposing gate, he broke into a lope.

Gravity and caution slowed him as the street angled up Esquiline Hill toward his destination. The Temple of Venus and Rome was a modest structure compared with Hadrian's breathtaking, domed pantheon, but it did not lack for ornately carved marble and cast golden adornments. Its peaked roof emitted a silvery gleam under the moonlight. As far as Jamil knew, it could be solid silver. Roman rulers set upon impressing the people spared no expense, and whoever had commissioned this temple certainly had subscribed to that philosophy.

The low hum of chanting and the spicy fragrance of incense wafted toward Jamil through the colonnade. A quick trip around the building's perimeter showed him that several dozen bronze fire-dishes, each perched atop a tall, three-legged stand, lit the temple's exterior.

And they prevented anyone from hiding next to the building. Jamil shimmied up a sycamore tree, took position on the lowest, fattest limb with his back braced against the trunk, and waited.

His precautions proved well worth the effort. In fact, Jamil could scarcely believe his good fortune. A lone figure moved stealthily from the shadows to loiter directly beneath his branch. He waited a few extra moments, to be sure this man was indeed the "patron's agent" Kynthos had told him about. When it became obvious the agent wasn't leaving, and he was indeed alone, Jamil quietly unsheathed his sword and jumped.

His prey looked up with a startled gasp but had no time to flee. Jamil landed atop his target to send him sprawling on his stomach with a whoosh of expelled breath. Jamil seized him by the hair, yanked his head up and positioned his sword.

"Shout for help, Rodo, and I guarantee it will be the last noise you ever make."

Better this had been Pugionis, but gods, it felt good to get the upper hand over this creature. Only following through with his threat would have given Jamil greater satisfaction, but he had business to conduct first.

"Illegal to go armed inside the city," Rodo gasped.

"Not for registered bodyguards, which I am." Jamil pressed the blade to Rodo's neck and could smell the reek of fear.

"You're interfering with a private matter."

Jamil couldn't recall when he'd laughed so hard. "Wrong again." He removed the sword and shifted his knee to let Rodo roll over. "I am the man Kynthos told you to meet."

"You! But you're—"

"Just the sort you have been ordered to recruit—a retired Praetorian guardsman."

Rodo had the gall to sneer. "No. Fa—my patron doesn't need you. It's too late."

Crablike, he tried to scuttle from Jamil's reach, but Jamil lunged forward, sword first. He stopped short of plunging it into Rodo's gut. "It will be too late for you if you fail to cooperate with me." He played a hunch, and grinned. "Of course, you are welcome to lodge a complaint with *my* patron—Senator Falco."

"If you've already hooked up with him, why did you arrange to meet me?"

"Don't be stupid. You cannot imagine how pleased I was to learn you were the senator's agent."

Rodo deflated like an emptied wineskin. "What do you want, Kalil?"

"Ownership of Libertas."

"Only her?" Rodo laughed. "Falco must pay you well if you're this easy to buy off."

None of the other gladiators mattered to Jamil in the same way Libertas did, but he wasn't about to admit it to this bottom-feeder. Instead he grunted assent.

"That bitch is more trouble than she's worth anyway."

Jamil grabbed the neck of Rodo's tunic and hauled him up. "Never refer to her like that again, unless you wish to feast upon your own testicles. Understood?"

Rodo nodded vigorously. With the sword pricking Rodo's back, Jamil guided him toward the temple. "Now what are we doing? Sacrificing me to the gods?"

Jamil smiled. "Pray you shall be that fortunate." Before stepping into the braziers' perimeter, he sheathed his sword and grasped Rodo's arm. "We are going to find a priest to draw up Libertas's transfer of ownership. The purse I know you carry, which was intended as my payment, shall make a fine donation for his services." He leaned closer to whisper, "And if you so much as squeak in protest, I will have your head on a plate so fast you won't have uttered half a word."

The priest who woke to Jamil's summons looked supremely annoyed until Jamil ordered Rodo to surrender the purse. Crafting the ownership transfer took but a few minutes. Jamil folded the precious document, tucked it into his pouch and marched Rodo to a shadowed alley he'd seen from the sycamore, a fair distance from the temple.

The gods served by this temple weren't the ones he honored, but he had no wish to desecrate sacred ground.

He forced Rodo to his knees, crouched behind him, yanked back the man's head and slid the sword under his chin.

"What are you waiting for?" Rodo's voice rasped from having his throat stretched. "Kill me and be done."

"You might save your neck if you tell me what I want to know."

That was all it took. Rodo didn't know much, nor was Jamil expecting him to, but he learned enough to heighten his suspicion that the emperor's life was in danger, and that Darius had been given the key assignment.

When his daughter's ex-tormentor was finished, Jamil gave a quick, deft slice, inflicting the mortal wound he'd taught to her and scores of gladiators before her. Blood spewed from Rodo's neck, spattering the paving stones. The spreading puddles glistened in the moonlight. Rodo toppled into them, facedown, with a soft splash.

Jamil bent over to whisper, "I said you *might* save your

life by talking. Take your complaint to your gods, if they'll have you."

He wiped his blade on the back of Rodo's tunic and sheathed it. Dragging the body, he scurried to the bushes. There wasn't enough room to hide it properly; so be it. He'd accept those consequences as they came.

At present, he had an emperor to save, and he knew of only one man who could accomplish the feat.

It took a while for Jamil to convince the soldiers on duty at the Praetorian barracks that he was who he claimed to be: a former guardsman with an urgent message for their commander. Caesius, when he arrived, settled the matter by hustling Jamil into a private, windowless room inside the gate tower.

"And you learned nothing more?" Caesius asked after Jamil had finished his report, including his concerns about the disaffection Kynthos had been spreading within the corps. "Such as, where the assassination attempt will occur, or when?"

"Come, my friend. You know as well as I do that besides the assassin, the only man who possesses those answers is the man who stands the most to gain."

"True enough. This is a start, at least." Caesius grimly smiled his gratitude. "The hour is late, Kalil. You are welcome to a bed here."

Jamil appreciated the offer but politely declined. "I must report to my patron so he can continue watching Falco."

"You never told me who that was."

"It's no state secret. Governor Agricola of Britannia."

Caesius regarded him strangely. "The same Agricola whose son is betrothed to Falco's daughter?"

"Yes…" It didn't surprise him that Caesius knew of the visitors at Falco's estate; Jamil would have been more surprised if he didn't. "Is that a problem?" he asked warily.

Caesius snorted. "Only if the governor is a coconspirator."

To say Jamil had never considered that angle was a gross understatement. "How well do you know him, Caesius?"

"How well do *you*?"

What a question. Agricola had defied public opinion to order the execution of Jamil's best provocator-class gladiator, and had tried to engineer the death of his gladiatrix, bribing Jamil heavily to look the other way.

"I've been in his employ less than a month," he elected to reply, "but I've had other dealings with him."

Caesius's expression lightened a little as he escorted Jamil to the chamber's door. "All I am suggesting, sir, is watch your back and be careful whom you trust."

Jamil enjoyed the second best laugh he'd had all night. "I hardly need a rawboned recruit—all right, an ex-rawboned recruit—to tell me that."

Jamil's first regret was that, by the time he'd finished at the Praetorian barracks, it was already midway into the night's final watch and too late to free Libertas from Ludus Maximus.

His second regret came as he realized his preoccupation over Agricola's possible involvement in Falco's scheme had returned him via the same route he'd come: past the alley defined by the blocks of priests' living quarters near the temple, where he'd left Rodo's body.

He recovered his caution in time to see flickering patterns of light emitting from the alley. He peered around the building's corner.

Rodo wasn't alone.

An athletically built, well-dressed man was squatting over the corpse, one hand cupping his chin in a contemplative attitude and the other holding a torch. His back, praise be to everything holy, was turned toward Jamil.

Playing a hunch, and knowing he'd be dead if he didn't, Jamil slowly unsheathed his sword and crept up on the man. By the time his presence was discovered, it was too late. Jamil lunged.

Squawking, Kynthos dropped the torch. It sputtered in the bloody ooze. In trying to leap up, he stumbled over Rodo's body and fell into the bushes. Jamil closed in, trapping his onetime barracks mate with the point of his sword.

"*Treason* is a word they never taught us in the legions," he grated out in his disgust. "Where did you learn it, Kynthos?"

"You don't need to know."

"You're in no position to judge what I do and do not need." He pressed his sword's point against the Greek's neck. "Which of the guardsmen have you subverted to join this 'new regime'?"

"Will you let me live if I tell you? For the sake of an old army comrade?" Kynthos sounded so pathetic that Jamil relented.

"Only if you have something tangible I can use." Kynthos nodded vigorously. "And only if you swear—" he nicked the Greek's neck to remove all doubt "—that you shall leave this city and never show your face here again. Because if you do, I will gut you where you stand. Understood?"

Nodding again, Kynthos withdrew a parchment leaf,

folded and sealed, from the pouch at his waist. It rattled as he passed it to Jamil, and the Greek laughed bitterly. "I was on my way to deliver it to the dead man's patron. I suppose it doesn't matter now if I don't keep that appointment."

Jamil was about to raise his sword but thought better of it. "By the way, if you're thinking of telling anyone about—" he pointed his chin toward Rodo's remains "—that mess, be aware that I've already spoken to the Praetorian Guard prefect. He knows of your activities tonight, too." Grinning, Jamil glanced at the alley's mouth. "A patrol should be arriving at any moment. I suggest you leave before they see you."

After sheathing his sword, Jamil helped Kynthos to right himself, and he watched the Greek sprint for the main road as the sky lightened. As a precaution, he pried open the layers of a sandal and laid the two small documents— Kynthos's list and Libertas's liberation—inside, sending up a quick petition for forgiveness as he worked.

All the lies he'd uttered tonight were for the noblest of causes.

A HORRIFIC CLANGING jangled Rhyddes from a sound sleep.

"Up, you lazy bitch!" The clanging, much closer now, made her head ring abominably. "Get up now, or join the criminals slated for execution!"

Her body moved before her brain could make sense of her surroundings; she scrambled off the cot, tugged her tunic past her thighs and lunged for the door before the guard could utter another threat. She remembered seeing Jamil, but the heat, already stifling at daybreak, and the shorter but wider cell told her this wasn't Villa Britanniae. And Jamil had owned only one gladiatrix, not the dozens trudging past her cell, prodded by guards.

Hand to temple and swaying in the cell's doorway, she shook her head. Of course she wasn't at Villa Britanniae. This was Rome, the thrice-cursed heart of the thrice-cursed empire, and she probably had dreamed Jamil's visit, too.

"Enjoy your man last night?" asked the guard who'd woken her.

"Sir?"

"Your visitor." With one hand gripping his spear, he used the other to rub his clean-shaven chin. "Though I swear by the gods he looked old enough to be your father."

*'Twasn't a dream!* Rhyddes coughed behind her hand to hide her elation as she joined her new sword-sisters silently trooping to the gods alone knew where. To break fast, she hoped.

She slid a glance toward her guard. "The man who came to my cell last night *is* my father, sir."

Sweet heavenly Epona, how good, how right it felt to think of Jamil in that manner!

The guard's expression seemed a cross between disbelief and revulsion. "Your father?"

Before she had a chance to reply, another guard joined them. "Indeed. I spoke to him last night. The man also claimed we would have Britannia's governor to answer to if any harm befalls this gladiatrix-slave." His breath reeked of stale wine as he leaned over Rhyddes. "Tell me, slave, why a favorite of the emperor would be interested in protecting the likes of you?"

An intriguing question. But surely, Jamil had not uttered

such a statement without reason. "In Britannia I was a popular champion," she said.

The guards shared a laugh.

"Well," said the first guard as he propelled her to follow the other women into the large, vaulted dining chamber that smelled of sweat and barley porridge, "we shall see how a provincial champion ranks against the imperial champions of Ludus Maximus."

Rhyddes didn't like the menace coursing freely through their laughter.

THE INSISTENT POUNDING on the door aggravated the pounding in Marcus's head. He extricated it from the pillows and glanced blearily toward the door.

"Time to get up, Son. Breakfast has been served on the terrace."

"A moment, Father." He had no idea whether Agricola had heard him and, frankly, he didn't care.

His father seemed to have moved on, for the door's rattling ceased. The pounding in his head did not, and he closed his eyes, willing himself to relax.

Recollection of the crucial task that awaited him propelled him fully awake. He rolled over, stood and padded to the side table containing a basin and pitcher of water. When a few splashes on his face didn't suffice, he tipped the basin's night-chilled contents over his head. He didn't envy the servant who would have to mop the water from the tiles, but at least he felt awake enough to accomplish his goal.

Failure could mean jeopardizing not only his life, but the lives of his parents and everyone in their entourage.

After shaking the excess water from his hair—and regretting the action, for it set his head to throbbing again—he shrugged into clean undergarments and a muslin tunic fit to be seen in public, but not so fine as to draw undue notice. He secured the tunic with a leather belt from which dangled a pouch that, gods willing, soon would be empty.

Stooping, Marcus thoughtfully fingered the soft woolen toga at the bottom of his clothes chest. Its drapes would hide the objects he was forced to carry. The toga also would add an air of respectability that would assist him at his destination, but it was out of the question. Not only would it be too hot, Marcus had no wish to fabricate a plausible excuse for deciding to wear it. He left the garment where it lay.

Before closing the chest, he retrieved the Anubis figurine and stashed it in the pouch, praying for the chance to return it to its owner.

While he tied his sandals, he considered whether to find Jamil, who probably had risen to join the house guards in their morning repast. Marcus wanted to learn how Libertas had received her former owner, and how she was faring, but the delay wasn't worth the risk of discovery.

To avoid the terrace he took a circuitous route to the library, hoping to be rid of the accursed parchment scrap before breakfast, but it wasn't to be. He found the library's double doors firmly closed. Although he couldn't make out Falco's words, the senator's voice seeped out in escalating levels of frustration.

Marcus felt himself blanch. Had the senator noticed the list's absence already?

He had no desire to find out. As quietly as possible, he bolted toward the nearest intersecting corridor, not a moment too soon. A door banged against the wall with a horrific thud, and Falco began shouting for his household staff. Men and women erupted from the nearest chambers and ran to answer their master's summons, paying Marcus no heed. After the tide of servants passed, he hastened toward the terrace.

Instinct convinced him to stop by his chamber for his money.

Falco, apparently having taken a shortcut, had already arrived at the terrace. Before Marcus came within range to make out the senator's words, he heard the towering fury behind them. Agricola was livid, and Loreia looked as if she would faint. Messiena, aghast, had wrapped an arm about Loreia's shoulders and was chafing one of her limp hands.

Marcus concealed himself behind a wide granite column while he decided what to do next.

"Papa, what are you doing? Can you not see this is upsetting Lady Loreia?"

"What I am doing is for you, Pulla. These citizens—" Falco made the word sound like an insult "—would jeopardize my efforts."

"This accusation is absurd, Falco." Though Agricola made an obvious effort to rein in his temper, the tension in his jaw was equally obvious. "I entered that chamber to speak with my servant after dinner. I saw no loose parchment leaves—the room seemed in perfect order. We took nothing."

"You must have," Falco cried, "for it is gone now!"

"What can be so damned important that you would call me a liar as well as a thief?"

"Something entrusted to me by the emperor for safekeeping. He'll have my head if it remains missing." Grinning humorlessly, the senator paced closer to Agricola. "And you and your family shall be guilty by association."

Marcus's first impulse was to charge forth and accuse Falco of being the liar. But he realized that would buy more trouble than he could afford, for his parents as well as himself. Reluctantly, he remained hidden.

Falco shouted for his guards. A sickening knot in Marcus's stomach told him what was about to transpire without having to watch the events play out. While the senator remained preoccupied with ordering his men to bind Agricola and Loreia, ignoring Messiena's shrill protests and his parents' shouts, Marcus slipped back into the mansion.

"You cannot do this to Roman citizens, Falco," he heard his father say as he shut the door on the terrible scene. "This is against the law!"

Marcus pressed his ear to the door frame to hear the senator's reply. And wished he hadn't:

"By midday tomorrow, I shall be the law."

Falco, emperor? Jupiter's balls! Not while he, Marcus Calpurnius Aquila, possessed the strength to fight him.

Marcus sprinted for the mansion's main door, and the liberty that lay beyond, as if all the demons of Tartarus had been unleashed upon his trail.

**27**

JAMIL PACED THE confines of the interrogation chamber, acutely understanding how the arena's big cats felt. And wondering, as perhaps those creatures did, how he had failed to see the trap before falling headlong into it.

"Noble causes" didn't matter to the gods, apparently, for Falco's bodyguards had arrested Jamil at the estate's gates.

The door banged open. Jamil whirled.

Senator Falco blustered in, flanked by a dozen guards. "Where is Aquila?" The implied threat prickled the hairs on the nape of Jamil's neck.

"I don't know, my lord," he replied cautiously.

"You're his bodyguard. Of course you must know!" At the sight of Falco's upraised hand, the guards surrounded Jamil, spears leveled. "There is no money in his quarters. Tell me where he went, or regret it for the rest of your miserably short life."

"Perhaps he went to buy a gift for your daughter."

"Useless Nile scumweed!" Falco backhanded Jamil, who could have ducked the blow if he hadn't been reeling from lack of sleep. "Lock him up with the others, and search the city for my would-be son-in-law."

"Lord Aquila has done nothing, my lord." Jamil hoped his protest didn't sound as lame to the senator as it did to him.

"Of course he has, Egyptian buffoon. He and his parents, and their entire household, including you, have dared to cross the new order." Falco grinned wolfishly. "I shall take great pleasure in attending your execution wearing my new emperor's toga. The only thing I haven't yet decided upon is which beasts will tear you apart. The Colosseum houses a splendid array from which to choose."

The senator's dreadful laughter was a sound Jamil never would forget.

After tightly binding Jamil's wrists, the guards quick-marched him to one of the mansion's outbuildings, a windowless grain storage shed that could have doubled as an oven. Governor Agricola, his wrists also bound, rushed at the door, but the guards backed him up with their spears. One blade sank into his left shoulder.

Jerking back, Agricola gasped and winced, color draining from his face. Lady Loreia cried out and rushed to him. Their servants stepped up to support her—and to attack the guards at Agricola's command, if Jamil didn't misread their tense muscles and the grim determination in their expressions.

"We are citizens! It is unlawful to hold us in this manner!" protested the governor. "I appeal to Caesar!"

He may as well have been shouting at a brick wall. The guards shoved Jamil into the shed, yanked the door shut and locked it. Jamil stumbled into a tall stack of grain sacks. The top sack slid off and burst open, emitting a cloud of barley dust and besetting the prisoners with coughing fits.

"Citizen Kalilus, are you all right?" Agricola asked after he recovered breath enough to speak.

Jamil nodded, righting himself, thankful that although the situation seemed dire, it had restored his faith in the governor's innocence. He braced against the grain and raised his left foot to slide free a knife concealed in his sandal's sole. The guards had overlooked it in their haste to follow Falco's orders. He held the blade steady for Agricola to slice through his bonds. Soon everyone had been cut free to rub sore wrists.

Hand to mouth, Loreia pointed at her husband, where an ominous red blot had appeared high on his chest. The governor glanced down, grimaced and started swaying.

"Help me!" Jamil shouted at the other two servants as he struggled to keep the unconscious Agricola from falling and injuring himself even more.

Galvanized into action, the men lent their strength to the task of easing the governor to the ground. Loreia removed his toga and balled it into a hasty pillow for Agricola's head while Jamil summoned his battlefield training and carefully but thoroughly probed the wound.

The guard's spear had sliced into the governor's chest near his shoulder, below the collarbone. The wound was deep but not mortally so, thanks be to all the gods. But the damaged flesh needed protection from the infernal dust, to say nothing of stanching the oozing blood. Jamil grasped the hem of his tunic, but Loreia stopped him with a firm grip on his shoulder.

"I have more fabric to spare." She shed her outer stola and deftly ripped off several long strips. "Will these do?"

Jamil nodded and set to work, first pressing a wad of linen to the wound, then wrapping it as best he could. He didn't have the heart to tell her that, with the blood loss and the mounting heat, if the governor didn't receive liquids and better care soon, he might not survive until his execution.

Midway through the ministrations, Agricola's eyes flicked open. "Many thanks, Citizen Kalilus. I suppose I shouldn't charge at spears."

"No, you shouldn't, dearest heart," Loreia scolded softly. Kneeling at his head, she bent over to kiss his brow. After she straightened, she regarded Jamil. "Where is Marcus? If he was still on the estate grounds, surely they would have delivered him here by now."

Jamil pressed a finger to his lips, and Loreia nodded. He crawled to the mound of spilled grain, smoothed it level with his palm, and wrote, "Ludus Maximus."

"Visiting Libertas?" she asked in the barest of whispers.

Jamil shrugged. "Possibly."

"Gods!" Agricola groaned. "We're going to be murdered by a host gone mad enough to believe he can depose the emperors, and all our son can think about is slaking his lust." Groaning again, he sat upright, hand to head and swaying.

"Sextus, what is it?" Loreia cried, gripping his shoulders to steady him. "Your wound?"

The governor gave his head a slight shake. "A document," he whispered, "that could damn me—all of us—if the wrong person finds it." As Jamil wondered what Agricola meant, the wounded man reached up to tug on the neck of Jamil's tunic. Jamil bent down until his ear was all but touching Agricola's mouth. "Months ago, our host recruited a century-sized band of mercenaries. That's too small a unit to be very useful in most situations, but there must be a reason. Can you think of one?"

"Distraction," Jamil whispered into the governor's ear, a thousand possibilities leaping to mind. But he dared not voice even one. Nor did he mention the document he possessed that might mitigate their situation if it could be brought before the emperor. No sense in raising false hopes. "My lord, our guards could be some of them."

Lying back down, Agricola nodded. "With our son off at gods-know-where, doing gods-know-what, we could use a miracle."

"Our son," Loreia said quietly but firmly, "may be the only miracle we have."

"Gods, help us." The governor closed his eyes and sighed. "And please help Marcus most of all."


BRANDISHING HER SWORD—a weapon honed for combat, not a blunted copy—Rhyddes circled her opponent, looking for likely openings and not finding any.

Gods, but the woman was huge! A great, lumbering tower of muscle, blond braids and mocking laughter.

Then again, everyone past the age of twelve appeared huge to Rhyddes. She tightened her grip, drew a swift breath and darted under the Gallic gladiatrix's guard. Her sword grazed the woman's thigh, and she yelped.

With her shield, she swiped Rhyddes back as if she were naught but a pesky bee. Rhyddes staggered amid the hoots and catcalls of the other gladiators, their foremen and guards.

Why this school's lanista had ordered Rhyddes and the Gaul to square off in full combat gear, alone in the center of the practice ground that had been built with encircling seats like a small arena, Rhyddes couldn't begin to fathom. Her only choice, as usual, was to obey or die. And mayhap, this time, she was fated to obey *and* die.

Not if she, Rhyddes ferch Rudd, had any say.

As the blond Gaul swaggered about the arena, collecting the admiration of her audience, Rhyddes readied her weapon and charged again. Her opponent lunged. Rhyddes dived and rolled into her legs, knocking her down with a heavy thud and explosion of breath. Sand sprayed everywhere, some into Rhyddes's face.

Spitting grit, Rhyddes flung herself atop her opponent, her sword pressed against the woman's gut. Deathly silence had engulfed the arena, the only sound the panting of the two combatants. As the Gallic gladiatrix closed her eyes in surrender, Rhyddes craned her head toward the lanista.

His thumb turned upward. Rhyddes relaxed her hold and helped her opponent rise. "Well done!" he called. "Libertas of Britannia, by defeating Lucerna, my best gladiatrix, you have proven yourself a most worthy addition to Ludus Maximus."

The reaction from the crowd, as Rhyddes had expected,

seemed negative. One voice of approval, however, rang out clearly. And it sounded too familiar to be a coincidence.

Could it be…?

She searched the crowd in vain. Surely, in her eagerness to find an ally in her new surroundings, she'd imagined the voice.

"Indeed, well done, Libertas," Lucerna was saying as she dusted sand from her wound and sheathed her sword.

Rhyddes gaped at her. "You are not angry for the loss?"

This time Lucerna's laughter held no mockery. A medic had run over to clean and bind her wound. After he finished, Lucerna motioned for Rhyddes to accompany her from the arena. "Lanista Laomedes tries every new gladiatrix against me and keeps only the best fighters. I see no shame in losing to the best of the best."

Rhyddes felt her cheeks flush, and not from the exertion. "I won with a trick I learned from a dear friend," she said, wondering how Gordianus was faring. "I don't deserve to be called the best for that."

Lucerna smiled. "You earned Lanista Laomedes's approval, and that's good enough for me." She clapped Rhyddes on the shoulder before a contingent of guards arrived to escort them to the armory.

Mayhap, Rhyddes mused as the glances thrown her way melted from disdain to acceptance, being a member of Ludus Maximus might not be so bad.

If she survived the prince's natal celebration.


"Papa, I am the lady of this household," Messiena said to a man she was ceasing to recognize, "not a child to be bundled out of sight."

His fingers dug even harder into her arm as he tugged her down the corridor toward her chambers, scattering terrified servants in their wake.

"I am doing this for you, Pulla, to keep you safe." The tense chords in his voice frightened her. "The less you know, the better off you will be."

As they rounded a corner, she latched on to the molding to halt his progress. He glared at her, but she ignored him. "Is that what you're doing to the Calpurniae, locking them in that shed for their protection?"

"No. I am cutting my losses." With a savage tug, he yanked her free and marched forward.

"Losses! They are human beings, Papa. Roman citizens. High-ranking, influential Roman citizens, in case you have forgotten. Not a gambling risk."

They reached the door to her chambers, and he paused with his hand on the bronze handle. "That is where you are wrong, Daughter. I did gamble in allowing you and that wastrel son of Agricola's to become betrothed, thinking I might gain important allies. But Agricola and Aquila have proven to be far greater liabilities than assets."

"Liabilities? What do you mean?"

She received no answer, for Falco opened the door, ushered her inside and closed it. Before she could twist the handle, she heard him turn the key in the lock, and he shouted for someone to bring his sedan chair to the front of the mansion.

"Papa, no!" She knotted her hands into fists and pummeled the door, tears stinging her eyes. "You cannot keep me locked in here forever!"

"Not forever, Pulla. Just two or three days. You shall emerge as queen of the world, and that useless Aquila will never trouble you again."

In shock she heard her father order the household guards to keep a man posted at her door.

Of course, she thought slyly, there was always the exit she used to escape this sort of punishment as a child: a window concealed behind the thick boughs of a hemlock tree.

The window's lock operated easily, but the sash wouldn't budge. Apparently the limed water used each spring to keep the mansion looking pristinely white had worked into the frame. She could grab something heavy to smash her way out, but only as a last resort. Instead she hurried back to her writing desk for the knife with which she sharpened quills and pried up wax seals.

After returning to the window to settle into the task of working the sash loose with the knife, she prayed it would quickly yield to her efforts. And that, once free, she could turn her father from the insane course of action he'd planned.

MARCUS DREW UPON every facet of his arena-honed cunning, cutting behind buildings and weaving among the pedestrians to elude pursuit. Soon the immense Forum of Trajan, with its myriad shops on four levels that attracted throngs of people from all social strata, loomed before him. He dashed into one end of the forum and up the nearest set of stairs.

The first order of business was buying a new tunic. He followed a knot of customers into a shop whose storefront displayed examples of what he sought.

"I need something plain," he insisted when the female shopkeeper, flirting outrageously, tried to sell him a silk tunic of robin's egg blue. "This is a fine garment, good woman, but—"

She held it to his torso. "But see how the fabric flows like water around your—" she batted her eyes "—rippling muscles."

Marcus had no time for this foolery. "Another day, madam." He withdrew two sesterces from his pouch and slapped them onto the pine table. "Today I need a tunic such as a common laborer might wear. It's for a special party I am attending." If the fib forestalled any questions she might ask, so much the better.

"Ah, a theme party. Very fashionable these days, I hear." The shopkeeper gave his feet a pointed stare. "I suggest plainer shoes, soled with hobnails, to complete the look."

Marcus glanced over his shoulder and out the door, but he seemed to have lost the senator's men. He added twenty-five sesterces. "Shoes and a hooded cloak, too. But please hurry. I fear I may be late already."

Nodding, the woman scurried off. To her credit, the items she brought were much better suited to his immediate needs. He took the undyed, coarsely spun tunic, scratchy woolen cloak and stiff leather shoes, and handed the women another ten sesterces.

"This is for the blue silk tunic," he said in response to her surprised look, "but I must return for it later. May I change into my purchases and leave my other clothes here?"

"Of course, my lord! This way, please."

From her vivid blushing, one might have presumed

Marcus had proposed a sexual liaison. She conducted him to a small storeroom partitioned by a thin linen curtain. Although she pulled it closed, it occurred to him that she probably could see his silhouette through the weave.

Chuckling softly, he made short work of stripping off his sweaty tunic and shrugging into the new one, cinching it with his belt, to which the pouch was attached. The shoes came next. After he finished donning his new attire, he draped the cloak over his left arm, gathered the discarded items, stepped from behind the curtain, and deposited the bundle into the shopkeeper's waiting arms. Her blushing had subsided, but only just.

"Good woman, I cannot thank you enough for your gracious service. May Fortuna richly bless you and your shop."

Marcus barely heard her stammered thanks, for he was already darting out the door.

On his way toward the forum's opposite end, he saw another shop featuring wares that promised to further his disguise.

If Falco had captured and interrogated Jamil, then it was possible Ludus Maximus was being watched already; perhaps the other gladiatorial schools, as well. Marcus hoped this wasn't the case but couldn't depend upon being that lucky. He needed someplace to hide until dark, when it would be easer to slip past Falco's men.

And Marcus could think of no better place to go to ground than inside the vast complex of Trajan's public bathhouse. He would have preferred Titus's baths for their proximity to Ludus Maximus, but Falco's men could be nearby, and Titus's bathhouse was but a tenth the size of Trajan's.

Submerging himself among thousands of bathers would be child's play compared with trying to submerge the rising tide of guilt for being fortunate enough to have escaped his parents' fate…at least, for the present.

MESSIENA SET A BRISK pace for the servants she'd recruited to bring food and drink to her guests. She refused to think of the parents of her betrothed as prisoners; that was her father's doing, induced by a brain fever. Accusing the Calpurniae of theft and lying, and calling Messiena "queen of the world"—clearly, Falco stood in dire need of Physician Galen's care.

That chore ranked second on her list. First came her gods-given duty to her guests.

She didn't have to direct the servants where to go; the location of the makeshift prison, and the identities of its occupants, had doubtless become common news within minutes of the incarceration. Her confinement apparently was not common knowledge, for no one she encountered seemed surprised to see her. However, she avoided the entrance to her quarters, where a guard had been posted.

Curiously, there seemed to be far fewer servants about than usual. Upon inquiry, she learned that a dozen men and women, escorted by a score of estate guards, had accompanied Falco into the city, but none of the other servants knew where the master had gone, his purpose, or when he was expected to return.

So much the better for helping her father's mistreated guests.

As she and her assistants neared the shed, the guards' postures stiffened.

"My lady, no one is permitted to enter," said the squad's highest ranking soldier. "Senator's orders."

She planted a hand on her hip to feign casualness. "Don't be ridiculous, Clareo. Surely my father didn't give orders for them to starve."

The burly blond Celt looked doubtful. "No, but—"

"But whatever these people may have done, they remain our guests until a legal trial can be conducted. And it is my sacred duty to see to their needs." Smiling sweetly, she asked, "You don't wish the gods to curse us for being inhospitable, do you?"

"Of course not, my lady!" Clareo snapped the order for his men to stand aside, and he unlocked the door with a key dangling among several on a ring threaded onto his belt. "But—please forgive me—I must lock the door while you are inside."

Messiena nodded. Beckoning the servants to accompany her, she stepped into the shed.

And was appalled.

Governor Agricola lay prone on the barley-littered floor, blood caking his shoulder and an alarming pallor to his face. Lady Loreia sat with his head cradled in her lap, massaging his temple with one hand and fanning herself with the other. The pox-scarred man Messiena recognized as the guard Marcus had called Jamil stood between the grain stacks, conversing with two men Messiena knew only as servants in the governor's entourage.

The gods alone knew what her father had done to the rest of Agricola's servants. Considering Falco's obviously unstable state, it was far too easy to imagine the worst.

Relief fought with worry when Messiena realized Marcus was not present. Surely Falco would have imprisoned him with his parents; perhaps her betrothed had escaped to find help. The thought of Marcus charging into the mansion, the district's prefect and a cohort of soldiers in tow, to rescue her from her father's madness, gave her spirits an unexpected lift.

It was quenched by the stiflingly hot air inside the shed. Everyone's skin was coated with a sheen of sweat, and their clothes—what they hadn't stripped off—had already begun to bear wet, dark evidence of their distress.

Conversation ceased, and all heads turned toward Messiena as she entered. The preternaturally loud sound of the lock clicking into place gave rise to a wave of panic, but she quelled it with a hard swallow and bade the servants to distribute the honeyed cakes and wine, which were accepted with gratitude.

"I am so sorry for this outrage," Messiena murmured as her guests partook of the refreshments. "I would love to set you free, but it was all I could do to convince the guards to permit me to offer this much succor."

"We heard, dear," said Loreia gently. "And we do appreciate your efforts."

Jamil squatted over a flattened area of spilled grain, gave Messiena a pointed look, and wrote, "How many guards?"

"XVI," she wrote, adding, "Fully armed."

Governor Agricola, whose pallor had been eased by the wine, said with a sad smile, "We know."

"Is that how you got hurt?" Messiena asked. When Agricola nodded, she said, "Are you in pain? Does the wound need tending? I might be able to arrange for the house physician to see you—"

"No need," insisted the governor.

"Unless your physician can incapacitate the guards," Jamil added in a hopeful, but resigned, whisper.

Their plight wrung Messiena's heart. "I will keep doing what I can for you." She couldn't bear to dash their hopes with the probable reality that her assistance, along with her liberty, would end as soon as the guards rotated posts and the entire complement learned of her confinement. But she felt compelled to add, sweeping an arm toward her servants, "I shall leave orders with the guards for Agna and Caius to bring you anything else you require."

"Swords would be helpful," Jamil muttered.

The door shook from the force of a guard's pounding. "Lady Messiena, you must come out now."

The sternness in the Clareo's tone made her stomach clench. Messiena didn't have to tell her guests that Jamil's request lay far beyond her power to deliver.

## 28

Rhyddes had to admit, even though she was sweating profusely under this land's relentless sun, it felt good to be exercising. Paired with a female sparring partner for the first time in her gladiatorial career, she traded blows with Lucerna in a standard drill pattern. As at Villa Britanniae, the trainers here at vast Ludus Maximus encouraged the gladiators to improve speed and accuracy rather than force.

But unlike at Jamil's establishment, the Ludus Maximus trainers delivered their encouragement with the tongue of a whip.

"Do they always do this?" she whispered to Lucerna after the group had repaired to the pine benches, set against the training ground's wall, for the evening meal. She flinched as a cut on her shoulder scraped against the rough plaster wall.

Lucerna glanced at a pair of fresh whip marks on her

shield arm and shrugged. "These are love taps compared to a flogging. You'll get used to it."

Jamil was no stranger to the whip, but he had wielded it judiciously. Rhyddes never would have believed that one day she would miss his school…to say nothing of her coming to regard him as the father of her heart.

An annoying voice in her head reminded her that she missed someone else even more acutely, though he had yet to grace her with his presence.

More annoying still, the voice was right.

MARCUS SAT ON THE tiled bench inside the dressing area, contemplating his situation as he donned his clothes. His body felt refreshed from having spent the day inside Trajan's bathhouse, with its boundless opportunities for swimming, soaking, exercise, massage and meditation, but despite the regal treatment, bands of worry and guilt constricted his soul. By sundown, he stood no closer to a solution.

He had struck up acquaintances with several other bathers to learn more about the names on Falco's list. As he'd suspected, many, like the unfortunate Ferox and two men who recently had suffered "accidental" demises, were senators. Agricola was the only provincial governor. The rest served as city magistrates.

Including Severus, the magistrate governing Templum Pacis, the district to which Falco's estate belonged.

Since Severus's name had not been crossed off, Marcus suspected that attempting to enlist his help wouldn't prove a viable option. Even though Marcus possessed a legitimate complaint with respect to his parents' mistreatment at

Falco's hands, the magistrate was probably a friend of the senator...if not outright in Falco's employ. For a coup to work inside the city of Rome, the fourteen district magistrates would have to be either included in the plan, or else bribed to look the other way.

Given Falco's temperament and financial status, the latter was more likely.

His best chance lay with the emperor, but a list of names scrawled on a scrap of parchment, even considering what had happened to some of those men, did not constitute proof of a coup. Marcus hoped the list would force Falco's hand, but he suspected the parchment had no power to get him past the front rank of the emperor's clerks.

Especially today, when all imperial attention seemed focused on the imminent celebration of Prince Commodus's natal day.

He finished tying his shoes, reached inside the niche for his cloak and gave it a shake. Too hot to wear now, it would be indispensable tonight. He withdrew from the niche his final purchase, a medium-length blond wig "crafted from the hair of a dead Germanic warrior," the shopkeeper had assured him.

Feeling absurd, even though many Roman men wore such trappings, Marcus rose to step in front of the polished silver mirror, adjusting the wig to hide every black wisp. With the leather cord the wig vendor had given him, he tied the fake hair behind his head in Gallic fashion, leaving the long bangs swinging freely.

From the bathhouse's main entrance, concealed by his disguise as well as the sea of bathers ebbing and flowing around the public pleasure palace, Marcus glanced about.

Not half an arena's width away marched a unit of soldiers with a sedan chair in their midst, trailed by servants lugging sacks and crates.

The procession, belonging to a senator, as indicated by the broad purple stripe adorning the sedan chair, headed toward the gates of Ludus Maximus.

*The gladiators will get their orders tomorrow....*

Remaining alert to the danger of being discovered, Marcus waited to the count of one hundred, while the procession filed inside the gladiatorial school, before following them.

WHEN LUDUS MAXIMUS'S servants failed to make the rounds with the usual meal of barley porridge and watered wine, the gladiators began to get restless. A trumpet blast halted their fidgeting, and all attention turned upward to the walkway that circled the top of the training arena. A portly man stood beside Lanista Laomedes, accompanied by a detachment of guards.

"A senator," Lucerna whispered to Rhyddes. "You can tell by his toga's wide purple band."

"Who is he?" she asked, more curious about how much her sparring partner knew than about the Roman's identity. "Is he important?"

Lucerna gave her a bemused grin. "They all think they are."

The crack of a whip sounded behind them, and Lucerna winced.

"Silence, woman," rasped one of the trainers. "Senator Falco is about to speak."

The senator raised both hands. "Put away your whip, good man. These excellent men and women deserve our respect, not our reproach, for showing us courage, cunning and honor."

That won him hearty cheers from most of the gladiators, though it left Rhyddes less than impressed. His eyes shifted often, as if assessing the gladiators' strengths, and his smile seemed flattened by insincerity.

Given a choice between trusting Pugionis or this senator, she'd have picked her noxious owner any day.

"Our venerable emperor, Marcus Aurelius," Falco went on after the cheers had died, "has bequeathed upon me the honor of establishing your pairings. I know it is customary for you to enjoy a feast hosted by the games' sponsor, but that is not possible today. There are far too many of you. However—"

Whatever he would have said was drowned by the gladiators' groans, boos and cruder expressions of disappointment. The senator's soldiers pounded the colonnade's cobbles repeatedly with their spears' butts to command silence.

"However," said Falco after order had been restored, "I have made arrangements to bring the feast to you!"

He clapped once, and a parade of servants filed into the training arena bearing platters and tureens of every size and shape, mounded with more temptingly fragrant delicacies than Rhyddes had ever seen. But when some of the gladiators surged forward in their hunger, the trainers' whips convinced them to remain seated.

Parched from the long training session, Rhyddes was more interested in drink than in food, but she took a moment to sniff her goblet's contents speculatively.

She felt an elbow dig into her ribs, not hard. "It can't be poisoned, if that's what you're thinking," scoffed Lucerna between aromatic mouthfuls of spiced beef. "They pay a fortune to watch us die bloody deaths."

If the woman had meant it as a joke, Rhyddes didn't find it amusing. And the lumps of lobster, crab and oyster on her plate, smothered in a tangy red sauce, no longer looked so appealing.

"SORRY, SIR. NO VISITORS. The gladiators are feasting in the training arena."

The guard's tone, expelled on breath acrid with garlic, carried strains of envy as well as boredom. He returned to the game of knucklebones with the other guards, not sparing Marcus a second glance.

"Libertas will not thank you for turning me away." He plucked a fistful of aureii from his pouch and let them tinkle from his fingers to the tabletop. "I am her husband."

The title came too naturally to his tongue and sounded too right in his ears for it to be a lie. He despised the fact that it could never become reality.

The guards regarded him with avaricious appreciation.

"Divide those among you," Marcus told the first guard, dipping his hand into his pouch again. He uncurled his fingers to show the guard another aureus. "This is yours if you conduct me to her cell without letting her see me." Marcus grinned. "I want to surprise her."

The man triumphantly regarded his fellows. "Easiest money I've ever made."

"And the easiest to lose!" jibed another, and the rest guffawed in agreement.

"This way, sir." He led Marcus through a side door, rather than the larger exit that undoubtedly opened onto the training ground. Once they entered the enclosed corridor, the guard set a brisk pace. "I have a game to win."

Marcus hoped he would win the game he'd been sucked into, too, although he felt as if he was playing blind, with no concept of the rules.

The stakes, however, loomed painfully clear. If Marcus failed to thwart Falco's plot, he and his parents would become the first aristocratic victims of the new regime.

AFTER THE BUZZ OF conversation was replaced by the sounds of gusty chewing, the senator raised his hands.

"Prince Commodus, whose natal day you shall be helping to celebrate tomorrow, enjoys military spectacles. To that end, I am pleased to announce another break in tradition in Prince Commodus's honor. You shall process through the streets, as some of you may have done in other cities, joining the gladiators and guards from Ludus Regis and Ludus Validus to march to Ludus Imperatorius, thence to take that school's tunnel into the Colosseum. Before the procession, attendants shall distribute your practice weapons, and you shall march fully armed, rather than carrying your helmets as in the past."

Falco paused to let the surprised muttering die down.

"But, my lord, the crowd likes to see our faces, since they can't when we fight," said one of the men, a heavyset brute who fought in the thraex class. Other gladiators expressed agreement by thumping their fists on the benches.

"The people will enjoy this spectacle even more, Carnifex," Falco replied. Rhyddes mistrusted the smirk that spread across the senator's face. "At the end of the tunnel, your guards shall leave you for their ready-rooms beside the Porta Vita…"

"Porta Vita?" Rhyddes whispered to Lucerna. She recognized the phrase as "gate of life" but had no idea what the senator had meant by it.

"The Colosseum architect's idea of a joke," Lucerna whispered back. "Dead gladiators never use it."

"…and you shall continue marching through the Porta Vita and onto the arena floor, as proudly as any legion. From there the true spectacle shall commence."

During the thoughtful silence that followed, Rhyddes wondered how many other gladiators had noticed the senator did not describe this "true spectacle," and how many, like herself, were itching to ask him.

The senator turned toward the lanista. "Laomedes, Ludus Maximus shall be the second contingent to enter the arena. I want your best guards and the criminals in the first ranks, followed by the rest of the guards, and the slave and contract retiarii, secutors, provocators and so forth, in the usual order."

Rhyddes wanted to ask where the women would be marching but decided against attracting attention.

Something about the senator's announcement stank like week-old anchovies, but the more Rhyddes pondered it, the faster the answer wriggled from her grasp.

Unlike at Londinium's Villa Britanniae, the encroachment of other public structures had necessitated that Ludus Maximus be built up, rather than out. As a consequence, the gladiators' stucco-plastered brick cells perched atop the school's common rooms surrounding the central training area.

This arrangement offered added security, for a leap from the cell blocks' iron-spiked perimeter fence constituted a perilous four-story drop.

Cloaked and hooded, Marcus sat on Libertas's hard cot. Since he was a free citizen—though for how much longer remained anyone's guess—the guard didn't lock the cell's door.

Falco's speech to the gladiators traveled readily to the cell blocks. Marcus listened with increasing dread.

The senator's mention of that many gladiators, from all the competing schools, marching into the arena like a legion, with their guards being instructed to leave them at the end of the route, caused certain facets of the plan to make horrific sense.

With so many unguarded gladiators crowded into one place, even armed only with practice weapons, too much could go wrong far too quickly.

He fingered the amber pendant inside his pouch, despising the choice he was being forced to make. That choice could endanger Libertas, which was the last thing he ever wanted to do. Her life as a gladiatrix was dangerous enough.

On the morrow that danger might prove fatal.

Since he and Libertas had parted in anger, she might want nothing more to do with him. Yet, with the fate of the Roman Empire and its coemperors teetering in the balance, Marcus's failure was not an option.

Slowly he pulled the leather cord from his pouch and slipped it around his neck, tucking the pendant into his tunic's neckline. With each breath, he prayed Libertas would forgive him at least long enough to accept his gift.

If she didn't…well, the lack of a woman's forgiveness wouldn't matter to a dead man.


LUCERNA, HAVING DRUNK too much of the senator's superb wine, fell asleep against Rhyddes's shoulder. Although most of the other gladiators were still laughing, drinking and eating as if they suspected this would be the last feast they'd ever enjoy, Rhyddes decided her sparring partner had the right idea. She signaled a guard to escort them to their cells.

"Vederi!" she gasped at the man who appeared from the shadows. "I did hear you this morning, didn't I?"

He inclined his head. "And a fine bout it was. Just as I expected of you."

They supported Lucerna between them and half carried, half dragged her toward the cell blocks.

"I thank you, but why are you here? I thought they turned you away."

"Not this morning. It seems the guard on duty before was misinformed. The lanista was seeking more guards because of the influx of gladiators."

That much made sense. However, "Didn't you try to become hired at any of the other schools?"

"Why would I, when the only charge I have ever enjoyed guarding resides here?" He slid her a shy smile.

She felt her cheeks flush and was thankful for the torchlit gloom. At the foot of the stairs, Vederi hoisted Lucerna over one shoulder and ordered Rhyddes to ascend first.

"You don't want me to help you?" she asked.

Vederi shook his head. "It's better for both of us if we don't appear as if we know each other overly well."

Sensitive to his laboring breath, and beginning to feel the soporific effects of the rich food and wine herself, she took her time climbing the three flights to the cells. Upon exiting the stairwell, near Lucerna and Rhyddes's cells, Vederi set down his softly snoring burden.

"I confess, Libertas," he whispered, "guarding you isn't the only thing I wish to do for the rest of...our lives."

"What do you mean?" she asked warily, suspecting she already knew the answer.

He glanced about. Lucerna was still slumped where he'd left her, and the rest of the gladiators and guards showed no signs of ending the merriment anytime soon.

"I know you have given yourself to Lord Aquila, but he must marry another woman soon, and..." He gazed at the ground. "And I was hoping you might consider marrying me."

Rhyddes clapped a hand over her mouth, cheeks aflame. She'd expected him to propose a sexual liaison, in truth, ever since her first day at Villa Britanniae. But marriage? Never.

"I am infamia, and a slave, Vederi. Neither are simple obstacles to overcome in this empire of yours." She gave him a frank look. "To say nothing of my occupation, which is dangerous at best. And—" she hated to be this brutal, but for his sake, she had to be "—lethal at worst."

He grasped her hands. "Who knows that better than I, Libertas? But I would be honored if you would merely consider what I propose."

"I..."

She stared at the hands holding hers, roughened and callused by countless seasons of service with a sword. Honest hands, hardworking hands. Not the hands of a pampered nobleman who held a sword only when he saw fit.

Not the hands of the man she loved.

Lucerna stirred, groaning, as if she might wake. Vederi loosened his grip, and Rhyddes gratefully pulled free. But the earnestness of his gaze wouldn't let her escape so easily.

She sighed. "What would you have us do? I cannot buy my freedom. I gave most of my winnings to my brother in April, and I haven't fought another bout since." Recalling this morning's trial, she smiled grimly. "Not for pay, that is."

"I can wait for you, Libertas," he insisted.

"And do what? Try to steal moments like this? How many do you think we could have before we're caught and punished?" Uncertainty stole across his face, and she pressed her advantage. "What do you think our punishments would be? The lanista might terminate your employment, but I, who must live under the specter of 'obey or die'…is that a risk you're willing to take?"

"Gods, no." He looked so forlorn, she felt her eyes moisten.

"But I am touched that you think so highly of me." Fist over chest, she bowed her head. "I thank you for the asking, Vederi."

Gently he pried her fist free, brushed his lips across the backs of her fingers, and withdrew with a sad smile. "Just being near you is enough," he said. She expected him to add, "For now," though to his credit, he refrained.

After Rhyddes and Vederi helped Lucerna to stand, Rhyddes resumed her position on Lucerna's other side, and the trio lurched forward. Once they got Lucerna settled onto her cot, Rhyddes was more than ready for hers.

The problem, she discovered when they reached her cell, was that someone else was already occupying it. By the figure's build, she could tell it was a man, but his cloak's hood cast his face in shadow. She thought she saw the glint of blond hair in the fickle torchlight, which confused her.

She glanced at Vederi but didn't get a chance to ask her question.

"Good evening, Libertas."

The hair was wrong, but she knew that voice. And before she could risk revealing how she felt about him, he had much to resolve.

Briefly Vederi looked as surprised as she felt. After locking them into the cell and bidding them, in strained tones, a pleasant evening, he departed. Rather hastily, Rhyddes thought.

Aquila seemed oblivious to Vederi's behavior. He rose, took Rhyddes into his arms and fastened his mouth to hers. She cocked her fist and punched him in the gut, hard. He dropped to one knee, clutching his midsection and gasping for breath.

"Roman pig! How dare you take such liberties!" She stalked to the cell's door to yell for Vederi.

"Libertas, wait! Please." He sucked in a few more breaths. "I deserved that punch, and I am sorry. For everything." His sincerity convinced her to look at him. He was sitting on her cot, head in hands. She leaned against the cold bars, arms folded and one eyebrow cocked. "I'm in trouble, and I need your help."

"Hah. Help you? After you refused to rescue me from men who would rape me, murder me and relieve themselves on my corpse? And after you tried to take me, just now, with no more consideration than if you were plucking a fistful of grapes?" She turned toward the door, gripping the bars, her heart once again at war with her head. Her head won. "I think not, my lord. I craved action from you, but not that sort of action."

She heard the cot's ropes creak as he rose and moved nearer, though he possessed sense enough not to touch her.

"I'm sorry! Please hear me out," Aquila whispered fervently. "If I leave now, and the senator's men are still here, I won't live to see the moon rise."

Was that what she wanted? To see him felled and dumped into the mass grave with the arena's losers, if his killers chose to accord him even that much honor?

She faced him. He smiled, and the intoxication of his nearness made her knees wobble. She couldn't afford that luxury, so she perched on her cot. She did not invite him to join her. That emotional luxury was too expensive.

He sighed, stepped to the rear of the cell, and slid down the wall to sit on the floor, arms wrapped around his knees.

"Start explaining," she growled. "My lord."

**29**

MESSIENA STARED OUT the windows of her gilt prison, watching the torchlight glint off the guards' spears, fuming at her father but mostly fuming at herself for being unable to convince them to let her out. They treated her courteously, but they patently refused to disobey their master's orders.

When the door opened, she didn't bother to turn around. Servants had not been denied her, so she had not lacked for care during this ludicrous confinement.

The same could not be said for her guests.

Regardless of whatever victory Falco thought he could accomplish, his madness had doomed them all for violating the sacred duties toward visitors under his roof. It was only a matter of time before the gods' judgment fell.

"My lady, I have brought your supper," said Agna softly.

"I'm not hungry." Not even the aroma of shrimp, crab and

lobster soaked in her favorite lemon-butter sauce could tempt Messiena from her black mood. "Give it to the Calpurniae."

"They have eaten already, my lady." The aroma wafted closer as Agna crossed the room to set the tray on Messiena's writing desk. "They received the kitchen's best portions. I saw to it myself."

"Bless you, Agna." Perhaps divine judgment might yet be averted. "How fare the Calpurniae?"

Agna sighed. "As well as can be expected, my lady. I did bring fresh bandages for the governor's wound."

"Well done. Any word of Aquila yet? Or my father?"

"Lord Aquila has disappeared," Agna said. "The master sent men out to find him, but no one's had any luck so far."

That Marcus had eluded capture was good news, but, "My father went with them?" It didn't sound like something Falco would have done, but yesterday Messiena never would have believed he'd have resorted to harming guests, either.

"No, my lady. The master had other business in the city today. Hosting feasts for the gladiators competing tomorrow, each in the gladiators' own school, so the other servants told me."

Messiena fingered her chin.

Falco hosting gladiator feasts meant he had a role in arranging the bouts—which, in itself, wasn't unusual. The fact that he had not hosted the event on estate grounds, as he had done so often in the past, however, was too irregular to stand above suspicion.

He'd told Messiena her confinement would last—what? Two or three days? After which time she would emerge as "queen of the world." Whatever in Tartarus he'd meant by that, he must have intended for her to miss the games' opening day "for her protection."

*Protection, hah.*

Whatever Falco had planned was going to occur tomorrow. Messiena would stake her virtue upon it.

Not even Jupiter in all his fury could prevent her from attending the games, for they represented her best and perhaps only opportunity to turn her father from his ill-conceived course. Surely he would back down when confronted publicly.

She rose and shifted to the chair behind the desk, where her supper awaited. It did look as delicious as it smelled, but more important matters needed to be resolved first.

Messiena regarded her servant speculatively. Agna's height and proportions were so similar to Messiena's that the servant had often assisted the estate's tailor in the fitting of Messiena's gowns.

"Is something wrong, my lady?" Agna's eyes rounded, and she blushed. "I mean, with the food."

"No, no. Please convey Coquus my thanks." Messiena beckoned the woman closer and dropped her voice to a whisper. "Come here early tomorrow morning. Bring a basket of clean linens, and two heaping bowls of cherries and cream."

Agna's disbelief looked comical. "But you don't like cherries, my lady. Except as lip coloring."

"Quite true." Messiena grinned. "I wish to reward my guards with a special treat. But they cannot enjoy it too much."

"My lady?"

Messiena briefly glanced at the door. "If someone swallows poison—"

Agna gasped. "Do—do y-you mean to poison them?"

"Of course not!" Messiena whispered harshly. "I just need to know if there's an herb that can make a person vomit."

"There is, my lady. It's—"

Messiena shushed her. "I don't want to know what it is. Just blend its essence into the cream." Before Agna could raise another protest, she added, "Bring your needlework, too. I suspect you are going to have a lot more time for it than usual."

BY THE TIME AQUILA had finished relating his tale, Rhyddes's head was spinning so badly, she thought it might fly apart.

"Let me see if I have heard you correctly. You think that senator wants to become emperor, and he's going to use the gladiators to accomplish this feat? Armed with fake weapons? Right under the noses of the emperor's bodyguards?" When he nodded, she pressed a hand to her throbbing temple. "That makes no sense. Even if a revolt was to break out, and enough school guards were killed to provide real weapons for the surviving gladiators, the emperor's men would intervene before the gladiators got too far out of control."

"Not if the guards are not stationed on the arena floor," Aquila replied. "It sounded as if Falco intends the gladiators to be the only ones in the arena, and he may have devised a way for them to storm into the stands. And, based on that conversation I overheard, I believe he may have paid some of the Praetorian guardsmen to stay out of the conflict."

"But that could mean—" Rhyddes clapped a hand over

her mouth, imagining the worst: hundreds of dead gladiators, perhaps spectators, too, being killed by rebelling gladiators or trampled in the panicked rush...mothers, children..." Gods, no! Why would he do such an evil thing?"

"It could be a means to prove to the people that Emperor Marcus Aurelius is unfit to rule if he appears unable to command the loyalty of his own elite guardsmen."

"Rome has two emperors, does it not?"

"Yes, but Emperor Lucius Verus is still off at war." Aquila's mouth thinned to a grim line. "And murder becomes laughably easy in the guise of combat."

"Why should I, a foreign slave, care who rules and who dies tomorrow?"

Aquila regarded her so intently she wished she could see his face to read it better. "You could die tomorrow, Libertas." A mournful quality invaded his tone to tug at her heart. "What emperor would begin his reign by allowing two thousand rebellious gladiators to live, especially if he instigated the rebellion?"

"I face death every day," she reminded him.

"I will die tomorrow, too." He looked down, resting his chin on his hands. "I'd hoped you might care about that."

Standing, she forced herself to examine her feelings for this man. In spite of the social chasm dividing them, she simply could not imagine a world without Aquila in it. Even when they'd been separated, and she wasn't sure she'd ever see him again, just knowing he was alive had given her the hope to survive each day's miseries.

But if Aquila were killed...spending a lifetime with

Vederi, good-hearted and stalwart though he might be, just wouldn't be the same.

The realization forced her to her knees, and she touched his cheek. A tingle raced from fingertips to shoulder. "I do care," she admitted, feeling her eyes moisten. "Very much. But what can I, a mere slave, possibly do to help you?"

Affection tinted his smile. "You may be many things, Libertas, but *mere* doesn't fit with any of them." When he lifted his hands, she expected him to reach for her face. Instead he pulled an amulet from around his neck and slipped the cord over his head. With the trinket resting in his palm, he presented it to her. "All I ask is that you accept this token of my love for you."

Did regret and worry skitter across his face? The lighting was too poor and the reactions disappeared too fast for her to be certain.

She picked up the amulet and tried to examine it but couldn't make out much detail other than its smooth, fingerlike shape and incredible lightness.

"I don't understand how my keeping this bauble could help you."

He enfolded her hand within his much warmer one, trapping the amulet inside. "It helps me to know you care enough to wear it. Will you, in the arena tomorrow? Please?"

She stared at his hand, trying to puzzle out his intent. Did it belong to someone else? His bride, perhaps? If so, why had he not given it to the woman for safekeeping?

While she wrestled with the mystery, Aquila released her hand. She uncurled her fingers, unsure whether she should keep it or not, especially if Aquila's betrothed was the rightful owner.

"I am deeply sorry that my decisions have brought you to this place, Libertas. More sorry than I can ever say." He tugged on the amulet's cord, and she let it slide off her palm.

In one fluid movement, he rose, yanked off the fake hair, slung it to the floor and kicked it under the cot. As if an afterthought, he pulled another object from his pouch, tossed it toward the cot and pivoted to clutch the cell door's bars. The wooden object bounced off the cot and hit the floor beside her with an echoing clatter.

She gasped. Gently, as if it were a babe, she picked it up and cradled it in her hands, reacquainting herself with its noble contours and smooth, cool finish.

Aquila had gone to the gods knew how much trouble to reunite her with Jamil's Anubis figurine—and was responsible for reuniting her with Jamil, she realized.

If not for Aquila, Rhyddes never would have learned how deeply her former master cared for her.

If not for Aquila, she'd have died at the end of Jamil's whip or in Londinium's arena at the hands of a gladiator dressed like a woman, and she never would have learned the glorious pleasures of love.

If not for Aquila, she never would have learned to love anyone outside her clan.

He had done all those things for her, and what was she about to do, ungrateful wretch that she was? Drive away, mayhap to his death, the man she loved to the very core of her soul.

Shame branded her cheeks, and remorse levered her to her feet. She padded up behind him and slid her arms around his waist.

"Please don't go," she whispered urgently. "My love."

MARCUS SLOWLY TURNED, unsure whether he'd heard Libertas properly. Her radiant smile confirmed it. She held up the enameled obsidian figure with the man's body and jackal's head. "Thank you for returning Anubis to me."

Standing on tiptoe, she reached up to lock her hands behind his neck and guide his face close to hers.

Poets were forever babbling about the qualities of the perfect kiss. The passion Libertas unleashed with her sweet, insistent lips could have given lessons to them all.

Feeling his body's heightened response, he slid his hands down her back to cup her buttocks, pulling her closer. The rest of the world seemed to melt in the crucible of desire, refined to just the two of them: lips to lips, body to body, soul to soul.

By the time she broke off to grasp his hand and tug him toward her cot, he wouldn't have cared whether every guard had run over to watch. Nothing existed beyond this goddess in his arms.

And even if Fortuna decreed their lives to end on the morrow, Marcus would express his thanks for this night with his final breath.

No, he decided as he enjoyed rediscovering her body's secret delights, watching her eyelids lower halfway and lips part in sultry pleasure as his movements quickened, that wouldn't be right. As thankful as he might feel for earning this incredible woman's love, he would reserve his last words uttered on this side of heaven for her: his goddess, his soul's mate and his only love.

SOME HOURS LATER, the screech of rusty iron hinges invaded Marcus's dreams. He opened his eyes to find himself lying on the chilly concrete floor, wrapped in his cloak, a guard opening the cell's door.

"Come, sir." The guard kept his voice low, but the tone brooked no disobedience. "Bid your wife farewell. It's time for you to depart."

Marcus gazed at Libertas, love swelling his chest. She slept blissfully through it all, a soft smile bending her lips, and he decided not to alter that.

*My wife.* How utterly right that sounded.

And how utterly impossible to achieve.

He rose to his knees, leaned toward the cot and laid the pendant across her palm. Her fingers convulsed around it. Her smile deepened, but she did not wake.

After lightly kissing her brow and murmuring an affirmation of his love, he stood and forced himself to leave the cell.

Other partners were being escorted out. Marcus and his escort fell into step beside a bleary-eyed man whose stumbling gait proclaimed how much wine he'd imbibed, as if the vinegary reek wasn't enough. Vederi was supporting him on one side. The guard accompanying Marcus wrapped an arm around the visitor to make sure he stayed on his feet.

Vederi avoided Marcus's gaze, whether because this school's rules forbade the guards from associating with visitors, or due to some other cause, Marcus couldn't be certain. But chilly waves seemed to emanate from the guard that Marcus surmised had nothing to do with Vederi's drunken charge.

One cell they passed in the men's section stood empty, its door thrown open and its walls smothered with battle pictures inscribed by former occupants.

*My wife.*

The solution to several dilemmas smote Marcus with divine clarity.

He stopped in front of the unoccupied cell. The guards halted with the other visitor. Marcus's escort turned awkwardly beneath his burden and regarded Marcus quizzically in dawn's strengthening light.

"I wish to join Ludus Maximus," Marcus stated.

"Sir?" The guard's gaze turned critical. "You don't seem the type."

Vederi's posture stiffened, but he said nothing.

Marcus felt too elated with his idea to take offense at either the first man's skepticism or Vederi's mute disapproval. "I have eight wins on my slate as a provocator in Britannia, and no draws or losses."

Vederi shifted to set down the drunken man, who had fallen asleep. Vederi's grin, as he faced Marcus, bordered on a sneer. "That is true, my lord, but your rank exempted you from contractual obligations. And from losing."

"Your rank?" The other guard took renewed interest in Marcus, scrutinizing him as if for the first time. "You are an aristocrat, sir? From Britannia?"

Marcus suppressed a groan, cursing himself for having abandoned the blond wig. Doubtless Falco's men had left Marcus's description with the staff of every gladiatorial school between here and Ostia.

"I hail from this city." He'd been born here and had lived in Britannia for only the past two years. Marcus hoped his glare would keep Vederi silent. He couldn't calm the hammering of his heart. "As for my being an aristocrat—" he sucked in a deep breath "—I renounce my rank to become a contract gladiator."

Vederi let out a low whistle. "You would sacrifice all that power for—" he jerked his head back the way they had come "—her?"

"I think it won't matter what this man is or isn't willing to sacrifice, once Senator Falco gets through—"

"No, you're mistaken, friend." Vederi stepped between Marcus and the other guard, arms crossed. "I know the man Senator Falco seeks." He gave Marcus a significant look before regarding his companion. "This man is not Falco's prey."

Marcus nodded vigorously, answering Vederi's question but letting the other guard make of the gesture what he would. "And I must be with Libertas today, of all days." He addressed his escort, "Please tell the lanista I will sign his contract later."

No decision had ever felt more right…or more harrowingly immense.

"Very well," said the guard as he stooped to assist Vederi with carrying the other visitor, who had begun to snore. "What name shall I add to the roster?"

"He fought as Aquila Britannia." Respect glimmered in Vederi's eyes.

"Here, I wish to be known as Aquila Roma," Marcus said.

"Eagle of Rome?" The other guard laughed. "Good sir, that ambitious inclination has been taken."

"Perhaps." After entering the cell and facing the guards, Marcus smiled in spite of the circumstances. "But not by another gladiator."

"Indeed not." Since Marcus was a freeborn volunteer, the guard did not lock the cell. "Welcome to Ludus Maximus, Provocator Aquila Roma."

Before the men moved off, Vederi pressed his face to the bars. "You plan to marry her?" It sounded closer to a statement than a question.

By *her*, Marcus presumed the guard was not referring to Messiena. "In my heart, Libertas and I are already wed."

Vederi pondered this for a long moment. "If you don't take excellent care of her, my lord…" He let the unspoken threat dangle between them.

Marcus raised his hands in mock surrender. "No worries there, Vederi." He leaned closer to whisper, "And thank you."

The guard cracked a smile. "Good fortune to you, then," he said, inclining his head, "and to your wife."

Marcus could not have agreed more heartily, especially for Libertas's sake.

MESSIENA HAD RISEN at first light but did not dress. Each time she checked, guards remained visible outside her windows, their spears at the ready, as they'd stood ever since her escape route was discovered the day before. She presumed the door into her quarters was still being guarded, too.

In her fist, as she paced, she clutched the gold token she always used to gain admittance through the Colosseum's imperial gate. It felt hot as a cattle brand in her palm.

A knock on her door interrupted her in midstride. She wheeled about and hurried to open it.

Agna, at last!

The maidservant stood with a wicker basket tucked under one arm, neatly folded bed linens stacked inside it. Behind Agna, two guards were each digging into his own bowl of pitted cherries and cream. When the men saw Messiena, they raised their bowls in salute.

Ruthlessly suppressing her mounting excitement, Messiena gave a stately nod, calmly beckoned Agna into the room and pulled the door shut.

"Hurry and change into this." Messiena held up one of her best gowns as Agna set down the basket of linens. "Just pull it over your undertunic."

Agna held the silver-brocaded crimson silk stola gingerly, as if she didn't feel worthy to touch such a fine garment. "My lady?"

Not having time to deal with the woman's objections, Messiena gently but firmly grasped her shoulders and propelled her toward the changing screen. "What of my father? Has he left the estate yet?"

Behind the screen, Agna nodded. "I beg your forgiveness, my lady, but he asked me to help drape his toga. That's why I was delayed." Her words became muffled as she removed her overdress and slipped the stola over her head. "His bearers should be carrying him down Esquiline Way even now."

The sound of retching and scrabbling footsteps in the corridor outside her door told Messiena the first phase of her plan had been a success. She snatched Agna's dress from where the servant had slung it over the screen.

The maidservant looked scandalized.

"Don't worry, Agna." Shrugging into the floor-length, unadorned linen tunic and tugging it into place, Messiena tried to sound more reassuring than she felt. "If anyone threatens to punish you, just tell them you were obeying my orders."

She bade Agna empty the basket, put another of Messiena's stolas in the bottom, and cover it with a layer of linens. Messiena expressed approval that Agna had brought her needlework.

Agna accepted the praise mutely, looking as resigned as the lamb being led to the slaughter.

"I should be the one to worry, Agna," Messiena insisted. "I have an estate full of guards to evade. We might resemble each other from a distance, but up close I don't stand a chance."

Agna swished over to the hour-candle, blew it out, pinched the charred wick between her fingers and lightly smudged streaks onto Messiena's face beneath her eyes, lower lip and cheekbones.

"As you say, my lady, even that won't protect you from close scrutiny. But anyone glancing your way won't do it twice—especially if you remember to keep your head lowered."

Messiena gave her a quick hug. "You are a blessing, Agna."

"May you walk with Fortuna, my lady."

It seemed an odd benediction, but Messiena nodded her thanks and picked up the basket. Upon retrieving Marcus's amber necklace from her jewelry chest, she thrust it to the basket's bottom. She opened the door and peered out. As she'd hoped, the corridor was empty, save for two pink, cherry-scented puddles of vomit, thanks to whatever Agna had added to the cream. The door clicked shut, and Messiena drew a fortifying breath.

With the basket tucked firmly under one arm, she slumped her shoulders, ducked her head and scurried for the corner before the guards could return, reviewing her escape options. She would have preferred passing the make-shift prison to check on Governor Agricola and his party, but she couldn't risk discovery.

Committing everyone's fate into the hands of the gods, Messiena darted toward the kitchens and the freedom, through one of the estate's rear entrances, which lay beyond.

RHYDDES WOKE TO FIND Aquila gone. That didn't come as a surprise; at Villa Britanniae, nighttime visitors were escorted off the grounds before the day's routine could begin, and she suspected the rule was no different at Ludus Maximus. The fact that she'd slept through Aquila's departure, though, did surprise her. Especially since he'd left her with a gift.

In her palm lay the strange, ember-colored amulet.

Her body atingle with the memories of their ardent lovemaking, she slipped the cord around her neck and tucked the pendant inside her tunic.

"Go with the gods, Aquila," she whispered as she heard the guards rousing other gladiators. "And go with my love."

The precombat routine in Ludus Maximus followed the same pattern as at Villa Britanniae: exercise lightly, bathe, eat and arm. Lucerna greeted her with muted friendliness, but the other gladiatrices scarcely spoke. Rhyddes wasn't accustomed to sharing facilities with women, so she couldn't tell whether their reactions were normal or not. At Villa Britanniae, the men trotted out their grim jokes about combat and death as a means of mentally girding themselves for battle.

Just as well that the women here avoided the subject of combat, even in jest. Rhyddes didn't feel in the mood for morbid humor. If Aquila's predictions came to pass, there would be little to joke about when this day was done.

Rhyddes had hoped to see Vederi again, but it wasn't to be. Her attendant, a grizzled but well-muscled man whose missing nose bespoke to an old arena loss, went about his work silently and efficiently, speaking in a pinched voice only to ask if he was cinching her armor too tightly. The leg and forearm greaves fit comfortably, as did the waistband of her battle kilt, but after inhaling a few deep breaths and feeling Aquila's amulet dig into her chest, she bade him loosen her breastplate. She'd have preferred fighting barefoot for better traction on the arena's sand, but this land's heat forced her to accept the pair of hobnailed sandals he'd brought.

The more she thought about what Aquila had said, the more convinced she became that he had to be right. If

Senator Falco had his sights set on the throne and wanted to incite a gladiator revolt as part of the coup, what better way to spread chaos than to bribe the emperor's guards to stay their weapons until the fighting spiraled out of control?

And what better way to be rid of two thousand warriors who might suspect the truth than to execute them as rebels?

The "legion march" had to be a trap.

A prolonged trumpet blast signaled the end of preparations. Her attendant escorted her to the marshaling area, where many of the other gladiators had already gathered, surrounded by what appeared to be every guard in the place, although she couldn't find Vederi in the throng.

Before she joined the column, a few ranks behind the criminal contingent, she thanked her attendant. He settled her helmet over her head, held her shield so she could grip it easily with her left hand, wished her good fortune and stepped back with the other attendants to watch the gladiators leave.

This represented another departure from the norm. In Londinium, the attendants marched with their charges, carrying the shields.

Rhyddes had a queasy feeling she would need all the good fortune—to say naught of wits, strength, courage and skill—that the gods chose to bestow.

The armory workers distributed the gladiators' practice weapons, just as the senator had said, but it did not allay Rhyddes's concern. Even with blunted edges and points, the iron copies were designed to imitate real weapons in balance and weight. In the hands of warriors bent upon killing their foes, practice weapons could be wielded to deadly effect.

If a revolt swept into the arena's seating, beginning with the nobility, the result could be catastrophic.

But since talking in the ranks was forbidden, upon pain of death, Rhyddes had no way of warning anyone.

Even when Vederi stepped into rank beside her, offering her an encouraging smile, the most she dared to utter, in the slimmest of whispers, was, "Be careful."

Vederi lowered his eyebrows in puzzlement, but she saw another guard glare at her, and she clamped her mouth shut.

To the fanfare of trumpets, punctuated by drums, the column of warriors and guards surged forward. Never had Rhyddes seen gladiators so eager to march toward their deaths.

Her heart clenched with mounting dread.

## 30

MESSIENA CHANGED OUT of Agna's clothes at the nearest public bathhouse. After fastening Marcus's necklace in place and leaving the basket beside the granite bench, she hurried toward the Colosseum as fast as the thickening throng would permit.

Since it was an unusual sight for Rome, she spared a few minutes watching the gladiators and their guards, who wore tunics in each school's color, as they marched toward Ludus Imperatorius. Between each pair of schools marched a small unit, no more than twenty gladiators strong. Their guards wore crimson tunics beneath their armor, which she thought odd. These gladiators and their guards must have been invited from one of the schools outside the city; Ostia, perhaps.

She had to admit she enjoyed the sight of the gladiators, their muscles alluringly enhanced by glistening sweat worked up during their march. It reminded Messiena of the moment she'd fallen in love with Marcus, and she touched the smooth amber beads, silently beseeching Venus that all would soon be set to rights between her and her betrothed.

But her top priority was saving her father from doing something foolish, mad…or worse. She hastened past the gladiators.

One of the provocators turned his head toward her, although it was hard to be certain to whom he directed his gaze because his helmet obscured his face. Something about him seemed familiar, and it gave her pause.

Mentally shrugging the puzzle aside, she pressed ahead of the procession, hurried across the red marble plaza, and on toward the gilt bronze colossus of Emperor Nero standing atop an alabaster pedestal, which, along with a similarly crafted image of Emperor Vespasian, who'd designed and commissioned the Colosseum, flanked the steps leading to the lavishly frescoed and perfumed imperial entrance. The gate attendants recognized Messiena and waved her through without asking to see her token.

The Praetorian guardsman of whom she requested an escort to the imperial box looked taken aback until she explained that her father had been appointed by Emperor Marcus Aurelius to act as the games' sponsor.

She saw it as a sign of Fortuna's blessing that the guard believed her. In appreciation, she pressed the gold token into the soldier's palm.

From somewhere came the disconcerting thought that she would need it no longer.

It felt exhilarating, and more than a trifle rebellious, to be armed in gladiatorial gear for the first time in a year. Marcus reveled in the familiar feel of the meticulous padding of his sword arm and differently designed leg greaves. The right leg below the knee bore a light harness to which a dagger's sheath, containing a blunted iron dagger, was strapped. The left leg was encased in metal plating that extended past the knee to protect it from being gouged by his tall rectangular shield.

Marching down Rome's streets was murderously hot under the helmet, fully enclosed except for the eye slits, its bib extending halfway down his chest in a crescent breast-plate. Since there had been no time to commission a crafts-man to paint the "Aquila Roma" eagle onto his helmet, it remained solid black.

The anonymity proved to be a blessing as well as a curse.

The blessing occurred in avoiding the notice of Falco's men, several of whom Marcus spotted in the crowds lining the procession's route. He saw Messiena, too, and noted with a guilty twinge that she was wearing the amber necklace he'd given her. She paused but didn't seem to recognize him. As she mounted the steps between the statues of Nero and Vespasian and passed through the Colosseum's imperial entrance, he prayed she would reach safety in time.

The curse: Libertas, who also had watched him fight Iradivus in his eagle-emblazoned helmet, wouldn't recognize him, either.

No matter. His heart would know her even with both his eyes gouged out. As he marched with the others of his combat category, he silently vowed to reach Libertas's side regardless of what transpired.

The trouble with such intrepid vows was that the gods

took perverse delight in throwing obstacles into the vow maker's path.

Marcus's height allowed him to peer over the sea of armored heads. The Ludus Maximus provocators marched with the heavier thraex and murmillo classes, in the school's rear ranks, which meant Libertas had to be marching in front of him, although she'd be impossible to see because of her small stature.

Marcus had expected the revolt to begin while the gladiators marched through the streets to capitalize on the terror ignited among people caught unawares. When the Ludus Maximus gladiators entered the grounds of Ludus Imperatorius and marched into the tunnel without incident, he was almost disappointed.

But the tunnel ran the entire width of the Colosseum's massive ring, sloping from street level to the arena floor, two seating tiers below, probably at least half a mile in total length, if not in crow's flight. Marcus suspected this structure followed the typical amphitheater pattern on a far grander scale, which meant the tunnel would be bisected at intervals with other tunnels that circled below the seats to provide access for the hundreds of arena workers toiling at the sundry tasks required for staging performances for the most demanding spectators on earth.

Marcus glanced behind him in time to see the Ludus Regis contingent enter the tunnel, also without incident, preceded by a tiny unit whose guards wore crimson tunics. He had no time to wonder about the unknown contingent as the sound of several hundred feet pounding the concrete, magnified by a million echoes, attained deafening proportions.

Approaching each smoky, torchlit intersection, Marcus's right hand twitched toward his blunted sword's hilt. On the other side of each intersection, his foreboding climbed.

After what seemed like hours, though were probably mere minutes, the tunnel began to lighten. Marcus's rank pressed on. They passed the final tunnel, where the guards had been ordered to leave the procession, and that maneuver proceeded according to the plan Falco had described.

As Marcus emerged, blinking, through the massively ornate Porta Vita into the brilliant sunlight and stepped onto the arena sands, he had convinced himself he'd been wrong.

Nothing was going to happen after all.

A series of muted clangs, coming from inside the tunnel behind him, sounded less like bells than…gates being shut!

He barely had time to draw his sword before rioting erupted around him.


FALCO DARED NOT REBUKE his daughter when she'd arrived at the emperor's box, breathless and fearful looking, escorted by one of the Praetorian Guards. Not only would it have risked raising suspicions, but there was no time.

The first unit of mercenary "gladiators" broke rank for their appointed tasks. Most attacked real gladiators to incite the melee. The rest sprinted for the ropes that had been let down into the arena by mercenary "guards," to take the fight into the laps of the aristocratic spectators.

As anticipated, the Praetorian guardsmen assigned to protect the imperial family whisked the emperor, empress and prince away at the first whiff of danger. Since Falco's status as the games' sponsor had afforded him the privilege of being seated beside the emperor, the Praetorian guardsmen allowed him and Messiena to accompany their exalted charges.

Falco would have loved to know whether any of these guards had been lured into his cause, but that damned Greek had failed to deliver the list. No matter; Falco had not risen to prominence in the Senate without being able to think on the run.

And run they did, literally, as safely within the cocoon formed by the Praetorian Guards' shield wall as a babe in its mother's womb. Falco could only imagine, from the escalating screams, what was transpiring as the gladiator riot spread to the other schools in the formation and more warriors scaled the walls to divert soldiers from the day's true central—if private—event.

He had intended to shield Messiena from the unpleasantness to come, but the gods had decreed otherwise. So be it.

In spite of the small bumps in the plan's execution, he'd received an unexpected boon: an intelligence report he'd found with Agricola's most important documents. The altered copy would redirect blame for the gladiators' rebellion and, by extension, the entire plot, quite firmly elsewhere.

Falco hoped he wouldn't have to wield the false document, but he saw it as a sign that heaven had sided with him.

The Praetorian guardsmen ushered the party, as he knew they would, into the Caesar Room, the audience chamber closest to the imperial box. While most of the guards established an outer perimeter, some accompanied the party inside.

This was unexpected. Kynthos was supposed to have learned who'd been assigned to guard the imperial family today and subverted those men to the cause, leaving the emperor unguarded at the pivotal moment. But that worthless Greek had vanished, and Falco had no idea whether he could trust these men.

When the Praetorian Guard prefect ordered two of his men to search the chamber, Falco knew the plan had careened drastically off course.

Hugging Messiena, who was trembling and swaying as if she might faint, he tensed for trouble.

"Praetorians, alert!" snapped their prefect.

The men surrounded the imperial family, swords cocked, as Falco's assassin was dragged from behind the frescoed door leading into the chamber's kitchen.

RHYDDES HEARD NO SHOUT, saw no signal to trigger the mayhem. One moment the column was marching, neat and orderly, into the arena to the roaring of seventy thousand spectators. The next moment, gladiators started going berserk.

While a skirmish broke out on the arena sands that built in scale and intensity as more gladiators poured in through the Porta Vita, a few raced for dangling ropes leading to the first row of seats. With Colosseum guards diverted to so many threats, some of the gladiators succeeded in scaling the walls. They attacked the spectators, inciting panic among the nobility, who stampeded, screaming and wailing, for the exits.

A sword sliced into Rhyddes's arm padding. She whipped around, bringing her blunted weapon to bear, and almost tripped over Lucerna's body. Shock battled dismay when she saw that Lucerna's killer was a gladiator armed with a sharp blade, dripping blood. And he wasn't the only one carrying a real weapon.

Rhyddes's choices shrank to two: fight or be slaughtered.

Although she chose to fight, it became a heroic struggle to fend off her attacker long enough for her to spin away until the next bore down upon her. Desperately she sought a third option.

She found her answer at the entrance to another tunnel. Its gates had been flung open as if daring her to enter. No guards patrolled within that Rhyddes could see.

The voice in her head urging caution was drowned out by the mental chorus insisting that the tunnel was her sole chance for survival.

"To me, gladiators, to me!" She pried a sharpened gladius from the hand of a dead man and swung it in a high circle. "Senator Falco has betrayed us! We must appeal to the emperor!"

She raced for the tunnel at a dead run, having no idea how many followed her into the labyrinth and praying with every stride that the gods would guide her feet to safe haven.

The scuffling of many feet, the clash of iron and steel, the thud of bodies and the shrieks of the wounded and dying, echoing off the dank stone walls and attended by the stench of sweat, blood and fear, told her more than she wanted to know.

Aquila's pendant pressed against her skin. She wondered if he was alive, wishing he could help her and cursing the futility of such a foolish wish.

Senator Falco had probably killed him, too.

She had no time to yield to grief as she rounded a corner, accompanied by several allied gladiators, and came face-to-face with Colosseum guards.

APPARENTLY OVERCOME BY the heat and stress, Messiena moaned softly and slumped in Falco's arms. He lowered her to the ground and crouched beside her, fanning her face with his hand.

If the assassin recognized Falco, the plan would crumble. But killing him would create a host of other problems, beginning with having to explain why Falco was carrying a concealed dagger.

He stayed hidden with Messiena behind the imperial family and their guards, while his mind raced to predict and counteract the likeliest contingencies.

After the searchers reported finding no other threats—which was true, according to Falco's original plan—they forced the assassin onto his knees, head held down. Falco fervently hoped it would stay that way.

"Who hired you?" Marcus Aurelius nodded, and the guard holding the assassin's head yanked it up.

Darius Caepio, never a cheerful sort to begin with, looked abjectly miserable.

"Your majesty, I know that man!" cried Falco, stepping away from his daughter to glide forward. "I saw him when you sent me to Britannia last year. He commanded the governor's staff."

"Senator! But you—" His guard cuffed him silent. Falco could have kissed the soldier.

"Yes, I saw you there, scum-licker, don't bother to deny

it." He faced the emperor, schooling his face into grave concern. "Your majesty, Governor Agricola must have conceived this heinous plot against your exalted person. I suspected something might be amiss yesterday when I found a disturbing document, so I took the liberty of detaining him and his entourage at my estate."

"Your majesty, no! I appeal to Caesar!" Darius's guard struck him again. His head lolled.

Mentally, Falco urged the guard to kill the assassin.

"Sextus Calpurnius Agricola is responsible?" The emperor sounded more sorrowful than enraged. "Do you have proof, Falco?"

"Oh, yes, my lord." Suppressing the urge to grin, Falco warmed to his topic. "According to the document I found in Agricola's possessions, he must have hired mercenaries to slip into today's procession to pose as gladiators and guards. Armed with real weapons, I'm sure your majesty can imagine the havoc those vile men must have wrought among the people."

Although the chamber's position and sturdy construction insulated its occupants from the main corridor servicing the nobility's tier, he fancied that he could hear panicked shouts seeping in. He hoped Marcus Aurelius could hear them, too.

The emperor gazed at Falco with those infernally probing gray eyes so long he began to fear that his web of half-truths had failed to ensnare its prey.

Finally, Marcus Aurelius returned his stern attention to the would-be assassin.

"Appeal denied."

As much as Falco knew Messiena enjoyed watching combat spectacles, he was grateful beyond measure that she wasn't awake to witness, at acutely close quarters, this execution.

And she was spared the sight of Darius's permanent, accusatory glare.

GODS, LIBERTAS WAS FAST!

But Marcus thanked them for leading him to her. After dispatching the last foe standing between him and the tunnel, using the real gladius he'd acquired, he tore off his stifling helmet, repeated Libertas's entreaties and rallied dozens more gladiators to follow her into the Colosseum's belly.

He earnestly hoped she knew what she was doing.

Marcus had never fought in close quarters, but the will to survive proved an excellent mentor. He'd abandoned his shield to free up his other hand for hurling opponents into the corridor's concrete-mortared travertine walls.

He lost count of how many men he'd maimed or killed.

Worried that he would lose Libertas in this gods-forsaken labyrinth, he attempted to track the sounds of her passage.

A horrific din broke out that couldn't be anything other than a skirmish. It seemed to be coming from in front of him. Tensing his grip on his sword's hilt, Marcus redoubled his pace as the cacophony grew louder. He prayed he wouldn't be too late.

RHYDDES FOUGHT FOR BREATH as hard as she fought the guards. Thrust, dodge, parry, kick, duck, leap, slice: over and over in a bizarre dance, changing partners every few blows. Her arms felt leaden; her legs, sluggish. She thought her lungs would burst. But she kept pressing upward, step by agonizing step.

If she didn't get to the emperor, she'd be dead, and everyone else with her.

A hard blow followed by excruciating pain forced her to drop to one knee. Probing the jagged tear in the leather of her breastplate, her fingers came away ominously red. Her adversary closed in, his face leering triumphantly.

She tried to summon the strength to jump clear, but her body refused to obey.

The guard, uttering a nasty chuckle, cocked his sword to finish what he'd begun.

"Libertas!" Unbridled anguish rippled through the cry.

Aquila, here?

*Alive?*

She squinted through the gloom but saw nothing beyond the guard's sword beginning its deadly descent.

Was she dreaming, or had she gone mad?

But hope—even if born of madness—lent her new strength. She raised her sword to block the blow. Iron met iron in a shower of sparks. The guard bore down with merciless force. Her arms trembled and began to give way.

Even hope had its limits.

MARCUS SPRANG AT THE guard attacking Libertas, knocking him off balance. As they grappled, she crawled away. Where she'd gone, Marcus couldn't tell; his opponent obscured his view.

She was hurt, and it was Marcus's fault. Fury drove his

hand to stab her attacker below the rib cage. As the guard staggered backward, Marcus's sword slid free, red to the hilt.

He stepped into the shadows, letting the other gladiators and guards rush past him.

After they had gone and the tunnel seemed clear for the moment, Marcus squinted into the gloom for Libertas. He found her in an intersecting tunnel, huddled among stacks of fake trees used in drama productions, clutching her midsection. She had closed her eyes, and her breath came in shallow puffs. Some of the blood splashed on her armor didn't appear to be hers.

The breach in her breastplate told a different tale.

Marcus knelt beside her, tore as much fabric as he could spare from his belted loincloth, and gently blotted her wound, thankful the breastplate had slowed the guard's sword. The cut would need more care than he was prepared to render but didn't appear to be deep.

He grasped her bloodied hands and squeezed. "Libertas," he whispered urgently. "Libertas, please come back to me!"

Her eyes fluttered open. "I must be dead." She disengaged her hand from his to touch his cheek, wonderingly, as if for the first time. "You're not supposed to be here."

"Neither are you." He placed her arm around his neck and levered her to her feet. "Your wound is not that bad. Can you walk? I think more guards are coming."

The escalating sounds of shouts and running feet confirmed his claim.

She tested her balance. "With you helping, yes."

He'd battle an entire legion single-handedly if she but asked. They edged down the side tunnel, which smelled as if it housed a wing of the bestiary but might lead to a staircase that would get them out. After a few steps, she stumbled. She might have fallen if he hadn't been holding her tightly.

"I'm so tired!" she whispered.

Gazing into her eyes, he summoned assurance to smother his worry. "We will get through this together, my love."

That was one promise he would not fail to deliver for her.

# 31

MESSIENA HAD TO be dreaming. Military commands, accusations, shouts, screams, the whine of swords being drawn, the clash of arms...none of it made any sense.

And, oh holy gods, her head felt insubstantial as air.

"Pulla? Are you all right?"

She opened her eyes to find her father kneeling beside her, cradling her head in his lap and chafing her hands.

The canopy of the imperial box had been traded for a stuffy audience chamber. The air reeked of death. Groggily, she glanced around but couldn't remember when she'd come here or why there were so many Praetorian guardsmen present.

Prince Commodus stood in one corner while a guard squatted beside him, allowing the young prince to examine his sword.

It was far too confusing. Groaning, she closed her eyes again.

"I'd like to get her home."

"Impossible, Senator." A crisp voice Messiena didn't recognize. "Order hasn't been restored yet."

"Senator Falco, shall I summon a physician?"

Messiena looked up into the beatific face of Empress Faustina. "My lady?" Falco hovered over her, too. "Papa, where are we? What happened?"

"Someone tried to kill the emperor, Pulla." Smiling, he patted her hand. "But do not fear. The nasty part is over. All shall be well soon." He helped her to sit up and pointed across the room. "See, his majesty is fine."

The emperor, accompanied by the Praetorian Guard prefect, was approaching her father.

But Messiena couldn't tear her horrified gaze from the glistening, bloody smear across the pristine white marble where a body recently had been dragged out.

Emperor Marcus Aurelius faced Falco. "Have Governor Agricola and his entourage brought to me at once."

"Why, Papa?" Messiena knit her brow as she regarded him, feeling as if something was gravely wrong. But for the life of her she couldn't think what it could be. "What is happening?"

"His majesty would like to ask the governor a few questions, Pulla. Nothing more." Falco kissed her brow and stood. "You rest there, Daughter, while I take care of everything."

If all was well, as her father claimed, why didn't she trust his smile?

FEELING MUCH BETTER FOR the brief rest, Rhyddes turned from Aquila to glance down the tunnel. And blinked, hard, refusing to believe what her eyes were telling her.

That oaf Furcifer was standing under a torchlit arch, fists on hips and a gloating grin painted across his accursed face. There could be no mistaking his impossibly tall, lanky build.

Jamil sometimes chose to watch his gladiators compete from ground level, usually to better determine where improvements in training needed to be made. Rhyddes couldn't envision her present owners being that consciencious of their human property.

Whatever Furcifer's intent, he'd selected an exceedingly bad day for it.

Rhyddes bolted down the tunnel, leaving Aquila to catch up as best he could.

Furcifer ducked around a corner. Nothing had ever pleased her more than his look of dismay. Gripping her sword tighter, she increased her pace, slowing only as the tunnel's shadows deepened. She had no desire to blunder into an ambush.

For where Furcifer was, the other two couldn't be far away.

And they had oh, so very much to answer for.

The only differences between this section of the Colosseum and the section Rhyddes had marched through earlier were the gagging odors and distracting noises of caged beasts.

It gave her an idea, but first she had to locate her prey.

Shouts and the thundering of many feet, somewhere in the labyrinth behind her, told her she didn't have much time. The Colosseum's workers so far had cowered in corners, but she wasn't sure if her luck would hold long enough for her to finish her vendetta.

To say nothing of the luck she'd need merely to find the monsters that called themselves her owners.

For once, the gods deigned to be kind to her. She rounded
the corner and spied two of the men pelting away.

"Furcifer, Pugionis—halt!"

They ignored her.

With the flat of her blade, Rhyddes banged on the bars of
the closest cage, causing its resident to snarl and swipe at
her. The beast raked her arm with a claw, though not deeply.

"I said halt! Or you can take your chances with this tiger!"

That got their attention. Pugionis was the first to face
about. As he moved slowly toward Rhyddes, grinning
smugly, Furcifer fell in behind him.

"That's close enough," she warned them, sword leveled,
when Pugionis had come to within a cage's length. "Where
is that weasel Rodo?"

"Ah, Libertas. A pleasure to see you, as always." Pugionis
spread his arms in a conciliatory gesture. "We were hoping you
might be able to enlighten us as to our associate's whereabouts."

"I am not his keeper."

"If you have a complaint about your treatment," purred
the fat man, "I suggest you discuss it with your new owner."

"My complaint is with—*new* owner?" She shook her head
but didn't lower her guard. "What do you mean, new owner?"

The smugness never left Pugionis's face. "Why, Senator
Falco. He's the one who paid for you to be brought here."

"That's impossible. You're lying!" She took a step toward
them. "No one bought Jamil's gladiators. You stole us from him.
Now Jamil can't buy one hour with a whore, thanks to you."

They chortled.

"Oh, no. You're quite wrong, bitch. The senator spoke of

using you to improve his fortunes," Pugionis said. "But I think the old goat means to rut you instead."

"Liar!" Roaring to make a lioness proud, Rhyddes spun and struck her target. Sparks sprayed everywhere. The cage's lock fell, sheared in half. She yanked the door open. The tiger bounded after the fleeing pair.

Rhyddes turned away, struggling to shut out the growls and screams, and the shouts of handlers trying to bring the beast under control. She almost felt sorry for them.

"Libertas!" Aquila stalked toward her, sheathing his sword, his chest heaving as if he'd just run from Marathon. A score of gladiators stood behind him, all struggling for breath. "Why in Tartarus did you do that?"

With battle rage still coursing through her veins, his resounding disapproval raised her hackles. "What? Did I deprive you of a kill?"

"Yes. No! I mean, I—" He opened his arms as if wanting to embrace her but seemed to change his mind and crossed them. "What I mean is, in releasing that tiger on your owners—"

"They claimed they didn't own me anymore."

"Regardless, they are—were Roman citizens. The penalty for killing them is—"

"Hah. I am dead already." She rammed her sword into its sheath. Upon hearing a rumbling growl, she glanced behind her to see several men loading the tiger into an undamaged, empty cage. The tiger was licking blood from its muzzle contentedly. The handlers glared at her. Not caring, she brushed past Aquila to go back the way she'd come. "Nothing I do can change that."

He gripped her arm and spun her around. "You carry something that may change the emperor's mind about you."

She hooked a finger through the cord at her neck, tugged the amulet free, flipped it over her head and flung it to the ground. It hit the slate floor with a brittle clatter.

"Save your own aristocratic hide with it, then." She continued her course toward the arena floor and the grim fate awaiting her there. "Whatever power that bauble possesses, it cannot protect an infamia slave."

Aquila scooped up the amulet and stepped into her path, his gaze growing earnest. "I hope it has the power to protect us both. I have renounced my heritage, my rank, my citizenship. Everything."

She felt her eyebrows climb her forehead. *"What?"*

"I didn't dress like a gladiator today only to gain access to the arena, Libertas. I promised to sign a contract—" he chuckled ruefully "—if I survive. For if Falco prevails, we are all dead."

Her palm found his warm, stubbly cheek of its own accord. "You would give up your wealth, your luxuries, your power—even your intended bride?" If Vederi had told her the sun had risen in the west that morning, she'd have believed it more readily than Aquila's claim. "All for me?"

He grasped her hand and guided it to his lips, sending a tingle racing down her arm. "Libertas, I would sacrifice my life for you." His fingers opened like petals of a flower to reveal the black-flecked orange amulet nestled in his palm. "Take this, and show it to the emperor when he asks for it. If he believes me—us, he may grant you clemency for your part in thwarting Falco's plot."

Aquila draped the cord around Rhyddes's neck. Before letting go, he bent to kiss her sweetly, though by necessity far too briefly. "And if your fate must end in death—"

She pressed a hand to his lips. "No, Aquila. Please say no more."

He pulled her hand away from his mouth. "I must finish, my love." Straightening, he looked around. "As all assembled here are my witnesses, I, Marcus Calpurnius Aquila, vow never to leave Gladiatrix Libertas again. I further vow to accompany Libertas in death, if that is to be her fate this day, even if the emperor pardons the rest of us."

"Aquila, no! I can't let you die because of me!" She twisted to regard the other gladiators. "This man's death vow is not valid. I refuse to accept it."

Aquila turned her to face him. A glow radiated from his eyes that seemed...*peaceful?* "And I refuse to accept life, Libertas, without you to share it. In death's halls I shall find you, and we shall be together for eternity. This, too, I vow to the very depths of my soul." The unbridled passion of his lingering kiss left no doubts about his determination to keep his vows.

Breathtaking wonderment kindled the fire of freedom, branding her soul.

"Very touching. But I doubt anyone is going to earn a pardon, Marcus Calpurnius Aquila," intoned a guard who had appeared from the corridor where Pugionis and Furcifer had met their demise.

The soldier was followed by the gods alone knew how many men. All Rhyddes could see sloping down into the shadows was an array of helmeted heads. More guards converged upon the gladiators from the other intersections, cutting off escape.

The only sound in the corridor was the mournful clatter of gladiators' weapons falling to the floor, followed by regret-weighted footsteps as they trooped toward Porta Vita.

Hand in hand, Aquila and Rhyddes approached the arena floor and the restive crowd, whose numbers had dwindled because of the riot but still included the most powerful man in the world. She prayed with all her strength that Aquila would not be called upon to sacrifice himself for her sake.

The gods ignored her plea.

WHILE RHYDDES AND THE others had been occupied in the labyrinth, soldiers had wheeled several dozen small platforms into the arena's center. Others labored to drag off the bodies of those fallen in the riot. The gleaming golden sands had become a stinking morass of sand-clotted gore.

Each platform held three spikes, a mallet, a coil of rope and an empty cross.

"I beg you, Aquila, don't do this. Recant your vows, and I will forgive you," she whispered as they walked slowly toward the grim structures.

Aquila gripped her hand harder. "But I would never forgive myself."

AS THE ARENA CAME INTO full view, Marcus discovered to his horror that his parents, Jamil and two menservants had been escorted into the center, surrounded by at least three dozen Praetorian guardsmen. Loreia was sobbing, and Agricola was hugging her tightly.

Not all the crosses were empty.

Obtego had already been crucified, and three soldiers were busily nailing Pyropus in place. His screams, punctuated by the sickening ring of mallet on iron, pierced the crowd's roar.

Jamil was next.

"Halt!" Marcus shouted.

The word boomed with the power of a battlefield command.

Astonishingly, the soldiers manning the crosses stopped, exchanged a glance and looked toward the imperial box. Emperor Marcus Aurelius raised a hand, ratifying the order…at least for the present.

Marcus shrugged off his captors and faced the imperial box. The spectators' noise dwindled as their curiosity swelled.

"I am a freeborn citizen of Rome!" Falco must have said something mightily damning to convince the emperor of Agricola's guilt, and Marcus didn't hold much hope that the legal formula would work. "I appeal to Caesar!"

"We already tried that, Son." Agricola shook his head sadly. "You see how much good it did us."

Falco, standing beside the emperor, grinned wickedly. "You have no proof, whelp."

Marcus pointed toward the woman he loved. "Gladiatrix Libertas has it!"

Libertas took the cue to yank the pendant from around her neck and hold it aloft. The amber glinted golden in the sun.

Strutting to and fro, Falco pitched his voice for all to hear. "His majesty is not interested in fabrications and lies."

"The only fabrications and lies, Falco, are the ones you have told him!" Marcus gazed at Libertas and made a twisting motion with his fingers. She removed the pendant's top and extracted the precious parchment scrap. Marcus took it and waved it overhead. "Your majesty, here is proof linking Senator Falco, in his own handwriting—" stretching the truth was a dangerous gamble, but with so many lives at stake, Marcus felt there was nothing to lose by it "—to a coup against the throne by subverting some of the Praetorian Guard—"

"Lies!" Falco's face flushed dangerously red.

"—and to the murders of senators Ferox, Scaevola and Quintilianus, who refused to become involved in Falco's coup." Although not explicitly reflected in the cryptic list, it was the only explanation that made any sense. "My father, Governor Sextus Calpurnius Agricola, also refused to support Falco, and our executions are part of his plan, too."

"Scaevola and Quintilianus suffered accidental deaths, and Ferox was killed by a thief in his home," Falco insisted. "Everyone knows that."

As Marcus gave the parchment to Libertas and she stowed it inside the pendant, Jamil stepped forward. "Your majesty, I spoke with Prefect Caesius at great length last night, warning him of the assassination plot I had begun to uncover."

"It's true, your majesty," said the bodyguard standing closest to the emperor, his uniform distinguished from the other men's by a crimson sash. "He warned me Darius Caepio would have a key role, and it did come to pass."

Marcus would have sacrificed his left arm to learn what had "come to pass." But at present he was fascinated by

Falco's reaction, which had started to resemble a carp, his mouth opening and closing reflexively but emitting no sound.

"I possess proof, too, your majesty," Jamil said. "I bear on my person a list of Praetorian Guard officers who had been subverted to Falco's cause. I intercepted Falco's agent, a retired Praetorian guardsman of my acquaintance, who admitted he was on his way to deliver the list to the senator."

"More lies! That Egyptian rabble is in the governor's employ. I saw them take counsel together, brazenly, in my home. And they had plenty of time to collaborate on their treason before arriving in Rome."

Agricola held up both arms, his soiled and bloodied toga folds hanging in tatters like desecrated banners. "Why would I betray your majesty, when you know how deeply loyal I have been to you all these years?"

"Your majesty, surely you cannot believe the traitors!" Falco protested.

Messiena, who had been sitting at the back of the imperial box, fanning herself, rose and rushed forward. "Papa, Marcus and his family are not traitors! Please don't do this to the man I love!"

"Child, do not interfere!" Falco brushed her aside and turned toward the emperor. "My daughter is wrong, your majesty. Marcus Calpurnius Aquila has blinded her with his charms. The traitors must be executed at once!"

While Empress Faustina's expression reflected growing alarm, and she hugged the wriggling Commodus close to her, Emperor Marcus Aurelius displayed an astonishing calm. "I know not whom to believe," he announced, "until

I examine the articles in question. Send the documents up here, Marcus Calpurnius Aquila."

Marcus bowed low and straightened. "Please forgive me, your majesty, but I believe it would serve your purposes far better for you to examine them down here. There would be less of a chance for the documents to go astray."

"Yes, your majesty, I think you should go." Falco stepped closer to the emperor, reaching into a fold of his toga. "Straight to Tartarus!"

"Emperor!" Libertas shouted. "He has a dagger!"

The emperor reared back, but the rail prevented him from dodging the blade. Caesius tried to shove him aside but his angle wasn't good enough.

Libertas whipped her dagger from its sheath and flung it. Her blade plunged into Falco's right shoulder. The blow's force sent him reeling backward, and he dropped his weapon. Bellowing, he ripped out Libertas's dagger and twisted to avoid capture as he charged at the emperor again.

Though Marcus could tell Libertas had aimed for Falco, the emperor's bodyguards only saw her as another threat. They released a barrage of spears into the arena, scattering soldier and civilian alike. Marcus threw Libertas to the ground, shielding her body with his, feeling the sting as a spear grazed his bare arm.

"Papa, don't!" Messiena cried.

Marcus turned in time to watch Messiena lunge for Falco's bleeding shoulder. But momentum carried her too far and she missed. Her body passed in front of the emperor as Falco's blow fell.

The empress screamed. Messiena's face contorted from fear to shock to agony. She clutched her abdomen, then regarded her hand wonderingly, as if it belonged to someone else.

It was covered in blood.

Head lolling, Messiena sank out of sight.

"Daughter!" Falco's anguish reverberated across the deathly silent Colosseum. "Messiena, my dearest little Pulla, I am so sorry!" Whatever else he said became lost in his sobs as he, too, disappeared behind the rail.

Nothing could be seen from the arena's floor after the bodyguards closed in.

## 32

AQUILA RECOVERED HIS stance, but he looked as if someone had gutted him as he stared in horror toward the imperial box.

Despite all he'd done and vowed, Rhyddes felt reality's crushing weight as surely as if she had been buried in a rock-slide. Because the stigma of infamia would taint everyone who chose to consort with her, it would be gross selfishness to imprison Aquila as a social outcast.

'Twas better to be thrice-cursed than destroy the man she loved.

With a heavy heart, she rose and faced the emperor. The men not guarding Falco leveled spears at her, and she sank to her knees, lifting her arms.

"Your majesty, I appeal to your wisdom and mercy. Senator Falco duped us with his false plan. When I saw him attack you, I threw my dagger at him, not at your exalted majesty."

"Indeed, Gladiatrix Libertas, and we are deeply grateful for your efforts." At Emperor Marcus Aurelius's upraised hand, the bodyguards lowered their spears.

Rhyddes bowed her head briefly as her cheeks heated; her part in thwarting Senator Falco's coup seemed absurdly small to be receiving such high praise from the master of the world. "Great lord," she addressed the emperor upon regaining her feet, "I humbly beseech a boon of you—not for myself, but for Lord Aquila and Lady Messiena, who deserve far more reward than I in this matter." A lump threatened to choke her, and she swallowed hard. "Lady Messiena is Lord Aquila's betrothed. If it pleases your exalted majesty, may he go to her?"

As Emperor Marcus Aurelius solemnly nodded his assent and ordered one of his guards to lower a rope, Aquila gaped at Rhyddes, slack-jawed. "Libertas, my place is—"

"Not with an infamia slave. I release you from your vows to me." She removed the amulet and pressed it into his hand. Tears branded her eyes. Anguish pummeled her chest. The tears slid free. A wave of weariness smote her, and her vision began to darken. By sheer force of will, she said, "Go to Lady Messiena, Aquila, with my blessings and love."

"No! Libertas, I…"

Anything else Aquila might have said was drowned by the furious buzzing in Rhyddes's head.

She felt a pair of hands grip her shoulders from behind and she whipped around, wishing she hadn't. Her head felt as if someone had cleaved it with an ax. Jamil had rushed to her side, concern carved into every pore of his face. She tried to respond to him, but severe leg cramps forced her to her knees.

"Libertas!"

Who said that? Aquila? Jamil? Somebody she couldn't see? Rhyddes had no idea. Faces pressed in around her, faces she failed to recognize. Oddly, their lips were working, but they said nothing. Odder still, the faces began to spin, faster and faster until they melded into a blur.

She closed her eyes against the whirling confusion, and knew no more.

"GO, AQUILA. YOU MUST show the emperor our evidence," Jamil said, holding the slumping Libertas with one arm and removing a sandal with his free hand. "The list of officers is tucked between the pad and sole. I will care for Libertas as best I can."

"Thank you, my friend." Aquila flipped the pendant's cord over his head, slipped the sandal's strap around his wrist, and helped Jamil lower Libertas to the sand.

Her wounds weren't life-threatening, but the heat, fatigue and blood loss, doubtless compounded by hunger and thirst, had exacted a cruel toll.

Jamil adjusted his stance to shade her face. As he checked her pulse, her graying skin felt dry and hot, and she was not sweating. The last gladiator Jamil had seen suffering this condition—years ago, before he'd fled Rome for Britannia— had died from it.

"She must be cooled soon, Aquila. If not…" Jamil couldn't bear to finish.

After raising her limp hand to his lips, Aquila gently lowered it to her chest, stood and faced the imperial box. "Your majesty, this valiant woman lies in dire need of medical care. Please forgive my boldness, but what is the imperial will regarding the gladiators and my family? I respectfully and humbly beseech clemency for being unjustly embroiled in Senator Falco's plot."

"Release the Calpurniae," ordered the emperor. Aquila thumped fist to chest and dashed for the rope. "Sextus Calpurnius Agricola, I restore you to the governorship of Britannia, with all its rights and privileges for you, your family and your servants. And I grant full pardon to all surviving contract and slave gladiators involved in today's debacle. Send in litter bearers for the wounded who cannot leave under their own power."

While Aquila climbed toward the imperial box, several pairs of litter bearers ran into the arena from their ready-rooms beside the tunnels' arches. Soldiers who had been assigned to execution duty pried loose the spikes to a mixed reaction from the crowd and more pain-wracked howls from the victims. After receiving tacit agreement from the governor, whose own wound didn't seem to be troubling him, Jamil diverted the first litter to Libertas and hovered over the bearers to prevent them from injuring her further.

The emperor raised his arms for silence. "If not for the timely actions of Gladiatrix Libertas, today might have had a very different outcome. Do not take her to the Colosseum's infirmary with the others. Carry her to the palace, where Galen, the imperial physician, shall attend her."

Jamil saluted his thanks and rushed to catch up with Libertas's litter. As they jogged past scores of curious people, Jamil thought of something else he could do for Libertas, if he could persuade the emperor to grant one more boon.

And if she survived.

Marcus hauled himself up the rope, bracing his feet against the wall and praying for time. He heard the emperor acknowledge again Libertas's part in the chain of events and felt grateful beyond measure that she would be receiving the medical care she needed.

Her willingness to let him go astounded him, but he harbored no intention of breaking his vow to never leave her. However, before he could fulfill it, one task remained. He reached the top of the railing, and two bodyguards assisted him into the box. Fist over heart, Marcus bowed deeply to the emperor and empress before turning toward Messiena.

She was lying on several cushions. Her face was deathly pale. The stain blazoned across the midsection of her gown was even deathlier red.

In spite of the blood, she smelled as if she were resting upon a bed of gardenias.

Marcus stepped toward a richly robed man, presumably the physician, who stood, shaking his head and wiping his bloody hands on a cloth.

"Is there nothing you can do for her?" Marcus asked.

"No," he replied softly in Greek-accented Latin, giving the cloth to a servant. "The blade damaged too many organs."

Empress Faustina released her son, who joined his father at the rail, and glided toward the physician. "Go, Galen, and minister to the gladiatrix as the emperor has commanded."

"Yes, my lady." Galen bowed and departed with as much haste as decorum permitted.

His throat constricting, Marcus knelt beside Messiena and

picked up her hand. It felt alarmingly cool. He chafed it gently. Her eyes flickered open, and she managed a weak smile.

"You came. Thank you."

Marcus swallowed thickly. "Messiena, I am so very sorry. I never meant to hurt you." He gripped her hand tighter. "Please believe me. And please—" he drew a breath and let it out slowly through pursed lips "—please forgive me."

"Oh, Marcus." She lifted her hand to touch his check, his temple, his hair. "Gladiatrix Libertas…is she the one?"

Gods, why did she have to ask that now, of all times?

"You should rest, Messiena. We can talk about this later—"

"Marcus, please!" The firmness in her voice surprised him. "There is no 'later.' My ancestors are waiting for me. Very close. My mother…" She stopped looking at him for so long, he feared she'd already passed through death's veil. It startled him when she began to speak again: "I don't need platitudes, Marcus. Before I join my mother and the others, I need to know you will be happy."

"Libertas is the woman I love," he whispered, loathing himself. Messiena had done him no harm, and had saved his life just as surely as if she'd taken a blade for him, too.

But lying to her would have been far worse, for all of them.

Her gaze grew unfocused. "I tried to hate you for loving another woman. But I—" A spasm wracked her body, and her face clenched. After the pain passed, she regarded him frankly, stroking with her free hand the amber beads he had given her. "I love you too much to ever despise you."

Blinking hard, Marcus kissed the back of her hand and bowed his head. "I am not worthy of such great love."

She returned his grip with astonishing strength. "Dearest Marcus, of course you are. It's just that we were never—" Another spasm left her panting. She lowered her eyebrows as if in intense concentration. "Libertas is your destiny. Prove your worth to her." She drew a deep, shuddering breath and let it out in a long sigh. "Go in peace. I forgive you." The corners of her mouth quirked upward. "Both of you."

Her gaze fixed, and her chest stilled.

Falco uttered an anguished wail.

Marcus felt too numb to say or do anything except kiss Messiena's brow lingeringly.

"Whom the gods love," murmured Empress Faustina as Marcus lowered Messiena's hand to her chest and stood, "they take early unto themselves." After sparing Marcus a sad smile, she turned toward her husband. "Lady Messiena sacrificed her life for the empire. Does that not merit special consideration when dealing with her father?"

"I don't want to live!" Falco cried, staring helplessly at his daughter's body while the guards held him fast.

"That shall be arranged," the emperor said icily. "However, I need more answers from you first. Beginning with how you were able to subvert any of the Praetorian guardsmen."

"The payroll," mumbled Falco. "I called in favors to have its distribution delayed."

"I ordered that to be distributed weeks ago." The emperor rounded on the prefect. "Why did you not come to me, Caesius?" He sounded more hurt than angry.

The prefect's posture stiffened. "My lord, the paymaster told me it had been diverted to the front. Prince Commodus was ill and the reason sounded plausible, so I didn't question it." He bowed his head. "I am deeply sorry, your majesty."

Marcus ripped apart Jamil's sandal. Two documents fluttered free. The first contained the list he sought. After handing it to Prefect Caesius, he tucked the second back into the sandal unread. "That should help you root out the traitors in your ranks."

Caesius stared at the parchment without registering surprise. "I had suspected many of these men, your majesty, and had confined them to the barracks. Had I but known about the others, none of this would have happened."

"Perhaps. But I might not have learned of Falco's treason until it was too late," said the emperor. "You have performed excellent work, Caesius, under difficult circumstances. In their final posting they shall accompany ex-Senator Publius Messienus Falco and the paymaster on the arena sands." His gray eyes glittered like twin diamonds. "Along with one out of every ten of the rest of the Praetorian Guard."

Caesius pressed fist to chest and bowed. "As you will, my lord." Upon straightening, he called over a subordinate and gave him the list. "Lock up these men, under heavy guard, and inform the unit centurions of the emperor's decimation order. I shall implement it as soon as his majesty is finished here."

The imperial box became a maelstrom of activity as the soldier saluted and left, litter bearers arrived for Messiena's body, and other soldiers dragged an unresisting Falco to his cross. The emperor rounded on Marcus, fists planted on hips and countenance stern as any god's.

"Am I to understand that the son of one of the empire's highest-ranking officials loves an infamia gladiatrix-slave?"

"Yes, my lord." Marcus dared not hope for for the emperor's understanding.

Emperor Marcus Aurelius lowered his eyebrows. "Even though consorting with her would condemn you to life as an outcast?"

Such austerity, freely chosen, ought to appeal to the emperor's Stoic beliefs, but that might not be enough to sway him. Squaring his shoulders, Marcus regarded his sovereign levelly. "Even should it condemn me to death, your majesty."

"Most intriguing." The emperor stroked his dark, curly beard and regarded Empress Faustina. "Your thoughts, my lady wife?"

The empress advanced with a soft rustling of her silken robes, coming close enough for the refreshing lilac scent of her perfume to conquer the reek of death engulfing Marcus. "Nobility has shown us many unusual forms this day, my lord husband. I believe that if the love this man professes for the gladiatrix Libertas is returned even a tenth as strongly by her—" she gave Marcus a radiant smile "—all of heaven's legions would fall powerless before it."

Marcus Aurelius seemed to ingest this pronouncement. At length he remarked, "You have asked boons on behalf of others, Aquila. Have you no boon to ask for Libertas and yourself?"

It was the issue Marcus had been wrestling with ever since this audience had begun, but he stood no closer to a solution. "My lord, I know Roman law is strict with regard to infamiae. As deeply as I love Libertas, I cannot in good conscience ask that she be set above the law. Such an action could pose more harm than good."

Slowly the emperor nodded. "It is refreshing to see a young man—any man, for that matter—place the empire's needs above his own. Your foresight and devotion deserve to be rewarded, Aquila."

"I thank you, my lord. I seek only one reward—the freedom for me and Libertas to live out our lives together." Marcus stiffened his posture and drew a steadying breath. "I am not prepared to give her up again, your majesty, but I stand fully prepared to accept the consequences of my choice. Even, as I stated before, death."

Emperor Marcus Aurelius scrutinized him for what felt like an aeon. "Go to your Libertas," he said. "Prefect Caesius shall escort you to the palace and see to all your needs before returning to his duties. If I require anything more of you, Marcus Calpurnius Aquila, I shall know where to find you."

Marcus looped a finger through the leather cord and pulled Libertas's amber pendant to eye level. "What of this, your majesty? It contains the other evidence we told you about."

"Falco condemned himself by his deeds, Aquila. That constitutes proof enough for me." A faintly sardonic look touched the emperor's lips. "Now, lad, must I command you a second time?"

"No, my lord!" Marcus bowed to the emperor and empress and followed Caesius toward the rear of the box.

Marcus saved his longest act of obeisance for Messiena. As the bearers finished bundling her shrouded form onto the litter, he beseeched the gods to welcome her kindly into their realm.

AGRICOLA WATCHED HIS SON leave the imperial box and returned, with churning emotions, to the horrific chore of helping Loreia bind their servants' nail wounds. With every rending of his toga's woolen weave, creating strips to blot the blood, he released more frustration and anger. The men had not been tortured long, fortunately, but Agricola doubted they would regain even partial use of their hands and feet.

Falco would pay. He'd paid some of the debt already, Agricola reminded himself, by causing his daughter's death.

"Poor Messiena," he murmured to no one in particular, and handed his wife another strip.

Loreia used it to tie off Pyropus's final bandage and beckoned over a pair of litter bearers. Obtego had already been carried off to be tended by the Colosseum's physicians. While the bearers loaded Pyropus onto the stretcher, Loreia laid a hand on Agricola's shoulder.

"Messiena would have been a fine daughter-in-law," she said wistfully.

Agricola agreed. "What I don't know is what sort of daughter-in-law we will be receiving in her stead."

"A far better one than you're expecting, Sextus, I'm sure." Loreia gave him her favorite enigmatic little smile that would have driven him mad, if he'd possessed the energy for madness.

MARCUS HAD NO TIME to gawk at the imperial palace's luxury. The soaring arches, towering red Egyptian granite columns and endless stretches of spidery marble passed in a blur of myriad hues as he and Prefect Caesius hurried toward the infirmary wing.

*Libertas is your destiny.*

Every step carved Messiena's words deeper into Marcus's brain.

*Prove your worth to her.*

He had a fair idea of what it would take to accomplish that directive, but first he had to see Libertas, to enfold her into his embrace and reassure himself that she was going to be all right.

Immersed in those thoughts and a thousand more, Marcus paid no heed to the barrage of looks, from mild curiosity to vehement disdain, thrown his way by the dozens of politicians, priests, soldiers, clerks and servants they passed. Doubtless none of them had ever seen a gladiator escorted through the palace by the prefect of the Praetorian Guard. To say nothing of the fact that Marcus, smeared crown to sole with gore, must have appeared as if he'd wrestled Cerberus to escape from Tartarus.

The cuts and abrasions he'd collected, along with the pervasive ache settling in every muscle, certainly made him feel that way.

Outside the infirmary's doors, an orderly denied him entry.

"But I am the son of the governor of Britannia," Marcus protested.

"It's true," responded Caesius to the orderly's doubtful look. "The emperor commanded me to escort Lord Aquila here."

"You know Master Galen's policy, Prefect," said the orderly. "I don't care if this man is Jupiter incarnate. He cannot enter."

"What policy?" asked Marcus, feeling his eyebrows knit.

The orderly gave him a measuring glare. "Anyone in your

grimy state, aristocracy or not, is forbidden inside these doors. You would put every patient at risk of infection."

"What? But the woman I love is in there. I must see her!"

"Not without bathing first." The orderly folded his arms, his countenance unyielding.

"Come, Lord Aquila." Caesius swept an arm back the way they had come. "He's quite right. I should have thought of that. While you bathe, I'll send for garments that befit your station."

Swallowing a sigh, Marcus turned from the ward to follow the prefect. He had no desire to risk inflicting further harm upon Libertas or anyone else today.

And there was only one set of garments befitting the station to which he aspired: the provocator's gear he was wearing.

"Prefect Caesius, I thank you for your assistance," he said after Caesius had ushered him into the changing area of the nearby bathhouse. "There is one other request I would ask of you—" imagining the grim task awaiting the prefect made him hesitate "—if you have time."

Caesius, kneeling behind Marcus to unlace his leg greaves, did not interrupt his work. "The emperor's orders were clear. You have but to name what you desire, my lord, and it shall be done."

"Please arrange for the lanista of Ludus Maximus to meet me here with the contract for becoming a volunteer gladiator."

Caesius's fingers stilled. "My lord?"

"You heard me, Prefect."

It was the most liberating decision Marcus had ever made.

SHRUGGING INTO A TUNIC woven of finer linen than anything Jamil had ever owned, he had to admit he felt immeasurably better after his enforced bath, though his worry for Libertas compounded during the delay.

"The orderly wouldn't let you in, either?"

Jamil poked his head through the tunic's neck to find Aquila standing before him, the white towel girded about his loins gleaming in contrast to his filthy skin like a pearl in pitch. Blood, sweat and grime had molded with arena sand over his chiseled muscles to create a grotesque sculpture.

If Aquila had been a god, thunderbolts would have shot from his eyes.

"He didn't tell me how long I had to bathe, if that helps you any." Jamil donned the new pair of sandals a bath attendant had brought him.

Aquila's face relaxed a little. He opened his hand to give Jamil the second document that had been hidden inside the old sandal, which he gratefully tucked into the new pouch at his belt.

"How is she?" Aquila asked.

"Unconscious." Jamil concealed the seriousness of Libertas's condition with a shrug. Aquila would find out soon enough, and by then, gods willing, Libertas would be starting to recover.

With a terse nod, Aquila headed into the chamber housing the warm pool. Jamil didn't stay long enough to hear Aquila's splash.

On his way back to the infirmary, Jamil passed several orderlies toting buckets heaped with lumps of ice. His worry mounted as he lengthened his stride.

This time the infirmary's door guard admitted him

without comment. Jamil followed a slick trail of melted ice past a series of small chambers, where people of all ages were being treated for sundry complaints, until he entered the main ward.

Jamil had no trouble locating Libertas's bed. She was the patient with more attendants flitting about her than flies on hippopotamus dung. Physician Galen seemed to be direct-ing the activities. The orderlies Jamil had passed arrived and began packing their cold cargo on top of the ice already heaped around Libertas's body.

After they finished and Jamil reached her bedside, the severity of her condition became alarmingly clear. She had been draped in sheets sodden from the earlier batch of ice. Her eyes were tightly closed; her face—what little Jamil could see between the compresses—looked pinched and dotted with reddish blisters. She seemed as if she were panting through slightly parted lips. Agony contorted her face as cramps racked her muscles. Several orderlies labored to massage her limbs.

"Are you a relation?" Galen asked Jamil.

"I own her." Although, if Lady Maat was feeling kindly disposed toward Jamil's prayers, that would not be true for much longer. If Libertas recovered. "She will recover, won't she?" Jamil tried to bleed the anxiety from his tone.

"If her body doesn't succumb to the heat," Galen said, crisply but not unkindly. "She must not be accustomed to this climate. Has she experienced another illness recently? A flux of the stomach or bowels, perhaps?"

Jamil crooked a shoulder helplessly, beset by a fresh wave of guilt. "She was born and raised in Britannia. She recently arrived here, but I did not accompany her." Gazing only at the young woman who had become the daughter of his heart, he asked, "What can I do to help, Master Galen?"

"Keep watch, and exchange the compresses on her head with cold ones when the cloth feels warm. Summon the orderlies if you need more ice or help with relieving her cramping. If new symptoms develop, inform me at once. If she wakes, have her drink as much as possible." Galen nodded at the pitcher and cup sitting on the table beside the basin. "I shall return to check on her later." With a swirl of his richly embroidered robes, he strode off to attend other patients.

Jamil scarcely heard the physician's promise; his mind fixated on a single phrase with gut-wrenching implications.

*If* she wakes.

As MARCUS ENTERED THE infirmary's main ward, his fears coalesced into sickening reality.

"Libertas!"

Mentally berating himself for ever having left her—especially at Forum Iulii, for if he'd purchased her then, none of the calamities she'd suffered would have come to pass—Marcus dropped to his knees at her side, ignoring the icy water wicking past the hem of the tunic Caesius had given him.

He reached under the sheet to find her hand. In spite of the ice, it felt far too hot. Tears burned his eyes. "Libertas, I love you! Please don't leave me," he whispered hoarsely. "If you die, I don't know how I could go on."

Jamil shifted from his seat at her head to lay a hand on Marcus's shoulder. "That makes two of us, lad."

An idea made Marcus regard Jamil. "What is her name?"

"Her name…" Jamil's brow lowered. "Ruth. No, wait. That doesn't seem right."

A memory stirred of another day when she'd nearly died in the arena. "Does it sound something like 'hree-dthes'?"

"Rhyddes, yes!" Jamil gave him an ironic grin. "I remember now. She once told me it means 'freedom.'"

"Rhyddes." Marcus squeezed her hand. "Rhyddes, I love you. Fight this illness, and come back to me. Please! I cannot bear to lose you, Rhyddes…."

**33**

"... RHYDDES. RHYDDES!"

Her brother, Gwydion, was running toward her, his arms flailing and his gray-banded, midnight-blue cloak billowing behind him like a sail. Gwydion! Gods, how she had missed him!

How silly to have thought she might never see him again. She held out her arms for his embrace, but, strangely, he stopped short. She regarded him, confused.

"You must fight, Rhyddes!"

Nay. She was done with fighting. Fighting had won her naught but pain. Her arms and legs felt like granite blocks. Her head hurt so badly she could scarcely make out Gwydion's face. If a flea had lit upon her, she wouldn't have had the strength to flick it off. No more fighting.

All she craved was sleep.

"Rhyddes, please come back to me! I love you!"

Why in the name of all the gods was Gwydion saying that? She hadn't gone anywhere and didn't intend to leave him, so how could she come back? And she knew he loved her. He had never needed to say it before. Why now?

'Twas all too confusing.

Better to simply sleep; deep, dreamless, undemanding, never-ending sleep.

Misty darkness engulfed Gwyndion's features.

"Rhyddes! Rhyddes!"

Gwydion hadn't gone, as she had supposed; he was gripping her hand so hard it hurt. Pain shot up her arm and coursed throughout her body. She attempted to pull free, to make him stop hurting her, but she couldn't summon the strength. If only he would leave her alone to sleep!

As if coming from a great distance, she heard someone moaning and wondered who might be suffering such plaintive distress.

Splinters of light pierced her brain as she opened her eyes. Wincing, she shut them again. The pain didn't abate.

Abruptly she felt as if she'd been locked outside, naked, in a blizzard. Shivering, she moaned again.

"*Excitare,* Rhyddes! *Amo te!*"

*Wake up?* And *I love you?* How very strange. Gwydion didn't know Latin. Did he?

When the phrases repeated, she recognized the speaker. A pit formed in her stomach.

"Go away. Please! Before it's too late." Her voice sounded as if she hadn't used it in a fortnight, and she cleared her throat. She didn't dare open her eyes, lest she behold him and lose her resolve. "For your own good, Aquila."

*I love you, Aquila! But I can never have you.*

Tears tried to strangle her speech. She gasped a breath and swallowed them. "I implore you to leave me. Forever."

Her heart ached as if someone had speared it. Crucifixion would have hurt less.


SHE MAY AS WELL HAVE RUN Marcus through. It wouldn't have felt half as agonizing.

"Rhyddes, you cannot mean that!" He shifted ice to press his cheek against her hand, grateful that the deadly heat had abated. The arena's stench clung to her, but he ignored it. "I vowed never to leave you."

He felt the fingers of her other hand twine in his hair, slowly, lovingly. Smiling, he lifted his head. Her hand fell heavily onto the ice mounded atop her coverlet. Infinite sadness clouded her gaze, and her chin was trembling. Panic tormented him with the thought that he could be losing her again. He gripped her hand.

"Think," she said softly but firmly. "Even if I could leave the arena, where would we live? A hovel beside a midden heap, where we would muck latrines all day?" She shook her head, tears moistening the blood caked to her cheeks. "For that is the best we, as infamiae, could ever expect."

"I don't care! That hovel would seem a palace with you to grace it, Rhyddes." He dried the tears with the fingers of his free hand, smearing the blood. "I shall not break my vow to you."

The ghost of a smile touched her lips. "You cannot break a vow from which you have been released." She drew a shuddering breath, and more tears welled. "I once told you that a Votadini Celt never begs. But I—" A strangled noise choked her words, offspring of a gasp and a groan. "Go, my lord, I beg you. Now. Please do not destroy yourself over me."

"Rhyddes, no! I love you—"

"If you love me—" her gaze hardened "—then honor my wishes."

He couldn't believe what he was hearing. "Is that truly your wish? That we never see each other again?"

She grimaced, her chin quivering. "It has to be," she whispered.

Reluctantly he released her hand. "I love you, Rhyddes, and always will."

She shut her eyes tightly. Her face contorted, though whether from physical or emotional pain, he couldn't tell. She turned her head away from him. Silent sobs shook her body.

No, not sobs, he realized, but uncontrollable shivering.

Alarmed, Marcus stood and yelled for the orderlies. They brought blankets, towels and sheets by the armload and swarmed about her to remove the ice and wet linens, wrap her in blankets, shift her to a dry bed and mop the floor beneath the first bed.

Marcus stayed out of the way, yearning for even the smallest sign that she would change her mind about him. She accepted the orderlies' ministrations so passively that she could have been a child's doll.

At last the shivering stopped. But when he returned to her side and picked up her hand, she did not acknowledge his presence.

He kissed the back of her hand and lowered it to the

coverlet. If honoring her wishes meant he had to let her go, then by all that was sacred he wouldn't fail her in that. Sighing, he trudged away. Jamil had left him alone with Rhyddes—probably thought he was doing Marcus a favor—to search them out some supper. Marcus hoped Jamil might be able to offer some advice.

"It's obvious she doesn't love you anymore, Son." Pausing, Marcus glanced up to see his father, divested of toga and his chest swathed in a clean bandage, standing in front of him. "If she ever did."

Marcus rolled his eyes. "What is it, Father? Didn't enough people stab me today?" He shouldered by to resume his course.

Agricola snagged his arm. "I'm sorry, Marcus. But Libertas was not a proper match for you. She is infamia—"

"So am I!" Into the silence spawned by his father's stunned surprise, he continued, "I will not return with you to Britannia. I report to Ludus Maximus to begin my five-year contract at sundown tonight. My lord."

"No, Marcus! I have given you wealth, status—"

"I didn't renounce my heritage to hurt you or Mother. I did it for love of Libertas. Rhyddes is her given name, and it, too, means freedom. Liberty."

"You're making no sense, Marcus. How can you possibly achieve freedom by signing it away to the arena—where, gods forbid, you might be killed?"

Marcus itched to grip his father by the shoulders and shake some sense into him. Instead he summoned his final shred of patience to say, "It was the only chance Rhyddes and I had of preventing another arranged marriage from separating us."

"If you were opposed to the match with Messiena, why didn't you tell me? I would not have signed the betrothal contract had I known how you felt."

"Somehow I rather doubt that." He saw Jamil approaching but had no interest in talking to him, and no interest in the tray of cubed pork, cheese, bread and peaches he was carrying, no matter how tempting it smelled. "The gods despise mortals who try to find happiness."

"Son, that's blasphemy!" Agricola shouted as Marcus stalked down the corridor.

"How else can I explain my failure to be happy with Rhyddes?" he retorted over his shoulder.

And yet, beyond all reason, Marcus's heart clung to the hope that as a contract gladiator, he might one day win Rhyddes back.

He could hear the gods' derisive laughter echoing in his every footstep.

JAMIL WATCHED AQUILA STORM away, his own fury threatening to boil over. He abandoned the platter on an empty bed to confront Agricola. "You are losing your son, Governor."

"You're wrong, Citizen Kalilus. I lost him long before this moment." Agricola's face sagged with resigned sorrow. "I was too blind to see it until now."

"Aquila was wrong, too. Volunteering as a gladiator was not his only chance at happiness with Rhyddes." Jamil pulled a crisp document from the pouch hanging from his belt, unfolded it and rattled it at Agricola. "This could have solved everything if I'd had the chance to show it to him."

"Everything?" The governor snorted his doubts and glanced toward Rhyddes's bed. "She rejected him. And I did not influence her, if that's what you're thinking."

"I know," Jamil said. "But—forgive my bluntness, Governor—if you hadn't driven Aquila off with your vain ambitions and arrogant snobbery, he might have fought harder for her love."

Agricola had the grace to look chagrined. "I suppose I deserved that, Kalil. But how would that document have made any difference?"

Jamil allowed the governor to read it. After a few moments, Agricola's eyebrows twitched. He apparently noticed the signature Jamil had obtained only minutes before. "You would do this for an *infamia*?"

Jamil expelled a noisy sigh. "That *infamia*, as you persist in calling her, helped prevent your *asinus* from being nailed to a pair of crossed beams today, and your family and entourage along with it. If you choose to forget that fact, my lord, I shall noise it about all Britannia that you tried to engineer the death of your people's favorite gladiatrix." He felt his eyes narrow to slits. "And I shall begin by telling your son."

"Aquila already knows." Agricola held up his empty hand. "But I have trouble enough governing those wild Celts without adding that decision to the mix."

"You might have an easier time ruling those 'wild Celts,' your lordship, if you start showing them more respect...as your son has learned with Libertas."

Lowering his arm, Agricola laughed. "I knew I'd rue the day I took you into my service, Kalil Al-Omar."

Jamil refrained from pointing out that, first and foremost, he had been hired as Aquila's bodyguard; direct service to the governor had come later. With Aquila bent on becoming a contract gladiator, it was a moot point.

"And though it pains me to admit it, you're right," Agricola continued. "There is much I can learn from Marcus. But how do we convince him and Libertas to speak to one another again?"

"Aquila's gladiator contract must be annulled. Since he is your son, I shall let you solve that problem, Governor." Jamil retrieved his document from Agricola, folded it and tucked it back into his pouch. "Leave the convincing of Libertas to me."

THE CLOSER TOWARD LUDUS Maximus he strode, the more furious he felt. He drew admiring stares from the women and jealous glares from the men he passed. Once he would have thrived on such attention. Today he couldn't have given a sour pomegranate pip for it.

Marcus Calpurnius Aquila was dead.

Dead to his family, dead to his past, dead to all the trappings of wealth, status, privilege, pleasure and power the Roman Empire had to offer her aristocratic citizens.

Marcus Calpurnius Aquila was dead to Rhyddes.

Long live Aquila Roma, this city's newest contract gladiator of the provocator class.

Perhaps he might one day earn her love again. If he survived long enough.

He reached the school's perimeter gates but found them locked—not entirely surprising, since the lanistae and guards at all the gladiatorial schools were probably still sorting out the rebellion's aftermath. He shouted through the bars to attract the attention of two guards emerging from the building's far side.

While one continued on his appointed rounds, the other ran toward Marcus—no, *Aquila Roma*, he ruthlessly reminded himself.

"My lord!" Vederi's greeting surged forth on the wings of relief. "Am I glad to see you! What happened? After we guards were let out of the rooms where the traitors had trapped us, we were ordered back here. We heard plenty of ugly rumors! What of Libertas? Is she—?"

"She will recover, Vederi, though I doubt she will be returning here." Vederi's elation sank into disappointment, and Marcus softened his tone. "She's safe with Jamil. And I am no longer a lord. I am Aquila Roma, here to begin my contract, as Lanista Laomedes ordered."

"What? But I thought you and she—"

Marcus raised a hand. "Long story. Maybe I'll tell it to you later. For now, let me in, please."

Vederi did not comply but gave him a cryptic look.

By this time another of Vederi's companions had joined them. "Lanista Laomedes did not mention anything…wait. What did you call yourself, sir?"

"Aquila Roma."

"Marcus Calpurnius Aquila," Vederi supplied.

"That was my name once." Squaring his shoulders, Marcus jutted his chin. "Now I wish to be known only as Aquila Roma."

"Either way, sir," said the other guard flatly, "you are forbidden to enter."

"What?" He eyed the men, who straightened under the scrutiny. "Vederi, is this a jest? Because it isn't the least bit amusing."

"No jest, sir." Vederi contrived to stand even more rigidly. "Emperor's orders."

"Impossible! I signed the contract only an hour ago! I watched Lanista Laomedes take it with him."

"That you did, Son."

Marcus whirled to see his father, elegantly attired in a purple-and-gold-banded white toga that had to be an imperial gift, cross the street from the wine vendor's shop where, apparently, he'd been waiting perched on one of the shaded chairs outside. As Agricola closed the distance, he held up a familiar looking document. Closer still, Marcus could make out the words, in bold red letters, "PACTUM TOLERE"—contract annulled, embossed with the Eagle of Rome stamped in purple wax.

"Still meddling in my affairs, Father?"

"Now who's doing the stabbing?" Sighing, Agricola lifted his hand. "Before you utter another word, Marcus, I want you to know you are absolutely right. For years I tried to tell myself I was making decisions regarding the course of your life for your own good, but in truth, they have been more for my good than yours. Especially that gods-forsaken betrothal contract." Hand pressed flat over his heart, he bowed his head. "I am deeply sorry, Son, and I ask your forgiveness."

"How can I forgive you, Father, when you keep interfering with my decisions?"

In response to Agricola's startled look, Marcus pointed to the annulled contract his father was clutching.

"This?" Agricola studied it, as if for the first time, before rolling it up and tucking it into one of his toga's folds. "Yes, that was meddling, too. But for far better reasons than for advancing my career at the expense of your life. Or your love."

"What do you mean?" Marcus asked cautiously.

Agricola's lips twitched into a shadow of a smile. "Come back to the palace with me and find out." As Marcus's skepticism scaled new heights, Agricola opened his arms beseechingly. "All I am asking, Son, is for you to spare me a few more minutes of your time. Regardless of the outcome—" he raised his left hand and placed his right fist over his heart as if delivering sworn testimony "—you shall be free to come back here and execute a new contract, or whatever you wish to do with your life. This I solemnly swear to you by all that is sacred."

Marcus turned, thankful to find Vederi and his companion still standing, agog, beside the gate. "You heard my father?"

"Every word, sir," said Vederi, and the other guard nodded.

"Good. Two witnesses make it legally binding." He shot Agricola a warning glance before saying to Vederi, "Please advise Lanista Laomedes he may not have seen the last of Aquila Roma."

"Just a few more minutes," Agricola repeated as they walked toward the palace. "That's all I ask of you."

"A few more minutes" was all the patience Marcus possessed.

RHYDDES, COCOONED IN A lamb's wool blanket, despised herself. She closed her eyes, but sleep eluded her. If letting Aquila go was the best decision, for his sake, then why did it feel so utterly wrong?

"Libertas—Rhyddes." Jamil's warm chuckle made her bury herself deeper into the blanket's folds. "I'm sorry. Please forgive an old Egyptian too long immersed in the common tongue. I promise to become better at addressing you by your true name."

Curiosity prompted her to poke out her head. Bathed, groomed, and wearing an expertly woven, scarlet-bordered saffron tunic girded with a finely tooled red leather belt and matching sandals, Jamil looked more affluent than she'd ever seen him during his days of presiding over Villa Britanniae.

"Why, master? Infamiae are never known by our given names."

"What happened to calling me 'Father'?" Her eyes widened, and he grinned. "Whatever you choose to call me, it needn't be 'master.' You are no longer an infamia—" his grin stretched wider "—Libertas filia Kalila Alomaria." The grin disappeared. "If you can forgive me for plunging you into a hell on earth."

"*Daughter?*" She could scarcely comprehend what she'd heard. Tears welled. She staved them off with incredulity. "You adopted me?"

"Yes, and being my legal daughter makes you a fully privileged citizen of the Roman Empire."

Her heart started racing, and she lowered her voice. "It cannot be."

"What do you mean?"

Willing her heart to slow down, and failing, she drew a breath and let it out. "I killed two of my owners today," she whispered. "I never saw the third."

"Oh, you mean the tiger?" Jamil waved dismissively. "I heard about what happened in the labyrinth from one of the witnesses. And I killed Rodo after he transferred your ownership to me and I learned all he knew of Falco's plot. Although you were a slave, you didn't kill your owners. When I described to the emperor what warts those men were on the buttocks of the empire—"

She couldn't contain her astonishment. "You gained another audience with the emperor? How was that possible?"

Jamil laughed. "My dearest Rhyddes, anything is possible when one has the right friends—or, at least, acquaintances who feel abiding gratitude for one's services." He dragged his chair closer to her bedside. "I wanted to free you two nights ago, but by Roman law you could not have become a citizen unless I adopted you. Only as a citizen would you have been permitted to marry Aquila. So, I—"

She clutched his knee. "I couldn't marry him now even if I wanted to. I—I sent him away." In spite of her aching muscles, she rolled over. "Permanently!" Her sobs erupted into the pillow.

Jamil's hand began gently stroking her back.

"Rhyddes? Do you still love him or not?" he asked.

Aquila had sacrificed every material thing he possessed for her; although she couldn't make out all of what he'd said, she'd heard that much. The purest, most faithful love she'd ever been offered, by anyone, and she had trampled it into the muck like so much hog slop.

It was she who deserved to be trampled in slop; she who deserved to suffer the ultimate penance of forever loving someone who would never, because of her foolishness, love her in return.

"I do!" she cried into the pillow. "I cannot stop loving him, even though he must despise me."

The hand on her back stilled and lifted. A moment later she felt its warmth caressing her cheek. "Must I, Rhyddes? I really would rather love you than despise you."

Her heart lurched. Still lying on her stomach, she turned her head toward the beloved voice.

Aquila was kneeling beside her bed, his head cocked like an expectant puppy's. Slowly, scarcely daring to believe what she saw, she reached out to touch his cheek. He leaned into her palm, his scratchy stubble a welcome reminder that she wasn't dreaming.

Love radiated from his eyes like sunlight warming her face.

She hated to ask the question that could destroy the moment, but she had to know: "What of your bride?"

He bowed his head, and sadness clouded his features. "Lady Messiena is dead. May the gods grant her peace." A thin smile conquered the sadness. "You were so wise to send me to her. I wronged her, and I never intended to. Before she died I apologized and begged her forgiveness." He regarded Rhyddes earnestly. "But please believe me, Rhyddes. You are the only bride I have ever wanted."

As Rhyddes sat up, she noticed Governor Agricola, arm in arm with his wife, standing beside Jamil, far enough away not to intrude, but close enough that she felt their influence, though they hadn't said a word.

"Don't you have to obey your father's will, Aquila?" she whispered. "That is Roman law, is it not?"

"Those closest to my heart call me Marcus." He grasped her hands. "My father has freed me, legally, to follow my heart. It led me straight to you, my beloved Rhyddes."

Gods, it sounded so sweet to hear him use her given name!

Before their lips could meet, a disturbing thought pulled her back.

"Your gladiator contract!" An ironic laugh burst from her throat. "Jamil adopted me. You are the infamia, now, and I am the citizen. Marcus, what are we to do?"

"What is your choice?" he asked.

"My choice?" As a slave, subject to the will—and whims—of everyone else, the concept had become all but incomprehensible.

"Of course. As I see it, you have three of them." Releasing her hands, he rocked back to sit on the floor, wrapping his arms around his knees. "If you renounce your citizenship to remain a gladiatrix, I shall return to Ludus Maximus to fulfill my contract obligations there, at Villa Britanniae, or wherever you wish to compete. If you keep your citizenship, I shall let the gladiator contract annulment, which my father obtained from the emperor without my knowledge, stand."

Just the two choices—to return to her life as a gladiatrix, though with a mote more freedom by being under contract; or to begin a new life as the adopted daughter of a Roman citizen, whatever in heaven's name that entailed—were weighty enough to make her throbbing head spin. She propped her face in one hand while she tried to sort out the benefits and drawbacks of each.

And yet, either way, Marcus would be with her.

Either way, that was the only factor that mattered.

Smiling serenely, she lowered her hand to her lap. "And my third choice?"

"Why, to keep things as they are, and let you worry about soiling *your* reputation by consorting with an infamia, for a change." Marcus's laugh boomed deep, genuine and contagious.

Chuckling, she rolled her eyes. "Gods, no! I don't think either of us could take any more of that foolishness. Jamil?" Expression sobering, she beckoned to her new father. He hastened to her side, and they shared a long embrace. "Will it disturb you," she murmured to him, "if your most profitable performer retires her gladius?"

Jamil broke the embrace but continued holding her left hand. "Not if my *daughter*—" he placed her hand into Marcus's, and closed both of his hands over theirs "—finds happiness with the man she loves."

Although Jamil let go, swiping at his eyes as he stood and backed away, Marcus did not. He twisted around to regard his parents. "Father? Mother? What say you to all of this?"

Her chin trembling and tears streaming past her smile, Marcus's mother clearly was in no condition to speak as she stepped forward to grasp Marcus's and Rhyddes's hands. The governor, blinking rapidly, seemed not much better off.

"What else can we say except—" Agricola's grip tightened as he inhaled deeply "—welcome to the family, Citizen Libertas filia Kalila Alomaria!"

The governor and his wife each kissed her on a cheek, straightened and rejoined Jamil.

"Rhyddes," said Marcus as he leaned toward her, gripping

her hands as if he never wanted to let her go. "My wife's name is Rhyddes."

"Your wife?" She felt her eyebrows knit. "Did I miss the ceremony?"

Marcus laughed. "Temple ceremonies are for Roman priests and priestesses when they marry. Between two aristocrats, it's a contract signing, followed by as many days of feasting as both families can tolerate. For everyone else, it's a handclasp blessed by the parents." He bent over her ear to whisper, "In my heart, Rhyddes, you became my wife last night."

To shed the stigma of a social outcast and receive the title bestowed upon her by a man who had chosen her as his daughter was astonishing in itself. But to gain the title representing her eternal connection to the first man of her heart left her speechless.

Fortunately, Marcus didn't seem to want a speech.

His lips met hers—not chastely, as she might have expected in the presence of their parents, as well as the physicians, orderlies, visitors and other patients, whose cheers erupted with the exuberance of an arena crowd—but with a depth of passion unlike anything she had ever felt before. As if of one mind, they liberated each other's hands to twine arms and bodies like mistletoe to oak, until not even the sharpest sword could have separated them. Their kiss deepened, promising a world of boundless delights in the days and nights to come.

For Rhyddes, bandaged and aching like fury in more places than she cared to count, it was the sweetest moment of her life.

# Epilogus

SIX WEEKS LATER, Governor Agricola proclaimed that he and his entourage, which had swelled with the addition of Rhyddes and included the two servants who'd been crippled by crucifixion wounds—though not Vederi, who chose to remain employed at Ludus Maximus—were ready to depart the Eternal City.

Rhyddes was going to miss her old friend, but not the city he'd adopted.

Oh, the emperor and empress had been extremely kind, gifting Agricola with Falco's confiscated estate, which Agricola promptly sold to split the profit with Jamil. The only item retained from the mansion was a marvelous portrait of Marcus dressed in his provocator's gear, a gleaming gladius clutched in his right fist and the eagle-adorned helmet tucked under his left arm. Rhyddes suspected the artist's identity, but chose not to ask.

In addition, the imperial family had hosted the Calpurniae inside the palace's dignitaries' wing as if they were
visiting royalty, held a nuptial celebration lasting a fortnight, and invited them to other lavish feasts and state oc-
casions. Learning how to comport herself like a proper
Roman lady was not too difficult with Mother Loreia for a
teacher, and Rhyddes had attended enough feasts as a gladiatrix that she wasn't surprised by the infinitely bizarre
combinations of food, drink and human behavior.

The pinnacle of Roman society was very grand, and no
mistake. But now that Rhyddes was no longer fighting
merely to survive, she missed Britain, especially the firth and
hills cradling her clan's lands. And her longing to see her
brothers and their families, to hug her nieces and nephews,
introduce her new husband, his parents and her adoptive
father and let everyone know she was alive and prospering,
grew more acute with each passing week.

The problem was, despite the fact that the governor's
barge was far larger and more stable than the other vessels
on which Rhyddes had sailed, she felt sicker than ever. The
main difference was that several servants, under the
watchful eye of Mother Loreia, attended Rhyddes's every
need.

By the end of their second week at sea, Rhyddes had developed enough of a routine that she could tell her father-
in-law they needn't put in at Londinium for her benefit.
They continued sailing up Britain's eastern coast as originally
planned. Agricola had promised Rhyddes and Marcus could
visit her clan, and he seemed pleased with the prospect of
not having to arrange an overland journey from Londinium.

The morning of their last day aboard, after spewing supper's stinking remains into a bucket and not missing too badly when the ship hit a swell, she could contain her frustration no longer.

"Why is this happening to me? My body should have grown accustomed to sea travel by now!"

Loreia listened with quiet patience, a maddeningly placid smile decorating her perfectly painted face. "My dear Rhyddes, when was the last time you had your monthly courses?"

"I—" Rhyddes felt her eyes stretch wide before narrowing in concentration.

"Since coming on board ship?" Loreia prompted. "Or before that, while we were lodging in the palace?"

"No, Mother Loreia. The last time nature, rather than an arena opponent, made me bleed—" Rhyddes laughed at her own foolishness "—was the last time I was on a ship, headed for Rome." She grinned at her mother-in-law's expression of surprised delight. "Congratulations, Grandmother Loreia."

Loreia clasped her into a long embrace. "Then Marcus doesn't know yet."

Pulling back, Rhyddes shook her head. Marcus had honored her request to rise and depart their cabin as early as possible each morning, so she could deal with her sickness in relative peace and spare him its full extent. "Please don't tell him, either. I want to do it myself."

"Of course, my dear." Loreia directed her stern gaze toward the woman cleaning up Rhyddes's partially digested supper and the other woman changing the bed linens. "Lady Rhyddes's secret stays inside this cabin until the time and place of her choosing, is that clear to both of you?"

Rhyddes giggled, not at the servants' earnest, bob-headed reactions but at the fact that she probably would never become accustomed to hearing herself called "Lady Rhyddes."

A knock rattled the cabin door. "Rhyddes, my love," called Marcus through the salt-aged oak, "are you almost ready? The ship's master says we shall be disembarking soon."

She thanked all the gods—Roman, Egyptian and Celtic—for that mercy. "Give me a moment, dear heart," she called back. "I will meet you up on deck presently."

His receding footsteps echoed off the planking into silence as the servants finished their work and Loreia helped Rhyddes don and pin her cloak.

Rhyddes climbed out of the ship's belly toward the breath-taking panoramic view of her homeland while the ship maneuvered closer to the dock. Marcus, resplendent in the pale blue silk tunic he had acquired the day after thwarting Falco's plot, slipped an arm around her waist and guided her to a spot along the rail amidships, where they could watch the proceedings and yet remain out of the crew's way.

"I had forgotten how beautiful this country is," Marcus murmured.

Nestling her head against his chest, she uttered a short, rueful laugh. "So had I."

Several dozen people, running toward the dock and shouting welcomes in a tongue she once had thought she would never hear again, caught her attention. Some of the shouting sounded familiar, and not just because of the language. She squinted and grinned, waving broadly.

"Hai, the clan!" she cried in Celtic as her brothers, sisters-in-law, nieces and nephews, surrounded by the rest of the village folk in a dancing, unruly mass, lined the docks to bring their lost sister home.

"Well come, Lady Rhyddes!" they shouted together as if they'd rehearsed it, not in Latin but in the Votadini dialect.

She shot an astonished glance at her husband. "Your doing?"

He tried to look innocent but couldn't shed the grin. "I had a lot of time on my hands while you were ill in our cabin."

"You shall need a lot more time when you become a father in the spring," she retorted.

"I—" His puzzlement looked endearingly comical. *"What?"*

"Father Aquila. Get used to it." She flashed a dazzling smile. "Now tell me, Father Aquila, how you managed to arrange all of this." She waved again at her clan, waving faster when she saw Owen push to the forefront.

"Very well, *Mother* Rhyddes." He gave her waist a light squeeze. "Our ship's captain knew the harbormaster. Arranging a proper welcome for you was simply a matter of finding a fast enough ship traveling this direction from our last port in Gaul to bear the message."

"Bribing that captain to make a detour, more likely," she said cheerfully.

Marcus bent to kiss her. "Wealth does have its advantages."

Rhyddes couldn't disagree.

Not only had her family contrived to be present for the ship's arrival, they had arranged a feast for the village to celebrate Rhyddes's homecoming. The roasted pork, pulled hot and juicy off the spit, surrounded by wild onions, leeks, lentil and barley porridge and stewed, spiced apples mixed with bilberries, washed down by rivers of potent, frothy ale, no doubt was barbaric fare for her husband, adopted father and parents-in-law.

As afternoon hastened toward evening, Rhyddes felt a restless hunger awaken within her that had naught to do with the food. Well did she ken its source, but she dreaded the thought of facing it.

To avoid dwelling upon this inner demon, she resolved to speak to her brother and tried to take her leave of Marcus. He insisted on accompanying her even though he knew he wouldn't understand the conversation.

"Practicing at being a protective father already, are you?" Teasing helped to keep the demon at bay.

He struck a statuesque pose. "By Roman law, it is my right." Saluting her as smartly as any centurion would have done, he continued, "As well as my honor and privilege."

"Come, then, privileged boy." She laughed, pulling on his tunic sleeve. "I'll translate for you later."

Owen saluted Marcus and Rhyddes in the Votadini way: a hearty backslap for Marcus, and a bone-crushing hug for Rhyddes.

"Hey, mind the bairn, Uncle Owen!" With an expression of love like that, she'd have preferred the backslap.

Owen backed off as if he'd been stung, and held her at arm's length. "My little sister is with child already?" After giving Rhyddes a far gentler, though no less heartfelt hug, he treated Marcus to another backslap. "A thousand blessings upon you all!"

"And what of you, Owen? Are there many women in your life?" Rhyddes asked with a grin. "Or mayhap just one?"

Her brother glanced at a woman watching them avidly from the shadows of a nearby doorway, smiled and shrugged. "Mayhap one." For a moment Owen's gaze filled with memories. "'Tis a tale for another day, not my dear sister's homecoming feast."

Too bad, Rhyddes thought, for a rousing tale might have helped her forget the issue hounding her. But she knew Owen better than to press him for details before he was ready to share them. And no matter how she might strive to avoid it, a crucial matter had to be resolved before she could enjoy true and lasting freedom.

Drawing Owen aside, she asked in a low voice, "Can you take me to him?"

"Him—you mean Da?" Incredulity overshadowed his tone. "Why, in the name of all that's holy, would you want to visit his grave? After every hateful thing he did to you your whole life...both our lives," he amended bitterly.

"I must try to lay the past to rest." She felt her gaze turn inward for a moment. "Even though I'll never know why he despised me so."

Gripping her shoulders, he regarded her solemnly. At length he asked, "Did you ever wonder why Ma named you 'freedom'?"

"'Twas her dying wish." She shrugged, and he lowered his hands. "No one would ever tell me more."

"Da had forbidden it. Maybe 'twas the only way he could express anger toward the priests when they refused to let him change your name. I was too young to understand, that day, but I asked Arden about it later. Da cared naught if we boys talked among ourselves, only that we never spoke of it to you." He gritted his teeth as if battling his own demons. "Da beat Ma, too. Only in death could she escape him."

His revelations, and its implications, hit her with the force of a blow. "Because of my name, he couldn't forget…and so he transferred his fury to me." She closed her eyes against the tears. "Gods."

"And you still want to visit his grave?"

"More than ever."

He raised his hands in surrender. "This way, then."

As they passed the gathering, Rhyddes beckoned Jamil, Agricola and Loreia to join her.

Owen led them across the village and up the hill that had served as the clan's burial place from time out of mind. Sunset's retreating colors bathed it in a warm, golden glow.

Gazing at the whitewashed rock plugging the pot containing her father's ashes, Rhyddes felt anything but warm and golden.

She knelt in the cool grass. "Father, at last I understand why you hated me so much that you felt compelled to sell me to eliminate me from your life," she began in Latin, as much for the benefit of her new family as for sparing Owen the pain of hearing what she had to say. "But the reasons are no longer important. I forgive you." Tears closed her throat.

Before she quite realized what was happening, Jamil and Marcus had knelt beside her. The rustling of fabric told her that Loreia and Agricola had followed their example.

"I thank you, father of Rhyddes, for your beautiful, valiant, wonderful daughter." Marcus wrapped his arm around her and pulled her close, and she hid her face against his chest, biting her lip in her struggle not to cry. "Know that I shall love her and care for her, and our children, forever."

"We have welcomed Rhyddes into our home and into our hearts," said Loreia. Rhyddes turned to smile her gratitude. "She shall always be welcome there, won't she, Sextus?" Loreia asked her husband with a nudge.

The governor, whose gaze had seemed distant, gave a startled grunt. "Of course." A genuine smile warmed his features as he regarded Rhyddes before turning his gaze toward Rudd's remains. "Your daughter has taught me much about your people, and the passions that empower Celtic souls. All Britannia shall prosper from what I have learned."

Owen, who had been standing off to one side, looking by turns confused and bored, stepped over and dropped to his knees beside Rhyddes. "What are they saying?" he asked, hefting a rock he'd plucked from the grass.

Inundated by a flood of emotion, she scarcely knew where to start. "Expressing their appreciation."

"To that bastard?" Tensing his jaw, he reared up and cocked his arm. "I'll show him appreciation."

Before anyone else could react, other than startled gasps, Rhyddes caught his hand. "Don't, Owen. Please." She tried to pry the rock free, but his grip was too strong. "Surrender to your hate, and he wins. He tried to enslave me. Please don't let him enslave you, too."

As he stared at the rock, his eyes widened. "Aye, Rhyddes, you're right. He deserves my pity, not my hatred."

'Twasn't much, but it was a start.

"And," Owen continued, cracking the lopsided grin she loved so well, "you deserve this." He dropped the rock into her hand.

"Nay." She gave it back. "You must bury it. Beside him."

His surprise gave way to frame-shaking laughter. "Gods! When did you become such a taskmaster?"

While Owen scrabbled in the dirt to obey her, she gazed fondly at Jamil, her chin quivering. "I had the best teacher."

"Believe her not, Rudd of the Votadins," Jamil responded, not in Latin but in Celtic, grinning at her astonishment. "You, sir, gave me the best student. And the best daughter a man could ever want." Solemnly Jamil touched hand to chest and forehead in the traditional Egyptian bow.

Nestled safely within the embraces of her husband and the father of her heart, Rhyddes celebrated her final victory. Mayhap the bairn she carried had weakened her defenses, but that scarcely mattered.

Her tears flowed hard and free, a fount of healing for her wounded but unconquerable soul.

# Author's Note

IN SEPTEMBER 2000, British archaeologists announced an extraordinary find: the cremated remains of a wealthy young woman buried in a Roman-era paupers' cemetery on the south bank of the Thames, outside the perimeter of 2nd century A.D. London. The ossuary was remarkable for its eight oil lamps, bearing gladiator and Egyptian motifs, evidence of an exotic feast that included almonds, dates and figs, and traces of stone-pine incense from the cones of trees that grew nowhere in Britain save for the grounds encircling London's amphitheater. The "Great Dover Street Woman," as the London Museum archaeologists prosaically named her, was either a gladiator's aristocratic consort, or else a superstar gladiatrix in her own right.

I chose the latter interpretation, and gave her a story.

I wish to thank my dear friend and fellow writer, Anne Shaw Moran, for clipping and mailing the original article to me as something that "just seemed like [my] kind of thing." Indeed!

Carbon dating placed Great Dover Street Woman's remains at about a hundred years earlier than I depicted, coinciding with the rebuilding of London's amphitheater following a cataclysmic fire, and at about the same time as the opening of Rome's Flavian Amphitheater, or Colosseum, as it quickly came to be known. Since I wanted to show an emperor who wasn't a raving megalomaniac, I employed literary license to set Rhyddes's story during the early reign of Emperor Marcus Aurelius and the governorship of Sextus Calpurnius Agricola.

Contemporary inscriptions show that Agricola was responsible for refurbishing an eastern section of Hadrian's Wall, and Roman lighthouses were built along Britain's northeastern coastline at approximately the same time. If those lighthouses weren't Agricola's idea, they should have been.

Other historic personages in *Liberty* include the emperor's wife, Empress Faustina, and their son, Prince Commodus—who did not grow up to murder his father, as shown in Russell Crowe's movie, *Gladiator,* although Commodus did enjoy fighting as a gladiator in later years and became arguably the worst of Rome's megalomaniac emperors.

The Greek physician, Galen of Pergamum, received his professional start treating gladiators, and cured Commodus of some unspecified childhood disease; I selected chicken pox, with complications. As a result, Galen became Emperor Marcus Aurelius's physician in Rome during the precise period depicted in *Liberty.* Galen's prolific medical treatises, which have proven to be about eighty percent accurate by modern standards, including essays about the dangers and avoidance of infection, formed the vast bulk of the Roman world's medical knowledge. Healers continued to consult them well into the medieval era.

Rome indeed had two emperors during the period described in *Liberty*, with the second, Lucius Aurelius Verus, kept busy overseeing Rome's frontier wars in what is now Russia, Germany and Armenia. The precedent of ordaining joint, equally empowered emperors, established by Marcus Aurelius, would be followed by some Roman emperors in later centuries.

Although it may seem strange to see the mention of concrete in my novel, ancient Roman engineers had developed at least five different grades of the substance, which accounts for the astounding longevity of buildings such as Hadrian's remarkable domed pantheon in Rome and the amphitheater in Nîmes, France—not shown in *Liberty* since it wasn't located at a port—that survives intact and is still used for bullfights and concerts today.

Regarding aspects of the Roman economy and monetary system, I have tried to reflect it as accurately as my research sources revealed. For example, it wasn't unheard of for a slave to be purchased for one hundred thousand sesterces—think "dollars"—as in Rhyddes's case, and gladiators, even the slaves, typically earned sums equivalent to today's sports heroes, with the superstars winning amounts to rival Michael Jordan in his prime, and the gladiators' owners receiving perhaps a hundred times more for each victory.

Some things never change.

Scholars exhaustively debate how many gladiatorial bouts ended in the death of at least one combatant. The games originated as funeral rites, so at first the mortality rate had to be one hundred percent. The bulk of current opinion leans toward the theory that, by the time of *Liberty*, it was so expensive to board, equip and train gladiators that perhaps only ten to fifteen percent of matches were fought to the death. Monetary penalties were levied against the games' sponsors—properly called "editors," although the term carries such a different connotation today that I chose not to use it—when certain gladiators were killed, as in the case of Agricola ordering Marcus to execute his opponent, Iradivus, who had been one of Jamil's top performers and a crowd favorite.

For a century and a half women fought in the arena, probably for many of the same reasons that gave rise to the modern sport of female mud-wrestling. Nero started the trend and even ordered "women of rank" to compete, although in A.D. 200, less than forty years after Rhyddes retired her gladius, the reigning emperor, Septimius Severus, permanently banned the participation of women.

My major written source for gladiatorial research was *Gladiators and Caesars*, edited by Eckart Köhne and Cornelia Ewigleben, University of California Press, 2000, and my research was supplemented by various television documentaries, produced by the Discovery Channel and History Channel, and aired between 2000 and 2004. For everyday details I found the *Handbook to Life in Ancient Rome*, by Lesley Adkins and Roy A. Adkins, Oxford University Press, 1994, to be indispensable. My research into the history and cultures of British Celts and Picts spans more than twenty-five years, and those sources are far too numerous to mention.

But, educational nuggets aside, my primary goal with *Liberty* was to create a story that inspires as well as entertains. In spite of historical inaccuracies that may have crept into the text, intentionally or otherwise, if I have inspired and entertained you, then I consider my task well and truly complete. Observed the newspaper reporter who interviewed James Stewart's character, Ransom Stoddard, at the end of *The Man Who Shot Liberty Valance:*

"When the legend becomes fact...print the legend."
kdih, XII June, MMIV
Soli Deo Gloria